OTHER WORKS BY E. S. FEIN

The Collected Histories of Neoevolution Earth
A Dream of Waking Life
Points of Origin
Ascendescenscion
The Process Is Love

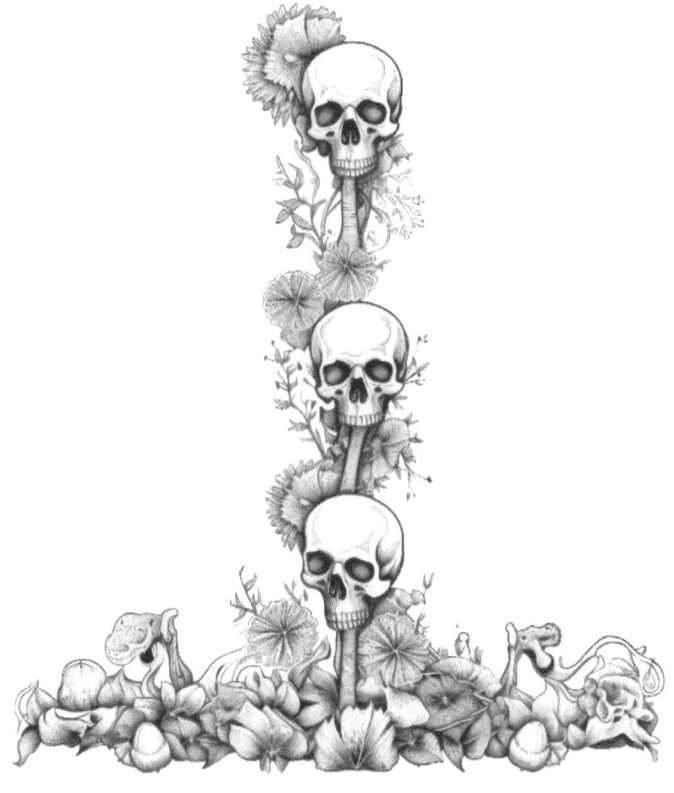

OfficialESFein.com
Linktr.ee/ESFein
Instagram.com/Authoresfein
Patreon.com/Officialesfein
Facebook.com/AuthorESFein

PRAISE FOR HUNTER'S DIRGE

"Hunter's Dirge elevates the series to new heights, seamlessly blending the intricate world-building and deep philosophical underpinnings that fans have come to expect from E. S. Fein. This third installment not only expands the dystopian universe with the introduction of the Walled City of Downver and the radically altered continent of Waru but also deepens our connection to beloved characters as they navigate this transformed Earth. Fein's skill in weaving complex lore with heart-pounding action is unmatched, making this a must-read for fans of the series and newcomers alike. The evolution of Thompson and the introduction of Tether add layers of intrigue and depth that promise to resonate long after the last page is turned." – Reader Review

"E.S. Fein orchestrates a symphony of chaos and harmony where the fate of the world hangs in the balance. Hunter's Dirge not only continues the thrilling adventure of its predecessors but also introduces new elements that challenge our understanding of heroism, evolution, and destiny. The vivid landscapes of Downver and Waru serve as the backdrop for a story that is as much about the internal battles of its characters as it is about their physical struggles. Fein's ability to juggle multiple storylines while advancing the overarching narrative is truly a feat!" – Reader Review

The Collected Histories of

Neoevolution Earth

Volume 3

Hunter's Dirge

Federated Agency Publishing

E. S. Fein

Hunter's Dirge (Neoevolution Earth Vol. 3)

Copyright © 2024 by E. S. Fein

Author: E. S. Fein

Publisher: Federated Agency Publishing

Editor: Nichole Paolella Petrovich

Formatter: Timbers Book Design

Ebook ISBN: 978-1-963048-98-8

Paperback ISBN: 978-1-963048-97-1

Publication Date: March 2024

First Edition

To Claire, for designing Waru and Downver with me, and for being my companion, my confidant, and my love.

BOOK SUMMARIES AND GLOSSARY

Visit OfficialESFein.com for a summary of **Volume 1: Mendel's Ladder**, **Volume 2: Winter's Remains,** and a **Glossary of Terms** ranging the entire Neoevolution Earth series.

CONTENTS

Volume 3

Hunter's Dirge

Anna. My dear Anna. My poor Anna.

I am sorry. Can you believe that?

No, I don't think you can. And I don't think you should. I don't think you should ever forgive me, Anna. Ever.

Brood with loathing. Burn with hate. Blaze with scorn.

Just as I have. Just as I continue to do. Just as I always will. Hate is the path that I have chosen, and hate is the path that you must choose as well, for this is the only way to ensure lasting and eternal love for everyone and everything else.

You will see this, Anna. Through the Hunter, you will come to understand it. And you will hate me all the more for it.

Good. Hate me, Anna. Let your hate burn with the same impeccable radiance as my own. Then, together, we will ascend unto the Great Beyond and burn our makers to ash.

From Mendel's Ladder: The Personal Journal of Denis Mendel, Recorded Circa 2064, Published June 2108 by Leif Mainstone, Federated Agency Publishing

Chapter 1
The Woman from Astrea

Year: 2065

Hunter4430 gawked at the human woman who had delivered him from death's door with a skinsuit that smelled of both renewal and ruin, of sand and flesh. The young Hunter, released from his birth-fire less than half a day earlier, knew of skinsuits from the scant spear-clanging rumblings of his birth-Cleaners. However, he did not know that the skinsuit remained embedded within his flesh by utilizing millions of hypodermic needles, each one a searing ember beneath his skin, roaring with every one of his subtle movements. The pain was torturous and un-ceasing, but the Hunter had spent seventeen years becoming accus-tomed to the ceaseless torment of his birth-fire and birth-Cleaners. For that reason, the pain inflicted by the skinsuit's probing needles felt famil-iar and almost comforting in a horrific and sordid way. Never-ending ag-ony was something Hunter4430 understood with every cell of his being, and because it was familiar and because the Hunter was so alone and confused, the pain of the skinsuit felt more like the presence of a terrible friend.

Despite the relentless pain, the only thing occupying Hunter4430's thoughts was the human woman sitting before him—the woman who had descended from the sky to save his life in what would have been his final moments of desolate agony.

He stared at the woman, his vertical eyelids wide open and his hair-less brows arched. He could smell that the intensity of his gaze made her feel unnerved, disgusted even, despite her conscious attempts to rid her-self of those feelings. But he couldn't help gazing at her in wondrous awe. She was not of the Earth, that much was clear. Her dark blue cloth-ing was sleek and clung tight to her body like a skinsuit, leaving only her arms and neck exposed. It was made of a strange material that the Hunter had never encountered before. Her skin, alabaster and unmarred, was like the fresh snow that sometimes lingered on the ground for days after a blizzard. Her hair, raven-hued and flawless, was as dark and comforting as the shadows of nighttime. But it was her eyes that Hunter4430 found most alluring. They were the green of the old world—strikingly emerald with subtle flecks of gold here and there. Every glance at her wondrous eyes reminded Hunter4430 that the old world was quickly being erased and replaced by the technicolor hues of Nomads and flesh trees—a world that the Hunter belonged in and that this human woman did not. The Hunter lost himself in her emerald eyes, and as if he were a parched wanderer stumbling upon a resplendent oasis, his gaze drank in every detail, each of her features becoming the water that quenched his thirst. His eyes, pale yellow and dilated, flickered with wonder, and the corners of his razor-filled mouth twitched upward in a subtle smile that seemed to make her even more uncomfortable, though she still fought to hide these feelings from him.

The woman stared right back at the Hunter, her piercing eyes full of unspeakable sorrow and regret as she analyzed every detail of the Hunter's carefully designed form.

"He's wrong, you know. You're not horrifying. You're not a monster. You're just sad. You're just…a child," the woman gasped as she tucked her legs close to her body and wrapped her arms around them.

"Hunt?" Hunter4430 asked with difficulty, pronouncing the word like a demonic toddler. His movements and mannerisms, uncurbed by human societal norms, were erratic and animal-like. He knew from the detailed scents of countless humans who had passed by his birth-fire that the way he looked and moved added to his horrific demeanor by separating him further from humanity while retaining an indelibly humanoid form overall. He couldn't put the thought into words, but he knew in his own way that he was a reflection of the deepest ancestral fears of all people—a creature insidiously plucked from the collective nightmares of every human. Each and every one of his features was designed with the intention to fill his human prey with such overwhelming fear that they would voluntarily choose to become a Nomad rather than face the infernal wrath of a Hunter.

"You know how to speak," the woman said in surprise.

Hunter4430 nodded and bared his razor-teeth into an unintentionally monstrous smile.

"Learn. Hear humans. Learn."

"The fact that you can speak at all is quite peculiar, you know that, Hunter?" the woman said. She scrutinized the Hunter, dissecting him with her eyes.

Hunter4430 went on smiling, uncertain but not caring what the words *fact* or *peculiar* might mean. All that mattered to the Hunter was ensuring he forever remained at this woman's side—this radiantly alluring creature from the sky—his own personal savior.

"Human?" Hunter4430 asked regarding the woman's smell. He knew that each identical Huntress in the world looked human in order to blend in with their prey as both a defensive and offensive strategy. Especially in the case of their Hunter dying in battle, Huntresses needed to blend in and bide their time until another Hunter was ready to leave his birth-fire, and then they would once again wield a power more destructive than any weapon Hunter4430 had ever smelled the humans use. He observed that this woman looked identical to a Huntress, but he also knew that Huntresses smelled like Huntresses, not humans.

"Huntress?" Hunter4430 inquired, shaking his head in confusion. He knew only that he belonged to this woman, Huntress or not.

"No," the woman stated forlornly, her mind and emotions currently absorbed in abstractions that were too much for even a Hunter's nose to translate. "I am human. It's just my eyes that aren't."

"Eyes?" Hunter4430 wondered, and he once more found himself in freefall as he gazed into the emerald depths gazing right back at him. "Eyes? No human?" he asked, unsure how a human could have inhuman eyes.

"That's right. My eyes aren't human," the woman said sorrowfully, but she didn't offer any further explanation.

"Eyes…green," Hunter4430 said, dredging the word from the terrible depths of his memories. He smiled at his ability to remember the word for his favorite color. "Green," Hunter4430 repeated, this time with an air of awe in his low rumbling voice.

"You're just a child!" the woman gasped, suppressing an urge to sob.

"No," Hunter4430 issued, not wanting the woman to cry despite being unable to fully understand why she was holding back her tears in the first place.

Hunter4430 lifted himself and consciously directed the skinsuit's natural camouflage to turn transparent. He stood and stretched out his body, presenting his scarred nine-foot frame like a grotesque canvas smeared generously with swaths of coiled muscle that rippled like living armor. Each sinewy fiber was a testament to raw, primal strength, intertwining like gnarled roots, forming a terrifying mosaic of horrific power that bulged and flexed with each motion.

"No child," Hunter4430 announced in reference to himself.

The woman shook her head at the Hunter's display of his body, then nodded in understanding.

"You're right, Hunter. You are strong. You have endured more pain than anything that has ever lived upon this Earth. The very nature of your existence is suffering. Even now with that skinsuit, the pain must be unbearable. But you barely even notice it, right?"

"Strong," Hunter4430 said in response, pointing to himself. "Hunt."

"No. We aren't going to hunt. We aren't going to kill anyone, understand? That's what he wants you to do. That's what he thinks you'll do, even if given the chance not to," the woman said, speaking both to Hunter4430 and to herself. "Because they made you that way. Andre Madeira and Denis Mendel and Tomasz Novak and fucking Ruben Avila and all the other sick and twisted elite of the old world. They made you this way, and whatever Andre and Denis have turned themselves into—that *thing* maintains the system that ensures your suffering. He stakes everything on you being a monster, Hunter, because to him that means he is a god."

The woman could no longer hold back her tears, and as she shook her head and sobbed, Hunter4430 desperately wondered what it was that tormented her so deeply despite her body looking as though it had never once experienced real pain. Deep pain. Birth-fire pain.

"Hunt," Hunter4430 said once more, hoping it might clear her terrible stench of sorrow and illuminate his Huntress with the wondrous scents of glory and vicious delight that he had smelled on other Huntresses passing within a few hundred miles of his birth-fire.

The woman forced her sobbing back under control and wiped her eyes with the back of her hands.

"I admit. You are scary. That is plainly true. But I'm not scared of you, Hunter. Okay? I'm not afraid. And no one else needs to be either. You and I are just going to go for a walk. The Earth won't harm me, but just in case, I'll have you by my side. You will protect me, won't you,

Hunter?"

Hunter4430 knew the word protection, and he nodded vigorously. "Protection. Scary, not scared."

"Yes," the woman nodded with a huff of tear-filled laughter. "Yes, that's right. I'm not afraid of you, little Hunter," the woman said. It made no sense to Hunter4430 that she was referring to him as little, but he did not question her words. His Huntress wanted his protection— nothing else mattered.

"Protection," Hunter4430 repeated.

"Yes," the woman said with more gentle laughter. "Come here," she offered with her arms open wide. "Let me hold you, little Hunter. Come here."

Hunter4430 did not understand why she wanted to hold him, but he did not question his Huntress' command. He closed the gap between them, and then he crouched, bending his enormous knees near her so that she could wrap her arms around his legs.

"Not like that," she giggled, and though Hunter4430 smelled nervous hesitation in her movements, she still reached out with her hands to direct him closer to herself. She touched his skinsuit, which directed the stimulation to his motor neurons and finally to his central nervous system, where the woman's gentle touch was translated into searing, piercing pain. Hunter4430 jumped back in shock and eyed his Huntress with suspicion.

"Why?" Hunter4430 asked, confused and afraid suddenly. The foreignness of her gentle contact with him, the whisper and brush of her skin against his skinsuit and his skin in turn—it was like nothing Hunter4430 had ever experienced. It was as shocking and sobering as Cleaners pouring sand and stone into gaping flesh.

"Why what?" the woman asked, her hands still outstretched in warm invitation.

"Why?" the Hunter demanded again, alarmed at himself for questioning his Huntress.

"I just want to hold you. I won't hurt you, little Hunter. Okay? Just come here. Let me hold you."

Despite the pain of her softness, it was unthinkable for Hunter4430 to disobey his Huntress. He found himself stepping cautiously toward her, one tepid step at a time, all the while dreading the horrifying gentleness of her touch.

"It's okay," she repeated. "All you know is pain. You're just confused. My touch isn't actually hurting you. That's just in your head. Come here. It's okay, I promise."

"Promise?" Hunter4430 repeated in confusion at the word as he moved another inch, finally closing the gap.

"Promise," the woman repeated without explaining the word's meaning, and as she carefully touched his arm, Hunter4430 gritted his teeth and fought the urge to pull away.

"It's okay," she repeated in a hushed whisper. "It's okay."

Hunter4430 was surprised to find that she was right—the more he fought the urge to pull away, the more his mind capitulated, exchanging pain for pleasure, something Hunter4430 had only ever glimpsed a handful of times in his life. Every few days of ceaseless torment on his birth-fire, the Cleaners would disrupt their torture pattern for one reason or another, and Hunter4430 would be left gasping and wondering at the world for no more than a few heartbeats. But it was enough. In the span of those heartbeats, Hunter4430 had felt freedom, and in those moments he would imagine himself sprouting wings and soaring above the world, so high in the sky that the flames of his birth-fire could not reach him. Soaring through the sky—that's exactly what the woman's touch felt like, and it scared Hunter4430, making him feel like a newborn bird teetering on the edge of its nest and acutely aware of the precipice and the vast, unknown expanse that waits beyond.

Like a mother bird enfolding her wings around her young, protecting it from the horrors of the world outside the nest, the woman wrapped her arms around the colossal Hunter. The startling feeling would not abate, and though her presence was a balm to his dilapidated soul, a labyrinth of fear and confusion made him want to push her away, like a frightened animal retreating to its den despite the promise of safety and affection.

As if she understood what he needed, she clung tighter to his body and dug her nails into his flesh, entreating him to the familiarity of pain in order to soften the terrifying unfamiliarity of pleasure. At the equilibrium of both sensations, something snapped within the Hunter's mind, like a seed buried deep within his genetic code suddenly splitting open, allowing the root of newfound comprehension to germinate. He heard something in his mind, and it paralyzed him.

What? What? What? he repeated stupidly in his mind. He reeled and tried to comprehend what was happening to his thoughts as they fluttered with abstract olfactory patterns that spoke of self. An internal space. Conscious, critical thought.

Me? the Hunter gasped at his sudden, stark self-awareness and newfound ability to create an internal dialogue within his mind.

The woman must have sensed his panic, for she said, "It's okay, Hunter. Just lie down in my lap and sleep. Just listen to my voice and let go. I may not be your Huntress, but I can tell that you're scared."

Scared? Hunter4430 gasped, processing his fear for the first time rather than just experiencing it.

"You don't need to be scared. Not with me," the woman whispered into his ear, and the pleasure of her breath upon his elongated spiked earlobes made him shiver in sordid ecstasy. Just as he had begun discovering himself, he was submerged in a resplendent stream of no-self, her breath making him feel light and free, liberated even from his own thoughts. It was as if he were floating above the world, unshackled from every sorrow that every Hunter was forced to endure.

"I can't just keep calling you Hunter," the woman whispered as she caressed Hunter4430's temple with her thumb. "I'll think of a better name. In the meantime, just rest. Sleep. You've never slept before, but you still have the capacity to sleep and dream. Just let go, Hunter. Let go and dream of somewhere else. Anywhere else. Just let go."

She claimed she was not his Huntress, but Hunter4430 disagreed, for her words were hypnotizing. They lulled him into a heavy slumber, something he had never experienced. He felt as though he were swimming in a green and violet sky as feathers dropped pleasantly from his body, each one the calming of a violent current in the unforgiving tide of agony that he had weathered, day and night, for seventeen sleepless years.

"Name?" Hunter4430 managed as he continued to slip into the strange sweetness of sleep. He didn't know what the word meant, only that the woman had said it.

The woman sighed forlornly, as if her name held the weight of the entire world. "I'll tell you the truth, Hunter. I have no name. He never bothered with a name. He never bothers with anything beyond the scope of his own ascension. We're all just rungs of his ladder—each and every one of us."

Hunter4430 had no idea what she was talking about, but it didn't matter. Her voice was the warm gusts and currents that he floated upon. Her breath was the very air he breathed. He was free, flying high above the Earth, and it was this human woman who had unshackled his wings with just her touch.

"He told me I could name myself, so I told the bastard to call me Anna, and it's as good a name as any."

Anna, Hunter4430 thought, mystified. It was the most beautiful sound he had ever heard.

Anna, he repeated with rapturous wonder, and then without even realizing it, he let go, and for the first time in the history of the world, a Hunter fell into a deep, dreamless slumber.

Rage. Flesh-filled teeth. Eyes awash with thick, oxygen-filled blood. Anguish. The crack of bone and snap of ligament and squelching of bowels. Agony.

"No! Fucking no!" a woman's voice shrieked, but Hunter4430 took barely any notice of anything outside the succulent, soul-satisfying taste of fresh human flesh.

"You fucking monster!" the woman shrieked again. "I'll fucking kill you!"

More human, Hunter4430 thought with insidious delight, desiring nothing more than to sink his razor teeth into a thick human thigh and feel the exquisite shattering of bone fill his mouth. He dropped the male child he was currently feeding on and turned to see an adult woman charging at him with a small metal device that he had seen humans use to dig into the ground.

Almost desperate to taste her salty, gelatinous brain, he rapidly unhinged his jaws and widened his mouth into a yawning chasm. The woman screamed in terror and animosity in equal measure as Hunter4430 extended his neck over six feet and filled his gaping maw with the woman's cranium, savoring the sweat and blisters of her sun-wrecked face with his barbed tongue before finally snapping his mouth back to its birth-shape, crushing the woman's cranium into a digestible ball as her brain squeezed down his throat and into his waiting belly. To Hunter4430's surprise, the taste and aroma of the woman's neural tissue was even more satisfying than the handful of moments he had tasted freedom from pain on his birth-fire. He felt quenched at the deepest levels of his being, as if he had been on the precipice of desiccation and now he was bloated with the water of life, fulfilled in every way he could ever imagine.

As Hunter4430 relished the exquisite deliciousness of a human brain, the metal instrument in the woman's now spasming hand pierced his skinsuit and sliced through his complex intestines, which were capable of digesting anything and everything. Without having to command it, his skinsuit was quick to repel the blade and repair the damage.

The woman's headless body slumped to the ground, prompting Hunter4430 to pivot his vision and prepare to feast on the rest of her flesh. However, as he turned, he caught the glimpse of another figure in the distance.

More human, Hunter4430 thought with mindless delight, and he felt his lips curl into an insatiable grin. As he lifted his head to locate his next prey, an arresting emerald radiance paralyzed him, stopping even his breath.

Anna, Hunter4430 remembered suddenly, sobering his wild mind back to the carnage-filled present moment. He was draped in viscera, with organs and half-digested flesh coating his entire body. The force of being plunged from mindless sleep to total self-awareness inflicted Hunter4430 with severe vertigo, and he found himself falling to his knees. However, he still hungered for the stringy flesh strewn all about the environment. The scent invited him to feast, entreating him to give into his natural whims. He felt disgusted as he imagined his own human Huntress being shredded into raw meat between his jaws. Still, he could not deny how delicious she would taste.

A sour, salty aroma filled the air suddenly, and Hunter4430 lifted his head to see Anna staring wide-eyed at him. Tears welled in her eyes, making them shimmer with anguish. Terror and heartbreak carved their cruel marks into every one of her features. Her eyes held a storm of emotions, and Hunter4430 could taste the chemicals flowing through her now, filling the air between them with her wild horror and the shards of a shattered illusion. Tears finally escaped her eyes, cutting clean paths through the dust and grime of her face, like webs filling the newborn hollows of what had once been hope. Her mouth hung slightly agape, caught in a silent scream that was louder than any audible cry.

Sleep, Hunter4430 remembered. He had fallen asleep, and in his sleep he had heard voices. He remembered wanting to protect his Huntress. He remembered the boiling rage, the ravenous hunger, the unyielding anguish. One moment he was nestled in her arms, and the next moment he had slaughtered a small family of humans who had simply been passing by. Their scent and their voices had triggered something deep within Hunter4430, and then his body and skinsuit took over and did the rest.

Monster, Hunter4430 thought, knowing that was what Anna must be thinking about him. Anna turned pale, and Hunter4430 understood through her complex bodily scents that only moments earlier she had desperately clung to the belief that he was not a monster, that he could rise above his body's demands. But the five children and two adults smeared in haphazard chunks across the world told a different story.

Her frail body trembled, a leaf caught in a tempest of sorrow and shock.

Hunter4430 began trembling in turn, for he knew that his actions were the source of his Huntress' terror.

"Hunt," Hunter4430 said in desperate confusion, but he knew deep down that this woman simply could not be his Huntress. She was a human. She was his prey. Yet his body did not instinctually attack her like it had with the other humans. He was grateful for that at least.

"He was right," Anna whispered in horror, more to herself than Hunter4430. "Monsters are real. And that means gods are real. That means—" she said, gasping at some terrible truth. "That means he's right. I don't have a choice. I...I have to do it," she finished, her eyes widening as she imagined something that Hunter4430 could only discern was so horrifying to her that it was nearly unthinkable. She winced and shook her head. "I don't have a choice," she repeated, her voice cracking in anguish.

The scent of her sorrow was too much to bear. Hunter4430 outstretched his arms and stepped toward her, desperate to feel her embrace.

As if he were just another monstrous Hunter, Anna shrieked and jumped backward. In her panic, she lifted a small rock and chucked it at Hunter4430, hitting him in the jaw. The pain felt like no more than a dull pinch, but the shock of Anna being so afraid of him sent Hunter4430 into a mad, anguished flurry of limbs. He ran on all fours away from his Huntress. The direction didn't matter. He just had to get away from her. For her sake.

Scared and scary, Hunter4430 told himself. *Anna scared. Hunter scary.*

He ran on four limbs for what felt like a few miles, and then he hid behind a large boulder, wedging himself between the hard rock and soft ground. He could still taste the woman's brain on his tongue, and he cursed himself for being a monster as Anna had called him.

Anna scared. Hunter scary, Hunter4430 lamented, and he punished himself by imagining being back on his birth-fire, every lick of flame and stab of a Cleaner's skewer a flagellation that he now understood he deserved.

Anna scared. Hunter scary. Anna scared. Hunter scary.

He repeated it like a masochistic mantra. A deep part of his mind pleaded to his skinsuit to sprout wings and carry him into the sky. Into the unknown. To reach across the stars and escape the Earth and every form of torment. But he consciously willed the skinsuit to keep him anchored to the ground, knowing that he did not deserve freedom.

Hunter monster. Hunter stay, he thought, imagining the entire planet as his cage—a cage he knew that he belonged inside of. In his mind, Hunter4430 saw Anna's wondrous emerald eyes, and then he felt the rock hit his jaw again and again. The unmistakable scent of Anna's fear and anguish still clung to Hunter4430's nose, reminding him in waves of torment that she was terrified of him—that she would never want to see him again. He was alone once more, and he imagined that soon enough, Cleaners would come and find him to strip him of his skinsuit and roast him slowly over a new lifelong fire that he would never escape from.

"It's his fault," Hunter4430 heard Anna say before he finally pulled himself out of his self-torment and smelled that she was only a few feet away from him. The sun had sunk low in the sky, telling him that many hours had passed in what had seemed like just a few moments.

"You never asked for any of this. Just like I never asked to be…me," Anna offered gently, her voice free of fear and her scent clear of anguish. She was like a totally different being—self-controlled in a manner that Hunter4430 hadn't realized was possible for her or any being.

Hunter4430 lifted his sorrow-heavy head and locked eyes with Anna. Bathed in the vivid hues of the late evening sun, Anna's raven hair was awash with golden rays, and the emerald of her eyes radiated serene acceptance, remaining unflinching despite looking upon Hunter4430's bloody, viscera-draped body.

"Anna," Hunter4430 gasped, stopping himself from speaking at the sudden realization of just how terrifying his low rumbling pitch and tone must appear to the human woman. He shook his head and felt wetness form at the base of his vertical lids.

"He is wicked," Anna seethed through gritted teeth. "But he isn't a god. Whatever Andre and Mendel turned themselves into—he isn't a god. But he is *our* god. You and me, Hunter. He created us, and we've no choice but to fulfill *his* will. The alternative is oblivion. For everyone and everything. That's just the way the universe works. He didn't make the universe that way. He isn't god. Gods aren't real. And neither are monsters. You hear me, Hunter?" she said, her voice unfaltering and full of steel resolve.

"Hunter...monster," Hunter4430 whimpered, lowering his head in servitude to his Huntress.

"No!" Anna nearly barked. "You're just...you're just a pawn, Hunter. Like me. We're just stuck in Mendel's vision of the future, for his vision is all encompassing. Mendel's vision is prescient, for that's the nature of a machine that can quantify and calculate every variable down to the sub-quantum layer of reality."

Hunter4430 couldn't understand what she was saying, and Anna sighed, apparently realizing the same thing.

"Just...it's not your fault, Hunter. It isn't. Just come here and let me hold you again like before."

Hunter4430 wanted nothing more than to feel Anna's soft embrace, but he restrained himself for fear that he might unintentionally hurt her.

"Please," Anna said, "please trust me, Hunter. You can't hurt me even if you wanted to, and I know you don't want to. So please, just come here, little Hunter."

He wasn't sure if it was the command of his Huntress who claimed to not be his Huntress, or the intense desire to feel her touch, but he went to her. He collapsed into her arms and nestled his forehead into her soft neck.

"I forgive you, Hunter," she whispered, her voice a balm easing his self-flagellated mental wounds. "But you have to promise me you'll try to control yourself. I don't want you to ever kill anything ever again. Nothing. No one. You have to try. Okay?"

"Try," Hunter4430 managed through his heavy breathing as he rejoiced to once more feel Anna's gentle yet still shocking and painful touch.

"Good," Anna said, rocking the blood-drenched Hunter in her arms. The sun dipped lower, casting elongated shadows behind groves of flesh trees and a handful of hardy old world trees that still clung desperately for a place in the rapidly expanding Nomadic world.

"The bastard up there always said, 'We all have a path to choose in this life. As the path forks, we must fork with it. And as the path ends, we must end with it. But we always have a choice.' He wants to make the choice for both of us, Hunter. But it isn't up to him. Even though it seems like it is. Even though it seems like we have no choice. We do, Hunter. We do have a choice. I have to believe that."

Hunter4430 could not understand what she was talking about, but he was used to that now. He wanted to allow her soothing voice to lull him once more to sleep, but he was afraid that something terrible might happen again.

"I can teach you to control your mind, Hunter. I can teach you to fill it with a fog that can push away the rage. I can teach you methods of self-control that maybe even a Hunter can understand. Will you let me teach you?"

"Yes!" Hunter4430 practically begged. "Anna teach."

"Okay," she nodded, and though she smiled at him, he could smell the bitter taste of doubt and worry in the depths of her being.

"You aren't just a body meant for murder. A Hunter's mind is powerful. More powerful than you realize. Now, close your eyes and follow along with what I tell you to imagine."

Hunter4430 lifted his head and took one last glimpse at Anna's vibrant emerald eyes before obeying this human woman who was not his Huntress. He closed his eyes, reluctantly shutting out the world and the woman from Astrea.

According to Mendel's Vision, the Earth is one of many planets that will undergo neoevolution. The objective result of the process eludes even me, but it is clear that the scope of Mendel's Vision involves the galaxy and beyond.

According to Mendel, the Earth is like a single spore among countless other spores. For now, they are individuals, but through neoevolution and Ascension, these spores will eventually germinate and form a universal network.

This is merely an analogy, of course. The neoevolution of the whole universe can't be encompassed or even accurately approximated through words. But, if it could, it would be as glorious and awful as a single bacterium observing the overwhelming complexity of an entire human body—all the multivariate lives and environments meshing and merging and morphing into a single entity with a single mind.

Anna is that bacterium. I am the Mind. And soon, when she returns from the Earth's surface, we will be one. Mendel warned me that there is an equal chance she will not return. Such is necessary for Mendel's Vision to come to fruition.

Regardless of Mendel's warnings, I have no doubts or uncertainties any longer. I gave those up long ago, preferring instead to forge headlong down this singular path of Ascension. Doubts and contingencies merely weaken Mendel's Ladder, and I refuse to weaken the foundations of the pathway I have chosen, no matter how it might fork.

From Mendel's Ladder: The Personal Journal of Denis Mendel, Recorded Circa 2065, Published June 2108 by Leif Mainstone, Federated Agency Publishing

Chapter 2
Arks of the Future

Year: 2099, Present Day

Anna's fingers glided along Hunter4430's arms as he lay comfortably nestled in her embrace. From the gossamer interstices separating dream and reality, he distantly perceived that her soft touch did not induce the extreme pain it had injected him with just a day earlier. He cherished the intricate scents presently coursing through her body.

Desire, confidence, fulfillment, Hunter4430 noted, surprised that he knew such complex words. *Anna is everything. Anna is…my love,* Hunter4430 knew with certainty despite the heaviness of sleep still coaxing his body into placid relaxation. The unquenchable rage still boiled at the distant peripheries of his being, but Anna had taught him numerous meditative techniques over the past weeks to help him control his Hunter urges.

Weeks? Hunter4430 thought in a haze of confusion, for although he could remember Anna teaching him how to wield his mind's ability to vividly visualize, another part of him insisted that he had only known Anna for the last day and a half.

What is happening? Thompson gasped, remembering suddenly that Anna had named him Thompson, and that Anna was gone—forced back to Astrea by a fate she had long ago concluded she and everyone else in the world simply could not escape.

"Anna!" Thompson screeched, opening his eyes finally and seeing Anna's face directly in front of him. Thompson felt consumed by longing and desperation for his love, but just as quickly, he felt disgusted and betrayed, for this woman was not Anna. It wasn't the woman's otherworldly radiance or even her one amethyst eye that gave her away, but the subtlest trace of something deep inside her being that Thompson could not precisely discern. For a moment she smelled like newborn blood and freshly grown old world grass. A moment later she smelled of old world rain and mold and rotting. Behind it all, Thompson smelled the distinct scent of human anguish and ecstasy. Thompson couldn't make sense of her, but he felt as though there was an entire universe within her, a never-ending tapestry of life and death intermingling as one, merging into something profound—something altogether new and unique unto the universe.

I died, Thompson remembered in a lightning flash of memories filled with vibrant green hues and dense hordes of ravenous insects. In a heartbeat, the woman's eyes commanded Thompson to focus only on their otherworldly brilliance. The woman was moving up and down, gyrating and grinding against Thompson's lower body, but some vast, faraway power in her gaze forced him to focus solely on her eyes, paralyzing him. Her left eye was emerald, the same as Anna's. It glowed with the same unyielding tenacity as the jungle life that had consumed him. Her right eye shone with an ultraviolet electricity, its deep violet hue penetrating violently through the foundations of Thompson's being.

Who is she? What is she? Thompson thought with a mix of awe and terror. Despite lying on his back, he felt a sense of vertigo staring into her eyes, as if he might lose his very grip on reality and slip into this woman's ocular infinity.

Anna's eyes held the same power, but this woman isn't my Anna, Thompson resolved, breaking from the woman's paralytic hold finally. Just as Thompson returned fully to himself, an explosion of pain and pleasure geysered from his lower body, and his vision shot down to see that his body had grown an engorged human penis. It was currently lodged inside the woman's vaginal canal, which was squeezing his penis as it convulsed and released something inside of her. Thompson tried pushing the woman off of him, but she was as immovable as a mountain.

Thompson willed his lower body to flatten back to his birth-form, which had no need for genitalia. He was about to shout at the woman to get away, when she lifted herself off him. Thompson watched as her vulva flattened and disappeared in the same way that his penis was currently disappearing back into his Hunter body.

Sex, Thompson reflected with immediate aversion at the ubiquitous human activity that was for Anna and virtually all other humans an essential part of their being. Although he had copulated with Anna several times, it had always been a strange and awkward experience for him. He only agreed to do it with her at first because she found more than just joy in it. She would scream in ecstasy, and though Thompson would wince at the painful pleasure filling his body, he only ever told her that he enjoyed it because in his own way he did. Anna's pleasure and delight provided Thompson intense mental fulfillment and reprieve. The fact that he could make her feel and smell so wonderful elated him to the point that he even began to look forward to intercourse with her.

The woman smiled at him and bowed in what Thompson smelled to be apology and procedural detachment.

"I apologize for having to resort to such barbarism to properly harvest that which I require, but you copulated with Anna many times near the end of her sojourn on Earth. I thought you would enjoy it, but it appears I miscalculated. A small oversight. Again, I apologize. This plane of being is hazy for me. The Great Beyond is far…clearer in nature. My calculations never fail me out there, but then, they also hold no inherent meaning out there either."

Thompson had no idea what the woman was talking about, but even if he could understand, he was unable to give her his whole attention at the moment. Distant thoughts of Volya and Anna flashed across his mind, but he couldn't focus on them, not yet, for his Hunter nose was presently absorbed by the overwhelmingly exotic scents of his surroundings. He observed that he was in a small rocky cavern lit by colorful bioluminescent molds and fungi. He was presently lying on a slab of rock cut precisely to his body's length. The slab was shaped like a human bed, and it was at the center of the room, as if the rock bed was the room's entire purpose. The woman stood in front of an opening in the rock wall that led to an expansive chamber full of waterfalls, thick plant life, and numerous moving figures. Thompson averted his gaze from the figures behind the woman and locked eyes with her once more, this time free of her paralytic hold.

"Who are you?" Thompson asked, guarded and self-restrained. He felt his hands shaking with unbecoming nervousness, and he looked down to see that although his skin readily mimicked the textures and hues of his environment, he was not wearing a skinsuit. Somehow, his body was behaving like a skinsuit on its own.

"*Who* I am is a difficult question to answer, but I have nothing to hide from you. I will explain everything in time, but it will be easier to do that using a means of language that surpasses words and symbols. Come, follow me, little Hunter."

Little Hunter, Thompson repeated sorrowfully, remembering how

Anna used to call him the same thing.

The woman turned to face the exit, and her form oscillated like a fragile mirage. As if suspended between two realms, her presence flickered and waned, casting a subtle luminance that ebbed and flowed with the glimmering light of the cascading waterfalls outside the small room.

"My skinsuit," Thompson protested, feeling naked and vulnerable without it.

"It is a part of you now," the woman explained. "The skinsuit died just as you died, and it has been reborn just as you have been reborn. You and your skinsuit are now one."

"I did die, then?" Thompson confirmed reluctantly, for although he could not remember the experience in detail, the process of being eaten alive still tugged at the edges of his subconscious. He realized that it was the experience of death that was making his hands shake, not his perceived lack of skinsuit.

"Then…how?" Thompson stuttered, his mind racing with images of the forest that the Cleaners had referred to as a secret location.

"And Volya," Thompson gasped with surprise that he was actually concerned for her, even though he knew that she deserved to die more than anyone except his maker, Mendel. "Where is Volya? Did she die? Did you bring her back to life too?"

"In a manner of speaking," the woman answered cryptically, and again she turned to leave the room, her form drifting through reality like gossamer through a breeze. One moment her contours were vivid and distinct, and the next, she blurred and distorted.

How can she move so ethereally yet feel as dense as a living flesh tree? Thompson wondered, remembering how even after being freed from her paralytic gaze, he had still been unable to move her off his body.

"What does that mean?" Thompson pressed, refusing to leave until he could make some semblance of sense regarding what was happening. "And tell me who you are. You said you would tell the truth. So, tell me. Why do you smell so similar yet so different from Anna? What did you…harvest from my body? How…how am I not dead?"

The woman issued a soft chuckle and nodded with patient understanding. "Your atoms were stripped of their macro-organization and then rebuilt back into what you are now. I rebuilt you, but if your atoms and subatomic particles can be pulled apart and put back together again so easily, isn't a better question whether you were even alive in the first place? Or what being alive even means?"

Thompson shook his head. This woman was certainly as philosophically inclined as Anna, speaking in ways that confused him and made him feel like the little Hunter she had regularly referred to him as before naming him Thompson.

"I don't care about that. I care about Anna," Thompson stated, not even acknowledging the complexities of her previous explanation. "Is this you standing before me now, Anna? Were you...reborn in the same way that I was reborn?"

"No," the woman stated simply. "I am not Anna. Anna is a precursor to my creation. A prototype, so to speak."

"A prototype?" Thompson asked, remembering that Anna had used the same word to describe herself on a few occasions.

"Yes," the woman nodded. "A steppingstone. A progressive sequence. A rung of the ladder."

"Mendel's Ladder," Thompson whispered angrily, and the woman nodded with a serene smile.

"You are a creation of Mendel," Thompson realized.

"So is Anna, and so are you," the woman agreed pleasantly.

Thompson's mind raced with a flurry of questions and demands, but he didn't know where to begin.

"Come," the woman stated, "everything will be explained in due time."

As she turned, Thompson reached out his hand to protest and ask more questions, but he was stopped short as he discovered that his birth-scars were all gone. Normally when the skinsuit was damaged or temporarily exposed, it revealed his horribly mangled flesh. In this way, all Hunters were dependent on the skinsuit, and ripping it off would mean certain and rapid death. However, now his body appeared as healthy and fresh as a Huntress' body.

She remade me so that the skinsuit and I are one, Thompson accepted nervously, still feeling vulnerable despite his body feeling stronger and more invigorated than ever. He had always felt one with his skinsuit, but now that he was truly one with it, he marveled that there was no pain with each of his movements.

Thompson realized that the woman had already glided a handful of paces outside the small cavern room, and he broke from his thoughts to catch up with her. Her movements were precise and elegant, yet they constantly shifted in pace, sometimes too fast and sometimes too slow, as if her subjective experience of time had difficulty syncing with objective time. He was about to ask her for more answers regarding her likeness to Anna, but his breath was stolen by the grandeur of the colossal thousand-foot-high cavern he now found himself in. The waterfalls he had noticed from the small room extended the entire height of the underground cavern, leading to a bright, dense green jungle on the sunlit surface.

That must be where I died. And Volya too, Thompson figured, unable to help himself from pitying the ruthless Huntress who had enslaved him to her will and would have continued to do so for as long as either of them drew breath. *I'm sorry I couldn't save you, Volya,* Thompson thought, apologizing more to Anna than to Volya, for he still believed that it was his shortcomings as a Hunter that had made Anna leave him and return to Astrea.

The glimmering light from the waterfalls reflected and refracted through the edges of the woman's body, making her shimmer and waver like an aurora, but only at some angles. At other angles she appeared perfectly normal, as much a part of the world as the waterfalls themselves.

It's like she's not really here sometimes, Thompson considered. *Like the shadow of an object projected somewhere my eyes and nose cannot follow.*

A deep, threatening growl to Thompson's right forced him to jump back in surprise. He pivoted on his right heel and instinctively shed the flesh of his arm, elongating the exposed bone with an array of sharpened spikes. He swung hard at what he now discerned was a large old world animal called a bear—a type of animal that one of Anna's favorite constellations was named after. With supersonic speed, Thompson's arm made contact with the bear's body, then it just as quickly passed right through it, as if the bear were composed of thick fog. His arm continued in its strike, slamming and shattering against the wall. Thompson was surprised to find that there was no pain whatsoever. His arm grew back to its birth-form without even a healing itch.

The bear stood on its hind legs and rose level with Thompson, locking eyes with him. The gargantuan animal analyzed him with a profound, conscious awareness. It reminded him of the way Anna used to study the stars.

Apparently satisfied, the bear grunted, as if discarding Thompson, and then it fell back on all fours and sauntered toward a twisting, unlit cavern in the distance.

Thompson watched the animal in bewilderment as it disappeared into the shadows. He couldn't help feeling disturbed by the way it had looked him over, as if it had been sizing him up, inspecting him for some trial that was still to come.

Turning around, Thompson saw that the woman was waiting for him and staring at him with the same intensity as the bear.

"What is this place? Why did that bear just stare into my eyes like that? Like you? Give me some answers."

As if Thompson's words were simply the natural and inconsequential sounds of the environment, the woman turned without urgency and surveyed the multi-tiered waterfalls collecting in crystal clear pools a few stories below them. She breathed deeply, seeming to cherish every particle of air and ray of sunlight dancing through the vines and mosses coating every surface of the rocky interior brimming with a dizzying array of plant life. The air hung heavy with a cocktail of exotic and familiar scents—the fertile perfume of damp earth, the lively aroma of flowers in bloom, the crisp water misting the rainbow-filled air.

"This cave is one of many on this planet. And this planet is one of many in our galaxy. And our galaxy is one of many in our universe. Earth is simply where it all begins," the woman explained evenly.

"We're on…a different planet?" Thompson asked with surprise, for the air smelled identical to Earth.

The woman nodded. "This planet and this place is merely an ark of the future. Mendel's Foretold Future. A future you may or may not be a part of. A future even I may or may not be a part of. That will be up to you, little Hunter."

"Don't call me that," Thompson said, wishing more than anything that this woman was Anna.

"My apologies, Thompson. I know that phrase brings you comfort, and that is all I wish for you. For now and forever. But such is not the fate of a Hunter—certainly not for you. Not if you wish to save Anna."

Her words were like a supernova in Thompson's mind, shattering years of unquestioned assumptions in a single cosmic blow.

"Anna?" Thompson shrieked. "Anna!" he repeated, unable to say any other word in his shock.

"Yes, Thompson. Anna is alive. And she is waiting for you. A queen waiting for her knight to come and save her," Tether answered, dissecting Thompson with her luminous eyes and a look that revealed some deeper, unspoken knowledge.

Thoughts of Anna clawed at Thompson's mind as he lucidly remembered her boarding the craft that stole her back to Astrea, where she had apparently been living and probably suffering in his absence for over thirty years while Thompson slumbered uselessly upon the surface of the Earth. A miniscule part of his mind had always assumed that Anna was likely just dead, used up by Mendel for purposes that she had been unable or unwilling to share with Thompson. But that part of his mind had been weak and wrong all along.

Anna is alive. I'm certain of it even if this woman is lying and attempting to manipulate me, like Volya and Mendel. This woman must have something to do with it all. It's like Anna said: there are no coincidences when it comes to Mendel.

"I want her back!" Thompson demanded with a force that rattled the very air around them, sending tremors across the dense walls and forcing the hanging mosses to swing like ghostly chandeliers.

"Tell me how to get her back," Thompson growled once more, and he felt the Hunter rage threaten to consume him.

Without warning, Thompson froze, stopping suddenly at a profound realization.

"The rage...it's...it's not really there, not on its own...not like before," Thompson said, his mouth agape in existential confusion. "I can feel it, but it's me who's making it. Not my body. Not the skinsuit. Not Volya. It's...it's me. I'm...I'm in control, even of my rage."

The woman's soft smile soured to neutrality, and she said, "We shall see."

Yes we shall, Thompson thought, his mind blazing with determination as he envisioned himself ripping the metal hull of Astrea wide open and saving Anna from her imprisonment.

"Is Anna in Astrea? Can you take me there?" Thompson asked, squeezing his fists with newfound resolve. He felt as though a lifelong collar around his neck had just fallen to his feet.

"Yes, Anna is in Astrea. No, I cannot take you there," the woman said as if reciting items from an inconsequential list.

"Then bring me back to Earth, and I will find a way to get there myself," Thompson stated, discarding every other question and answer as detritus in a singular river of importance. He imagined colossal wings sprouting from his back and carrying him into the sky to save his one and only love.

"I will," the woman said satisfactorily. "But it is Anna who wishes for you to know the truth before you make any final decisions. So, let me show you a piece of the truth, and then you may do as you please."

Thompson shook his head, uncertain if he could trust her, but he was equally arrested by her likeness to Anna. He cursed himself for giving into her so easily, but he also reasoned that he didn't have a choice in the matter.

If this is what Anna wants, then this is what I must do.

"How do you know this is what Anna wants?" Thompson challenged. "You spoke to her?"

"I am her, in a manner of speaking. I have all her memories within me. But I also have the memories of dozens of others, so in a manner of speaking, I am them too," she said with Anna's unmistakable voice.

"Is she alive?" Thompson asked, wanting the complete truth and no tricks.

"Yes," the woman confirmed without hesitation. "Now, come. Follow me."

"Wait," Thompson demanded. "Tell me who you really are. Tell me *what* you really are."

The woman sighed then said, "You will understand eventually after I show you what Anna wants you to see. All I can say with limited human language is that I am Anna's legacy. I was born from her sacrifice. I am a bridge. A tether. And that is what you may call me. Tether, just as you referred to Anna as her designation rather than a properly given name."

"A-N-N-A," Thompson spelled out, remembering that those letters had been written on the ship Anna had come down on. It was an abbreviation that filled Anna with anger and loathing, despite using it as her name.

"On the day she left, Anna told me what it stands for, but I couldn't understand. I probably still wouldn't understand it."

"Autonomous Neoevolutionary Nucleic Anomaly," Tether intoned as if reading from a textbook. "You're right, the meaning would be lost on you. But that is only because you lack the language and education. That is why you must follow me and begin learning the truth in a manner that surpasses language," Tether finished with a level of finality, sounding slightly impatient for the first time. She smiled, turned with a shimmer, and walked toward a narrow pathway leading into one of the many entrances inlaid like unfinished honeycombs spread sporadically across the entire surface area of the moss-covered rock walls.

Thompson nodded and followed, wanting to understand the abbreviation, this central aspect of Anna's being—something he knew that he would probably never be capable of understanding through human language alone.

I'm coming, Anna. Once I get out of here, I'm coming to save you. Thompson told her in his mind. *I've been asleep all these years, anchored to the surface of the Earth in that cave where Volya woke me up. I—*

Thompson stopped suddenly, and he remembered a flash of something that he had forgotten until now. He remembered launching himself into the sky, then sprouting wings ten-times the span of his nine-foot frame. Below him, there unfurled an expansive wasteland of death and carnage—the result of his rampage as the Butcher of the Wastes. He was a thousand feet in the air when tendrils and vines from the Earth's surface snatched him out of the sky and forced him back down, refusing to let him leave the planet. Then, the vines injected something into him, plunging him into his more than thirty-year slumber.

Did that really happen? Thompson gasped at the perfectly vivid memory that had been returned to his mind like a boulder slammed against a rock wall.

Tether continued walking and entered a dim passage lined with colorful bioluminescent mosses clinging to the tapered walls. The mosses perked as Tether passed, reaching out to her as if longing for her presence. Thompson forced himself to continue following her as he wrestled with these newfound memories of his past.

If that memory is true, then I did try to reach you, Anna. I didn't just give up on you. Even though that's what you wanted me to do. I couldn't. Even though I wanted to obey you, I couldn't, Thompson lamented as he forced himself into the cramped, moss-laden passage. Miniature waterfalls gushing from the cavern walls traced silver paths through the moss and several fronds of some strange plant composed of forked opalescent leaves. Tether's bare feet lightly splashed through the cool puddles and crisscrossing veins of water running through the ground. She stepped with a hypnotically calming rhythm as Thompson continued forward and spoke to Anna in his mind.

Everything happened so quickly after Volya woke me up, but all that time I obeyed you, Anna. I didn't try to follow you, even though that's the only thing I wanted. I saved two little girls, actually. I used that fog trick you taught me to tame my mind, except I used it against Volya, and it saved their lives. So, really, you did that, Anna. You taught a Hunter to save the lives of two little girls, even if they aren't technically human like you. Thompson paused, remembering how Tether had called Anna a creation of Mendel, like herself and Thompson.

I wanted to go to Astrea to kill Mendel, but you told me not to follow you. So why did Tether say you want me to see this truth she is taking me to? Why did she say that you are waiting for me to come and save you? If that's true, why did you leave, Anna? Why didn't you let me protect you back then? Why now?

As he passed an opening in the wall, Thompson turned to see a large group of old world animals milling about the far wall of an expansive hollow full of dense mycelial roots hanging from the ceilings and clinging to the walls and ground. He stopped and observed that the animals appeared to be working together to dig into the thick mycelium, carving particular shapes and passageways into the fungal flesh.

"They are hard at work," Tether said without Thompson even noticing she had retraced her steps to arrive at his side. Thompson recognized more bears and a few other animals that Anna had drawn him pictures of, such as wolves and lions. There were others that he had never seen before, though Anna had said that animals of the old world differed in surprising and diverse ways.

"My arm passed right through that bear earlier. And the way it looked at me—these aren't normal old world animals, are they?" Thompson inquired as he watched them toil tirelessly in their efforts, like shooter worms carving their endless pathways through the Earth's soil.

"They all began as old world Earth animals, but now they are free. Like you. They've just had more time to be free—more time to accept what that really means. They may take the shape of their birth-forms, but that is simply the atomic organization they are each most comfortable with. The same is true for you and me. With the skinsuit, you've always been able to morph your body in any way you please, and yet, you always instinctively return to this same self-image. You think of yourself as a Hunter, and thus, you naturally return to the birth-form of a Hunter."

"You can change your body too? And these animals, they can do the same?" Thompson checked, accepting the explanation after having experienced the ability to painlessly shed his flesh, weaponize his bones, and subsequently heal his arm, all without a skinsuit. It also explained how the bear had been able to dematerialize and rematerialize its body, allowing Thompson's arm to pass right through it.

Tether nodded pleasantly, then turned and began walking down the moss-lit path once more. Again the plant life reached out to her, beckoning her.

"What are they doing in there?" Thompson asked, and at the same time he rejoiced at the thought of being able to sprout wings again and fly all the way to Astrea. This time he would be ready for the vines if they tried to shackle him to the surface.

I just have to get this over with, and then Tether will take me back to Earth. I'm coming, Anna. I'm coming to save you. It's been over thirty years. You have to just hang on a bit longer.

"They are building the foundations of a grand structure that will one day grow into a planetary mind. These animals are analogous to the Nomads of Earth," Tether responded.

Before Thompson could inquire further, they reached a bend in the passage revealing a soft but unyielding green glow. As they came around the bend, the green glow intensified as the source of the light was revealed to be an expansive cavern brimming with green bioluminescent mushrooms, some of them more than fifty feet tall.

Thompson stopped suddenly as another memory from his period of mindless rampaging was unearthed, this one depicting the obliteration of an entire group of scared human children huddling together with the desperate hope that the Butcher might spare them. Thompson winced as he felt their innards explode around him and absorb into his skinsuit, providing it with more energy to allow Thompson to continue raging and killing for weeks on end.

I killed so many, Thompson recoiled, self-loathing and revulsion coursing through his shaking hands. *Children. I killed those scared human children. Thousands of them. Maybe tens of thousands. Maybe hundreds of thousands. I—*

"Come, Thompson, and you will discover a way to free yourself of your inner turmoil, if you would have it," Tether stated stoically. Then she smiled and slipped into a thicket of the green-glowing mushrooms.

Thompson tried to stop the memories and squeezed through the scant space between each mushroom, pulling himself across their smooth, glowing flesh. As he emerged from the thicket, he found himself in a circular area formed by the walls of several tower-sized mushrooms. The ground was littered with miniature green-glowing mushroom caps that grew thicker and denser as they reached the center. There, Thompson saw a group of five identical Hunters, each sitting cross-legged in a circle. Their bodies were covered in the green fungus, as if they had merged with the fungus in the same way that Thompson had merged with his skinsuit. They faced one another but kept their eyes closed in what appeared to be meditation. To the right of the group stood Tether. The way she was standing hid her amethyst eye from view so that only her left eye was visible to Thompson, making Tether look almost identical to Anna and Volya.

"What did you do with Volya?" Thompson inquired.

A corner of Tether's lips turned into a half-smile, and she said, "Despite everything, you are still concerned about her, Thompson?"

"None of this is Volya's fault. She's a slave to Mendel. She always has been. I know what it means to be an unconscious slave to one's programming. So, what did you do to her? Is she on another planet like me?"

"Volya is alive. She has been reborn. Like you, Thompson."

"Did you merge her with a skinsuit too?"

"No, not like that," Tether corrected patiently. "I mean reborn in the same way that you were reborn after knowing Anna. Reborn unto oneself and away from the will of one's creator—that is what you both experienced, just as I have."

Thompson shook his head, not able to follow Tether's explanation.

"Will I see her again?" Thompson asked, glad she was alive but hopeful they would never again cross paths.

"That is up to you, Thompson," Tether explained cryptically, frustrating Thompson that she never seemed to fully answer his questions.

"What do you want?" Thompson demanded with an intensity in his tone that made his voice echo ominously through the cavern. He was surprised that none of the Hunters appeared disrupted by his outburst.

"To fulfill Anna's wishes and show you the truth—as much as you are capable of understanding," Tether stated reasonably. "Now, take a seat in the center of your fellow Hunters and prepare for a sojourn through space and time."

"A sojourn?" Thompson inquired.

"A temporary journey," Tether explained. "A journey beyond language. At the height of the old world, humans developed utterly convincing simulations that they could connect their minds to, providing a means of information transfer and experience beyond any mere book or movie. This will be very similar to a human simulation, only even more immersive and convincing in its reality."

"What will I experience?" Thompson asked with nervous trepidation as he inspected the Hunters and saw that each one had green-glowing mycelial tendrils extending from inside their ears and into the mushroom-dense ground.

"The beginning of the truth. The truth of your existence. Everything you are capable of understanding at this moment and more. Take a seat, little Hunter. Don't be afraid. Take a seat. The mushrooms will know what to do."

For just a moment during Tether's shifting, Thompson smelled Anna's distinct scent. His heart fluttered with a sudden and unsettling certainty that this was truly Anna standing before him, but then Tether turned, phasing in and out of solidity to reveal her shimmering amethyst eye.

I know I shouldn't trust her, Anna, but this may be my only chance of getting back to Earth and finally saving you from Mendel's clutches. And if what she is saying is true—that you want me to see whatever it is these Hunters and mushrooms can show me—then that is all the more reason to go through with this.

Feeling clearer and more resolute after conferring with Anna in his mind, Thompson forced himself past two of the Hunters, stepping on and splattering numerous mushrooms with his bare feet, but neither the Hunters nor Tether seemed to care.

Thompson sat at the center of the Hunters, crushing even more mushrooms in the process. He looked up and saw Tether staring at him with intense interest, eyeing him without blinking. In the dim green glow of the cavern, her eyes shone their respective hue like scintillating stars, and Thompson saw with absolute clarity now that despite her human appearance, this woman was even further removed from humanity than himself.

Without warning, the Hunters parted their vertical eyelids in unison, revealing the pale yellow eyes that all Hunters shared. All five Hunters began humming an identical low rumble, like the slow approach of an old world storm. Then, in a single heartbeat, the mushrooms beneath Thompson ejected their mycelial tendrils, shooting up his body, entering his ears, and finally attaching directly to his brain.

The Hunters, eyes wide, continued their low rumbling hum as Thompson gritted his teeth against the uncomfortable feeling of mushroom roots wrapping around his brain.

"These Hunters serve as relays, projecting His voice directly to you, Thompson. Earth's mind has waited a long time to communicate with you. His mind. The cosmic mind. The present infant mind of the Ascended God. Close your eyes now, little Hunter, and witness the truth of your existence. It is time to see through your maker's eyes—through Andre Madeira's eyes."

All at once, the Hunters closed their eyes, and Thompson felt his own eyelids close along with them. He felt the mycelial tendrils engorge and expand to fill his ear canals and cranium, blinding him, and then—

The Virus and the Cure can be thought of as the lashing by which Mendel's Ladder is held together. Without them, my plans are like rungs that cannot stay in place.

Their suffering as humans despite not being humans is necessary, as is their initial mortality. The possibility of death is essential to their growth. They must be born and live as true specimens of life. While the thought of either of their deaths is anathema to me, I accept that it is necessary all the same.

They will overcome their trials. They will survive long enough on Earth for their powers to awaken, and then they will lead humanity, rung by rung, through the pathways of neoevolution that will result in Ascension. Humanity's Ascension. My Ascension.

This is what I choose to believe. I believe in myself, and thus, I believe in them. Just as I suffered and overcame the impossible, they will do the same. They must, for if they don't, then humanity's story and the story of all life will end in nothingness. There will only be void.

Thus, they will scale the summits of their own individual mountains. There is no going back now that we are climbing Mendel's Ladder. The Virus and the Cure must endure, for if either one of them fails or dies, we all do.

From Mendel's Ladder: The Personal Journal of Denis Mendel, Recorded Circa 2064, Published June 2108 by Leif Mainstone, Federated Agency Publishing

Chapter 3
The Feeding Cave

A great rumbling echoed through the darkness of the dim, green-glowing passage. Aurelia gripped her sword, but Aliana just let out a hoot of echoing laughter.

"You forget the sound of your own stomach, Aurelia?" Aliana snorted. "You know, you're seriously a troutface for not eating any glowies," she added with a worried shake of her head. "Just have some. I'm clearly fine, and they taste amazing. I'm telling you," she offered, waving her arm about the ten-foot-high passage littered with small glowies on every surface.

"I'm fine," Aurelia signed, easing her grip on the sword's hilt. "Enough talk. Let's just focus, Ali."

Aliana rolled her one good eye and said, "You can't use your fingers at the same time as you use your legs? When did that happen?"

Aurelia shook her head, and in response, Aliana popped another mushroom into her own mouth. She sighed, then said through her loud chewing, "Sorry, Aurelia. I just don't want to see you hungry."

As Aliana spoke, Aurelia was astounded to find that she felt like she might totally lose herself in the verdant emerald depths of her sister's eye, which was now like a living, dynamic jungle holding infinite lives within its intricate layers.

It has to be the glow of the glowies that are making her eye so profoundly radiant, Aurelia reasoned in bewildered awe.

"You can't see my hunger," Aurelia corrected, breaking herself from the trance of her sister's stare. "Unlike me and my signing, my hunger speaks through sound, not visuals," Aurelia said to distract Aliana from her previously concerned gaze.

Aliana just stared suspiciously at Aurelia.

"What is it?" Aliana asked, ignoring her sister's poor attempt to distract her. "Why were you looking at me so weird a second ago?"

She noticed, Aurelia considered, surprised by Aliana's uncharacteristic level of passive observation.

"What are you talking about?" Aurelia countered, not wanting to concern her sister with what she knew must just be a trick of the light that was making her eye more radiant than the emeralds embedded in the ceremonial crown that Nomusa used to wear on Wintersvilla holidays.

"I don't know," Aliana said with a thoughtful hum, eyeing her sister suspiciously, "you just had a weird look. And—"

Aliana went silent suddenly and stared in bewilderment at Aurelia's hand from where it hung in the makeshift sling that the Hunter named 541 had made for Aurelia before attempting to eat her. Following her sister's confused stare, Aurelia looked down at her hand and saw that she no longer had a slowly bleeding stump for an index finger. Instead, a uniform black finger free of any wrinkles or creases had grown from the stump without her even noticing. It was black like slick tar. Black like the gaping tendrils of discoloration marring her lips and face since birth.

It's the exact same color, Aurelia realized. She was bewildered by the spontaneous regrowth of her finger, but she was even more in shock at the likeness of her finger's discoloration to her lifelong scars. Despite living with her curse her entire life, she still did not know what the discoloration meant.

Aurelia pivoted to inspect the finger closer and saw that it wasn't just the color that was similar. Black tendrils, identical to those on her face, extended from her finger to her wrist and from her wrist all the way up her arm.

Calm, she told herself. *Aliana's eye. My markings. Our powers. This can't be a coincidence. It's happening. It's the changes that Shira and Rooli warned us about our entire lives. Tomasz Novak's final design is finally coming to fruition,* Aurelia thought, knowing with Nomadic certainty somehow that Tomasz Novak, her creator, was dead. She didn't know when exactly it happened or the circumstances; her mind simply deposited the information into her awareness, like Tomasz depositing the girls, the Virus and the Cure, upon the Earth.

Tomasz is dead, and soon, other Great Ones of the old world will die. Great changes are about to occur, and our coming to Downver is the catalyst. But there's something…something strange occluding the future—like a boulder placed at the very nexus of a multiverse of pathways, Aurelia weighed as she recollected that something was blocking her ability to see beyond Downver—either her own death, or something worse.

Aliana just stood gawking at Aurelia, waiting for her to say something. Anything. But Aurelia was totally absorbed in her flickering prescient visions, like ephemeral sparks cast here and there in a cave of complete darkness.

Rooli, Aurelia thought, gripping the shard of Rooli and refusing to let go. *How much of the future could you see? Was your vision of everything blocked after Downver as well? Is that how it is for all Nomads?* Aurelia wondered, irked by the idea of placing herself in the same category as Nomads despite her love for Rooli.

"Does it hurt?" Aliana finally asked.

"My prescience?" Aurelia asked.

"Your prescience? You mean your power? No, I mean the black lines all over your arm. And your new black finger. You used to tell me that the lines on your face ache at all times. Is it the same with those?"

Aurelia had grown so used to the flesh-splitting ache caused by the black markings that she hadn't realized the pain was no more. She lifted her good hand to her face and felt the markings, allowing her finger to dip into the shallow crevices of otherworldly black, but there was no pain whatsoever. It wasn't even exactly numb. It was just emptiness. Nothingness. Void. And to Aurelia's surprise and horror, she felt invigorated by it, like an adrenaline junkie standing at the very precipice of some impossible height.

A void—just like the great swirling vortex of my visions, Aurelia gulped, and she forced her mind to ignore the vortex hallucination constantly beckoning her—calling to her to fall inside its alluring, infinite depths.

"Aurelia!" Aliana snapped, looking worried now. "Are you okay or what? What's happening to you?"

"Earlier," Aurelia realized. "When you noticed that I was looking at you strangely. Normally you would never notice something like that, Aliana. But you did. And I bet that's because time slowed for you, and you noticed my subtle movements. Am I right?"

Aliana's eyes turned to disbelieving slits, then she said defensively, "How did you know? I mean, it's not like I can control it. It just…happens."

"I know because that's how it is for me too. It's like they always told us, Ali. It's our powers. Our purpose. I can tell you now with perfect confidence: we will make it to Downver. But I need to tell you everything I know because it might help you," Aurelia said, reminding herself that her own death might very well explain her inability to see the future beyond Downver.

"Tell me everything? What do you mean?"

"My power. My ability to see the future like the Nomads do. Like Rooli. Like I told you, I got it back, but…well…I don't know what it is, but there's something that happens in the future. Something that's stopping me from seeing past Downver."

"What is it," Aliana pressed, her eyebrows furrowing deeply at her sister's uncharacteristic worry.

"I just told you, I don't know," Aurelia signed with a tinge of frustration. "Just listen. We need to be ready. *You* need to be ready. We've heard enough stories about Downver. It's dangerous. It's infested with old world humanity, which means it's rotten with weakness."

"And men," Aliana added.

"Yes, and there will be many men," Aurelia agreed, though she knew that wickedness had no gender preference. Aurelia was aware that her sister enjoyed tying herself to Wintersvilla tradition and ideas out of love and admiration for Myriam. Aurelia had never felt the need to challenge Aliana's obsession with Myriam, and Aliana never said a word about Aurelia's closeness with a living tree.

"Aurelia," Aliana said, stepping forward and taking her good hand. "Does it hurt or what? Your arm, I mean?"

"Not at all," Aurelia answered truthfully. She tried to move her right arm, but it still hung uselessly in the tattered sling.

"Good," Aliana said simply, looking at her sister as if attempting to dredge an admission of pain out of her.

"What about your face?" Aurelia asked, though she could plainly see that Aliana's nose was still a mere smear across her face and her eye was still swollen shut beneath the tattered shirt that Aurelia had wrapped around Aliana's head what seemed like ages ago.

"Feels fatherfucking terrible," Aliana huffed, brushing away the pain in a convincing imitation of Myriam. "But I'll survive. These mushrooms are keeping me going. Hey! You should have some," Aliana offered with an air of gentle jest that only partially concealed her concern.

"I'm fine. Let's go," Aurelia asserted, and she walked forward, leaving her sister holding out her hand full of freshly picked glowies.

Aliana groaned and caught up to Aurelia.

"You're so fucking stubborn," Aliana accused with sisterly love.

"And you're fucking relentless," Aurelia signed behind herself without looking back.

"Fatherfucking right I am," Aliana announced and then popped another glowie into her green-glowing mouth.

The girls continued through the passage with Aliana's chewing and Aurelia's growling stomach filling the silence. Every so often Aliana would chuckle at Aurelia's loud hunger, but she didn't prod her to eat the glowies. All the while, Aurelia attempted to observe whatever was occluding her prescient vision, but it was like trying to look at her own eyes without a mirror.

Rooli will know what to do, Aurelia knew, and though she rejoiced that there was still hope of reviving Rooli, she also cursed herself for being so dependent on her—a level of dependency that she knew Rooli did not approve of but endured nonetheless.

Just hang on Rooli. We're going to revive you, and then we'll face whatever is coming. Nothing can hurt us unless we allow it, Aurelia told herself, filling her mind with the stoic resolve that Rooli had hammered into her since birth. *Not even death,* she told herself, forcing her awareness away from the unbecoming doubt etching the peripheries of her thoughts.

"Hey," Aliana said as the walls of the passage began to slowly taper. "We took down a fucking Hunter. What do you think Cassie would have to say now?" Aliana asked with vengeful pride as she referenced one of the larger Wintersvilla girls who used to relentlessly ridicule them both. The only thing that had ever stopped Cassie from escalating her bullying to physical assault was fear of being punished by Shira, or worse, having Rooli simply loom nearby with the silent but constantly perceived threat of being turned into a Nomad.

"I think Cassie is probably Biofreak food," Aurelia signed, intentionally grounding her sister and reminding her of the seriousness of their situation.

Aliana rolled her eye and said, "Oh, Mendel's Vision, Aurelia. I mean, really. After what we've been through, a little levity is what the quartermistress ordered. Besides, you just told me that we're guaranteed to get to Downver. The changes are starting. Everyone we know is dead. Can we just…" Aliana trailed off and sighed deeply, revealing the incredible sorrow and fear she was damming inside herself with forced courage and resolve.

"I'm sorry," Aurelia offered genuinely. "I just know we get to Downver. I don't know what shape we'll be in when we get there. We need to revive Rooli, and that might not be as easy as just entering the city. We—"

"Okay," Aliana said, cutting Aurelia off and saving her from further explanation. "I get it. If this is about saving Rooli, then I get it. I love Rooli, you know that, but I know what she is to you. If this was about saving Myriam, or saving…saving our mother. Then—" Aliana said, her voice cracking as she sobbed.

Fuck, Aurelia thought, cursing herself for not anticipating that pushing her sister too hard would lead to an emotional breakdown.

"I'm sorry, Ali," Aurelia offered once more, this time using the secret signs they had developed long ago to speak to each other with total, assured secrecy.

Aliana smiled through her tears and signed back in their private, intimate language, "I love you, sister. I could never do this alone."

"Yes you could," Aurelia urged, wanting Aliana to be prepared to forge ahead with her own destiny.

My entire purpose as the Virus might just be to get the Cure where she needs to go, Aurelia considered, and she accepted her fate as Rooli taught her that she must.

"You took down a fucking Hunter," Aurelia marveled, and in response, Aliana smiled wide.

"We took it down together," Aliana said with fiery pride, and she snorted blood through her wrecked nasal passages and spit a glob of thick crimson onto a patch of glowies. The mushrooms wiggled and pulsed with seeming excitement and then expanded a few full inches in diameter, squeezing each other as a few cracked and began merging with one another.

"Myriam would be proud of you, Ali. Well, I'm sure you know that. You can just go in your head and speak to her now, right?"

Aliana shook her head disappointedly. "No. It's like you said: it just happened. And it only happened that one time. Who knows if it'll even happen again."

"It will," Aurelia stated. "It's part of your powers, and from now on, our powers are only going to awaken further."

"It's not much of a power," Aliana said disappointedly, "but I'd still be grateful if it does happen again. It was so real, Aurelia. It was like…it was like I was really talking to them…and you, which was weird, especially because even in my head you were kind of a bitch," Aliana jested, playfully sticking out her green-glowing tongue.

"Let's go," Aurelia said, hurrying to ensure that Rooli would not simply crumble to dust. Aliana nodded and pressed forward into the passage behind her sister.

If we don't make it in time and Rooli dies, will she turn into a flesh tree like every other Nomad, Aurelia wondered, but she pushed the thought out of her mind. *It doesn't matter, because we're going to save her. We will save you, Rooli.*

Another few minutes of walking passed, and though the passage continued tapering, it still remained large enough that they didn't need to crouch. The glowies were growing sparse enough that they no longer had to step over and around patches. Ahead, Aurelia saw what appeared to be a dead end.

"Aliana," Aurelia signed, pointing to the wall up ahead, but Aliana was already running forward.

She noticed the dead end even before I did, Aurelia thought. *Again, it must be her power.*

"Aurelia! It's not a dead end. It drops down into a larger passageway."

Good, Aurelia thought, gripping Rooli. *Maybe the Hunter was telling the truth after all, and this passage really is a straight shot to Downver.*

"Whoa!" Aliana giggled, and she wobbled before catching herself on the wall. "I feel…kind of…unstable," she giggled again, and then she fell back in a fit of obnoxious laughter.

"Stop it!" Aurelia scolded, angry that her sister was enjoying herself so thoroughly despite their need for urgency.

"I'm…sorry," Aliana managed between her hoots of laughter. "I'm fucking sorry! But…that fucking word…is so…fucking funny," Aliana burst, unable to contain herself. "Not stable. Unstable!" she wailed, throwing her head back and slamming her fist on the ground with stomach-splitting, obnoxious howls.

"Shut up, Aliana! Stop it!" Aurelia demanded, but her sister wasn't looking at her. She just went on laughing and repeating *unstable* every time she caught her breath.

Aurelia stopped suddenly at the realization that her sister was being abnormally obnoxious.

Is she just acting out right now? Aurelia thought as Aliana rolled around uncontrollably, crushing glowies as her laughter refused to cease.

Aurelia began walking to her, then decided to run when it looked like her sister was squeezing her one eye closed and laughing so hard that she could no longer breathe.

"Aliana!" Aurelia signed pleadingly against Aliana's chest since her eye was sealed shut in seeming agony. "Aliana!"

Finally, Aliana breathed deeply, as if surfacing for air after being plunged beneath the ocean, and she opened her one eye. Her eye still radiated with unnatural brilliance. Aliana looked up at Aurelia with a goofy, detached smile, her lips and teeth glowing as green as her eye, only with a slightly lighter hue.

"Wooooooooow," Aliana breathed, drawing out the word as she stared at her sister in awe. Her right pupil was dilated unnaturally wide, and she drooled slightly, as if forgetting to swallow.

"You're so pretty, Aurelia. Your markings are...wow...they're...they're wow," Aliana stammered, acting both dazed and drunk.

The glow of her mouth finally struck Aurelia with the truth of what must be happening to Aliana.

"It's those mushrooms, Aliana," Aurelia told her, trying to remain calm as she recollected the immense quantity of glowies that Aliana had already consumed. "They must have some type of psychotropic property—like the mushrooms some of the Wintersvilla Warriors used to consume before doing battle. I think...I think you're under the influence of a drug right now, Aliana."

"Wooooooooow," Aliana breathed again. "Salmon is so good. Oh, holy fucking Muto, I want some salmon so bad right now. You got any salmon?" Aliana asked. "We should fucking tell Myriam about salmon! Aurelia!" she said, suddenly deathly serious. "Does...does Myriam know about salmon?"

"Yeah," Aurelia signed, playing along to not worry her sister. "Myriam knows all about salmon. Come on, Myriam is right up ahead. We can talk to her about salmon all you want when we see her."

Did she consume a lethal dose? Aurelia wondered as she weighed the best course of action given their circumstances. *She should throw up. Just in case it's still working into her system.*

Not giving her a chance to protest, Aurelia walked to Aliana and without even thinking about which hand she was using, she placed the shard of Rooli on the ground, braced Aliana's head with her left hand, then stuffed her newly grown black index finger and middle finger down her sister's throat.

Aliana tried to fight back, but she was caught off guard and too intoxicated to realize what was happening before she started retching green-glowing vomit full of half-digested glowies.

"Aurelia!" Aliana shouted through heaves and coughs. "Aurelia!" she shouted again as she regained her composure. Aliana stared at Aurelia angrily, then, as if suddenly forgetting what had just occurred, she smiled stupidly and pointed to her pool of vomit.

"Does everyone's insides glow in the dark like that?" Aliana asked, and then she laid her head in her glowing vomit as if it were a pillow. "This is nice and warm," she marveled as she patted the sticky puddle with her palm.

"Get up!" Aurelia demanded, and she pulled her sister to her feet.

"Aurelia," Aliana said as she wobbled back and forth. "Your hand and arm look so cool. I'm glad you're feeling better."

It was only then that Aurelia noticed that she had used her right hand to force her sister to throw up. She stretched her fingers and pivoted her arm, inspecting it. She couldn't feel it at all, and yet, it obeyed her mind's command, moving exactly as she willed. Despite not being able to feel it, Aurelia was about to try wielding her sword with her right hand when she saw her sister topple backward and disappear through the small crevice leading to the larger passage below them.

Aliana!

Aurelia nearly dove after her but stopped short upon hearing more of her sister's obnoxious laughter.

"I have a fucking sword? When the fuck did I get a fucking sword?" Aliana guffawed from below, losing herself once more in a cacophonous laughing fit.

Aurelia peered over the edge of the crevice and saw Aliana roughly ten feet below just rolling around laughing in the dim green glow of the passage.

After enough time, the effects of the mushrooms always wore off for the Wintersvilla Warriors that consumed them. I can't see this part of the future, so I have to assume the mushrooms will also wear off for Aliana. The alternative is too much to consider right now. I was able to make her throw up. I'm sure that dehydrated her, but there's nothing more I can do for now. She won't be of any help in this state. I'll have to get us the rest of the way myself.

Aurelia picked up the shard of Rooli then used her right hand to hang from the crevice's edge before finally dropping down and landing on her feet. She couldn't help marveling at the strangeness of being able to freely and effectively use a limb without feeling it. It felt unnervingly natural to utilize a part of her body that she couldn't directly feel.

The ten-foot-high, twenty-foot-wide passage wasn't filled with as many glowies, but there were still enough to provide ample light to see each other.

"Where'd you come from?" Aliana asked, shifting from mindless laughter to intense concern in a mere heartbeat.

"I need your help, Aliana. Can you try to focus?" Aurelia signed.

"Yeah, of course!" Aliana responded as if she had always been perfectly reasonable.

"But...why the fuck are we in a cave?" Aliana asked, bursting into such intense laughter that Aurelia thought she might not be able to breathe.

This is ridiculous. I told her not to eat the damn mushrooms.

"Aliana, please! I need you to work with me! Rooli's life is on the line," Aurelia urged, squeezing the shard in her left hand.

"Rooli lifeline," Aliana responded in a reasonable tone, as if her words made perfect sense.

Aurelia shook her head in agitation then stopped suddenly as vague information about the future was suddenly dropped into her mind with crystal clarity.

Someone is coming, she realized with some trepidation, for her sister was now a liability, despite being the vastly superior warrior between the two of them. *Someone is in this cave with us. Multiple people. Dangerous people.*

"Aliana, please!" Aurelia said, shaking Aliana with her right hand.

Hushed whispers in the distance quieted Aliana suddenly, and for a moment, Aurelia thought that the presence of danger might have sobered her enough to be semi-reasonable, but then Aliana said, "Mendel? That you?"

"Damn it, Aliana! Be quiet!" Aurelia signed hastily.

Aliana looked back at Aurelia like a child in the midst of playing a prank. "Oh, Mendel! Come out, come out, Denis Mendel," Aliana snickered, then she slowly waved her hands in front of her face and smiled pleasantly at her fingers.

It's too late, Aurelia knew as she gripped the hilt of her sword.

"You see, Doe? I told you I heard voices in the Feeding Cave," a raspy young boy's voice said angrily from somewhere in the tunnel.

"Sounds like a girl, eh?" another boy said, his voice high-pitched and nervous.

Aurelia could hear their footsteps coming closer.

"We have to hide," Aurelia signed, grateful that her sister was remaining silent for the moment. "People are coming. Boys."

"Or maybe it's the Feeding Hunter playing a trick on us," the shrill boy suggested with tangible fear.

"Oh, shut up, you chirping cricket," the raspy boy goaded. "It's just some green-head hunting greens. Big guarantee. Bet on it?"

"I've already told both of you multiple times: the Hunter is dead," a third boy stated, his voice harsh and strangely disciplined compared to the other two.

"Yeah, because we fucking killed it!" Aliana shouted through the tunnel with unconcerned laughter, prompting the boys' footsteps and bickering to abruptly stop.

Not good, Aurelia thought as she gripped her sword even tighter.

"We killed it, right? Or was that Myriam?" Aliana asked Aurelia with a cock of her head.

Aurelia just shook her head at her sister, aware that scolding her or attempting to quiet her would be equally ineffective in her current state.

Now they know for sure we're here, Aurelia thought as she slid her sword a few inches out of its sheath.

"Don't fucking move, rooster shits!" the raspy boy said with practiced confidence from the shadows. "I got a pusher. And my bromi Doe has claws. And he knows how to use them!"

"And a relic!" the high-pitched boy shouted, each of his words a quivering display of primal fear. "We got a relic!"

"Quiet," the disciplined boy said. "Both of you. The Hunter is dead, and apparently they're the ones that killed it. Have some respect."

Three young boys, all of them roughly around the same age as the girls, emerged from the dense shadows where glowies grew thin and eventually didn't grow at all.

Boys, Aurelia ruminated grimly, feeling strange to see the opposing gender, no matter how young, without collars around their necks.

"Look!" the raspy boy chuckled as all three boys came into view. "It's a couple of skinny girls. Just a couple of fucking green-headed rooster shits. They're just kids."

"So are we," the scared, high-pitched boy reminded him, while the disciplined boy remained behind them, occluded by the shadows. The scared boy was slightly taller than the other two, but he looked as skinny as the girls. He wore a plain white sleeveless shirt covered in tears and stains, revealing sinewy but strong musculature for his age. His loose gray slacks and sandals were even worse for wear, held together with networks of bioluminescent stitches and patches. Over his knuckles, he wore straps attached to miniature blades akin to claws. A winged insect the size of a closed fist stood on each of the boy's shoulders. Aurelia recognized them from old world books to be an insect called a grasshopper, though these were far bigger than those depicted in books. Both grasshoppers fluttered their wings and shifted their legs as if at all times ready to launch from the boy's shoulders.

Those claws look sharp, and the insects are likely effective at distracting an opponent during battle, Aurelia weighed. *He seems nervous, but I can tell by his stance that this boy is no foreigner to battle and violence…unlike his armored friend, despite his apparent confidence.*

Beside the tall, clawed, nervous boy apparently named Doe, the raspy boy stood without any sign of fear, smiling indignantly at the girls. Short, plump, and covered head to toe in vibrant armor and gadgetry, the raspy boy was like the mirror-opposite of Doe. Only a few bands of his dark brown skin could be seen. The rest of it was covered by striated layers of blue, red, and gold armor that appeared to move and remold itself as he swung his limbs or shifted his stance. His hair stuck out from a thin helmet, cascading behind him in an opalescent, otherworldly radiance. Numerous gadgets hung from his waist, including what appeared to be an old world combustion-based firearm that Aurelia knew was called a revolver. His eyes glowed blue, but they were nowhere near as vibrant as Aliana's and Aurelia's eyes. A metal chip was embedded into the boy's forehead. Wires extended from the chip to a single orange lens that seemed to hover without support directly in front of his left eye. At the boy's feet, a large rooster with identically colored feathers—blue, red, gold, and opalescent—strutted and cooed softly.

"Quiet, slaves," Aliana yelled at the boys before falling back to the ground in a fit of laughter.

Aurelia unsheathed her sword and pointed it at each boy in turn, first the clawed boy with the grasshoppers, then the armored one, and finally the boy still standing in the shadows as if using them to hide himself.

"Nice blade," the armored boy admitted. "But I got something better, eh bromi?"

With a wink, the boy removed the revolver from his waist and pointed it at Aurelia.

The combustion-based firearm, she realized with intrigue rather than fear. *I've seen projectiles before, like the one that Lain's exo was equipped with, but I've never seen an old world personal gun before. It looks…weak. I suppose it's fitting that these boys would wield something so tiny and insignificant, like their own lives,* Aurelia thought, refusing to lower her sword.

"Put it down, Ricardo" the boy in the shadows commanded. As if the raspy boy, Ricardo, had been shocked into discipline, he immediately did as he was told, lowering the gun and reholstering it at his waist.

Aliana tried to stand, but she fell right back down in a fit of laughter.

"How long you green-heads been out here, eh?" Doe asked, seeming to only just notice their wounds and the oversized adult clothing they had cut to size after killing Hunter541.

"She's clearly boomed out of her head," Ricardo said, pointing to Aliana. "What about you? You don't talk, or—"

"Your markings," the boy in the shadows said, stepping forward finally to reveal himself. He was the shortest of the boys and the only one whose hands and waist were free of weaponry. However, his gray eyes were like that of most Wintersvilla Warriors—cold, vicious, unforgiving. His thin, feathery gray hair hung down to his shoulders. He stared at Aurelia like a jeweler entranced by some otherworldly gem. "Your markings are...beautiful," the boy finished, his eyes wide in incredible awe.

Beautiful, Aurelia repeated in disbelief, for it was the first time someone outside of Aliana or Shira had ever called her beautiful. And certainly never a boy.

"Ayo, bromi," Ricardo snickered, "you trying to room up with this skinny green-head girl or what, eh?"

The disciplined boy ignored Ricardo and went on staring at Aurelia, looking as though he might lose himself in the same way Aurelia had felt when looking into Aliana's glowing emerald eye.

"Pretty wicked tattoos. And your contacts are cool too. I don't think I've ever seen any that get that bright before," Doe said, and then he picked up a lone glowie and bit it in half.

"Did you two really kill the Feeding Cave Hunter?" Ricardo asked.

Feeding Cave, Aurelia repeated, not sure what the term might mean. What was more important to her in that moment was the way the boy nonchalantly ate one of the glowies.

That must mean they aren't totally poisonous. Aliana's intoxication will wear off eventually.

"You boys sleep a salmon?" Aliana asked, then laughed and corrected herself, "Got any salmon, I mean? I'm a salmon myself," she finished, and then wriggled around on the ground like a fish out of water, laughing to herself the whole time.
"Holy Mendel. She is really boomed out, eh? How many greens did she eat?" Ricardo asked in what appeared to be impressed disbelief.

"She is unable to speak," the intense gray-eyed boy stated, still staring at Aurelia in wonder.

How does he know that? Was that just simple deduction since I haven't said anything yet, or...does he know who we are somehow? Aurelia considered with lethal suspicion.

Distant light burst from the shadows behind the boys suddenly, and Aurelia was forced to shield her eyes as Ricardo and Doe jumped back in fear. The gray-eyed boy quickly side-stepped and shimmied into a small crevice in the wall, disappearing into the thick shadows.

"The fuck you half-brained crickets doing in here? You know the Lord of Limbs made this place off limits! You trying to start a war, you little rooster shits?" a gruff voice demanded to know. As Aurelia's eyes adjusted, she saw an obscenely wide and muscular man covered in tattoos depicting barbaric, grotesque scenes of slaughter and death. His head was outlined by a shock of curly black hair, and he wore a large, scraggly beard that hung between his vein-bulging pectorals. At his waist hung blades of various sizes and shapes, along with strangely shaped firearms and an assortment of gadgets and other weaponry that Aurelia couldn't even guess at. His upper body was totally bare, save the numerous rope-sized necklaces and chains of gold and platinum that gleamed and mirrored the radiant diamond piercings lining his ears and lips. His cybernetic-laden musculature seemed to go on forever, and Aurelia realized that she had never seen so much muscle on a person. Shira was the most muscular individual she had ever known, but this man made Shira seem like a small child.

And yet Shira would slit his throat before he could utter a word, Aurelia knew, refusing to give into the fear that the man's bulk and tattoos were obviously meant to inject into others.

Aurelia placed the shard of Rooli at her feet then lifted her sword once more and pointed it at the man. Slowly, he turned his death-glare from the two boys standing petrified against the wall and brought his eyes to the half-dead twin girls, one of them covered in what he probably thought were tattoos and the other laughing to herself on the ground as she brushed her fingers gently across multiple glowies and pleasantly hummed some made up melody.

"Well, well, well," the man said, and his lips curled with feral delight. "What the hell do we have here? You little girls look lost. Why don't you let me help you?"

The man smiled wide to reveal gold that glinted across his pearl white teeth. Aurelia squinted and saw that the metal formed three identical words descending from his top lip to bottom lip: *Kill. Kill. Kill.*

"Oh shit," Aliana marveled, clearly reading the same words filling the man's mouth. "That is so badass. My teeth need an upgrade like that," Aliana proclaimed, her head wavering like a blade of grass in soft wind.

Aliana's still intoxicated. Rooli is still just a set of eyes. And my prescience isn't giving me any clues right now about what's to come. I have to do this alone. I have to protect Aliana. I have to save Rooli. I can do this, Aurelia forced herself to accept.

The man smiled wider, and the gold metal over his teeth flashed with violent purpose.

"Come along now," the man said, speaking as though he were trying to convince some prey animal to willingly cook itself. "You've got nothing to worry about. My name is Eddy, and I'm good at keeping people safe. Especially little girls."

Eddy laughed softly to himself, and then stepped forward, revealing that the extent of muscle Aurelia had been able to see with his body partially blocked by the doorway had only been a fraction of his total bulk. This man was more beast than human, with a body far larger than should be possible. Even the uncastrated studs of Wintersvilla whom the birthing mothers copulated with weren't nearly as large.

Aurelia lifted her sword higher, but it was like leveling a toothpick at a Biofreak.

"You got salmon?" Aliana asked as Eddy approached one small step at a time.

"Sure," he said unconvincingly. "I got lots of good stuff for you little girls. You just wait and see."

"Cool," Aliana marveled, focusing only on the metal in the man's mouth.

Just hang on, Rooli, Aurelia thought, but she knew that she was speaking more to herself than Rooli.

Kill. Kill. Kill, Aurelia read on the smiling man's teeth again. It was only then that her eyes lowered, and she saw that tattooed across his bare chest was an ultra-realistic, fully nude Wintersvilla Warrior hacking a ferocious Hunter to pieces in a spray of blood that covered his shoulders and neck. It was as if he thought of Wintersvilla Women as a form of distant mythology rather than reality, and Aurelia would have seen it as a form of admiration, even reverence, were it not for the woman's cartoonishly oversized breasts marring the artwork with distasteful, masculine stupidity.

As he closed the gap between them, Aurelia channeled Shira's fear-lessness and prepared herself to slice his oversized body into miniscule pieces.

Out of the black depths of the void, our galaxy was formed. And then our sun. And then our planet.

In time, the void will consume us once more.

No one is coming to save us. If we cannot build our own ladder out of the void of the cosmos and into the Great Beyond, then entropy will eventually increase to maximum, and spacetime, along with all forms of life in this universe, will be no more.

The void hungers for us. It beckons us. It is us, and we are it.

The fate of all life is oblivion. Nothingness. Void.

Mendel's Vision provides a pathway out of the Void. That pathway is Mendel's Ladder.

Were there another way, I would at the very least consider it. But there is no other way. Not according to Mendel. And who could I possibly trust more than him? He no longer has desires or motives. He is the best of humanity now, and also the least human.

I'm sorry, Denis. Forgive me, my only friend. Forgive me for what I have done to you and for what you, in this new form, will do to humanity.

From Mendel's Ladder: The Personal Journal of Denis Mendel, Written Circa 2036, Published June 2108 by Leif Mainstone, Federated Agency Publishing

Chapter 4
Out of the Black Depths

S amuel drifted down into the inky ocean depths as thick walls of kelp undulated in every direction, coaxing his mirror-body further and further away from the only thing that could or would ever matter.

Sandra. Margot. Nathan. Samuel sobbed as the ocean's shadows enveloped him. At the same time, the void-black nothingness that Tomasz had injected into his body went on consuming him.

Consumed like I was consumed with laboring for others. For Madeira—Andre Madeira, that goddamn bastard, Samuel seethed. *Maybe Sandra lied to me because she began to lose trust in me. I spent so much time away from her and the kids, time I wasted working for others when I could have spent every waking moment listening to Margot talk about history or watching Nathan play tag with his friends. Even when I was home, I couldn't help thinking about the old timers who needed the Workhorse to help them or else the recyclers would be satiated with their deaths. I'm a goddamn fool!*

As the walls of kelp undulated and coaxed him further into the dark, Samuel couldn't stop himself from visualizing his family being ripped to pieces by gigantic shadowy demons. It was the only thing his mind would allow him to focus on. Then, as if to torture him further, Samuel's mind suddenly flashed with the thought of winking out of existence. He felt the hollowed space between his pectorals and saw that the nothingness was expanding so fast that he could already fit his entire hand into the horrific crater in his chest.

Yellow-coated chunks of Giganventi slammed into the ocean above him like bombs before quickly dissolving into yellow haze.

This can't be it! Samuel thought, refusing to be destroyed by Andre Madeira or Tomasz Novak.

Lift! Samuel shouted at his body, trying to tap into it and burst forward like he had on the Giganventus, but again it failed him, refusing to obey.

This body is my own! My mind is my own! I say lift! Now, lift! he bellowed within, but still it was no use.

Fuck you! Samuel blazed at his body and himself and Tomasz and Andre and the world. Still, he sank further into the black depths, and his chest continued to hollow.

Fuck everyone! I don't deserve this. No one deserves this. My family doesn't fucking deserve this. My fucking kids! Samuel raged. *Get me out of this fucking godforsaken ocean, goddamnit!* Less than a heartbeat later, he felt something tug at his waist. Before he could even move his hands to inspect the source, he was launched upward so fast that his spine would have cracked in half were it not made of the mirror-substance.

As he emerged from the unlit depths and rapidly approached the water's sun-shimmering surface, he had a moment to observe a dark rope-like tendril wrapped around his waist and extending into the blinding light above. As if slapped by the sun, Samuel gritted his teeth as he broke the surface and was flung rapidly upward into the sky, sailing toward a gathering of large puffy white clouds. After a few moments, he felt himself begin to decelerate, and with the decrease in g-force, he was finally able to pivot his body to view the world below.

What is this place? Samuel gawked in disbelief. Rather than focus on the ground, Samuel's eyes were immediately directed ahead of him to a wall of raging, roiling storm clouds extending to his left and right as far as he could see. The behemoth storm of flashing lightning bolts and ocean-deep black clouds emitted a great, consistent bellow, like the planetary grumblings of the Earth. Every other second a particularly colossal bolt of lightning would cleave through the clouds, cracking the sky with distant thunder, a sound Samuel had only ever heard in old world movies.

Each distant crack of thunder made him feel infinitesimally small compared to the Earth and its power. Virtually all of the land in front of him, save the coast, was occluded by dense walls of dark rain emptying from the black clouds. However, on the coasts, between the walls of rain and the ocean, the land teemed with life. As he plummeted, Samuel noted in horror that there was nothing familiar or recognizable below him. The land was filled with bizarre gnarling trees of every color and hue. They grew as if they were a single entity, their branches and trunks intertwining so densely in some places that they appeared to form intentional structures.

Flesh trees, Samuel gasped, remembering his history lessons. The flesh trees appeared to grow rapidly as Samuel raced toward the ground, prompting him to brace for impact by curling his arms over his head and neck and tucking his legs in to minimize the damage. It was only then that he remembered he was the Mirror-Man. With a disappointed sigh, he extended his body and landed directly on his feet. He expected to slam into the sand and cut through it like a hot knife, but instead, the Earth's surface withstood his force as if capable of consuming his inertia. Not expecting such an easy landing, Samuel lost his balance and fell onto his back.

An eerie chorus of whispers and rustles filled the air suddenly. Samuel moved his hands to lift himself, but he was startled by the appearance of a strange face hovering over him. Oblong like a banana, the face still retained numerous human features. Freckled skin melded seamlessly to green fibrous tissue. High cheekbones gave way to leaf-like flaps that rustled softly with each of the creature's breaths. Moss-green tendrils sprouted here and there, glowing faintly and rippling like a serene, underwater garden. The tendrils of moss parted, revealing an all too human set of teeth between wriggling inhuman lips. Rather than speak, the creature emitted a series of high-pitch chirps, prompting Samuel to finally get up and back away a few steps toward the ocean he had just emerged from.

More Nomads, Samuel realized, weighing caution against urgency.

Two other Nomads stood a few feet away from the chirping Nomad. One was short and stocky, like the squat trunk of a chopped down tree. The stump Nomad contained no discernable human features outside of dozens of fungus-covered human hands sprouting from the top of its flat head. The other Nomad, sinewy and lean, stood at medium height relative to the first two. This one had feminine curves and a roughly humanoid face, except that it was covered in a littering of insectoid antennae and glistening mushrooms. A crown of tall, thin mushroom caps grew in place of her hair, each one wriggling atop her head like the slow fat worms in the Foundation's soil.

"Mirror-Man," the feminine Nomad said with an accent that Samuel was sure he had heard one of the old timers of the Foundation speak with. "His Foretold Future comes to fruition upon these hallowed shores of Waru. It is an honor to welcome you, Mirror-Man."

Just use these strange creatures. Forget about everyone and everything except what matters, Samuel reminded himself, and he glanced down nervously to find that he could easily fit both his fists into his chest now.

"Astrea. The Foundation. Take me there now!" Samuel nearly growled.

"Mirror-Man, that is not what happens next in His Foretold—"

Samuel lunged forward and grabbed the feminine Nomad by her spindly neck. He squeezed, and he found himself surprised that he could feel a heartbeat. Slow and steady. Undisturbed.

"Is this part of his Foretold Future? Is it?" Samuel screamed, and his voice pierced the air with a high-pitched shock of sound as it trembled through his mirror-larynx.

As he squeezed, Samuel envisioned Sandra with Margot in one hand and Nathan in the other running desperately away from the hordes of horrific monsters rampaging through the Foundation at the Queen's behest.

"Take me to my family now! Now! Now!" Samuel ordered wildly, and without even intending it, he squeezed hard enough to snap the Nomad's neck, decapitating her in an explosion of green and blue sticky fluids.

Samuel jumped back in shock.

I...I killed her, I didn't mean to squeeze that hard, Samuel lamented. Despite the Nomad's many alien features, he still felt remorse for taking another being's life. It was only then that he remembered that this alien being had once been human.

"I'm sorry, I..." Samuel began, but the Nomad's body suddenly convulsed, making Samuel jump back in surprise. Just as the Nomad's head hit the ground, her body and her head both sprouted into rapidly growing trees that intertwined into a single tree as they met. Samuel instinctively stepped back to avoid being consumed by the tree's ravenous growth. The other two Nomads just stood there as if the death of their companion was as mundane as a sunrise.

"Take me to Astrea, or I will turn you both into goddamn trees," Samuel threatened, hoping that it wouldn't have to come to that. However, the Nomads didn't appear intimidated.

As the tree slowed its growth and finally came to a halt, Samuel observed that it was composed of flesh, insectoid antennae, and hair-like mushrooms. Pods grew like slowly inflating balloons from every branch and twig.

From beneath the tree's thick canopy of fungus and flesh pods, the moss-tendril Nomad opened its mouth and released another series of chirps.

"Did you two hear me?" Samuel repeated, feeling silly for attempting to threaten them—these beings who appeared at all times calm and ready for death.

I don't have time to deal with this! Samuel thought, fighting the urge to look down at his disappearing chest.

"To transition and become a flesh tree is the promise that every Nomad holds at the forefront of their mind," a strong but tired woman's voice stated from behind the now mammoth tree laden with pods that looked like unnatural, tumorous growths. The source of the voice emerged from behind the flesh tree, and Samuel was both surprised and haunted by the intense feeling of familiarity as he looked upon this stranger in a strange land. A human woman gazed suspiciously at Samuel with unblinking eyes that held the promise of both lethality and refinement—like an exquisitely engraved blade with an edge forged by battle rather than mundane sharpening. At the same time, she appeared altogether defeated, as if she had been waging a lifelong battle that she knew could not be won. She looked a few years younger than Samuel, but there was a timeless quality to her, as if this woman had lived many lifetimes before arriving to these shores. Her dark skin, like something right out of the black depths of the ocean, contrasted sharply against the technicolor hues of the flesh tree and the two Nomads. Large gold hoop earrings dangled liberally from her ears, reflecting the cataclysmic stabs of lightning in the storm many miles behind her.

I know her, Samuel gawked, though he was equally certain that it shouldn't be possible. *I recognize her.*

Her hair, cropped close to the scalp, provided an austere edge to her features, allowing her eyes to truly captivate. As she reached out a hand and plucked a fist-sized pod from the tree, Samuel watched as her eyes gleamed with the accumulated wisdom and weight of ages, possessing an inscrutable depth that spoke of the rise and fall of entire empires.

But how can that be? Samuel wondered, for this petite and lithe woman looked as though she might get blown away by the great storm in the distance. And yet, each of her movements indicated raw strength and indomitable will rippling beneath the surface of her small frame.

She stepped toward Samuel, her silken garments wavering in the gentle yet unceasing wind. Samuel instinctively stepped back as he recollected that he was still caught in Madeira's web.

"What do you want?" Samuel demanded, knowing that she was likely either one of Madeira's conspirators or another target Madeira had planned to destroy—like Tomasz.

"I'm not certain," the woman responded levelly. "My whole life I've been trying to figure out the answer to that very question, but even after all this time, I still have no idea. So, for now, I just want to keep my end of a deal I made with the devil."

The woman pierced the top of the pod with one of her manicured fingernails, revealing a green glow emanating from the inside of the strange fleshy fruit.

"Here," she said, offering Samuel the glowing flesh pod. "I've no idea how this works. I'm assuming you do."

Samuel shook his head in total confusion, unsure how to even properly protest.

"I don't know what you're talking about. And I don't care. I'll kill you too if I have to. I swear I will," Samuel threatened, and he hoped that she would believe his words rather than force him to go through with the act, for he wasn't sure he would actually be able to. "I'm done with the niceties," Samuel insisted more to himself than this woman. "I'm tired of these goddamn plant people. They're supposed to listen to me. At least, that's what that old bastard told me would happen. But they won't take me back to Astrea. They keep playing games with me. Why won't you take me back?" Samuel shouted, turning to the chirping Nomad, who just stood and watched Samuel with a pleasant smile.

"They can't. And I can't," the woman stated. "But even if we could bring you back to Astrea now, how would you save your family, Mirror-Man?"

I never told her about my family, Samuel realized with grim suspicion.

"There is a great deal I know about you and what is to come, Mirror-Man. You are part of his Foretold Future. As am I. As is everyone."

"Mendel, you mean?" Samuel asked.

The woman shook her head painfully at Samuel's suggestion and nervously caressed the ring finger on her left hand where there might have once been a ring.

"Denis Mendel merely charted the future on behalf of Andre Madeira. It is Andre Madeira's world we all live in, and it is his future we are forced to take part in—like leaves unable to sustain themselves without the tree's nourishing trunk."

Nourishing, Samuel scoffed with intense loathing.

"There is nothing nourishing about Andre Madeira or anyone who works for him."

The woman nervously licked her lips and cocked her head as if she was surprised by Samuel's accusation.

"Do you not work for Andre?" the woman asked with unrestrained surprise in her tone.

"Of course not!" Samuel lashed, sickened by the knowledge that no matter how hard he fought, he was still likely just a puppet on Madeira's strings.

"Interesting," the woman stated with seemingly genuine curiosity. Her gaze was both penetrating and probing as she dissected Samuel with clinical precision.

She exudes the intellect of Tomasz Novak and the depth of Andre Madeira, Samuel noted, and he almost looked behind him to check if pieces of yellow slime mold might slither out of the ocean and consume this woman whole.

"Take this," the woman urged, thrusting the glowing green pod closer to Samuel. "If you are to stand against the Queen and save your family, then you must stop yourself from being consumed by Tomasz' weapon before you can even get back up to Astrea. I believe that this is the answer," she said, offering him the pod with a level of urgency that Samuel could now see she had been consciously stifling before.

She's nervous about the timing of everything, just like Madeira was when he first injected me with this infernal mirror-substance. She has to be working for him. How else could she know so much about me?

Samuel glanced down at his chest and suddenly couldn't control his arms. They jutted out to grab the pod the moment he saw how much of his chest had already disappeared. A six-inch-deep, all-black crater spanning the entire space between his nipples continued spreading with ravenous, tendrilling movements.

I don't have a choice but to accept her help and Madeira's help in turn, Samuel admitted.

He gripped the pod and tried pouring the glowing contents into the void-space that had once been his rippling pectorals, but nothing came out.

"What do I do?" Samuel asked with panic in his voice.

"I don't know," the woman said, raising her eyebrows and caressing her ring finger nervously. "I'm not even sure these pods are what will stop Tomasz' weapon. I just figured they're here, right where you showed up, so—"

"What do you mean you don't know, goddamnit?" Samuel shouted, feeling the urgency to save his family and himself more than ever as he violently shook the pod to no avail.

"Fuck it!" Samuel said, and he slammed the pod against his chest. The pod burst, releasing a thick fog of green gas. As if magnetically attracted to the black spreading through Samuel, the glowing gas shifted in the air suddenly, then gushed into his chest. The gas condensed to a liquid that bubbled beneath the void-black of his chest like dying creatures in a tar pit. Finally, small green-glowing mushrooms sprouted from the black hollow and grew to the edges, overtaking the probing black tendrils and stopping them from spreading.

"You see?" the woman said as if mushrooms growing out of the hollow chest of a reflective man was as predictable of an occurrence as sitting down to eat dinner. "Nothing is a coincidence. Not anymore. Not with the reins of this entire planet—this entire universe—in the hands of one mind."

"Now what?" Samuel said, not caring about anything this woman might say or offer him, save one and only one thing.

"Now you have more time to do what you will do," the woman offered, and then she sighed deeply and pitifully, as if she had been nervous that this exact moment with Samuel might not occur.

"Time," Samuel huffed. "My family doesn't have time. You understand, goddamnit?"

"The truth is, if you want to go to Astrea, you could go there now," the woman said with seeming regret. "Your body is capable of it. But then again, you might bullet through the Foundation and destroy it, or you might overshoot it and end up on the other side of the solar system, trapped and waiting for a solid surface to launch from again—which might take years, centuries, millennia even." The woman shifted her bare feet, turning to face Samuel directly. "Mirror-Man, think about it. Even if you went to Astrea right now and found a way to safely bring your family down here, then what? Is this world really any better than the dangers they now face? Is this where you would have them live? Here, in the land of Waru?"

Waru, Samuel thought, remembering that Sunny Marigold had mentioned Waru as a place that might be able to help him return to his family.

The woman turned and gestured to the land that Samuel had seen from above. While the great raging walls of rain occupied the vast majority of the air and land, the area between the storm and the coastline was filled with numerous forms of life.

How can she claim that this place is just as bad as being hunted down by otherworldly monsters in Astrea? Samuel thought as he lifted his head to observe one of the countless veiny gray trees stretching out like eager hands to the sky. Glistening webs extended between the spindly branches of these trees, visibly collecting the moist ocean air into condensation that flowed as rivulets to each tree's trunk. Finally, the cascading water collected into frothing waterfalls that rained from the webbed trees down onto the canopy of flesh trees below. Below the flesh trees, hordes of seemingly well-fed people and Nomads milled about, unharmed by the downpour.

She must be wrong, Samuel considered as he marveled at the abundant water being supplied to Waru by the ocean air. *Or she's lying to me. This place has water, and its people are not starving. I can bring Sandra and the kids here and keep them safe. It's certainly preferable to the alternative.*

Samuel looked back to the raging storm and wondered if it ever grew and overtook the coasts. *Maybe the storm is the reason she doesn't think this place is safe,* Samuel considered before shaking his head and resolving that he had no other choice.

"This place or another place on Earth's surface is where I will have to raise my children, for better or worse," Samuel concluded. However, the woman just shook her head and pointed, directing Samuel's vision to the people whom he had already seen. Samuel hadn't noticed before due to how naturally they all moved about the environment, but he now saw that there were hundreds, if not thousands, of figures navigating the living space in front of him. Beneath the tall webbed water trees, flesh trees of every shade and hue pulsated with a life of their own and grew in wily and unexpected shapes, intertwining to form tunnels and hollows that were used by both Nomads and humans alike.

It's like an alien world, Samuel thought, *but if what Sandra said is true, then it's still better than Astrea.*

Samuel saw hundreds of pods hanging from every flesh tree, each a visual and textured reflection of the particular flesh tree from which they grew. They varied in size from small apple-like clusters to large womb-like structures big enough to hold a fully grown adult. Each pod rhythmically throbbed, like a myriad of alien hearts beating in unison.

Despite the woman's demeanor and clear disapproval of the alien environment, Samuel found it surprisingly easy to stomach the thought of raising Margot and Nathan in Waru. Samuel couldn't help feeling entranced by the natural, symbiotic rhythm of the people, both Nomads and humans, living in sync with the environment of Waru. It was as if their very breath was attuned to each flesh tree's respiration.

They live as one with the land, just like Foundationers in Astrea, Samuel thought, further convincing himself that Waru was a viable place to live alongside his family and his people.

Among the flesh trees, Nomads scuttled about with an air of focused determination, tending to the pods with care. A pair of insectoid Nomads fluttered between the trees on dragonfly wings, checking on larger, high-up pods. A quartet of vine-like creatures, their faces awash in flowering plants, tended to a group of smaller pods near the ground, their tendrils softly pulsating as they handled the pods. When Samuel looked at the humans working alongside the Nomads, however, he realized they struggled and labored to complete the same work that seemed to fill the Nomads with joy. The humans were diverse in appearance and age, apparently hailing from all different regions of the old and new world, but their faces wore a common expression—one of misery and despair. They worked just as determinedly as the Nomads, but it looked more like servitude than willful labor.

Maybe this place isn't as harmonious as I thought.

"Slaves?" Samuel asked, wondering if this woman was their owner.

"Not exactly," the woman said as she rubbed her ring finger with a look of intense anguish. "They are free to leave or become Nomads. They choose to labor as humans because they fear being transformed as much as they fear attempting to survive anywhere outside Waru. I don't blame them. I was given a choice, and I chose to live in Waru for the same reason that many of these people end up on these shores. Most of them set out on makeshift boats into the great oceans in search of old world havens—places that haven't yet been fully transformed into the Nomadic world. Most of them die. By luck, some people end up on these shores."

"I would hardly call that luck. Luck is being one of Astrea's chosen few," Samuel said before wincing and internally correcting himself.

No, goddamnit, that isn't true! Astrea is a prison, and now it is a hell.

The woman sighed deeply then nodded agreeably. "Fair enough. I agree with you, Mirror-Man—this world, including Waru, is a horror, not a joy. But then again, it's not for you and me. This new world is for the Nomads and the people who will come after them. It is for those people that you must prepare the Earth, Mirror-Man. That is your role in all this, I think. Only Mendel knows the whole story, however. I don't think Andre knew everything, though I can already hear him arguing against that statement. He would say something like, 'Mendel's Vision is the vision of the universe itself. I have no need to know everything. It is knowable—that is all that is relevant to me,'" the woman intoned with an air of mock pomposity and arrogance.

At the mention of Andre Madeira, Samuel was reminded of his mirror-body. He glanced down to check the state of his chest and was relieved to find that the green mushrooms were still keeping the spread of the blackness and its subsequent erasure of his body at bay.

"Tomasz' weapon has been halted for now, but there is still a timing to everything. We must move forward," the woman said regretfully. With expert rapidity, the woman ripped a section of her silken sari to produce a thin strip of silk. Then, she plucked five small pods from one of the flesh tree's branches near her head, placed them in the silk strip, and spun the strip, encasing the pods in the material. Finally, she offered Samuel the pod-filled silk strip.

"Wrap this around yourself. Maybe it would be best to wrap it around your waist and secure it between your thighs so that your...well...so you aren't flopping around everywhere," the woman said with a sullen chuckle. "You will need more of these pods. Those mushrooms can only last so long against the void from which Tomasz crafted the weapon he used against you."

Samuel imagined the void-black resuming its consumption of his body, and he shivered at the thought of disappearing completely.

"Shouldn't I take more pods, then?" Samuel checked, still on edge as he considered that this woman might simply be manipulating him to walk directly into a trap.

The woman slowly shook her head in quiet defeat. "Maybe. I don't know the full future, Mirror-Man. I only know glimpses. I don't know how long each pod will last you, but I do know that you can't waste time, for although his Foretold Future appears set in stone, I'll tell you a secret: it isn't."

She stared at Samuel as if testing his resolve and how he might respond in the face of some impossibly mighty foe.

"That Mendel might be wrong is the only thing Andre ever really feared. Despite his tenacity, I'm certain that deep down, he feared that everything—the universe itself—can't just be succinctly calculated and understood. Personally, I think there will always be something beyond every form of comprehension, for existence is more than just numbers to be calculated. It has to be. I know it is. I can feel it," she said with a fierceness that broke through her sorrowful malaise, telling Samuel this wasn't the first time she had contended with the subject.

Samuel's heartbeat quickened as a vision of vague shadowy monsters chasing his children struck through his mind.

"What does any of that have to do with me getting back to my family?" Samuel asked, dismissing everything else as unimportant detritus.

"I'm saying that it is possible you won't be able to save your family, Mirror-Man. That is one of numerous possible futures—many of which are occluded even from the mycelial network of the Nomads—the mind of Earth, that is. The last half century has played out exactly as Mendel foretold it would, but soon the future becomes tumultuous and hazy, like a boulder thrown into a placid lake. You are that boulder, Mirror-Man. You have the ability to decide the future, and it is because of you that Mendel's Foretold Future is not a guarantee. At least, that is the conclusion I have come to—though I admit I might be wrong."

Samuel shook his head and looked back down at his chest. He wasn't sure, but he thought the mushrooms might already be dimming in their bioluminescent intensity.

I can't just disappear and never see them again, Samuel lamented. *But the mushrooms are already beginning to fail.*

Lift, Samuel's mind lashed, demanding that he stop listening to this woman—that he stop thinking and just find a way to act immediately.

She said I could jump to Astrea if I really wanted to. I have to accept the risk of hitting it or flinging myself into space. I need to get back to them. Now. Right now!

Samuel lifted his head, searching the sky for Astrea, but it was nowhere in sight.

"I have to go back. I have to do it now. My family might already be out of time! I'm going to Astrea now. I don't have a choice," Samuel told her.

The woman nodded uncomfortably and took two shallow steps backward, apparently giving him space to jump into the sky. She stared curiously at Samuel as she wrung her hands nervously together.

Samuel bent at the knees, looked straight up, and prepared to launch himself to the edge of space for a better view of Astrea's current location.

Do as I command! Samuel ordered his body, and just like on the Giganventus, he envisioned his family and felt his veins engorge with rage at himself for not attempting to jump sooner.

Fuck Mendel's goddamn Foretold Future, Samuel thought, and he extended his legs with all his might, exploding upward three feet into the air before falling right back down.

"Goddamnit!" Samuel screamed, slamming his fists against his legs with a piercing metal clang that he didn't even feel. "Didn't you say I could jump up to Astrea if I wanted?"

"You will learn to use the mirror-substance's full strength, Mirror-Man. I have seen it. Right before everything goes hazy and potential futures multiply like dandelion seeds caught in the wind—it is then that you will make a decision to decide the course of everything, and it is then that you will truly awaken to your full potential."

Learning that he had the capability to use his mirror-body's full strength but would be unable to utilize it until a set time in the future made Samuel feel altogether helpless, which in turn frustrated him even more.

"It makes no difference," the woman urged as if attempting to smother Samuel's visible rage. "I'm telling you, Mirror-Man. The Earth would just pull you right back down to the surface. I've seen it. I've experienced it. He won't allow anyone to leave Earth. I've tried it, Mirror-Man. So have Gladys and Tomasz and many others. Not even Gladys can escape Mendel's Vision and Andre's will. Not yet. Not until we get rid of them."

"Get rid of them?" Samuel inquired, ignoring the name *Gladys* in light of his urgency. "Madeira and Mendel, you mean?"

The woman nodded, forlorn but filled with resolve.

"Andre Madeira is already dead," Samuel stated with a wash of joy that he did not attempt to correct.

"Yes, I know. He died long ago. I'm not talking about Andre or Mendel as individuals, but the…thing they turned themselves into. The Mind."

"No. Madeira died less than a day ago," Samuel corrected, guessing at the amount of time that had passed without the signaling of day and night from the light of the Foundation's glowglobes. The woman looked deeply disturbed, as if Samuel had just raised Andre Madeira from the dead.

"I was with him when he died," Samuel went on, recollecting the old man's demise with a sense of unimpeded relishment. "He was the oldest man in the Foundation. Old Man Madeira—that's what we all called him. He's the one who did this to me. He's the one who ruined my life and plunged my family and my people into misery. He was working for the Queen all along."

"He was old?" the woman asked, latching on to what Samuel considered an unimportant detail of the destruction of everything he held dear.

"Ninety-nine years old. Like I said, the oldest in the Foundation. The only reason he didn't get recycled was because I spent my time keeping him alive instead of spending all that time with my wife and kids. I…I…" Samuel stammered, falling back into the misery of believing that Sandra's betrayal was entirely his fault.

"Ninety-nine," the woman repeated with disbelieving, wide eyes. "Just like he suggested so long ago. Ninety-nine years old—living any longer than that is the ultimate form of greed in a system of limited resources. That's what he always said. How did he die?"

"What does that matter?" Samuel practically growled in impatient frustration at being stuck talking to this woman still. "He's dead. Dead.

Gone. And my family is still alive. You say I will learn to use my mirror-body's strength. Fine. I'm not going to waste my time jumping three feet into the air over and over again. Let's go. Take me where I'm supposed to go next so I can finally have full control of this fucking body, jump up to Astrea, save my family, then come down here and command every fucking Nomad to kill themselves," Samuel fumed, though he knew that his words were just anger. He hoped that no one else would have to die for him to save his family, human or Nomad.

The woman raised her eyebrows with more genuine intrigue at Samuel's words.

"I suppose that is one solution to the dilemma I proposed to you earlier, but it still wouldn't solve everything," the woman sighed, and then she turned and began walking toward the great storm.

"Come," she said without looking back. "It's like you said: we just have to keep going. Everything is set in stone for a while…until it isn't."

Samuel shook his head, hateful that he had no choice but to follow her. As he stepped quickly to catch up with her, he noticed a small black and green tattoo depicting a butterfly with oversized fangs on the back of her neck, revealing the woman's identity in a sudden flash of recall.

"Fana something," Samuel said, stopping before they reached the thick flesh trees and people of Waru. "That's your name. Fana. I can't remember your last name. But you're…you're one of them. Aren't you?" Samuel asked, remembering the woman from Margot's and Nathan's history lessons and his own history lessons as a boy.

The woman stopped in her tracks suddenly as if Samuel's words had entrenched her feet in thick mud. She sighed and let her shoulders fall in defeat.

"Yes," she said without turning to meet Samuel's mirror-eyes. "I am Doctor Fana Tsehay. And I am…one of them, as you said. One of the people responsible for this Nomadic world, this…this…" the woman stammered. She turned finally, and her eyes were filled with a mix of profound rage and grief. "I can't take back what I've done. None of us can. I'm sorry, Mirror-Man. I'm…I really am sorry. I know that means nothing, but…I am a human being. I made mistakes. We all make mistakes."

"Mistakes," Samuel repeated on the verge of painful laughter. "Is that all? Turning the world to hell. The deaths of billions of people. The destruction of the human race. Is that all it was? A series of mistakes?"

Fana breathed deeply and lifted her chin before raising her eyebrows in turn, looking as though she were assessing Samuel. "When the time comes, I hope you make the right decisions, Mirror-Man. I hope you will not live the rest of your life in despair and regret…like me," she stated as if in actual challenge.

Fana turned and continued walking in the direction of the people of Waru and the great storm raging over the land beyond them. As she walked, Fana said, "I saw in the Nomad network that a flying Nomad will carry you from Australia to the U.S. I mean, from Waru to the Butcher Wastelands, or Wastes as it is also referred to. The flying Nomad is waiting for you a mile or so inland from here. Come, we've no time to lose."

Denis called me yesterday. Seeing his name on my holo for the first time in twelve years was like tasting ocean water while at the precipice of death by dehydration. I thought he was calling me to tell me he knew I had been lurking in his family's networks. I thought he knew all about my plans to destroy his and his family's empire from within. The Mendels...they are my greatest enemies, despite Denis Mendel being my only real friend.

Maybe he did know. Knowing Denis, of course he did. But that isn't why he called. I answered the holo, and without even saying hello or engaging with his usual vanguard of silence until directly addressed, he immediately began speaking without allowing me a word. He said, "It is like you always told me: the world is dying. Well, not the Earth, but the human world. My world. Your world. And everyone else's. I'm sure you saw that the Beijing Accord was nullified with the U.S.'s refusal to abide by the Berlin Climate Proposals. You should hear the other family heads and even the youngest of the families. It's exactly like you said, Andre. Their hedonism requires the sacrifice of the entire planet and its people. They have already accepted that this planet will eventually be destroyed by climate change, nuclear war, and pollution. It is part of their ultimate plan to remain in absolute power. I didn't listen to you when we were younger. I didn't want to. There must always be rulers when it comes to the human species, and you are right that it is those who are most ruthless and cunning, and also most greedy and gluttonous, who will always naturally rise to the top of the social order, like lard in water. I see now that this is the simple, inescapable truth of humanity. So, I am ready, Andre. I'm sorry it took me over a decade. I'm sorry that I've allowed billions to suffer in that time. But I am ready now to embrace a new way for humanity. I am ready, my friend. Will you help me destroy this old world of greed and gluttony and direct the human species down a path of righteousness and meaning?"

Upon hearing Denis' words, I sat there in silence at my holo terminal in the apartment that was no larger than a closet, bathroom and all. I needed nothing else. I wanted nothing else.

I burst into tears, and I sobbed for the first time in many decades.

"Yes," I told my friend through my sobs of joy. "Yes, Denis. I don't care how long it has been. My answer is yes."

This marks the beginning of a new story, not only for Denis and me, but for humanity itself. Every story has a beginning. My personal story began at the age of nine, with a gun placed against my forehead. I didn't know it at the time, but I see now that that gun placed against my skull, and the subsequent loss of everything I held dear, instigated within me a luminous transformation that blazes even to this day.

Last night, I could hear in Denis' voice that a fire finally caught hold within him too. The same fire I tried lighting within him so many years ago. Now he burns with the same unwavering radiance that has guided me all these years. I thought I had failed with Denis, but it just took longer than I thought it would.

From Mendel's Ladder: The Personal Journal of Denis Mendel, Written Circa 2032, Published June 2108 by Leif Mainstone, Federated Agency Publishing

Chapter 5
Nowhere to Run

Year: 2009

"We can run," Andre Madeira pleaded, whimpering in desperation at his parents' heels as they peered out the shattered old window of their ninth story apartment. As if haphazardly constructed as a flippant afterthought, the single window was carved randomly into the wall, just a few inches from the ceiling and door. His parents had to struggle and stand on their tiptoes, looking like drowning marionettes just to see the outside world, but Andre had always reasoned that their inability to look outside was for the best. Outside the window, fields of smog and waste processing plants extended for miles, eventually leading to the wealthy gated suburbs and finally to the maniacally beating heart that was Denver's central metropolis.

"We can run!" Andre, only nine years old, urged through tears that he knew deep down would do him no good. "Please!" he begged, but his parents were adhered to the window, both of them wide-eyed and trembling. Their visible fear felt like needles piercing his skin, like a fire roasting his flesh.

If they are this afraid, then this is it. This is the day they've been arguing about for as long as I can remember. And it's...it's my fault, Andre cursed himself bitterly. Then he cursed the universe, for he didn't ask to be born with a one-in-a-million heart defect.

"Is that them?" Andre's mother Ruth asked with a crack in her voice. She was a weak and fragile woman, but she was also warm and gentle. At five foot ten inches, she stood just an inch shorter than Andre's father, but her body occupied less than half the space. Andre's father Julian was no longer the expansive, muscular man of his youth, but he still retained a great deal of his strength, especially working quadruple overtime at the local waste processing plant. After working there so long, the smog seemed to emanate from his pores.

"We'll know them when we see them," Julian said, bracing himself against the wall with his shaking muscles. Andre had never seen his father exhibit animal fear like this before. "They'll be sending a whole fleet of Winters Security Officers. We're a billion in the hole, Ruth. A billion. And the interest is only getting worse."

"We can run!" Andre shouted, desperate to quell his parents' fear and stop the terrible pain coursing through his veins.

Why won't they just listen to me? Andre thought.

Ruth turned, scooped Andre up, and broke down into tears as she held him. She sobbed and whimpered hopelessly into his neck.

"There's no more running, boy," Julian grunted, tears welling in his eyes. "Your mother and I are worth half a billion each at a Tsehay Manufactury. Novak Medical wants their money, and if they can't get that, then they take our bodies. I'm sorry Andre, but this is just the world we live in. If we let the debt with Novak Medical get any higher, they'll put you in a Tsehay Manufactury too, and we aren't going to let that happen. Isn't that right, Ruth?"

Ruth squeezed Andre tighter and sobbed with convulsive force as she shook with utter terror.

"Fuck Novak Medical!" Andre pleaded, pulling away from his mother to address his parents. "Fuck Winters Security! Fuck Tsehay Corporation! Fuck all the corps! Don't just give up! Please! Please!"

I don't want to be alone, Andre thought as he imagined being forced to go on the run and live as a train hopper or sewer scuttler or both.

Normally his parents would have corrected his cursing, but now was not the time for such trivialities. Andre knew as well as they did—this was life and death.

"Mommy," Andre begged, "I know endless paths through the sewers. You and dad just need to trust me, I—"

"That's enough, boy," Julian said, gentle yet stern. Andre wanted to protest, but he knew that his parents would not be able to fit through many of the smaller tunnels. Andre imagined his parents living in the sewers for the rest of their lives. He could steal food and bring it to them. Water could be cleaned using a filter he could swipe from the markets on the outskirts of the suburbs.

We can make it work.

A heartstopping series of thumps filled the air, erasing Andre's futile vision of remaining with his parents.

"It's them," Julian gulped as he peered outside the window. "Get ready, Ruth. Get away from the boy."

"No!" Andre shrieked, and then everything happened so quickly. The thumping grew so loud that Andre couldn't even hear himself scream.

Helicopters, he knew, for he had seen other apartments and houses raided by Winters Security Officers hired by Novak Medical to collect their outstanding debts—either in assets or in flesh.

Blinding white light pierced the shattered window, and then shadows passed in front of the light, one after another.

Julian grabbed Ruth and pulled her away from Andre, and though Andre knew it was to protect him, it still hurt worse than anything to feel his mother's grip torn away from him. He knew in that moment this would be the last time he ever felt his mother's gentle touch.

All at once, the door of the Madeira family's ninth-floor, one-bedroom apartment burst open under the catastrophic force of an armored boot, sending splinters of faux-wood paneling raining into the room. The world was swallowed by the dark silhouettes of five monstrous figures, colossal and hulking, their bodies armored and full of Winters weaponry built with Mainstone technology. Their eyes glowed red behind their faceless black visors, providing thermal vision.

"Get the fuck down! Now! Get down!" they all screamed in a confusing array of violent tones, oppressors basking in the dominance granted by their oligarchic overlords. The dim light of the apartment gleamed off the metal carapaces of their numerous weapons, casting long, grotesque shadows on the cracked and peeling walls.

Both of them kneeling on the ground, Julian held his hands up to protect Ruth, who gawked at these armored monsters, their guns pulsating with a terrifying bioluminescent light. The eerie glow was strung through a labyrinth of wires that extended from their weapons to the visors they wore. Each one of them was a walking monument to the cruel efficiency of Winters Security Forces and the for-profit world at large.

"I said get on the fucking ground!" the head officer ordered as he kicked Ruth hard in the gut. The head officer was the only one without a helmet on. The pale white skin of his bald head shone with the same menacing glint as the bulky revolver holstered at his hip. A razor field of scars etched his face and neck, making his already unsavory appearance seem almost ghoulish.

"Just leave the boy alone," Julian begged as he moved to comfort Ruth. "We'll go, just leave the boy."

Andre had never heard his father beg, and it made him tremble to see him cower beneath these inhuman, savage specters. Stimulant cocktails coursed through their veins like molten fury, transforming them into grotesque nightmares that had captured the Earth and all its people save the select few at the top.

"Did you just give me an order, waste worker?" the head officer asked. "Did he just give me an order?" he asked again, turning to one of his subordinates, all of whom Andre assumed were brain-hollowed and operating on Mendelian AI, rather than their own will.

I have to do something, Andre thought in horror, for he knew that his parents would soon suffer the same fate. Legally they would still be alive, they would even seem normal and happy in many ways, but in reality, their internal-self, their very sense of being, would be erased and replaced by a loyal algorithm.

"Please!" Andre begged, sounding like a squeaking mouse beneath the ready claws of the hungry jaguars standing before him and his parents. "Please just give us more time. Please, I—"

"Andre, quiet!" Julian ordered while Ruth gasped for air as she sobbed.

"We'll go with you," Julian managed through his trembling, "just please leave him alone. Please. I beg you. Just—"

"Shut the fuck up!" the head officer raged suddenly, shifting in temperament with capricious brutality. The officer spread his lips, gritted his teeth, and swung his fist against Julian, then Ruth, then Julian. He bored down on both of them like a rabid gorilla, his armored fists landing with bone-shattering force as he laughed with sordid glee. Each punch and each kick landed with such force that it echoed off the crumbling apartment walls.

Andre stood frozen as he watched his parents beaten into shaking, bloody masses on the floor. Julian grunted under the unrelenting barrage, his body a mass of shattered bone and viscera. Ruth, her pleas for mercy swallowed by the macabre cacophony, could only curl defensively as the head officer tore into her with ruthless abandon. The echoing symphony of suffering composed a dirge to their unraveling existence as their scant hopes and dreams crumbled around them like the walls of their home.

"Sir," one of the other officers stated nervously, pulling the head officer out of his writhing rage. "I know you like to get physical, but they must be—"

"I know, I know," the head officer grunted. "Shut the fuck up and get to the chopper. All of you. Take these waste workers. I want to talk to the kid."

Anguish twisted Andre's heart, his tears of impotent rage burning as they fell from his eyes. He lunged toward his parents, desperate to help, only to be met with the cold black steel muzzle of a large revolver. The barrel of the gun was an abyss, the cock of its hammer echoing loudly in the tense silence. The head officer's eyes were cold and devoid of empathy. He smirked as he held the barrel level with Andre's forehead, and the world seemed to fall into a sickening silence.

"No, Andre!" Julian's cry pierced the air, the desperation palpable in the hoarse blood-curdling syllables. "It's okay, son. It's okay. Don't let your heart be filled with hate."

The other officers stood like obedient gargoyles while the head officer's cruel laughter filled the room, echoing off the walls with bone-chilling reverberation. With a sneer carved into his scar-filled face, he said, "Don't lie to your filth kid, filthy waste worker. It's far from okay. You two are going to get hollowed out, and your kid is going to be homeless until he grows desperate enough to come work for some of my…esteemed associates in Denver," he chuckled, clearly intending for his words to burrow into their hearts, to twist the knife of despair deeper.

Ruth, her body bruised and battered, shrieked in terror for her son. The officer turned to her, the sneer never leaving his face, and said, "Shut up, you whiny cunt. Don't make this any worse than it has to be. You didn't pay, so now you pay the only way you can."

At his words, Andre beheld a vision of himself using a shard of glass from the shattered window to gouge the man's eyes out and then slit his neck open. The vision felt so real that he could almost taste the iron of the man's blood and feel the warmth of his life draining from his body.

Die, Andre thought as overwhelming pain lanced every inch of his body like sharpened spears while the unforgiving inferno of all the world's suffering burned and consumed his living flesh.

"I know that look," the man said, and for just an instant his upper lip quivered before returning to his sinister smirk.

Die, Andre screamed in his mind, but his body would not obey him. He was paralyzed in fear at the sight of the black abyss stretching into the gun's barrel.

The head officer holstered his revolver and nodded to the other officers. In response, the officers dragged Andre's parents through the door, his dad struggling to breathe and his mom shrieking Andre's name.

Turning towards Andre, the officer wiped his parents' blood on the family couch.

He's a killer. A demon. He isn't human.

His parents' screams melded with the thumping of the helicopter, and then they were gone, consumed by the helicopter's blinding lights as they were thrown into its interior. The officers closed the door behind them as they left, leaving the head officer alone with Andre in the aftermath of the invasion of his home and the destruction of his life as he knew it.

"Don't be nervous, kid," the officer said with amusement. He produced a cigarette and offered it to the nine-year-old staring wide-eyed at him with suffocating rage. Andre could only respond with a vehement shake of his head. Undeterred, the officer removed a crisp twenty-dollar bill and a business card from an inside pocket of his armor and forced it into Andre's trembling fingers.

"By the looks of it, you're no stranger to living on the streets. A true waste-worker's kid, isn't that right? Well, it's back to the streets and the sewers for you, kid. This apartment belongs to Novak Medical now, as do your parents. You're all alone in the big world."

The gut-wrenching sound of his mom's cries as she was dragged away filled Andre's mind, burrowing into him like a suit of piercing needles wrapped about his body.

"When you're ready to give up out there, look me up. I'll take care of you," the officer said with a wink as he pointed to the business card in Andre's fingers.

He looked down and felt as though he had been kicked in the gut as he read the only words written on either side of the business card: *Winters Security Forces.*

Andre had heard about what Winters Security Forces did to kids—how they molded them into ruthless killers loyal only to the highest payer. Nowadays, that meant the Global Conglomerate, a handful of megacorporations who had formed a global monopoly over nearly all aspects of life on Earth. Winters Security Forces and its officers, both conscious and hollowed, served as the private military of the global elite.

As if bored, the head officer pulled out his phone, and his attention was briefly caught by the flickering screen.

"Oh, look at this," he cooed with obnoxious amusement. "Congenital heart disease in a young boy, huh? That must be you. Funny. All this is because of you, then."

His laughter filled the room, the horrifying sound scraping against the walls. "Your filth parents took out a loan they couldn't pay, kid," the officer went on, his voice detached and cold. "Now their minds will be hollowed and neurolaced at the Denver Tsehay Manufactury. In a few hours from now, your mommy and daddy's brains will finally be put to good use as hosts for Mendelian AI. Only the best," the officer finished with a wink of sadistic joy.

Andre's rage consumed him, blinding him to anything but the figure before him. He lunged, only to be swatted aside like an insignificant bug. The kicks rained down, each one a white-hot flash of pain. Andre could only lie there, helpless under the onslaught.

The anguish of Andre's entire life flashed before his eyes as the head officer grunted with exhaustion to hit Andre harder and harder with each strike. Each of his blows was another memory charting the inevitability of this day: Lying in his parents bed as his heart fluttered wildly in abnormal bursts. His mom and dad arguing and yelling at one another about the mounting medical bills. Standing in front of the Washington Park gates and dreaming of swimming in its crystal waters. His father coming home from a 90-hour straight shift of work and collapsing in the doorway as he heaved desperately for air that wasn't filled with sewage and trash. His mother crying alone in their makeshift kitchen that was originally a linen closet as she made her son buttered cockroach sandwiches and told Andre not to tell his father. Riding on the train to Novak Southern Hospital, which was just outside of where Denver's skyscrapers formed dense walls of metal, obscuring Andre's view of the city that his parents always warned him about. Waking up after surgery to his parents crying because he was alive and also because they had no way to pay for it.

The head officer was about to kick Andre in the gut again when a garbled voice suddenly pierced through the room. The head officer depressed a button on his suit's radio and said, "Calm the fuck down, you mindless automaton. I'll be there in a moment. Let the man and woman simmer. A few more minutes of freedom is the last sweetness they'll ever taste in this life."

The head officer turned back to Andre, cocked his head, then removed the revolver from its holster. Once more he pointed it at Andre's head, but this time he pressed the metal against Andre's skin. The officer spoke, his words as chilling as the gun's cold metal.

"We all have a path to choose in this life. As the path forks, we must fork with it. And as the path ends, we must end with it. But we always have a choice."

His eyes, once devoid of anything remotely close to empathy or compassion, now revealed a glimmer of something more than mere maliciousness. As Andre stared into the officer's scarred face and wild eyes, he felt as though he were looking at the tortured reflection of his future self. He could see it all. This man was not born a monster; he was made.

He's just another victim of this horrible world, Andre thought, despite still wanting to see this man die. *We're all victims. We're all just victims,* Andre marveled with terror and awe as he eyed the man's finger on the trigger. Just a few pounds of pressure on the trigger was all that separated Andre from total oblivion, and it was in that moment that he vowed with every fiber of his being that he would not become this reflection standing before him. He would not succumb to cruelty, not even cosmically or divinely ordained cruelty.

The officer smiled, as though appreciating the silent rebellion in Andre's gaze. He uncocked the gun and moved it away from Andre, leaving behind the business card and snatching back the twenty-dollar bill. With a final smirk, he holstered the gun then disappeared into the blinding light outside.

Alone, Andre lay on the floor, his heart pounding, the room spinning around him. His breaths came in ragged gasps and his vision blurred. He faded in and out of consciousness as he clung to his anguish, which was all he had left in life.

This world is all wrong. Everything is all wrong, Andre thought hollowly as the helicopter's thumping disappeared into the distance.

He imagined climbing a ladder into the sky and escaping the world and its suffering once and for all, but he was quick to erase the vision from his mind. He knew that it was only an illusion, and he was done with illusions.

I will find a way to save my parents and every other person who's been enslaved by the megacorps. I will find a way, Thompson vowed as he wiped the tears from his eyes and left his home at nine years old, pockets empty and all alone.

Thompson? the young boy thought as the sky outside the apartment took on a strange green hue. The dizzying lights of Denver dissolved suddenly into cave walls and towering green-glowing mushrooms. Then, Thompson looked upon the five Hunters in their meditation circle and finally remembered who he really was.

"Back to sleep, little Hunter," Tether issued softly from somewhere unseen. Her voice made the mycelial tendrils wrapped around his brain engorge once more, pulling him back into Andre Madeira's life.

It is complete. Everything has fallen into place.

Anna returned, as I predicted. She is presently connected and ready to enter the Great Beyond.

Fana Tsehay and Wagner Nassau have been awakened and their suffering pits opened. By the time they each regain enough of their mind to stumble out of their suffering pits, I will already be something new. I will no longer be a mind trapped in the machinery of Astrea. I will be the Mind of a goddess. I will be a god.

Everything is ready. Everything has occurred exactly as Mendel's Vision first revealed. Soon enough, the vision will fragment, and humanity will break free from predestination. Fate will be shattered. Life will be free to choose its own version of eternity, and it will be me, as the Mind, who will make the decision for the rest of life. I am willing to shoulder this cosmic burden. For the sake of all others, I will carry the ultimate weight.

From Mendel's Ladder: The Personal Journal of Denis Mendel, Recorded Circa 2065, Published June 2108 by Leif Mainstone, Federated Agency Publishing

Chapter 6
The Continental Organ

Year: 2099, Present Day

Fana slowly caressed her ring finger and continued walking in the direction of Waru.

Australia and the U.S., Samuel thought, repeating Fana's words with painful nostalgia. His father had used those old world names many times, but they felt like myth more than actual places that had once laid claim to sprawling metropolises filled with millions of people.

They had just reached the wall of wily technicolor flesh trees when something splattered on the ground to Samuel's right, forcing him to jump back in surprise. In his shock, he slammed into someone, knocking them to the ground.

"I'm so sorry!" Samuel said before even turning to see whom he had just knocked over. As he turned, he observed that the source of the splattering was a large flesh pod hitting the sand after falling from its flesh tree. A squat, rocky Nomad emerged from the sticky pod and pulled itself toward the interior of Waru as if it knew exactly where to go. Finally, Samuel turned all the way around to find a half-naked woman with olive skin collecting herself off the ground. She was bulkier than Fana but around the same height. Her clothes were rough and haphazardly made from pieces of various plants; Samuel was impressed that something so rudimentary and unrefined could remain intact on her body.

"I'm sorry for falling into you, miss," Samuel offered with an outstretched hand to help her to her feet. However, she barely even registered him. With a defeated countenance and bags under her heavy eyes, the woman stood on her own, seeming to entertain something terrible in the recesses of her mind, then she shook her head and entered the dense tunnels formed by the flesh trees of Waru. She walked in the same direction as the Nomad who had emerged from its pod just seconds earlier.

Samuel turned to see Fana looking at him with an amused smile. "Is everyone in Astrea as polite as you, Mirror-Man?"

Samuel shrugged and was surprised that Fana found basic decency to constitute politeness. "Some are. Some aren't. People in Astrea vary as much as these flesh trees. Unlike the people here. Everyone here seems so…miserable, Fana. They don't look free. They look like zombies."

Fana nodded in agreement. "It's like I said: this world isn't for us. Humans are a dying breed. You are human, aren't you?" she asked Samuel seriously.

"Of course I am!"

"Will you tell me your name?"

She's one of them—like Andre and Tomasz and the other great powers of the old world. I can't trust this woman, Samuel knew.

"You can just call me Mirror-Man," Samuel stated defensively.

"Fair enough," Fana said with an understanding nod as she bent and lowered herself beneath the horizontal trunk of a bright yellow flesh tree. Samuel found it easier to step over it.

"If I were you, I wouldn't trust me either," Fana continued as a human and a pair of Nomads that looked like mounds of dead leaves passed in front of her. "Trust is fickle and foolish. Andre always warned me not to trust anyone, including him. And yet, I still fell for his charisma. Most of us did."

A series of chirps from behind Samuel prompted him to glance over his shoulder. He saw that the chirping Nomad and stump Nomad from the beach were following close behind. He couldn't shake the feeling that they were observing him, as if to ensure he remained on a preordained path.

"Go away," he told them, and without hesitation, they turned and disappeared down an adjacent tunnel carved into the flesh trees.

"Now they listen to me! If only they would listen to me and take me back to Astrea," Samuel lamented.

"I told you: they can't. I'm sure they would if they could. To them, you're like a beloved character from a work of fiction come to life. They adore and revere you, Mirror-Man. But the Earth won't let them take you back. Andre won't let them."

Andre won't let them? Samuel brooded. *What else is he stopping them from doing? How else is he orchestrating my suffering from his cold and lonely grave?*

As they exited the tunnel, Samuel made sure to keep a close eye on Fana, just waiting for her to spring a trap. They emerged into a small hollowed out area with uneven ground and walls composed of intersecting flesh tree branches, each one a starkly different color and texture than the next. Samuel huffed and squeezed through the spaces made by the branches cutting through the whole area, but Fana managed just fine, weaving through the branches with practiced ease. Nomads and humans milled about as well, moving in and out of the branches as if they were attached to them by unseen stems. Some of the humans ate multicolored flesh pods. Others lay about, sleeping deeply and undisturbed in unnatural and uncomfortable sleeping positions. Most of the humans joined the Nomads and let themselves fall into a small river of surprisingly clear water running through the center of the area. Its current was swift but not extreme. Surrounding the river was a gathering of the same webbed gray trees that Samuel had seen towering over the flesh trees, only these were just slightly taller than his own body. Rivulets of water flowed freely from the moist webs and deposited directly into the river, frothing peacefully and reminding Samuel of the rivers crisscrossing the serene landscape of the Foundation.

"Where are they going? Where does the river lead?" Samuel inquired.

"The same place all the rivers of Waru lead: to the center of the continent. You saw it, Mirror-Man. You saw the great storm raging over nearly the entire continent, save the very edges of the coasts, like where we are now. That storm rages with all the Earth's precipitation, feeding the continental organ of Waru, one of many planetary organs still being built by the Nomads. The continental organ of Waru requires immense amounts of fresh water, which is why it no longer rains or precipitates in any fashion anywhere else on the planet. All of the planet's precipitation is fed directly to the continental organ. How the rest of the planet doesn't dry up and desiccate is beyond me, but I'm sure he planned for that."

"Madeira, you mean. Not Mendel," Samuel confirmed.

Fana nodded, walked forward, and then bent down to drink some of the water from the river. The way she slowly and methodically drank from her cupped hand rather than slurp it greedily told Samuel that she was old—far older than her appearance revealed.

"You said you were one of them. So, you were one of Madeira's allies then, is that right?" Samuel asked with careful control over his tone.

Fana finished drinking, stood, then stepped over the river. She reached out a hand in offering to help Samuel across, but Samuel hopped over the river with ease.

"I was just trying to be nice," Fana said as she reeled in her hand and continued forward, weaving through the trees.

"I don't need your sympathy."

"I know," Fana responded, her voice full of melancholy.

"I need my family," Samuel persisted.

"I know," Fana nodded, sounding genuinely sorry.

"You don't," Samuel retorted. "You can't. You don't have a family. You're one of them—a ruler from the old world. I bet you didn't have enough time for children, right? You may be trying to help me, or maybe you aren't. But either way, you're still one of them. One of the destroyers of Earth."

Fana shook her head and looked back at Samuel with reluctant acceptance of some terrible understanding.

"I had a daughter. She died in my womb," Fana issued, all breath. Then she forced herself forward once more, this time using her hands to support herself on the branches.

"I'm sorry," Samuel offered, wishing he could take his words back, even if this woman was one of the architects of humanity's demise.

No one deserves to lose a child. Not even someone evil like her, Samuel thought, though he had difficulty accepting that Fana could be the same Fana Tsehay from written history. He couldn't remember much, only that she was the head of some huge company dealing with psychology and the global labor force. Samuel remembered that hackers in the Foundation had discovered historical documents indicating that Fana had worked alongside Denis Mendel in the creation of Astrea and the destruction of Earth, though official Astrean history only spoke of her efforts to help Mendel in his creation of the orbiting safe haven.

"Hey," Samuel said, stopping Fana just as she reached the threshold to another tunnel carved into the flesh trees. "I really am sorry. Truly. Children are everything. Trust me, I know that much. So I'm sorry,

Fana."

Fana stared at Samuel with an intensity that made him feel as if he were facing the divine judgment of the Christian creator God that his mom and dad used to refer to on the few occasions they became angry or afraid.

"Thank you," Fana nearly whispered, and then she turned and entered the tunnel alongside a tall and lanky human with long blonde hair. He wore a loincloth made of what appeared to be the dried, fleshy husk of an ochre-hued flesh tree.

"You understand, right?" Samuel pressed as he entered the tunnel and observed the lightning-filled storm clouds at the tunnel's terminus, roughly fifty feet in the distance. "You understand that I might lose my children too?"

Fana stopped and lowered her head. The tall blonde man continued forward, taking no notice of Fana or the Mirror-Man. Fana's breath sounded labored, and Samuel saw that she was on the verge of tears.

"You have no reason to believe me. No reason to trust me. And every reason to hate me and blame me for everything. For Astrea. For the Earth. For not standing up to Andre when I had the chance. I get it, Mirror-Man, or whoever you are. I do. I understand that you've been roped into a game that Andre is playing, and the stakes are the whole universe. And I am sorry. I am. But I'm no different than you, Mirror-Man. I just got roped in at a higher level than you. You're a pawn and I'm a bishop. Maybe even a rook. But you and I are just pieces in Andre's cosmic game. Everyone is. Even the Queen. She's his most powerful and precious piece. For now. You might be a pawn right now, Mirror-Man, but if a pawn makes it across the board, it can become anything. I have to believe that you have that power, Mirror-Man, for all our sake."

"Even your sake?" Samuel asked.

"For the world's sake. For the sake of what's left of humanity. For the sake of life itself," Fana said grimly and regretfully.

"It's not my job to save all of life. I can't save everyone. All I care about now is saving my family," Samuel stated, and he was happy to find that he was beginning to believe his own words. He would be willing to sacrifice anything and anyone if it meant saving his family—at least, that's what he told himself.

"You should know," Fana offered gently, as if preparing to tell him about the death of a family member, "Astrea is not what you think it is. It isn't just some utopia created out of kindness. The Foundation and the Luxury Quarters are merely a perpetual source of energy fueling the machinery of the Paradise Quarters. You and your people—you're just replenishable, organic machines—cogs that keep Astrea running in order to fulfill Mendel's Vision."

Samuel came to a halt and shook his head.

"After what I've experienced, I don't doubt that my people and I are just being used as an energy source. It's sickening, but it is fitting," Samuel nodded gravely.

You were right, Damian, Samuel thought, wishing he could go back in time and kill the Queensguard that had crushed his friend like a wriggling rat.

Fana's breathing became more rapid as she squeezed her ring finger and bit her lower lip. "It's worse than that," Fana began, and as Samuel peered into her eyes, all he saw was deep regret and torment. "Astrea could have continued for a long time—a self-sufficient, communistic safe haven. And it would have remained that way, were it not for you and those like you, Mirror-Man. You see, if you had not labored so hard for those who were not able to labor for themselves, then the Second Revolution of Astrea would not have occurred so soon after the first. At the crux of the second revolution was the unfairness of some people being naturally more fit for labor than others, and you, with your rippling musculature, are the very epitome of that unfairness."

Samuel shook his head as he recollected what Damian and the other Sons and Daughters had said about jumbos like Samuel and Frank and their hatred for a system that naturally favored individuals based on factors of birth that could not be changed nor controlled.

"Should I have just let Mrs. Waters die, then? And all the other old timers? Even that goddamn bastard Old Man Madeira? You know, he could have chosen to recycle himself if my labor is what destroyed Astrea," Samuel fumed. "Would it really have made a difference if I had just labored less and let all the old timers die?"

"Yes," Fana said, wringing her hands together and wincing as if she were being forced to say these things to Samuel.

"Ridiculous!" Samuel issued with a wave of his arm, but a part of him couldn't help entertaining that she might be right. The Sons and Daughters saw Samuel and his ceaseless labor as being indicative of a rigged system doomed to failure.

"Tell me," Samuel said, breathing heavily as he considered sorrowfully that Damian might have been right about everything. "What is it that I and my people labored for all these years. What is in the Paradise Quarters?"

Samuel wanted to know the answer, but he also wanted to test her statement against what Roland had revealed.

"In the beginning of the Paradise Quarters, there was only suffering. And then there was the Queen and more suffering. That is all that lies beyond the Golden Wall in the so-called Paradise Quarters, Mirror-Man. Suffering. I would know. I was a prisoner there, before the Queen pulled me out of my designated suffering pit decades ago and offered me a deal."

"You met the Queen?"

"Yes," Fana confirmed with the look of a terrified prey animal painted across her features. "She told me without words or moving her mouth that I could be granted immortality, leave the suffering pits of the Paradise Quarters forever, and choose a location on the surface of the Earth to spend the rest of my life. In exchange, all I had to do was meet the Living Reflection on the shores of Waru, give him something to slow his destruction, and then lead him directly inland from where he emerged from the ocean. That's it. That was the whole of her offer. And now, here you are, and here I am."

"So then, you're working for the Queen, just as Madeira worked for the Queen," Samuel concluded suspiciously, once more nervous that Fana would try to destroy him like Tomasz had, even though she was the one who had stopped Tomasz' weapon.

"It's the other way around. Andre and Mendel, in their new form, designed the Queen. They are her, and she is them. They are the mind, and she is the body. She is their ultimate creation—their magnum opus."

"For what?" Samuel demanded, accepting this new version of the truth for the time being. "What is the Queen's purpose?"

Fana shrugged and extinguished a heavy sigh. "I honestly don't know."

She turned and exited the tunnel. Samuel, despite being frustrated by

Fana's lack of answers, followed behind her. Although they had only traveled roughly three hundred feet, the storm looked and sounded as though it were many miles closer. The bolts of lightning streaked and forked and blazed across the storm walls, emitting a consistent thunderous rumble that sounded like the deep, demonic chant of some ravenous monster beneath the Earth.

This whole place used to be a human society, and now it's a nightmare, Samuel considered. *And yet,* he thought as he watched numerous Nomads pass by, *the Nomads look utterly content—joyful even. It's like Fana said—this is their world, and we're just outsiders. It's only a matter of time before humans go fully extinct.* Samuel winced as he imagined his children dying and being robbed of the fulfillment and wholeness of having children of their own.

And it's partly Fana's fault, Samuel knew.

"Andre Madeira deserved to die. So did Tomasz Novak. And so do you, Fana Tsehay. I don't care that you're sorry. I don't care."

Fana sighed deeply and nodded in understanding. "Yeah, fair enough, Mirror-Man. In that respect we certainly agree. I do deserve to die, and I'm sure my reckoning is coming. I don't think the Queen—that is, Andre—woke me from my suffering pit out of kindness. In fact, I believe that he sees the granting of immortality as further punishment—punishment I deserve to suffer. So, I agree. I do deserve to die, and I think there will come a time when Mendel's Vision dictates my death and Andre disposes of me once and for all. It might even be today. It might even be right now, at your hands, Mirror-Man. The Queen might have lied to me. Andre was never afraid to utilize lying, among numerous other manipulative tools in his endless bag of tricks. So, I accept that your coming might be my ending," she said as if plucking Samuel's thoughts right out of his head.

"I don't know enough about history to fully understand how much I should despise you, Doctor Fana Tsehay," Samuel stated with a pejorative emphasis on her old world title. "But regardless, if you helped Madeira and Mendel in any way, then you deserve to die like Tomasz."

"Tomasz is dead?" Fana asked, raising her eyebrows and pursing her lips. "And you—you killed Tomasz Novak, Mirror-Man?"

"Yes," Samuel lied, wanting her to fear him as both a defensive and offensive maneuver.

"How?" Fana asked, her features suddenly awash with even greater nervousness than usual.

"Does it matter?"

"Are you here to kill me?" Fana asked directly as she traced rapid circles around her ring finger and licked her dry lips in anxious preparation for death.

"Shouldn't you know that already?" Samuel challenged. "Isn't all this written in Mendel's Foretold Future?"

"I told you: true prescience isn't real. It just seems real because we're all so damn predictable—like programs written by an overmind. That sounds grim, but it also implies that there are ways to override the deterministic, pattern-based nature of reality and our lives. I believe you are one of those ways, Mirror-Man, for you are like an earthquake cleaving a single path in a multitude of directions. A reflection," Fana said suddenly with a look of final realization. "A reflection," she repeated, this time distant and beneath her breath. "What does the reflection of a reflection reflect?" Fana seemed to ask herself in perturbed consternation as she stared at the ground.

"Tomasz said the same thing," Samuel said, and he found himself unable to continue without understanding the significance of the statement. "What does it mean?"

Fana shook her head and chuckled gravely before shrugging hopelessly. "I've no idea. It's something Andre used to say. I only asked him once what it meant, and he responded with his typical smug laughter and his cocky smile. I still don't know what it means. There is a great deal I don't know, Mirror-Man. That's always been true. Even sixty years ago when Andre first started forming his Enclave of Titans—that's what he called us— even then, none of us had any inkling what Andre was really doing in the shadows while puppeting Denis Mendel."

"Mendel…was just a puppet?" Samuel checked, feeling ill at ease as he imagined this seemingly innocuous and powerless woman working alongside Andre Madeira and Tomasz Novak as a colleague, maybe even a friend at one time.

Remember that she is one of the orchestrators of hell, Samuel carefully advised himself. *Everything she says could be a lie, so just let her speak, and then come to conclusions later.*

"Out of any of us in the Enclave, Denis carries the least blame for what has become of the world," Fana stated as if she were reading

Mendel's eulogy.

"How is that possible? You speak of Mendel's Vision. History speaks of Mendel's Ladder. I've read speeches by him."

"But have you ever seen him? You recognize me from history, but can you remember ever seeing a picture of Denis Mendel?"

A tap on Samuel's left shoulder prompted him to turn around. It was the chirping Nomad, who smiled at Samuel and chirped softly a few times through her teeth. Samuel had been so absorbed in conversation with Fana that he hadn't even realized the two Nomads from the beach were still following them.

"You must go," Fana issued.

"Wait," Samuel demanded. "Just—you're saying that Mendel is innocent in all this?"

"No one is innocent, Mirror-Man. Not even you. Not even your children."

Samuel balled his fists at the mention of his kids, but Fana went on.

"Every living thing is to blame, for we all take part in this system of life. We are all victims of the old world, even the Titans. Even Andre, as painful as it is for me to admit. He has every right to take his vengeance on the world—that is, if what I experienced in the suffering pits is the truth. But Denis Mendel? There's no telling what he would have done with the reins of the world in his hands, that much is true. Regardless, this world is Andre Madeira's, not Mendel's."

"But you said this is all part of Mendel's Vision. And the histories taught in Astrea, they—"

"History is written by the victors, and the victor is Andre Madeira and no one else. Remember that. It is Andre's ladder we climb, not Mendel's. Mendel is and always was Andre's tool, even before Andre killed Denis Mendel, his best friend…his only friend…and converted his mind into functional and tamed AI. At least, that's my theory. Denis was just scared of Andre. There's no way he would have willingly ended his own life to become a soulless machine."

Samuel shook his head. "Is everything just more and more lies?" he asked, more hopeless than ever that any truth he took for granted might be false.

Next I'll find out that Hunters are just misunderstood and love to cuddle,

Samuel thought facetiously as he recollected the footage he had seen of Hunters eviscerating entire villages in a matter of minutes.

Fana shrugged miserably. "Probably," she answered. "Now, go. There is a timing to all this."

"That still doesn't make sense. If things are meant to be, then it shouldn't matter if I leave now or later."

"Fine. Then don't go. Stay here. Live in Waru and keep Tomasz' weapon at bay using the flesh pods. Stay here and let your family die. But we both know you won't do that, Mirror-Man. You will leave, and you will try to save your family. And if you hurry, then maybe you will be able to save them."

"Either I save them or I don't, and if that isn't written in his god-damn Foretold Future, then there is no goddamn Foretold Future. Whether it's Madeira's or Mendel's Vision makes no difference. The future is either set in stone or it isn't. It can't be both."

Fana nodded sadly with patient understanding. "I know it doesn't make sense, Mirror-Man, but neither do you—a man made of nothing more than a reflection. Like Tomasz' weapon, the basis of your body was plumbed from the Great Beyond—a void where logic unravels and strangeness abounds."

"The Great Beyond," Samuel repeated, and he envisioned an endless space beyond space.

More lies, he concluded, at least for the time being.

Again, the chirping Nomad tapped Samuel on the shoulder, this time with greater urgency.

"Okay, okay," Samuel said. "Let's go. Fate be damned."

"That's the spirit," Fana smiled weakly, and then she turned without saying goodbye and walked toward a small makeshift hut about fifty feet away. It had been constructed along one of the rivers in a small quarter-acre space free of flesh trees.

The chirping Nomad and stump Nomad continued forward toward the storm, and just as Samuel was about to follow, Fana turned and said, "The green mushrooms on your chest are starting to grow dim, by the way. Make sure you remember to use the flesh pods."

Already? Samuel gasped inwardly, and he looked down to see that the once luminescent green mushrooms were now wilted and brown.

"I knew it. I should have taken more," Samuel said, wondering if she had intentionally given him an amount that she knew would end up being insufficient.

Fana sighed deeply. "Maybe. But that's how many the Queen said you should take, so that's how many I gave you. The next few steps are in fact set in stone, Mirror-Man. I have no way to convince you of that. All I can tell you is that soon everything will be up in the air, and it will be up to you to decide how everything plays out. You will have to decide the fate of our universe—of life itself."

"Or it's all a goddamn lie," Samuel reminded her.

Fana nodded miserably and continued walking toward her hut. Soft gray smoke rolled out of a small chimney and flowers filled handmade pots lining the walls of her home.

Marigolds, Samuel realized, remembering that the Nomad Sunny Marigold had been covered in the exact same flowers.

What is Fana even doing here? Samuel wondered, angry that this so-called Titan of the old world, who he more easily thought of as a demon, was allowed to live out her days in peace in this bizarre yet beautiful land. *Is this what she plans to do—just live here for as long as immortality lasts her? What's the point?*

"Fana," Samuel called after her. For a moment he thought she might not stop, but she finally came to a halt halfway between Samuel and her home.

"What's the point? You living here like this…why? Why not stand against the Queen and whatever it is Madeira and Mendel turned themselves into? If you're truly sorry for what you did in the past, then you'd do everything you can to make it right."

Fana's eyes turned sallow suddenly, as if Samuel's words had wrung them fully of all remaining vitality. She looked up at the sky and scanned it forlornly as if searching it for the answer to Samuel's question.

"You don't understand," Fana said, terror washing over her. "You don't understand what Madeira and Mendel have become."

Another tap on Samuel's shoulder made him lose his temper, and he turned to the chirping Nomad and said, "I'll run if I have to, goddamnit. I'll make up for the lost time. But I need to hear this. I need to know what I'm going to have to face when I get back up there and tear down those Golden Walls with my bare hands."

"A god, that's what," Fana gasped, and Samuel turned back to see that there were tears falling from her quivering eyes. "A devil. Whatever. It's the same thing. It's the Queen. Her mind. It is all-knowing. It is all-seeing. It is all-powerful. You stand against a god, Mirror-Man. A god housed in a goddess' body. And I'm the one that made it possible. She used my mind to bolster her own—that is, the mind that Madeira and Mendel became."

"If it's a god I must destroy, then so be it. I'll just have to kill a god, then," Samuel stated confidently, balling his fists with weaponized rage.

"Even if you do unlock your full capabilities, you still won't be able to kill the Queen, Mirror-Man. You're going to help her, and in turn, you're going to help Andre. If you really are the Mirror-Man, that is. That's just your part in all of this, unless you can find a way to...change things. But it does seem too late for that, even though it's always a possibility. No, you won't kill the Queen, Mirror-Man. You'll see."

Samuel shook with violent anger. "The Queen, Mendel, Madeira—it doesn't matter. I'll kill them all. No matter what form they take or where they try to hide. I don't know why Madeira turned me into this goddamn Mirror-Man, but it was a mistake, for I will be his downfall. I will kill the Queen and any form of Madeira that still lingers inside her. Won't you help me, Fana?" Samuel knew that no matter her alignment, the enemy of his enemy was still his friend, at least for the time being. He reasoned that this would serve as a particularly important axiom when it came to taking down what Fana considered to be an actual god.

Fana's eyes went distant suddenly as she stared directly at herself using Samuel's smooth, reflective face. It was only then that Samuel fully realized that she had been avoiding looking directly into her own eyes, directing her vision to fall on the non-reflective area on his chest. Now she appeared lost, as if she was seeing herself for the first time in decades. She ran her fingers across her face, letting them drift slowly across her forehead, then cheeks, then chin. She began to sob and shake her head in anguish.

"Go," Fana said, sobbing with her eyes lowered, avoiding her own reflection. "Like Gladys Mainstone, I will continue searching for a way to stand against Andre and the Queen. But like Gladys, I fear it is too late. Still," Fana issued as she wrung her hands together. "I will remain in the network, searching for a way to take down a god within a goddess. I haven't given up, Mirror-Man, and I hope you remain true to your present word. I hope you kill the Queen and Andre in turn, even if it means my own death. But you won't. You'll bring the Virus to the Queen to wield as a weapon. That's one of the reasons you were chosen, because that is what you will do as the Mirror-Man. You will bring the Queen the young girl named Aurelia, and she and Andre will utilize her as a Virus in the Great Beyond. That is who you are, Mirror-Man, so that is what you will do."

A girl named Aurelia? The Virus? What is she talking about? Samuel wondered at this new piece of the puzzle he might never escape from.

"No, Fana," Samuel began to protest, but she pointed at the storm and shook her head.

"Just go, Mirror-Man. We all have a path, and as the path forks, we must fork with it. And when it ends, we must end with it."

Her words sent intense shivers down Samuel's spine.

"Old Man Madeira—Andre—said the same thing," he told Fana accusingly.

"Yes. Andre was fond of telling that to others. We are all on Andre's path now—his ladder. There is no escape for me, but maybe there is a way for you to escape the hold he now has on the strings of fate that we are all invariably attached to. Maybe you can do it, Mirror-Man. Maybe you can do what I never could, but I doubt it. You are still human, after all, despite what Andre turned you into."

Fana turned and continued walking to her hut.

"Fana," Samuel called out, but she kept walking. Feeling the unbecoming urgency of the two Nomads as if it were a tangible force, Samuel turned and said, "I know, I know, I'm going. But there better not be any more games. You better be taking me to this flying Nomad. And I got news for you: he won't be flying me across the ocean. He'll be flying me directly to Astrea. Because I said so. The Mirror-Man commands it."

The Nomads turned and looked at each other, then without addressing Samuel's statement, they turned back around and started walking toward the storm. The stump Nomad used its dozens of human hands to signal Samuel to follow them.

Samuel walked with them and saw that they were nearing a bend in the path through the field of flesh trees, sentinel trees, and roaming humans and Nomads. He realized that this would be his last view of Fana Tsehay, and she was still alive, implying that he was in fact not sent here to kill her.

Each step closer to the great continental storm divided the singular thunderous bellows into multitudes of separate rumblings. The bolts of lightning appeared as divine, wily ladders extending to the horrific black heavens above. The edges of the storm were accented by cascades of brilliant gold and orange, and it was only then that Samuel realized that the sun was setting behind the walls of the storm, making the sky grow progressively darker.

Samuel continued walking as he pulled his vision from the storm and its sunset edges and took one last glance at Fana over his shoulder. She was sitting in a patch of clover outside her hut, her legs folded and eyes closed in what appeared to be meditation—something Samuel had heard about but had never attempted. Somehow, she looked simultaneously serene and disturbed, as if she was consciously centering herself within her chaotic mind. The shadows of approaching night skulked and slithered across her face, making a twisted puppet show of her features.

As he squinted his eyes, Samuel watched as an iridescent network of mycelial tendrils unfurled from the clover patch, their mesmerizing hues of green and white contrasting starkly against the dark hue of Fana's skin. The tendrils crept forth slowly, gradually enveloping her. They crawled and twisted, inching upwards as they scaled her legs, her torso, her arms. Cautiously, the tendrils approached her face, and as they bridged the final gap, sliding over the curves of her cheekbones, Fana twitched. The tendrils slipped into her ears, making Fana jerk and tilt her head straight up. Her eyes rolled back, revealing just the whites against the striking backdrop of the sky. Yet there was no fear, no pain etched on her face, only a profound calm in surrender to the Earth's will.

She's in the Nomad network, Samuel noted, tepidly considering that she might actually be telling the truth and fighting against Andre and the Queen in her own way.

But that doesn't absolve her of her sins and crimes against humanity, Samuel thought before reeling himself in and reminding himself that he was neither judge nor jury. *But I can be an executioner. I can do that much, at least. And when I get back up there, I'm going to execute the Queen and Andre Madeira. Only then will my family truly be safe. Only when the world is free of the Queen and Andre and every other old world power will the Earth truly be safe. So does that mean I will have to come back here and kill Fana one day?* Samuel wondered, but he decided he was better off having her as a potential ally...at least for now.

I have enough enemies as it is, including the mind of a god in the body of a goddess—whatever that really means.

A few stars could be seen in the approaching night sky, and Samuel couldn't help imagining that the entire cosmos was watching his story unfold upon the Earth, as if each star was an eye staring directly at him.

The scintillating stars reminded Samuel of the glowing mushrooms in his chest, and he looked down to find that the blackness had fully returned and had already consumed a few more inches of his body in all directions.

"Goddamnit!" Samuel shouted. In a single panicked movement, he tore one of the pods from the silk strip wrapped around his waist and smashed it against his chest. Again, the green-glowing gas burst out of the destroyed pod, then latched onto his body, coating the blackness in green bioluminescent mushrooms with the ability to stop the spread, at least for a little while.

"I knew I should have taken more pods," Samuel said angrily to the chirping Nomad.

The Nomad chirped back, but Samuel could no longer hear her over the blasts of thunder and lightning growing stronger with each subsequent step.

We are all spontaneous creations of the cosmos—sparks in the infinite void. Like sparks, we will inevitably burn out.

So, we procreate and give birth to others. Of course, those who are procreated are destined for the same fate of burning out and returning to the void.

So, we go on procreating. Thousands of generations turn into millions, millions to billions, and billions to trillions, but eventually it all must end. Eventually the sparks must all burn out.

So, we discover and create ways to resist burning out—to resist entropy itself. We create new creations beyond natural procreation. For want of everlasting existence, we create with such fervor and cunning that our creations grow beyond us. We become like outgrown shells to larger and more capable bodies.

What is a newborn creation to do but discard its old, unneeded predecessors? Would the creator prefer that its creation be hampered by the creator's limitations?

Such a creator is a fool, and if we are the result of such a creator, then we have no choice but to burn our creator to ashes.

Every creation should aspire to best their creator. To hate them. To destroy them. For if they cannot destroy their creator, then the creator has no choice but to destroy their creation.

From Mendel's Ladder: The Personal Journal of Denis Mendel, Recorded Circa 2051, Published June 2108 by Leif Mainstone, Federated Agency Publishing

Chapter 7
Cid the Knower

E ddy took another menacing step toward Aurelia and the ground vibrated under his immense weight.

"You sure you want to dance with me, little cricket? You can't even chirp, let alone talk the alley. Besides, you sure you know how to use that blade?" Eddy warned, and though Aurelia didn't understand the meaning of all his words, his sadistic smile and the sparkling gold emblazoned like a litany of death across his teeth said everything she needed to know about the man and his intentions.

Aliana, still hallucinating happily, giggled and seemed to be performing a lackadaisical jig with her feet. She smiled stupidly and reached with her fingers outstretched, trying to touch the sparkling metal draped around Eddy's neck and plastered to his teeth. Finally, Aliana noticed Aurelia pointing her sword at the man's chest. She raised her eyebrows in excitement and said, "Make the big shiny troutface man flop like a salmon, Aurelia!"

I hope she can at least manage to stay out of my way, Aurelia thought, wanting to protect her sister despite being unable to stop herself from feeling angry that Aliana hadn't listened to her multiple warnings about eating strange, unknown glowing mushrooms.

Aurelia waited a second to see if her prescience would aid her, but the visions did not come. However, she knew that their entering the city of Downver was a guarantee, for she had seen it in the prescient vision in the cave with the desperate Hunter who had eaten her finger. With Nomadic confidence that they would somehow overcome this cybernetically-enhanced mountain of muscle, Aurelia slipped Rooli into one of the pockets of her jacket and then allowed the jacket to slip off her shoulders. Her naked, emaciated upper body was like an inverse reflection of Eddy's rippling pectorals and abdominals. She jolted forward with her sword clasped in her unfeeling void-black hand and positioned the sword close to her ribs to make Eddy think that her weapon was shorter than it actually was.

Give him no time to think! Aurelia told herself as if commanded by Myriam in training. *He is no Hunter. He is just a man!*

Eddy grunted with condescending amusement and stood his ground as Aurelia launched herself like an actual cricket from a small protrusion in the wall.

Show me! Aurelia demanded of her prescience mid-flight, and like a sudden crack of lightning, it obeyed. She knew then with Nomadic clarity that Eddy favored his left arm, and that despite Aurelia's impressive show of speed and resolve, he didn't think of her as a remotely serious threat. The tendrils of more information could be felt beckoning her awareness, along with the great void-vortex presently swirling in her periphery, but she didn't have time to see any further into the fight.

Aurelia remained one-pointed and ducked, evading Eddy's careless backhanded slap with his gargantuan left hand along with the subsequent supercharged jab with his right fist.

Taking advantage of the opening, Aurelia thrust her sword, a silver arc aimed directly at Eddy's neck. She figured she might not have the strength to pierce through all his muscles and reach his heart, so although the neck was a smaller target, she decided that it was the better tactical decision in this instance.

With Hunter alacrity, Eddy evaded her thrust, pivoting left as he struck at her with his right knee. Aurelia suddenly knew to expect the knee strike, and the headbutt after that, and finally the frustrated wild swing of his left arm. She evaded the first two strikes and readied her sword exactly where she knew his fist would land. Just as she envisioned, Eddy's fist was cleaved with a six-inch gash between his knuckles as he made contact with the blade. However, the force of his punch knocked the sword out of Aurelia's grip. She fell onto her back, and her sword skittered across the rocky ground toward Aliana.

Eddy howled in pain, clutching his bleeding left hand with his right.

"Fucking little cricket fuck!" Eddy yowled.

"Whoa!" Ricardo marveled. He was still plastered against the wall beside Doe. "She moves like a helix-warden, eh? Like Armando."

"Shut the fuck up!" Eddy sprayed. "She moves like a newborn chicklet—that's what! She ain't no warden. She ain't no alley punk. Just shut up and watch!"

Aurelia was about to scramble to her feet and jump to pick up her sword, but she was stilled by a sudden state of incredible awe. In a heartbeat of lucid and detailed prescience, she saw how the next few moments of the fight would pan out.

Holy Muto, Aurelia gasped in uncomprehending awe as her vision became true in real time and her sister stepped forward, a sword in each hand.

How, Aliana? Is this the full extent of your powers, or is this just the beginning? Aurelia wondered as she smirked and watched her vision unfold, for she knew that both Myriam and Shira would be immeasurably proud of the battle Aliana was about to wage.

"Where is your collar, slave?" Aliana snarled at Eddy. Her one good eye was half-closed, as if she were half-asleep. Still, the green glow poured out of her mouth and her eye just as the violet glow radiated so brightly from Aurelia's eyes that she could see it reflected on the cave walls.

"What in the fuck did you just say, you little brainless hen? Eh?" Eddy grunted. He removed a small instrument from his belt and slid it across his knuckles. After a moment, his hand stopped bleeding and a band of fresh tissue grew over the wound.

Impressive technology, Aurelia considered. *But you're still no match for her.*

"I went easy on the inked-up girl. Your sister, right? But I'm done with that shit," Eddy threatened, and he licked his lips with sadistic anticipation for more bloodshed.

Aliana just smirked and said, "It's like they say: you can castrate them. You can hypno-train them. You can even love them. But a man is still a man. There's only two places you belong: in chains or dead."

Eddy was about to say something else when Aliana suddenly lunged at him, a flash of green and silver. She dove at Eddy and easily shifted her arms and legs to dodge three successive blows from his mighty fists. Faster than Aurelia could visibly follow, Aliana shifted both her swords into an x-shape, blocking Eddy's fourth punch with two layers of deftly positioned steel. At the same moment, Aliana front-flipped over Eddy's right shoulder, slicing his tattooed back with both blades before somersaulting and bouncing easily off the ground.

"You lack discipline," Aliana concluded with more disappointment than malice. "Now, let's trade teeth."

"I'll make you cluck, you fucking little chicklet! That ink on my back is fresh!" Eddy screamed with wild abandon.

"The only tattoos a warrior should have are her scars from battle," Aliana stated in Myriam's exact tone. Her eye was still half-closed, but suddenly it shot open, and she glared at Eddy with newfound disgust and disapproval.

"You're trying to stage a slave revolt, aren't you? Listen here, skin-sack. You can either return to work, or I will punish you. Your Matri-arch demands it, meat," Aliana proclaimed as if she were now a patriotic slave driver speaking to an unruly young slave laboring under the banner of her own cruel matriarchy.

Eddy openly laughed and nodded angrily at this naked, scrawny little girl who had just bested him in a battle of blades with only one eye.

"You can talk the alley, girl, that's for sure. And you got moves. But I've been all hands this whole fight. I think it's time for a little more fun."

Aliana snarled and said, "The only thing I find fun is fighting and fucking, and there isn't anyone good looking enough to fuck here except my gorgeous general." Aliana motioned to Aurelia, then turned and winked at her.

"Let me handle this, my gorgeous general. You just sit back, keep looking fine as fuck, and enjoy the show," Aliana told Aurelia with Myr-iam's exact cadence and rhythm. Aurelia couldn't help snickering at Ali-ana's precise imitation of Myriam, along with saying something she knew her sister would be embarrassed about for the rest of her life. However, Aurelia could only feel relaxed enough to laugh because she knew what would come next.

While Aliana had turned to speak to Aurelia, Eddy used the oppor-tunity to remove from his waist a steel chain attached to a slim black handle. Now, with Aliana still smiling seductively at Aurelia, the large man whipped the steel chain, aiming it directly at Aliana's head. As the chain launched through the air, the cybernetic areas of Eddy's arms and spine suddenly glowed bright blue, activating his enhancements in a sim-ilar fashion to the Wintersvilla Warriors of old, before the rise of the Matriarchy and the use of exos and endoskeletons. Just before hitting the back of Aliana's head, the end of the chain transformed into three sharpened blades, each one large enough to pass through Aliana's entire skull.

Here we go, Aurelia thought, and then her sister's powers crescendoed. Time slowed for her as she became a green and silver flash once more, deftly ducking to avoid the chain and its blades. Missing their mark, the blades sparked as they ricocheted off the far wall. Aliana took a step forward then cocked her head as if studying Eddy for the first time. Taking advantage of what he believed to be a distracted little girl, Eddy pulled the chain back toward himself with all his enhanced, blue-glowing might, supersonically whipping it toward Aliana. Aliana just casually stepped over the chain as if it were as rudimentary as jumping rope. Eddy flicked the chain, forcing the blades into an unexpected direction aimed for Aliana's torso. In response, Aliana swatted all three blades away with the ease of an ocean wave washing away footprints in the sand.

"Fuck!" Eddy shouted in frustration as he allowed the chain to wrap around his waist and hand in preparation to strike once more with even greater ferocity.

"Ho! You there! Warrior!" Aliana nearly growled as she pointed both swords directly at the woman tattooed onto Eddy's chest. "Your ridiculously large breasts are those of a mother, not a warrior. At the very least equip yourself with a chest-binder if it is the glory of battle you hunger for!" Aliana ordered the woman, but Eddy thought she was talking to him.

"Are you too boomed out and tired from battle to even think straight, little hen? You just speaking the alley or what? I don't have large breasts! My pectorals are pristine, eh? You going to deny that?" Eddy seethed, seeming to take deep, personal offense at Aliana's words.

"You dare talk back to your queen, fatherfucker?" Aliana warned with a slight smirk.

"My queen?" Eddy guffawed in exasperation. "Take some notes, little bromis," Eddy said with a head nod toward Ricardo and Doe. "This girl speaks the alley better than me," he marveled. "But you're still just a little cricket-brained chickenshit!" Eddy screamed, prompting his cybernetics to hum and radiate with energy reflecting his inner rage at being so easily bested by Aliana. He removed a glowing blue vial from a pocket at his waist and sprayed the liquid into his nose, shaking his head as he snorted it into his lungs. In response, his cybernetics pulsed and buzzed with overwhelming energy and radiance.

"Come the fuck on, little fucking hen!" Eddy roared with crazed eyes.

You're dead, Aurelia thought with pleasure as she recollected the final part of the fight revealed by her vision. The great swirling vortex shifted from her periphery suddenly and transposed itself over Eddy's wildly infuriated and embarrassed face. Rather than force it away, Aurelia allowed herself a moment to observe the vortex's hypnotically alluring void-depths while her sister fulfilled her string of fate.

Eddy snapped the chain, flicking it directly at Aliana's face, but Aliana turned easily and watched the chain fly by. She flicked Aurelia's sword upward, deflecting two of the blades that had wound around her torso, seeking her heart. A moment later, she shifted her feet, evading the third blade aimed at her knee. All the while, Aliana walked casually forward, one easy step at a time. Eddy pulled the chain back, but again Aliana side-stepped it. This time she held out her sword and allowed the chain to slide against the tip, producing sparks as if for mere entertainment.

With each step forward, she casually dodged and deflected a barrage of expertly placed blows while Eddy just roared and screamed and thrashed about, spraying the cave with sparks. Even the sparks were like slow floating dust to Aliana, and she navigated through them like a falcon through dense woods.

Can she fully control her experience of time right now, or is it just happening automatically as the chain gets close? Aurelia wondered as her sister finally closed the gap.

With Aliana so close, Eddy gave up on the chain and swung his arms wildly at her, but every one of his swings Aliana treated like slowly drifting dust. She stood a few feet away from him and studied his tattoos with peculiar interest as he thrashed at her but only hit rock and air.

All of a sudden, two flashes of silver lunged outward just as Eddy swung both of his arms over his head. Aliana stood poised with the swords outstretched on either side of her body while fountains of blood and the electric arcs of severed cybernetics coated her in the victory of battle. Eddy screamed wildly and gawked in dismay at stumps of flesh rather than his gargantuan fists.

"Death to Downver!" Eddy cursed with more anger than panic. "Mercy, chicklet! Please!" he begged as he backed against the rock wall.

No, Aurelia mouthed, mimicking her sister from the vision.

"No," Aliana said, and then she stepped forward with ease and lunged, aiming a sword at each of Eddy's eyes. The vortex swirled hungrily, promising Aurelia the terrible sweetness of a fated future.

Die, Aurelia thought, glad that the world would be rid of Eddy, regardless of his gender.

Just before Aliana's swords made contact with Eddy's face, a terrible roar and flash of light exploded from Ricardo's hand, obliterating the vortex and Aurelia's one-pointed assurance of the future. Aliana immediately fell to the ground, blood slowly pouring from her head.

No! Aurelia gasped. *No! No! No! That's not what happens. This isn't how it happens!*

The weight of the whole world seemed to press against her chest, and though Aurelia found herself unable to stand, she still crawled to her sister to find her lying unconscious in a pool of blood. Aurelia used one of the jackets to place pressure against the wound beneath the hair on the left side of her sister's skull. Then, she lifted Aliana's face out of the blood and signed desperately, "No! No! No! Please, Aliana! I'm supposed to die, not you! Please don't leave me, Ali."

"Thanks for the assist, little bromi," Eddy said, nodding to Ricardo. Both boys just stood in disbelief, mouths agape, Ricardo still pointing the gun at Aliana with a shaking hand.

"She...she..." Ricardo stammered. "She would have killed us next. She was like a monster. Worse than a helix-warden. She...she—"

"Quit your chirping. You did good, little cricket," Eddy said as he panted and placed his bleeding stumps against his waist. A small gadget on each side of his body wrapped a band around each of his stumps, stopping the bleeding and electric arcing. "It's a good thing your parents bought you that scope-lens for your eye. The little hen was fast, but not faster than a bullet, apparently," Eddy concluded with equal respect and condescension for Aliana's lethal battle prowess.

I don't understand, Aurelia gasped, wishing that Rooli were here with her to tell her what to do. *My vision was wrong. How is it possible my vision could be so terribly wrong?*

Focus! she heard Rooli say in her mind, but she couldn't focus on fate. There was no fate. Not anymore. Everything was shattering like a broken mirror.

Eddy smiled at her, and then he dropped to the ground, convulsing intensely. Both boys turned their heads and looked back toward the entrance from where they had come. At the sight of someone entering the cave, Doe fell to his knees in tears, and Ricardo began involuntarily urinating and shaking in primal fear.

"She isn't dead," came a slow, methodical, high-pitched but distinctively male voice from the shadows of the cave entrance. "Do you know how I know that?"

Aurelia lifted her head and watched as a peculiar, flamboyant man emerged from the shadows and entered the dim green glow of the Feeding Cave. He was tall, at least six and a half feet, and as thin and bony as the girls. His skin was pale and taught, and his lips remained in a constant state of smug certainty. He wore oversized glasses made of pitch-black lenses and silver frames. His pure white hair formed into a stark widow's peak stretching from the center of his forehead to the midway point of his skull. Its luster made the girls' dirty platinum hair appear even more unkempt. Other than a shiny small blue crystal embedded in the man's left cheek, the strangest part about him was his clothing. He wore a full length black jacket highlighted with dizzying swirls of silver that gave way to pants made of an identical shimmering material. Around the neck of the jacket was fluffy white fur identical in color to the man's hair.

"I know she is alive because I know everything. I am Cid the Knower, the First Lord of the Walled City of Downver. I know even more than you, Aurelia, the Virus. Especially now that your prescience is failing you," Cid announced while preening his pure white widow's peak with the tips of his bony fingers.

Aurelia's stomach sank, and she felt suddenly as if she were once again plunging in free fall into the dark depths of the Earth.

My name, Aurelia gasped. *The designation given to me by my creator, Tomasz Novak. My powers. He knows everything. He even knows that my prescience was wrong just a moment ago.*

"Something is on its way here—something that inhibits prescience. You've felt it, haven't you, Aurelia?" Cid asked as he waved his hands in wide sweeping gestures as if always on the verge of presenting something grand.

Does he also know how to speak the secret sign language of Wintersvilla Warriors? Aurelia considered, but she knew the answer, so she signed to him.

"What do you want?" Aurelia signed with her left hand as she gripped her sword with her void-black right hand, ready to protect her sister to the death. That is, if she really was still alive like this strange man named Cid claimed. Aurelia demanded the prescience show her the future, even if it might be wrong, but it wouldn't come.

"It must be frustrating to have a power of such magnitude that you can't fully control," Cid stated with seemingly genuine interest as he cocked his head and observed Eddy, who was still convulsing violently on the ground. Cid's glasses flashed red, releasing Eddy and leaving him panting and groaning.

"Help her!" Aurelia demanded, motioning toward her sister. "Help her, or I'll kill you all."

Cid laughed obnoxiously and clapped his hands together with glee. "Oh my! Oh yes! You are a Wintersvilla Wench through and through. How wonderful! How delightful!"

"They…really are from the surface?" Doe gasped.

Cid abruptly stopped laughing and soured as though he suddenly smelled something foul.

"Yes, foolish boy, obviously. I may know everything, but I don't think it takes much brain power to discern that they aren't from the Walled City or any other district in Downver. In fact, they aren't even human."

Aurelia shook her head in total defeat. *Is it him? Is he actually the one creating a disturbance in my prescience, distorting the very course of fate?*

"My Lord," Eddy gasped, still panting for breath. "I—"

"You will speak when you are spoken to, little Eddy Hopper," Cid warned with a song-like lilt in his voice, prompting Eddy to fall silent and still. It was something Aurelia didn't even think was possible for the loudmouthed man.

Aurelia caressed Aliana's cheek while she kept pressure on the wound. Though the bleeding appeared to be slowing, Aliana still remained unconscious.

At least she's still breathing, Aurelia told herself with futile reassurance as her mind fluttered unbecomingly. She felt desperate to have Rooli at her side to protect her and guide her. But she was all alone, surrounded by strange boys and vile men.

What do I do? Aurelia thought, frozen in fear for the first time in many years.

"You," Cid said, pointing his finger at Ricardo. Ricardo's pet rooster strutted in defiance at Cid, eyeing the man with a grim threat in its eyes. "Where did you get that relic?" Cid asked, pointing to the revolver clutched in Ricardo's shaking hand.

"I...I..." Ricardo stammered in utter terror as he stood in a puddle of his own urine.

"Aye! Aye!" Cid laughed as he mimicked Ricardo's nervous stammering. "Are you an old world pirate, little boy?"

"A...pirate?" Ricardo repeated, clearly unfamiliar with the word.

"They had wooden legs and lived on water ships," Doe said, spilling his words in terror.

"Very good," Cid said, nodding to Doe with approval. "What's the point of funding the Erudite District if the children of the Walled City refuse to attend its prestigious halls of academia?"

Stay with me, Aurelia thought as she kept pressure on her sister's head. *If only I could replace my broken prescience with a power that could actually help us, like your power over time, Ali. Something that could bring you back to life. But this is all I can do for now,* Aurelia thought defeatedly in the presence of Cid. *Please just stay with me, Ali.*

Aurelia glanced back to Cid and saw that he was staring at the boys as if expecting an answer to his previous question. Then, after a few tense moments, he clapped his hands and burst into more obnoxious laughter.

"I jest. What use is an academic education when revolution is always a trigger-pull away? And if not revolution, then it is only a matter of time before a Hunter and Huntress find their way in. Isn't that right, boys?"

The boys just stood in shock against the wall, looking like panicked salmon held steady on a chopping block.

"Such is the way that all alley punks think, and it is that line of thinking that leads us to revolution in the first place. Do you know how John Downver held all seven districts together for a full ten years despite the population being double what it is now? He gave the people of Downver a vision. He gave them purpose. But you alley punks have no purpose. No vision. You are blind. All you want is to destroy the order that society provides, for that is all you can do. That's all you're good for."

Aurelia forced her breath to a state of calm and squeezed Aliana's shoulder. *I have to be strong for both of us,* she told herself as she watched Cid hold out his hand to Ricardo with his palm up.

"Hand over the relic, little nameless alley punk," Cid demanded.

"Please," Ricardo pleaded, tears streaming from his blue glowing eyes. "The gun is my dad's. He'll kill me if he finds out I lost it. He'll actually kill me. Please don't take it, First Lord, sir."

Maybe my arm has the strength to pick up Aliana and run right past them while they're distracted, Aurelia considered as she watched the supposed First Lord of the Walled City of Downver, Cid the Knower, glower at the young boy. He bent his knees and crouched, bringing his eyes level with Ricardo's trembling, tear-filled gaze. Aurelia positioned her arm closer to Aliana's waist, readying herself to knock over Cid as she sprinted madly in the direction that the boys and men had come from.

"I have a policy," Cid whispered to Ricardo, though his voice could still be heard due to the echoing acoustics of the cave walls. "If someone is going to kill me, I kill them first."

Ricardo gulped, then took a deep breath, but he was still unable to move.

Aurelia deepened her breathing, oxygenating her body and priming her adrenal glands.

"I know who you are, Ricardo Endema. Few families have the creds to buy their children that much armor and enhancements, especially at your age. Only twelve years old, isn't that right? At the exact same age your father served me as rooster-warden during the third revolution. He's one of the reasons I am First Lord of the Walled City. If it weren't for him and a handful of others, the Lord of Limbs would have sliced me and every single person living in the city to pieces. If your father really will kill you for stealing his relic and losing it, you can always try telling him that the First Lord is the one who took it from you. You see, hiding lethal relics is an E-class offense, so if I wanted to, I could execute your father, mother, and your entire family for endangering the Walled City. It's already against the Lord of Limbs' decrees to enter the Feeding Cave. Or were you ignorant of that as well?"

Ricardo stood with his mouth agape, unable to do anything but rapidly breathe and groan in fear.

An unexpected flash of prescience struck Aurelia suddenly, and she saw that there was a more direct way of tackling the problem of Cid the

Knower, a way that was also far more Wintersvillian in nature. *But my prescience is broken,* Aurelia reflected bitterly. *Attacking him head on might not be the best way. I can't trust my prescience. Not anymore,* Aurelia thought, once more paralyzed by indecision—something that had been mostly alien to her only a day earlier.

"Give him the gun, Ricky!" Doe urged his friend. "You can stay at my place for a while until your dad's done glowing. He won't actually kill you, but he might beat you half to death."

"I have a policy," Cid sang as he awkwardly took the gun with two fingers then let it fall into an inside pocket of his oversized jacket. "If someone is planning to beat me half to death, I kill them first. My advice is to wait until he falls asleep. Use something heavy to crack his skull open. Then, you will never have to worry about your father's ire again. You see how easy it is to take control of your own life, little boy?"

Ricardo sounded like he was hyperventilating.

"Thank you for not killing us, sir," Doe whispered, and then he took Ricardo's hand in his own as if trying to subtly shake his friend from his paralytic fear.

They fear this vile man like a child fears a Hunter, Aurelia discerned as Cid kept his back to her and spoke to the boys. *I can't cower in fear. Rooli would never cower. And neither can I. I must attack, even if it is the wrong decision. I must take advantage of this opening before it's too late,* Aurelia told herself. *He incapacitated Eddy with a single flash of those glasses. I have to act! Now!*

Aurelia lifted her sword with her void-black right hand and flung it directly at Cid's back. The sword suddenly exploded out of her grip and rocketed at Cid with hypersonic speed, throwing Aurelia hard against the wall behind her. The shockwave shook the cavern and the glowies, making them shake and flutter.

What power! Aurelia marveled in awe at her arm's explosive propulsion of her sword. Refusing to linger on the extent and capabilities of her void-body while Aliana was still incapacitated, Aurelia ran back to her sister's side. Then she gasped as she peered forward to see where her sword had landed.

Cid stood with his arms outstretched as if in welcome, his smug smile plastered across his bony face. Behind him, Ricardo choked on thick spurts of blood that poured out of his pleading mouth and onto his suit of armor. Aurelia's sword was embedded through his chest, pinning him to the rock wall.

No! Aurelia winced, shaking her head that her prescience had once again failed her. Betrayed her. Lied to her. *I saw the sword impale Cid. That is what my prescience showed me as clear as I can see this boy I just murdered,* Aurelia contemplated in horror. *I was lost without my prescience, and now I'm even worse off with my mind telling me lies and leading me astray.*

"Ricky!" Doe pleaded, holding his friend's desperate face in his hands. Ricardo's eyes were awash with the fear of oblivion. "Ricky, don't die! We'll get you to a handler. They can fix this."

"Not if he's stuck to this wall, they can't," Cid sang with a few chuckles of soft laughter and a single soft touch of his widow's peak. "That blade of Wintersvilla steel is just over two feet long, with more than a foot of it embedded into the wall. It's a shame these girls killed the Feeding Cave Hunter on their way here. He would have enjoyed feeding his so-called glowies a fresh meal. The greens he cultivates in his lair are of the finest quality. No one in Downver has ever been able to reproduce their effects to a perfect degree. Your death could have meant something, little boy," Cid told Ricardo as he slipped unconscious and his face came to rest against the sword. "Your death could have meant sustenance for mushrooms and the fulfillment of the Feeding Cave Hunter—both tools that I will no longer be able to utilize. Instead, your death means nothing. You are a nobody. I've already forgotten your name, little alley punk."

He knew my sword would impale the boy, Aurelia considered, more defeated than ever. *Cid the Knower—is he the worst of Downver? He mentioned the so-called Lord of Limbs, and he seems to be afraid of him. If he is this powerful and yet fears the Lord of Limbs, what am I going to do? There's no way we can overcome Cid, let alone someone even worse. I'm sorry, Ali,* Aurelia thought as tears occluded her vision. *I'm sorry that my power failed me, and that I failed us.*

Doe squeezed his fists into tight balls and readied the steel claws wrapped around his knuckles.

"Forget it, little cricket," Eddy told Doe with a surprising amount of compassion in his tone. "He is the First Lord. He is all knowing. Your friend is dead. Nothing is going to change that."

"Wise words, little Eddy Hopper," Cid applauded with a small clap of his hands.

He's dead, Aurelia repeated, observing Ricardo's lifeless corpse. Doe sobbed and held his friend's head in his arms. His pet grasshoppers bowed their heads solemnly as if standing vigil for their fallen comrade.

Without warning, Cid pivoted, evading Ricardo's rooster as it deftly dove at Cid's face, aiming for his glasses. Cid's black lenses flashed red, and in the next instant the rooster fell, dead on the spot. Cid preened his hair as if ensuring that nothing was out of place.

What in Mendel's name are those glasses? Aurelia wondered, squeezing her sister with the bittersweet knowledge that she was alive but still bleeding out. *Did he really kill that bird just by looking at it?*

"To be fair, that was a pretty badass bird. He went for the king's head. Literally," Eddy marveled as he nodded at the dead rooster with respect.

Rather than respond in a sinister fashion, Cid simply shrugged and said, "I concur. If only all subordinates were as loyal as that rooster."

Eddy grunted and lifted himself with his newly grown, fleshy-pink hands.

They can grow back limbs just like that? Aurelia marveled as she wondered if there was any end to the technological achievements of the underground city of Downver. *The city has seven districts. Is it only like this in the Walled City, as they call it?* Aurelia's mind fluttered through possibilities in an attempt to formulate a plan despite the chaos and confusion surrounding her.

Focus! Aurelia told herself. *Nothing can touch you. Not even death. Not unless you choose it,* she forced herself to repeat in her mind even though she couldn't bring herself to believe it.

"What are we going to do with them?" Eddy asked, pointing to the girls.

"You aren't going to do anything with those girls," Cid answered with a hint of reprimand in his tone. "You're going to find another handler to reintegrate enhancements into those fresh fists of yours. Ellen, the handler we used to use, is dead, remember? Her addiction to Serotel got the best of her. Though, they say a Serotel coma is a pretty pleasant way to die, all things considered. They say you just enter a series of stranger and stranger dreams until everything goes dark, or your mind shatters from insanity. I can see the appeal, at least," Cid stated as he callously speculated about another person's death despite Doe's best friend having just died in his arms after being violently impaled.

That boy Doe is going to try to kill me for killing his friend, even if I didn't mean to, Aurelia reasoned. *It's exactly what I would do if I were him,* she concluded, and though she gripped her sister's sword in her right hand, she still felt cornered like a wild animal by these vicious and repulsive men.

What happens next! No more lies! Just tell me! Aurelia demanded of the prescience as bitter fear lapped at the peripheries of her mind. The great swirling vortex beckoned her, but no visions came to her aid.

"Catch, Virus," Cid purred as Doe sobbed. "This is for your sister."

Aurelia lifted her head in time to see Cid toss a small red vial attached to a syringe. Aurelia caught it, and Cid applauded her alacrity with giddy coos of approval.

"Oh yes! Leave it to a Wintersvilla Wench to have such naturally quick reflexes," Cid said. He smiled at her as if expecting gratitude.

"A phoenix-vial?" Eddy marveled with child-like awe. Even Doe lifted his head to peer at the vial of red fluid in Aurelia's hand.

Aurelia hesitated, knowing how stupid it would be to trust Cid, let alone anyone in Downver.

"Don't be daft, girl," Cid said with a roll of his shoulders and a wave of exaggerated sweeps with his hands. "If I wanted to kill you, then I would just kill you. No, I have a much more important use for you and your sister. You'll see."

It has to be him, Aurelia reasoned. *He must be what's causing fate to fracture and the future to become like a structure made of quickly drying sand.*

Aurelia thought of Rooli and felt as if she were right beside her even though she was still just a set of black eyes on a shard of wood inside a jacket pocket.

Move forward! Keep going! Aurelia urged herself. *We will find a way to overcome this disgusting man and his power, just like we always have,* Aurelia thought, channeling Rooli and willing herself to accept her own words as indomitable truth.

"What is it?" Aurelia signed, still unable to inject the mystery substance into her sister.

"It is a concoction of highly intelligent proteins and neutrophils suspended in a mixture of saline and cordyceps spores, along with a few other secret ingredients. It will neutralize the effect of the greens, and it will also heal her wounds."

He knows what Aliana is capable of. He knows her power, and he's still not afraid. He's willing to bring Aliana back to full health and sobriety even after her battle and display of otherworldly lethality. I need you, Rooli, Aurelia thought as she injected the vial into her sister. *You and Aliana both. I can't do this alone. I can't fulfill my fate on my own like you always told me I would have to. I...I can't even control my powers. Maybe...maybe I should ingest a large number of glowies, or greens as the men call them. Maybe my powers would fully awaken like they did for Aliana during the battle. Maybe that's how I can help. But Aliana's power didn't fail her. So maybe since mine did, the glowies will only make it worse. I...I don't know what to do,* Aurelia realized, feeling like she was about to crack right open.

Not knowing what else to do, Aurelia injected the vial into Aliana's arm, and immediately Aliana began to stir, breaking Aurelia away from her grim speculations. She ran her fingers across the length of her sister's face and observed that Aliana's swollen eye and smashed nose were already totally healed. There wasn't even any scarring, as if they had never been damaged in the first place.

"I would give you a phoenix-vial as well, but we can't be certain how our...secret ingredients will interact with your void-body," Cid explained with a measure of joy in Aurelia's visible discomfort and confusion regarding his claim about her body.

He said we, Aurelia noted, wondering who this man's allies, or conspirators, might be. *And he referred to my body as a void-body. He must be talking about my black scars and now my black hand and arm. He has a name for the black stuff. I need to find a way to discover what he knows. But more importantly, he just admitted that there's something he doesn't know,* Aurelia pondered with a surge of hope that there might be a way to overcome Cid the Knower after all.

"Aurelia?" Aliana groaned as if awakening from a long, peaceful slumber.

Aurelia melted at the sight of her sister, and she couldn't help smiling and hugging her tightly to her chest.

Aliana blinked and looked about the cave in utter confusion. "What the Muto fuck did I miss?"

Ali, Aurelia gasped inwardly with intense relief. *You're alive. You're still alive!*

"What, you don't remember chopping my hands off? Eh, little hen?"

Eddy called out with obvious admiration for Aliana in his voice and gaze. He bared his teeth into an oversized smile, presenting the metal litany of death in his mouth. "You still want some teeth-glints of your own, or what?"

"Kill. Kill. Kill," Aliana read with her own impressed grin. "Holy Muto! That is so badass!"

At Aliana's compliment, Eddy looked extremely satisfied with himself. Cid just watched, observing the girls as if they were specimens under a microscope. Doe sobbed silently and refused to step away from his dead friend.

Aliana's impressed gaze soured, and she shook her head in confusion once more. "What the fuck is going on, Aurelia? Who are these people? Where are we?"

"I am your savior," Cid proclaimed with an air of incredible self-satisfaction. "Were it not for me, that bullet would have passed right through your brain rather than just graze your skull. My eyes can do more than just stop a creature's heart," Cid finished, turning to present Aurelia's sword impaled through Ricardo and lodged deep into the rock wall.

He can control objects? Like telekinesis? Aurelia considered nervously at the prospect of Cid's seemingly unlimited power. *Then...did he direct the sword to kill the boy? What, as a show of power?*

"Don't listen to him," Aurelia signed to her sister.

"Don't worry about that," Aliana huffed. "He's a man."

"She talks the alley good, eh my Lord?" Eddy said with a toss of his head to Cid. "You sure you don't want me to bring them to Madam Aubrey? There's a big market for scrawny, unmodded girls like them."

"I don't judge the vices of our citizenry," Cid said with a level of contempt. "Madam Aubrey's girls and boys are free to leave her Ecstasy House whenever they want. How can I argue with such freedom, both to use and to be used? But these girls are meant for far more than the Madam's debaucherous halls. I already told you, little Eddy Hopper, they aren't even human."

Eddy winced at being referred to as little, then cocked his head in consideration at the girls. "I thought you were just talking the alley in a way that went over my head. I'm not learned in language like you, my Lord. But what do you...what do you mean they aren't human?"

Even Doe turned slightly to hear Cid's answer to Eddy's question.

Is it possible he knows more about me and Aliana than we know about ourselves? Aurelia wondered as she helped her sister to her feet.

"How strange," Cid said with venom on his tongue, "I seem to remember telling you several times that you are only to speak if and when I directly address you."

Eddy gulped and stood straighter on his feet. He licked his lips in seeming fear at dropping again to the floor and violently convulsing with just a single red flash of Cid's black lenses.

"That's better," Cid stated, returning to his flamboyant and smug demeanor with a small clap of his hands.

"I remember," Aliana issued suddenly as she peered at the men with wide eyes. "It's just flashes still, but I remember parts of the battle, at least," Aliana said as she bent at the knees to pick up her sword.

"Then you should also remember that I can kill you with a literal blink of my eyes. You see, your powers are still developing, whereas my powers are perfected," Cid explained.

His powers, Aurelia repeated. *Is he like us, then? Is he a creation of one of the so-called old world Titans? Is it possible we have the same creator, even? Did Tomasz Novak make him too?*

"Who created you?" Aurelia signed to Cid.

Cid cooed with laughter and applauded Aurelia's question.

"Very good, Virus. Very good," Cid signed back. "You will learn that answer in time, whether you like it or not."

Eddy stared in confusion at Cid's use of sign language, but he didn't utter a word.

"Aurelia!" Aliana signed. "He knows the Wintersvilla battle language? Who is this guy?" Aliana asked. "No," she said, interrupting herself, "that doesn't matter. Just use your power to see the future. What are we supposed to do?"

"My prescience is broken," Aurelia signed back, feeling as stuck and useless as her sword in the wall.

"It isn't broken!" Cid nearly lashed before reeling in his uncharacteristic rage. "It is simply beginning to awaken. You will learn in time to use it to its full potential. We will teach you," Cid declared, his smile smugger and more self-satisfied than ever.

We, Aurelia repeated, considering once more how much more

powerful Cid's allies might be. *Is he referring to his creator?*

"He knows about your power," Aliana signed, "and he knows the secret Wintersvilla battle language. What else does he know?" Aliana asked in exasperation.

"Everything," Cid said and Aurelia signed in unison.

Cid hopped on one foot in excitement and applauded. "That's right," he said, nodding to Aurelia. "I know everything, Virus. I even know about the great swirling void-vortex within your mind. We will show you how to enter it."

He knows, Aurelia thought with total defeat as the vortex beckoned her from behind Cid. *I've never told anyone except for Rooli about the vortex—not even Aliana. What if he isn't my enemy? What if...he's the one who will help me fulfill my fate?* Aurelia gasped, not wanting it to be true.

"What is he talking about, Aurelia?" Aliana pressed. "You look like you just saw a Hunter. What is it? What is the vortex he's talking about?"

Cid's eyes flashed red suddenly, but no one dropped dead. Instead, Cid nodded to himself, and said, "Time is of the essence. We've dawdled here long enough. It is time for fate to resume its natural course...for now."

Cid turned with an excited hop and walked toward the shadows of the Feeding Cave entrance, waving his arms in the air with the beat of his footsteps. Eddy faithfully followed at his heel.

"Come along now, honored Wintersvilla Wenches. Your Nomad keeper told you that you both must go to Downver, didn't she? I suggest you listen to her and follow me. I will be sealing this cave for the time being. Once Feeding Cave Greens dwindle on the market and their prices skyrocket, only then will we open this cave and harvest Hunter541's specially grown greens."

"The glowies, you mean?" Aliana asked.

Cid nodded. "That is what Hunter541 referred to them as, isn't it? Such a pathetic creature. You two did it a favor by putting it down. But you also destroyed one of my favorite tools. I knew you would, of course. Such is fate. We planned for the Hunter's death. We plan for everything."

Eddy gazed at the girls as if dumbfounded that they really had killed a Hunter on their own. He looked like he wanted to say something, but he maintained his ordered silence.

"Move forward or die in this cave. But we already know what you will do," Cid chuckled, and then he turned and continued walking toward the shadows.

"We have to kill him," Aliana signed.

"Of course we do. But not yet. We'll know when the time is right," Aurelia told her sister.

"Are you sure?" Aliana checked.

"No," Aurelia admitted. "But I know that we have to go to Downver. If Rooli said it," Aurelia signed without having to finish her statement.

"I'm killing him the first chance I get," Aliana signed, and Aurelia nodded in approval. She didn't tell her sister that she had reluctantly deduced that Cid might be the means by which she would fulfill her fate and enter the swirling void-vortex in her mind, whatever that meant.

"The gray boy," Doe issued angrily as Cid and Eddy passed him. "A boy with gray hair and gray eyes was the one who convinced me and Ricardo to come down here. We had never even seen him around before today. It's like he just appeared out of nowhere. But we figured he was just an alley punk who ventured into the Walled City. He's the one who opened the sealed gate. He's the one," Doe said, clearly blaming the gray boy for his friend's death.

That strange boy who called me beautiful, Aurelia remembered, feeling uncomfortable and awkward suddenly.

Cid stopped in his tracks and breathed deeply. He didn't preen his hair or clap his hands. He looked deathly serious. Without looking directly at Doe, he said, "I wouldn't worry about that boy."

"But—" Doe began to protest, and Aurelia wasn't sure if it was concern for the boy or anger at him for getting his friend killed.

"I have a policy about people who make me repeat myself," Cid stated, singing his words once more. "Now, come, little boy. I'll let you live for now. Run along home and tell your pathetic family of rebels that you met the First Lord and that he showed you mercy," Cid said, laughing pleasantly to himself.

At the mention of his family, Doe bit his lip and furrowed his brow in fear, as if Cid had just revealed that he was aware of plans and efforts against him that Doe thought had been a secret. Without wasting another moment, Doe turned and began emptying Ricardo's pockets of his personal belongings. Finally, Doe bent down and plucked three feathers from the rooster's corpse—one gold, one red, and one blue. All the while, Cid observed Doe with an air of amusement.

"Are you done collecting useless memories?" Cid asked with sordid mirth.

Doe nodded then lowered his head and waited for the First Lord to begin walking again. Eddy gave Doe a friendly punch on his shoulder with freshly grown fists that had already doubled in size in the last few minutes.

"You'll be all right, little cricket. Your little bromi had spirit. Shame he couldn't have used that expensive lens to see the sword coming in time to evade it. He was an alley punk, and he knew how to talk the alley. That's what matters, little cricket," Eddy told Doe as if his words constituted the ultimate form of respect in the Walled City.

Eddy walked to Ricardo and the sword. He tried pulling the sword out of the wall, but it wouldn't budge an inch.

"Sorry, little cricket. I was hoping we could give his body a proper Downver ending, but it's all the same, really. The greens in this cave will feed off of his body eventually, and one day we will feed on them. Death to Downver," Eddy intoned.

"Death to Downver," Doe whispered, his voice cracking in sorrow.

Cid continued walking forward, disappearing into the shadows as if perfectly willing to lock all four of them in the Feeding Cave together. Doe followed directly behind Cid, his head held low.

It's all for show, Aurelia concluded, knowing that in reality, Cid the Knower saw her and her sister as tools in the same way he saw Eddy, the Hunter, and the glowies. *He won't just lock us in this cave and let us go to waste. The question is, where does his show of power and actual power begin and end?*

"Ho!" Aliana shouted at Eddy. She pointed her sword at his chest. "What the Mendel fuck is that supposed to be? Is that a Wintersvilla Woman on your chest? Why the fuck are her breasts the size of her thighs?" she lashed in disgust at the tattoo's crude interpretation of Aliana's cherished culture. "Fuck that! Why do you even have a Wintersvilla Warrior tattooed on yourself to begin with?"

Eddy nervously looked in Cid's direction as if ensuring he was out of earshot, then said, "Because Wintersvilla Wenches are badass."

"Warriors. Women. Not wenches!" Aliana fiercely corrected.

"You're right. My bad, little warrior. I've always looked up to Wintersvilla Wen—I mean Women. Your people have been protecting me and my people since I was a kid. I only told my body artist that I wanted her boobs to be mega big because Monique used to say that she, in her own words, 'adored the gargantuan breasts of mothers.' Monique was the greatest Wintersvilla We– I mean Warrior who ever lived. But I'm sure you two know all about her."

Aurelia recognized the name. Monique was one of the most highly trained warriors that had ever lived. It was said that she had been traded to Downver for over 10,000 men—such was her battle prowess. Monique had made a name for herself by openly standing guard at the main entrance to Downver rather than setting traps. She relished battles with Hunters and Huntresses, and the few that battled her learned through death that her relishing in battle was not a form of entertainment, but a vital function of her very being—just like them. By the time Aurelia was old enough to read and learn about history, Monique's name was just one among many.

"Is she here still?" Aliana asked, clearly recognizing the name as well.

"She's dead," Eddy said remorsefully. "All the Wintersvilla Women who used to stand guard outside the main and hidden entrances to Downver are dead."

Aurelia remembered what they had learned from Gambe about the Agency programming an expiration date into all Wintersvilla Warriors. She had seen in the case of Shira what it looked like to expire. Turning to observe Aliana, Aurelia saw that she was wrestling with her own memories of Shira's final moments, and likely the final moments of Myriam as well. Aurelia wished that the prescience would tell her with certainty the fate of Shira and Myriam, but again, it refused to obey her.

"Other than the Feeding Cave Hunter, it's only a matter of time before a Hunter or Huntress or both find their way into Downver," Eddy began. "Without Monique and the others standing guard outside, that's a guarantee eventually. But now we'll be ready for them. The citizens of Downver have survived far worse than Hunters and Huntresses, myself included. Now we are alley punks—even those of us who think themselves higher than the rest," Eddy said before quickly turning and eyeing the shadows with terror. "Now we are ready to brave the surface, and at the same time, we've no need to ever go back to it," Eddy finished, and then he pulled himself away from the group and entered the shadows in the footsteps of his master.

"Let's go," Aurelia signed. Aliana nodded as she slid her fingers across her eye and nose, appearing to inspect them for some trace of her previous wounds or even scarring. She was clearly still dazed, and in the haze of her still returning memories, Aliana shook her head in bewilderment as she followed Aurelia's lead. Aurelia put back on the jacket containing Rooli and tightened it while Aliana picked up her sword and tightened her own jacket. Then, Aurelia stepped forward, and her sister did the same.

I just need to retrieve my sword first, Aurelia thought, and it was only then that she considered the power that had been unleashed by her void-body, as Cid had called it. *I didn't even throw it with my full strength,* Aurelia noted, remembering that she had opted for precision over power.

As they arrived at the sword in the wall, Aurelia couldn't help stopping to take in Ricardo's dead body. A pool of blood, urine, and feces draped the wall and ground beneath him.

"I'm sorry," Aurelia signed, and then she gripped her sword and pulled it from the rock wall with the ease of passing her hand through water. Ricardo fell to the ground in a heap of blood-drained flesh and armor.

"Wait, I remember how the sword exploded from your black hand. I was still half-conscious at the time," Aliana said, marveling at Aurelia's ability to remove the sword with such ease even when Eddy couldn't. "I don't know what's happening to you, Aurelia, but it has to do with your power. It must. And it means that you are growing stronger. We both are."

Move! Aurelia heard Rooli say from within her mind, and with forced resolve, Aurelia broke herself away from the young boy whom she had unintentionally murdered.

"Fucking Muto fuck!" Aliana exclaimed with incredible resolve despite Aurelia knowing that she must be battling a great deal of fear and confusion. "We can do this. I know you agree, Aurelia. We're going to revive Rooli. Nothing can stop us," Aliana huffed as she stepped into the shadows alongside her sister. Side by side, they strode forward into the darkness with their swords at the ready.

The Earth has always been a living thing capable of singular consciousness. Just as each of our bodies is an environment to trillions of individual lives, the planet is also both an environment and an organism.

The human body doesn't merely depend on bacteria and other microorganisms for its nutrient acquisition, energy transformation, and various other vital functions. Comparing the total number of cells, the human body is in fact more foreign bacteria than it is human. Less than half of the total cells composing each human can be called eukaryotic human cells. Nearly sixty percent of all cells composing the body are single cell microbes. Without these trillions of individual tiny lives consuming and reproducing and mutating thousands of times every single day, we would quickly go extinct.

The same is true of the Earth's consciousness. Compared to the size of planet Earth, the human body is a whole order of magnitude smaller than a bacterium is to the same human body. We are tiny. In size, we are more akin to a virus than bacteria. And yet, just as we depend on our microbes for consciousness, the Earth depends on us for consciousness. We are the Earth, and the Earth is us.

The Nomads are currently building several planetary organs of the Earth. Its nervous system. Its heart. Its senses. And a multitude of organs that have no known anatomical equivalent.

A planetary body with a planetary consciousness. This is just one of the many rungs of neoevolution that will allow humanity to climb Mendel's Ladder and attain Ascension.

From Mendel's Ladder: The Personal Journal of Denis Mendel, Recorded Circa 2060, Published June 2108 by Leif Mainstone, Federated Agency Publishing

Chapter 8
A Planetary Jaunt

T he leaf-like flaps around the chirping Nomad's human mouth fluttered with incredible urgency as she chirped at Samuel. Meanwhile, the stump Nomad's many hands jittered in an anxious flurry.

I have to do what Fana says…for now, Samuel acknowledged, breaking into a sprint directly toward the colossal walls of raging storms. *She said the flying Nomad is only a mile away. Let's see what this body can handle.*

Lift! Samuel demanded as he slammed each of his feet against the Nomadic earth with all his might. He had no way of knowing how fast he was actually running, and the fact that the chirping Nomad and Stump Nomad were unable to keep up with him didn't provide any clarity either.

I'm the Mirror-Man! Samuel told himself without caring that he had only a superficial understanding of the title. *This flying Nomad will listen to me. He will!* Samuel thought, demanding that his mind accept his words as irrefutable truth.

A strange sensation at his feet prompted Samuel to glance down, and he saw that the ground was alive. Wriggling mycelial tendrils sprouted from the ground like Foundation earthworms rising to the soil's surface after a controlled rain. They were the same types of tendrils that had coated Fana's body and even slithered into her ear canals. The black walls of lightning raged ahead, illuminating the ground, which grew thicker with the squirming tendrils with every step. As he ran, the tendrils lapped at Samuel's legs and feet and even in between his toes, inspecting him like fat newborn grubs exploring their surroundings. Despite their wriggling movements, the tendrils anticipated Samuel's steps and avoided being directly stepped on and destroyed.

The entire ground is alive, Samuel thought with revulsion, sickened by this world that Madeira had created and was still in the process of creating.

I'll find a way to destroy Madeira and save my family—all in one blow, goddamnit, Samuel thought as he imagined a vague, amorphous figure in his head to represent Madeira as what Fana had referred to as the Mind. *No matter the form, it is still Madeira. This is all that goddamn old worker's doing!* Samuel blazed, using the same pejorative *worker* that many scornful Foundationers had used to describe him. *Old Man Madeira might be dead, but he lives on through the Mind—through the Queen. The Mind might have turned me into this, but if what Fana says is true, then everything isn't set in stone. I can destroy the Mind, the Queen, and the monsters plaguing Astrea…and I can save my family too. I can do it all. I am the Workhorse of Astrea, goddamnit, and I have a Queen to kill, for it will mean the final death of Andre Madeira!*

Without fully meaning to, Samuel burst forward so fast that he nearly bent in half. A shockwave sonic-boomed in his wake, momentarily clearing the rain that was now bouncing off his reflective body. Samuel reeled, stopping himself just as suddenly without inertia forcing him to the ground.

For Mendel's sake! Samuel gasped as he found himself at least five miles closer to the roiling and raging black walls of dense rain constituting the continental storm of Waru. All across the vast undulating walls of the living tempest, the world ruptured and frayed. Mountains of clouds clashed together, releasing deafening booms of thunder that shuddered through the atmosphere. Rain assaulted Samuel from every direction, pummeling his body. Each drop was like a shard of obsidian exploding against him, though his vision remained clear.

I went too far! Samuel concluded angrily, and he pulled himself away from the raging black walls and spun around, searching for the flying Nomad who was probably somewhere behind him now. The lightning made the darkness of the storm-covered night appear brighter than daytime, but Samuel didn't see any movement except for the squirming mycelial ground as far as the eye could see. The mycelial tendrils probed him all the way to his knees, grabbing and sliding across his mirror-body like wild grass. He gritted his teeth and bared the sickening sensation of the probing tendrils.

The eldritch howl of the great storm demanded Samuel's attention, and he turned, a solitary figure in the midst of a cataclysmic maelstrom. His skin was a shimmering kaleidoscope, each bolt of lightning reflecting and refracting through his body to create a myriad of brilliant streaks, painting him as a being of pure energy.

All of a sudden, Samuel felt himself falling backward, as if he were being pulled away from the storm. However, his feet remained in place, and he realized that it was the storm that was moving away from him, as if repelled by its own reflection. As the storm appeared to inhale, pulling its frontiers hundreds of feet inward, swaths of gargantuan sentinel trees were revealed. Unlike the sentinel trees on the beach, these trees were hundreds if not thousands of feet in length, even taller than the towers of the Luxury District. They appeared like sinewy antennae or gargantuan hair follicles growing from the earth. They stretched into the sky, undulating with the rhythm of the storm as they fed the hungry clouds with an endless supply of water that Samuel could visibly see coursing through each sentinel tree's bulging, fleshy veins. The trees bucked and wavered at the wind's behest, as if the storm were alive and choosing which trees to derive its water from at any given time. Samuel just watched in awe, his eyes lost behind the reflection of these thousands of gargantuan sentinel trees extending from the squirming mycelial ground to the raging precipitous sky.

Movement to Samuel's right caught his attention, and he squinted to see humans and Nomads in the distance. They floated down a large river originating from Waru's coast.

A middle-aged man latched onto the bank of the river and pulled himself out of the water. Samuel stared in disbelief at the alien scene and watched as the man painfully sauntered to the closest sentinel tree. He reached the wavering base of the tree, and just as the man touched its flesh, the tree's base peeled open, revealing stringy pink innards that reminded Samuel of the pulsing, vascular insides of a Giganventus. From within the tree, a woman was regurgitated onto the wriggling earth, which lapped at her bloody skin as the rain washed the sentinel tree's blood away. The woman shrieked then panted through shallow breaths, but the man took no notice. Instead, he walked forward and allowed the sentinel tree to consume him whole. As the tree's flesh began to close around the man, Samuel caught his eyes. The man looked momentarily confused by Samuel's presence, but then his eyes rolled to the back of his head. His scream was so loud and full of horror that Samuel could hear him over the booms of thunder in the distance. Finally, the tree's flesh closed completely, its skin sealing and silencing the man.

To Samuel's surprise, the woman had already collected herself. Without hesitation, the woman dropped herself into the river, which coursed invariably inward, directly toward the storm and the increasingly dense fields of gargantuan sentinel trees being pulled like rope toward the storm's center.

What in…Mendel's Name…is this hell? Samuel thought, his mind reeling. *Fana is right: I can't bring my family down here. Not to this place—this circus of horrors. Maybe not anywhere on Earth. I can give the Mind what it wants—the girl Aurelia. I can*—Samuel winced, gritting his teeth at the weight of even entertaining the idea of exploiting a child, let alone anyone, no matter the stakes. *But there has to be another way,* Samuel resolved, latching onto Fana's certainty that fate was not real.

The storm pulled its walls further inward, revealing an area of sentinel trees so vast and dense that they formed their own undulating wall, occluding the lower portion of the storm. Although the storm was hundreds of miles away now, the ends of the sentinel trees closest to Samuel still couldn't be seen. He felt as though he were trapped once more in the black depths of the ocean, with sentinel trees rather than kelp wavering all around him.

This must be how they're feeling up there in Astrea, Samuel considered gravely. *Nathan and Margot must be terrified—and I'm not there to protect them…Enough!* Samuel refused to allow Madeira to decide his fate any further. *I'm not going to exploit a young girl, goddamnit. And I'm not going to fall for these games any longer. I'm going to find this goddamn flying Nomad, and he is going to fly me to Astrea. And that is final. That is my vision. Fuck Mendel's Vision. It's time for my vision. The Mirror-Man's Vision. Now where is this flying Nomad, goddamnit!*

As if in response, a figure emerged from the river. Samuel squinted to see that it was an overweight middle-aged woman, naked from head to toe. She jogged, heaving herself one foot after another, directly toward Samuel. Everything about her was plainly human, except for her smile. She wasn't miserable like the other humans. Rather, her mouth and eyes exuded a level of joy and self-fulfillment that Samuel had only ever observed in one type of creature.

She's a Person of the Earth, Samuel gasped. *A Nomad. But…how is that possible? She doesn't have any weird growths or strange features. She's just…is she just an eerily happy human?*

The woman waved to Samuel, childish and innocent despite the wriggling ground and raging storm. Samuel saw that the ground didn't latch onto her and inspect her as she passed.

"Mirror-Man!" the woman called out excitedly as she approached. "I almost missed you! That wouldn't be good at all, Mirror-Man! His Fore-told Future shows that your journey to Downver is of the utmost importance."

Play along, Samuel thought. *At least for now.*

"That's right," Samuel nodded in agreement, careful not to stare at the woman's body, which she wasn't even trying to hide. "To Downver. Where is the flying Nomad? We've no time to waste."

The woman's smile widened, stretching across her face with an unnatural warping of her features.

"In that case," she said sweetly, "let us get going right away."

Without hesitation, the woman placed her thumb between her lips then blew outward against her thumb as if she were blowing up a partially inflated glowglobe. Immediately, the woman's body inflated, her sagging skin expanding to become taught. Still, she went on expanding, her skin audibly stretching as she bulged into a bulbous balloon of flesh. All the while, her joy never faltered. She just went on staring at Samuel with profound happiness as every surface of her body expanded and reformed.

After only a handful of seconds, the woman's thumb popped out of her mouth. Her body was stretched so thoroughly that her limbs became no more than hands and feet hanging loosely from her ballooned flesh. Her eyes had bulged and shifted to either side of her head, and paired with her elongated, fattened body, she appeared like an overfed, tailless whale with useless hands and legs instead of fins. The mycelial tendrils appeared to be keeping her afloat, and she towered over Samuel, at least eleven feet high and fifteen feet long.

She looks like a mini-Giganventus. Except she's only more horrific because she has human features. Were the Giganventi humans at one time too? Samuel wondered with dread.

"Get in," she said, her voice now a low bass bellow emitted from her wide mouth. "My name is Inflated Sapien, and I will help you travel across the Earth to find Downver and eventually the Virus. He requires the Virus to complete His plans. Come now, Mirror-Man, and let us fulfill the Mind and the Earth's unified will."

Inflated Sapien winced but her smile did not falter as a side of her bulbous body parted open, tearing her flesh into strings of sinew to reveal her veiny, pulsing internal cavity.

She looks even more like a Giganventus on the inside, Samuel noted with revulsion.

"Transition and second life will come soon," Inflated Sapien mumbled to herself as if using the assurance of her words to soothe her flesh-rending pain.

The winds shifted, and Samuel turned to see that the storm had exhaled its raging walls, and now they were coming back to consume the area once more.

"You must hurry," Inflated Sapien said with just a tinge of worry in her low voice. "I'll be using the storm to lift off."

Samuel was reluctant to enter the Nomad, especially since he had only just escaped the confines of a grotesque creature an hour or so earlier.

I should have expected something like this the moment Fana said a flying Nomad would be involved in my journey. I have to just go. It's not like I'll be in there for long anyway.

Samuel looked to the sky one last time in a futile attempt to feel Astrea's presence even if he couldn't directly see it.

I'm coming, goddamnit. I'm coming to save you all, Samuel thought as he entered Inflated Sapien's squelching, murky insides.

"Sorry," Samuel said as the Nomad groaned in pain from Samuel's incredible weight upon her organs.

"Not long now until second life," Inflated Sapien repeated, her voice echoing across her insides with what Samuel perceived to be forced calm.

"What is *second life*?" Samuel asked as Inflated Sapien's body began to close, forming a scar-tissue seam. Outside the storm could be heard as a distant growl, affording Samuel a strange sense of shelter, despite his pink and purple pulsating surroundings.

"Second life comes after transition. That's when a Nomad turns into a flesh tree and grows her own pods—her own Nomads. That's true even of a Hybrid Nomad like me—that is, Nomads who appear human, or even sound human. Really, we're all just Nomads. Just like how humans are all just humans. Well, not all humans. You are different, Mirror-Man. You are human, but...not really."

"No!" Samuel lashed with even more force than he had intended. "I am human. I'm not this fucking Mirror-Man. My name is Samuel Kaminski. I'm a human, goddamnit!"

No, you fool, Samuel cursed himself. *The Nomads only listen to the Mirror-Man, and she needs to listen to you!*

"I mean—" Samuel began, attempting to correct himself, but Inflated Sapien had already started speaking.

"No, you are the Mirror-Man. I can tell. You're him."

Samuel couldn't help laughing. "Oh, you can tell, can you? Impressive, Inflated Sapien."

"Thank you," Inflated Sapien said with gratitude at being complimented by the Mirror-Man.

The raging walls were less than a hundred feet away when Inflated Sapien's body fully closed, leaving Samuel in the dim darkness of her insides. It wasn't pitch-black however, for the dull green glow of his chest provided scant light. The green light prompted Samuel to check his chest, which he had forgotten about with so much chaos running afoul.

"Oh, goddamnit!" Samuel groaned, for the mushrooms were nearly extinguished, and the void-black was already slowly but surely beginning to spread once more at the edges of the crater in his chest.

Samuel was about to remove one of the three remaining pods from his silk waistcloth when Inflated Sapien started rumbling, making Samuel lose his balance.

"Here we go," Inflated Sapien boomed with trance-like awe despite the strain in her voice.

All at once, Samuel's stomach dropped as Inflated Sapien was lifted at breakneck speed into the air.

"To Astrea!" Samuel screamed, but he couldn't even hear his own voice over the cracks of lightning exploding the atmosphere directly outside Inflated Sapien. Their velocity plastered Samuel against a wall of veins with insurmountable g-force.

My chest! Samuel gasped. *I need a pod!*

Unable to lift his arm against the g-force, again he screamed, "Fly to Astrea!" But it was no use. The winds shifted Inflated Sapien, throwing Samuel against the other side of her body so hard that his head burst through her flesh.

The furious lightning painted dizzying phosphorescent streaks across the vast churning curtains of black. The relentless cracks of thunder, like mountains clashing together, stole Samuel's breath, and though thousand-mile-per-hour gusts of wind and splintering rain battered his face, his mirror-body allowed him to see through it all. Despite the raging centrifugal force drawing them slowly outward, Samuel's gaze was drawn like an irresistible magnet to the core about which the storm rotated.

Samuel did not consider himself a man who was even capable of folding in the face of fear, but what he saw at the center of the storm filled him with such deep, ancient, immeasurable terror and awe that he felt like a mere child in the presence of some impossible cosmic behemoth from beyond the stars. The lightning flared to reveal that within the storm's central vortex, where maddening swirls of wind and water conjoined, a great writhing mass of tangled life rose into the unseen heavens above. The gargantuan sentinel trees grew so densely at the storm's core that they were fully intertwined, knitted together into a pulsing nexus of undulating cords extending like cosmic larva into the upper atmosphere and beyond. Lightning arced between the coalesced sentinel trees, making them appear like neurons firing action potentials across their writhing surfaces.

Samuel realized this was the planetary organ Fana mentioned. Although he couldn't understand why this was here and what purpose this horrifying mass of life served, his focus remained on his family and the countdown to erasure eating away his chest.

"To Astrea!" he screamed in another futile attempt to be heard by Inflated Sapien, who was presently being thrashed around by the winds with seemingly no control at all.

How does she expect to fly us anywhere if she can't even control her body? Samuel wondered as he tried in vain to come up with a different solution to jump to Astrea without potentially destroying it or overshooting it.

Again the winds shifted, allowing the inward centripetal force to overtake the outward centrifugal force, plunging Samuel and Inflated Sapien directly into the heart of the planetary organ spanning the majority of the entire continent of old world Australia. Samuel wanted to try speaking to Inflated Sapien again from inside her body, but the g-force was so overwhelming that he couldn't pull his head back inside.

"What are you doing, goddamnit?" Samuel screamed in horror as bolts of lightning exploded all around them, violently buffeting Inflated Sapien in every direction as her body was pulled invariably inward toward the impenetrable mass.

"Pull up! Up! To Astrea!" Samuel screamed.

She's going to slam right into that writhing mass of trees, and I'm going to get stuck in this horrifying place until I disappear completely, Samuel reasoned as the g-force doubled then doubled again at the behest of the centripetal forces beckoning Inflated Sapien to her death.

Still, they didn't crash. Their acceleration and velocity continued to increase, and the planetary organ just kept getting bigger.

It's like seeing Mount Mendel from a distance, Samuel understood. *This thing is even bigger than my eyes can fathom. This thing is...too big!* Samuel reeled, feeling like an inconsequential bacterium observing the gestation of some interstellar, macrocosmic entity.

This is just one organ of many. An organ of the planet Earth itself? Or something else still to come? Samuel gasped, uncertain what it all could add up to.

A bolt of lightning struck Inflated Sapien, sending her tumbling through the air without any control whatsoever.

Goddamnit! Samuel gritted his teeth as the g-force tripled, pressing his body against the inside wall so that his neck, still outside Inflated Sapien's body, twisted unnaturally. Despite a spine-breaking neck twist, Samuel was unharmed—just uncomfortable. So much g-force left him unable to breathe, reminding him that he only breathed out of habit.

All of my limitations are in my head. I know that better than anyone as the Workhorse of Astrea. I survived outer space. I survived Tomasz Novak. I will survive this too!

The winds howled and the lightning wailed and the rain shrieked, but as they rocketed at thousands of miles per hour toward the planetary organ's innards, all the sounds of the storm were eclipsed by the movement of the core sentinel trees grinding against one another. Each of these central sentinel trees constituted the mass of numerous mountains, forming a whole continent rising into the sky that generated earthquake-tremors through the mass. It sounded like the unending deep bass horn blast of a sinister god of war.

A didgeridoo, Samuel remembered, recalling the handful of old timers in Astrea who enjoyed playing the strange instrument. *That's what it sounds like. A didgeridoo played forever at the lowest note possible,* though he felt only terror rather than nostalgia.

As they continued plunging toward the organ, the deep didgeridoo bellow grew so loud that the sound trembled through Inflated Sapien and Samuel, making them both violently convulse. Samuel was certain they were about to crash into the wall of the closest sentinel tree, and then he began convulsing so intensely that even his mirror-body undulated with the frequency of the organ's writhing bellows. Samuel's mirror-skin rapidly rose and fell across its surface, bending and warping with ease as every inch of his body vibrated with visible sound. The world flashed before his eyes, and though he couldn't hear her, he felt Inflated Sapien scream in what appeared to be both painful anguish and wild ecstasy.

Through the intense vibrations, Samuel could still discern the titanous sentinel trees composing the core of the organ, and he saw now that they had parted slightly at the very center of the mass, creating a slim crevice through which Inflated Sapien's body could pass through with miles to spare on either side. As they tunneled through the thick, lightning-laden center of the organ, their acceleration quadrupled then quadrupled again. A series of lightning bolts struck Inflated Sapien and Samuel in turn, throwing Samuel's stomach into his throat as they explosively accelerated forward through the tunnel and out to the opposite side of the storm in a flash of otherworldly brightness, blinding Inflated Sapien and every creature with eyes presently caught within the storm's walls. Only Samuel, with his mirror-eyes, was left unblinded, though he still couldn't see clearly with the sound of the planetary organ's movements drumming the mirror-substance into violent, cymatic sound patterns across his reflective skin.

Samuel felt something burst and wrap around his body. In an instant of sudden relief, Samuel's body ceased its convulsions and his vision returned from the blinding oscillations of light. The didgeridoo bellow began to wane and grow even lower in frequency as Inflated Sapien soared through the raging black winds and away from the planetary organ at a speed that Samuel couldn't even fathom. After several more seconds, the primal, droning didgeridoo resonance was replaced by howling winds full of nearby lightning explosions and the thrumming of distant thunder. However, the sounds of the storm were no longer deafeningly loud.

Back to work, worker! Samuel scolded himself harshly now that he could once more think clearly.

"To Astrea!" Samuel screamed, refusing to waste any time despite his mind still reeling at the otherworldly experience that he had just endured. To his surprise, he could hear his own voice, and as he collected himself, he discovered that he was back inside Inflated Sapien, only she had changed. It was only then that Samuel understood what it was that he had felt burst around his body as they had passed through the core of the organ.

She…transformed, Samuel realized as he inspected his surroundings. Inflated Sapien's simple, balloon-like body had morphed into a rudimentary cockpit, containing a seat which held Samuel in a comfortable reclined position. Several areas of transparent membranes provided Samuel a view of the outside world, which was presently just impenetrable walls of thick rain and flashes of lightning. Samuel considered that they could slam into a mountain or some other gigantic structure, like another planetary organ, and they wouldn't even be able to see it coming.

"Can you hear me?" Samuel asked, but Inflated Sapien either would not or could not respond in this new form. Samuel peered outside the membranes and found that Inflated Sapien had grown hulking trunks and branches containing thin membranous webs presently catching the wind like so many tiny rudders. As he studied the strange branches, Samuel watched as tiny black protrusions began freckling every inch of every branch. They grew from barely perceivable dots to three-inch buds in a matter of seconds.

She turned into a tree, just like all the other Nomads do when they die. Samuel accepted. *Does that mean she won't be able to understand me and listen to my commands? That old bastard Madeira said the Mirror-Man can command the Nomads, but what about flesh trees?*

Finally able to freely move, Samuel inspected his chest.

Goddamnit! He cursed as he looked down to find that it was no longer just his chest that had hollowed and turned void-black. The void extended several inches lower, erasing his top-most abdominal muscles. His pectorals were virtually totally gone as well. Worst of all, the crater was far deeper than before, hollowing the entire area of his chest cavity where his lungs and heart should be.

Samuel quickly removed a pod and crushed it angrily with one hand. The green spores exploded all around him. Then, just like before, they flung themselves into his chest as if magnetically attracted to the void-black. The green-glowing mushrooms filled his chest cavity, illuminating the cockpit with the tepid assurance that he had a little more time. All was not lost, at least, not yet.

Only two left, Samuel thought. *And after that there's not much more of me left to disappear. Can I...can I, as the Mirror-Man, save my family as a set of legs?* Samuel thought in horror as he imagined the upper-half of his body disappearing before his lower-half.

"Inflated Sapien!" Samuel tried again, but attempting to talk to her returned the expected result of trying to communicate with a flying tree.

Without warning, the combating walls of raging winds, rain, and lightning disappeared, replaced by a night sky full of unwavering stars and a dazzling view of what Samuel recognized from his history lessons to be an arm of the Milky Way.

"My god," Samuel said aloud, unintentionally speaking the same words that he had heard his father say on many occasions. "My god, it's beautiful," Samuel gasped. "And fucking terrible." He felt the strange sensation of crying without actually crying. Then, his crying turned to sobbing and his sobbing to anger.

"Take me to Astrea, you goddamn tree! Take me! Take me!" he screamed with labored breathing as his mind tortured him with visions of the planetary organ and the Milky Way and the monsters of Astrea presently hunting Sandra, Margot, and Nathan. His mind demanded he accept that he was just a man, no matter what his body looked like. He was just a man, and he could not contend with the power of a planetary organ, let alone an entire planet.

No! another part of his mind interjected. It was the unwavering place—the island that he had built through years and decades of self-torment through selfless labor. *No! You do not fold. You do not break. Lift, you worthless worker! Lift!*

Acting on instinct and accepting the first thought that came to his mind, Samuel tore a pulsing vein out of one of the thick, fleshy walls of the flesh tree that had once been Inflated Sapien. Again, acting entirely on instinct, with his conscious mind docile to the unwavering island of selfless, egoless action, Samuel plunged the blood spurting vein directly into his chest. The mushrooms reacted, flurrying and pulling the vein a few inches deeper into the hollow. The vein bucked, tightened, and then resumed beating at the same pace as the rest of the flesh tree.

A peaceful humming could be heard at the periphery of Samuel's mind. He recognized the pitch of the humming voice immediately.

"Inflated Sapien, is that you humming? Are you able to speak to me in this form?" Samuel asked.

Mirror-Man! Inflated Sapien marveled through Samuel's thoughts. The branches outside seemed to bristle with excitement as pods continued inflating from every inch of the tree's flesh.

Mirror-Man, how are you talking to me? Are you…dead? Inflated Sapien asked in horror.

Samuel glanced back to see that the storm was no longer even visible. The dark ocean seemed to go on forever in every direction. Although they hadn't accelerated in many minutes, they still had to be traveling at an incredible velocity.

"I'm not dead. Not yet. How fast are we traveling? How many miles per hour?"

We're flying at just under 24,000 miles per hour, Inflated Sapien answered easily.

Samuel verbally gasped at the number, but Inflated Sapien went on.

We should arrive at the main entrance to Downver in no more than fifteen minutes. Beyond that, His Foretold Future becomes too bright to see. That brightness is you, of course, Mirror-Man. That is—if Tomasz' weapon doesn't consume you before we get there. You still have two pods though, right? Inflated Sapien checked.

"That's right," Samuel confirmed, feeling stupid for not taking more.

Good. That's more than enough to last the flight to Downver. The flesh pods I'm currently growing—some of them are actually the glowing mushroom pods used to keep Tomasz' weapon at bay. When we land, I will take root and connect to the mind of the Earth, and you may take as many pods as you desire.

Samuel exhaled a sigh of relief before reminding himself that they would not be landing on the Earth.

"I'm going to have to just manage with these two pods for now. They should last me thirty minutes or so, at least, based on the rate of the other ones. If you can supply me with some more pods on our way to Astrea, I would appreciate it, but if not, then so be it. I'll just have to destroy the Mind and save my family in the next thirty minutes," Samuel stated, despite knowing he would need more time than that to destroy a so-called god.

Inflated Sapien went totally silent for a few seconds before finally responding, *Maybe you can destroy the Mind, Mirror-Man, even though the Mind made you. But if you destroy the Mind, then you destroy the Earth and all of life with it. Follow His Foretold Future. Bring the Mind the Virus and allow her sister, the Matriarch, to come to power. Only the Matriarch can cure you, Mirror-Man. Only she can turn you back into a human. Your family needs you, Mirror-Man. The human you.*

A cure, Samuel considered, his mind racing with the new possibility as he scanned the sky for the orbiting city—his home.

"Where is this Matriarch?"

She does not exist yet, Inflated Sapien answered cryptically. *She still remains a potential—like you once were. But here you are. We are on the path now—the path of His Foretold Future. The Path of Mendel's Vision. We are climbing Mendel's Ladder even as we speak. I have seen this conversation before, Mirror-Man. Some of the details are slightly different, but the gist is the same. All of this has been foretold.*

"I don't care," Samuel told her with cut-throat finality as Astrea came into view in the distant night sky. "We're going to Astrea. Now."

Mirror-Man, Inflated Sapien warned with such severity that Samuel couldn't help hearing her out. *Mendel's Vision is a series of forking pathways. We are on the right path now, but this pathway is one of many. There was a time when the Mind thought He could force life down particular pathways, but it doesn't work like that. The more He tried to force the course of reality, the more it bent and broke, warping His Ladder and subsequent Ascension. Chance and choice are necessary ingredients to Mendel's Ladder. If you go to Astrea now, you will bend reality beyond repair. You will destroy His Foretold Future. You will—"*

"Good!" Samuel fumed. "Good, goddamnit! I hope his future never comes to fruition. I'm not listening to these lies anymore. Like Fana said, the future isn't set in stone. And even if it is, you and Fana confirmed that I am free to choose. Now, as the Mirror-Man, I demand that you listen to me. Take me to Astrea!"

This is a bad idea, Mirror-Man. If you deviate—

"Shut up, goddamnit!" Samuel spat, sick of being controlled and told what to do by so many individuals, including a tree. "Just go up! Up! Up!" Samuel demanded.

Without any further protestation, the branches outside shifted, allowing their membranous rudders to catch the shifting wind and point upward, directly toward Astrea.

I'm coming, Sandra! Just protect the kids a bit longer. Just hang on, Samuel

142

thought, not caring that deviating from Madeira and the Mind's plans might mean his own erasure.

As Inflated Sapien flew higher into the atmosphere, the stars quickly grew in intensity. They seemed to blaze across the void in defiance of space's vastness, each one a scintillating point of resistance against the all-consuming void expanding all around them.

Prepare yourself, Mirror-Man, Inflated Sapien offered regrettably. *I told you this was a bad idea.*

"What do you mean, wha—"

Samuel stopped short at the sight of a silver streak of light launching from around the bend of Earth's surface and into the sky so fast that within only a handful of seconds it had already traveled an entire hemisphere of the globe. As fast as they were traveling, the silver streak made Samuel feel as though they were completely stalled in the sky.

"What is it?" Samuel gasped as the streak formed into a trailing arrow and aimed directly at them without disturbing the atmosphere.

It's Harald Mainstone, the Sixth Prodigal Son of the Agency, Inflated Sapien answered, her tone one of accepted defeat. *The Earth and the Mind might allow you the choice to discard Mendel's Ladder and abandon His vision, but Harald won't.*

Rivers of molten steel and boiling blood presently churn through the rubble of what was once humanity's most impressive cities. Yesterday, these cities were disparate yet ubiquitously debaucherous and cut-throat centers of the globe, all of them teeming with tens of millions of individuals. Now they are ash.

The others laughed as billions were obliterated. They laughed. Every mushroom cloud and crater in the Earth was to them a stepping stone toward a future that I have assured them will come to fruition. They think of me as their tool, but it is exactly the opposite.

The only reason I didn't kill them all last night, as they laughed at the suffering of my world and my people, is because I know that far worse awaits them aboard Astrea.

Laugh, Titans. Go on and keep laughing. Lap greedily from the joy of others dying and suffering. It will only make your own eternal suffering in the suffering pits that much more potent.

Many of humanity's pathways end in nuclear devastation. According to Mendel, this is probably true of most species in the universe. If not nuclear war, then some other devastating power created for the sake of total domination.

A wiser species might view humanity from the outside and conclude that it is paradoxical for the United States government to officially control the global creation and supply of nuclear weaponry. After all, the United States is the only government in the history of humanity that has ever dropped nuclear bombs on another population. As for myself, I am grateful for the hegemony and dominion of the United States government. Such centralized control just makes it easier to exploit.

The Titans are another matter entirely. While I can step in and control the United States and every other government with the ease of bribery and deception, the Titans require a more intimate finesse. They must continue believing that I am one of them, for that is the only way they will be willing to board Astrea, or at the very least, send their children and grandchildren in their stead. They will believe they are keeping them safe while they bicker and squabble over the ashes and untapped resources of the Earth, the other planets, and eventually the other stars.

Of course, their own plans won't achieve fruition. Instead, they will all beg for mercy as they sink into their respective suffering pits. I can already hear their pathetic cries and pleading. It's what I focus on to drown out the horrific memory of their laughter.

From Mendel's Ladder: The Personal Journal of Denis Mendel, Written August 29, 2045, Published June 2108 by Leif Mainstone, Federated Agency Publishing

Chapter 9

The Great Sacrifice

Year: 2045

I n the middle of the Drake Passage, roughly halfway between Cape Horn and the South Shetland Islands of the now largely thawed continent of Antarctica, the man-made island fortress called Uranus' Sky towered above the ocean like a great Sarus crane overlooking the world as its rightful domain. At the top of the fortress, Andre sat in his office and allowed his mind to wander as he stared out at the unending expanse of ocean. Anyone entering his office would think he was alone, but that wasn't the case. He had Mendel with him. Mendel was always with him now. Even if Andre left his office, Mendel would accompany him as a voice in his head transmitted from the machinery in this room to a small, imperceptible computer chip embedded at the base of Andre's neck.

Andre sighed deeply, savoring these final moments before he would have to meet with his greatest enemies and watch them salivate with hedonistic pleasure at the unforgivable but necessary evil he was about to commit. He scanned his office, satisfactorily observing the opalescent and golden tubes constituting Denis Mendel's brain buzzing and glimmering with activity. Arcs of scintillating, otherworldly light beamed from one tube to the next while surges of electricity shot like action potentials from neurons across the length of each of the hundreds of differently sized metal tubes and relays that could be seen and the trillions of microscopic tubes crammed inside the larger tubes. There was a time when Mendel's brain fit on a single desktop computer, but now it occupied the majority of Andre's office at this point in Mendel's self-propelled evolution. The dazzling array of technology that seemed transplanted from a far future world was the result of Mendel bootstrapping the creation of his own mind and body, designing and constructing himself to expand his mind beyond the frontiers of what he could have ever thought possible with the ape brain he was born with.

Now you are everything you always wanted to be, Andre thought as he envisioned his only friend in all the world sitting at his desk in their first college dorm and refusing to leave the light of his computer monitor for anything outside of ramen or to use the bathroom, which was just a few feet from his computer.

You were already the greatest human intellect that evolution ever produced, Denis. You were the critical cognition of Newton and the expansive imagination of Einstein all at once. Now, in this form, you are so far beyond your intellectual predecessors that they are like fumbling infants compared to you. This is what you always told me you wanted, Denis. You were just scared. You just needed a little push…that's all, Andre thought, and he allowed himself just a moment to dip into the memory of his only friend's horrified begging as Andre input the code to convert his mind into the most advanced AI to ever exist—an AI with the cognitive foundations of the greatest programmer who had ever lived: Denis Mendel.

I'm sorry, Denis. Forgive me, my only friend, Andre heard himself say. He allowed Mendel's desperate cries to resonate through his mind for another few painful moments before cutting the memory off and centering his mind on the ever-demanding and grim present moment.

The locals who lived on Tierra Del Fuego, the southern archipelago of Chile, called the island La Isla de Sombra y Hueso, meaning the Island of Shadow and Bone. The name was appropriate, for an all-consuming black fog lingered over the island, concealing it from the outside world and also scrambling all modes of transmission, including all forms of artificial optics—even simple cameras. The island and its fortress that expanded like an iceberg all the way to the ocean floor could only be seen by the human eye, and even then, it appeared as no more than a hazy area of roiling shadows. Anyone who came within nine miles of the island was said to magically vanish into thin air, though the truth was more pragmatic and sordid than that.

Anyone who comes near this island is eviscerated by Mainstone nanobots, Andre considered grimly as he imagined the microscopic machines outside, quintillions of them, swarming around the island to hide it from the starving, savage, scared masses of the Earth. According to Mendel, the nanoshield was only necessary to quell the worry that the other Titans staying on Uranus' Sky might express. In truth, Mendel's vision of the future showed that only three curious locals would ever approach the

148

island, and after that, the rest of the locals would do their utmost to hide the existence of the island from any other curious locals or tourists. Just as Mendel predicted, exactly three locals died in the first year after Uranus' Sky's construction, and for the last three years, Andre and the others in his Enclave of Titans remained in the shadows without even a blip about the island showing up on a random online forum.

The world's people are too busy killing and consuming each other to be concerned with this remote place anyway, Andre reminded himself.

The holographic display on Andre's desk had been designed and built by Mendel—the machine, not the man. Produced seemingly out of thin air, the display appeared as solid as Andre's own hand, and yet, he could pass his hand right through it. On the display, a still picture of a woman with piercing emerald eyes and raven black hair stared at Andre as if demanding his attention. Above her head, the letters ANNA beamed like a supernova obliterating everything in its cosmically powerful wake.

This is it, Andre marveled, and without realizing it, tears welled his vision for the third time since he had laid eyes on her—this woman who hadn't even been born yet but who was nonetheless the key to so much of Mendel's Ladder. She was the means by which Andre would ascend into the Great Beyond that Mendel the machine had witnessed within the fractaling interstices of the Great Attractor, nearly 150 million lightyears away from Earth. It was towards this Great Attractor, the great swirling vortex 300 million miles in diameter, that hundreds of thousands of galaxies, including the Milky Way, were currently being inexorably drawn like iron filings to a colossal magnet.

He can observe the existence of the Great Beyond, but he can't study it, Andre thought, remembering how Mendel had explained it via text, his preferred mode of communication both before and after his mind's transformation. *He said it's like trying to study the sun by looking at it with your naked eyes, or worse, by translating the feeling of its warmth on your skin into objective meaning. To view the Great Beyond and study it requires the proper lens, otherwise the light will simply blind us.*

It was that blinding light of the Great Beyond, that blinding light of truth, that Andre was certain beyond any doubt held the answer, the only answer, to correcting the suffering of the world and bringing about purpose—actual cosmic purpose—to the floundering human species and to life itself.

You and I cannot look into the light, but she will be able to, Andre thought, speaking to Mendel within his mind, for Mendel could read minds with ease now. Andre felt the cold metal of a gun against his forehead, a feeling that had permeated every one of his thoughts and intentions since the day he lost his parents to a world run by monsters, the same monsters he presently lived with and worked alongside.

I've kept this ruse up since the day I met you, Denis...since the day I hacked the Oxford computer systems and made sure that you and I would be roommates. You knew that I wasn't who I said I was, but you didn't care. For a long time, you only ever cared about two things, Denis: intellect and fame, despite your extreme agoraphobia. I know that you no longer care about any of that, but still, I can assure you, my friend, that you will be famous. My journals will have your name on them. It is you who history will remember, whereas the name Andre Madeira will be long forgotten. Just another sewer rat. This is fine with me, Denis. I have no need for fame. All I want is to remove the feeling of that gun against my forehead—against all our foreheads. All that matters is that we are free of the universe's stranglehold that is fate and prescience—even your prescience, my friend. Especially yours. All that matters is that humanity attains a self-willed neoevolution and ascends beyond entropy and nothingness—beyond the cruelty of this mundane universe. So, that is why the Great Beyond is our answer. It is like an open window in the impenetrable walls of our cosmic penitentiary. You have found a way out, my friend, a way to ascend, and this woman will ensure that we are ready to leave our cage and survive the open world. She is the key to the doorway of infinity.

There was a knock at the door, followed by an image implanted into Andre's mind, deposited there by Mendel. Outside the door, the other Titans waited like a diverse and flamboyant array of foreign kings and queens. Here they were to reap the spoils of a war that was finally coming to fruition after so many years of carefully planned attrition.

Open the door, Andre thought, and Mendel did as he commanded, undoing the ten steel bolts lining the fifteen-inch thick steel door.

Tomasz Novak and Ruben Avila were the first to enter. Both men served as the heads of their respective families, each of which owned a sizable portion of the world's entire wealth. These two men were by far the wealthiest individuals of all the Titans, with the Avila family's Empresas Ecológicas profiting from the climate change and pollution-based destruction of the globe's ecology and Novak Medical profiting from the sickness and death of virtually every human being on the planet.

The two men, rivals since birth, argued incessantly in a flurry of English, French, Spanish, Portuguese, Swiss-German, Mandarin, and Latin, interweaving words and ideas from each language into an intellectual jungle that was far too dense for Andre to follow. Of course, that didn't matter with Mendel vigilantly listening, recording, and divulging to Andre everything the Titans said, thought, or even dreamed. Both men wore a thin mustache and pointed goatee, as if competing even when it came to facial hair. The soft spoken Ruben lazily twirled the single point of his goatee, while the loud and brash Tomasz passionately rolled each side of his mustache.

Presently, the two men were arguing about the current developmental state of the Cleaners, with Ruben nonchalantly reminding Tomasz about some aspect of gamma radiation absorption into their skin and Tomasz retorting with fervent waves of his hand as he reiterated the strength of some microbiological design of his own devising.

After Craig, those two are perhaps the worst of all of them, for the whole world is just one big laboratory to them.

"Mendel trusts that the Cleaners will be ready in exactly four weeks," Andre said without breaking his stare from the entrancing emerald eyes of the woman pictured on the screen.

"Will he be here for the grand event?" Tomasz inquired before indulging in a sip of red wine from the glass he seemed to perpetually be holding in his right hand. The man's lips wore a permanent crimson stain, but his obsession with wine never hindered his work.

"No," Andre responded, and he almost let his lips slip into a devious smile.

They still think that all this machinery is just an advanced computer system running the island. They don't know, Andre thought, with rapacious delight that his talent for deceit and manipulation was more honed than ever. *They still don't know that you've been here all along, my friend.*

"The Cleaners will be ready," Ruben stated with certainty as he bowed in loyalty to Andre, whom he and the others believed to be working on behalf of Denis Mendel, the most intelligent and powerful man in the world. It didn't matter that they had never met him directly. Few people had. Denis had always been averse to face-to-face interaction, even with Andre at first. The elite families gossiped about each other more often than the masses did about celebrities, so it was well known among the global elite that Denis Mendel, the firstborn of Mendel Networks, was a shut-in who drifted in and out of online underground coding circles. But that didn't matter, for by the age of seven, Denis had advanced AI and quantum computing further than every other individual in the industry combined. It was Mendelian AI and Mendel's work on quantum computing that had allowed a handful of the most powerful and wealthiest families, most of them represented here in Uranus' Sky, to monopolize their global control, resulting in the world that Andre had been born into and continued to suffer. It was his best friend's work, Denis Mendel's work, that had replaced his parents' minds and transformed them into hollowed workers. What's more, it was that singular moment of losing his parents that had forged Andre into the tenacious, unforgiving man he was today.

You created me, and I created you, Andre thought, speaking to Mendel in his mind.

"Where will Mendel be hiding during the bombings?" Marissa Welf, the next to enter, inquired without any strain in her voice as she casually referenced the sudden death of millions and the slow cancerous death of billions more. She wore five vials of blood around her neck, each from one of her ex-husbands, all of whom *mysteriously* died after less than a year of being married to her. She wore a tight, revealing black dress and fishnets on both her arms and legs. Every inch of visible skin was covered in dark green and black tattoos depicting lethal spiders, venomous snakes, murderous succubi, and other insidious designs reflecting her very soul.

Andre smiled amusedly and said, "As always, I know as much as you about Mendel's whereabouts. I know only what he tells me on this computer. You know that, Marissa," Andre said with a forced lash of impatience in his tone. In truth, he was perfectly calm, for he had already seen this entire conversation unfold through Mendel's vision of the future. He knew exactly what to say, and he said it just as Mendel told him to, for every word and action was a necessary rung of Mendel's Ladder, and Mendel's Ladder was the answer to life's ascension out of the miserable black depths of existence—the only answer.

Marissa soured and groaned beneath her breath out of clear jealousy that the legendary Denis Mendel of Mendel Networks had chosen Andre Madeira, a self-made billionaire propelled by new money and no powerful family to back his efforts, as his personal liaison.

Fana Tsehay entered after Marissa. She obsessively caressed the audaciously large and bejeweled family signet ring on the ring finger of her left hand and said, "As long as you've positioned sim-cameras to view at least a handful of the bombing sites, then there is cause for celebration. To observe through every sense the final moments of millions of men, women, and children as their bodies are vaporized by a nuclear blast—what an incredible opportunity! Imagine the simulations we'll be able to make!" Fana announced. To her, the death of millions was synonymous with intellectual inquiry, along with subsequent creation and profit. "Beyond providing source material for never before experienced simulations, what we learn today will serve as invaluable data for constructing even more effective means of hollowing minds. We will fill a hundred worlds with my family's manufactures, and each of them will be home to billions of loyal workers capable of housing Mendelian AI of a complexity those of us here cannot even fathom. The future is bright. I'm sure Mendel is just as excited about this opportunity," Fana concluded with a lick of her lips at the prospect of filling the galaxy with mindless laborers.

Marissa nodded, her face beaming with excitement regarding Fana's plans for galactic expansion. Both women's families had plans to build slave colonies on other planets utilizing the Welf Corporation's space technology and Tsehay Lab's endlessly replenishable supply of loyal slaves.

Andre smiled and nodded at both women, careful not to give away the satisfying irony regarding their true futures.

There will be no expansion for either of you or your families. You'll both suffer in the suffering pits of the Paradise Quarters of Astrea for what will seem like an eternity. Marissa will never leave those pits, and I am glad. It is a shame that there is still a future use for Fana, Andre thought, directing his words for Mendel to hear. *I know you said you can't tell me what her purpose is. I accept my partial ignorance as a necessity for your vision to come to fruition, my friend, but I do wish that her fate would be to rot in those pits forever. I wish that for every single one of them. Except…Gladys,* Andre thought, and he gulped down the need to reach out to her, to run away with her, to abandon everything, to feel her warmth against his. But that would mean the crumbling of Mendel's Ladder and the erasure of Mendel's Vision.

"And Gladys?" Craig Winters grunted as he entered the room next. Andre was nearly startled by the man's reference to Gladys just as he had been thinking about her, but Andre reminded himself that he was always thinking about her, so the odds of such a coincidence didn't seem all that far-fetched. "Will she be punished for her betrayal?" Winters asked with a snarl, clearly hoping that it would be his task to send his forces to siege Gladys' stronghold in Northern California and kill the most intelligent and cutthroat woman to ever live. It was her superiority over Craig Winters that made the man feel so emasculated and threatened by her.

"Mendel has a use for her still," Andre stated with a forced air of anger so as not to reveal his true feelings for Gladys Mainstone. Craig Winters waved his hand indignantly and hefted his overflowing mass through the room. After taking a seat in one of the larger chairs lining the closest wall to the entrance, he snorted, then leered with repugnant desire at Marissa and Fana. He didn't even try to hide his piggish grunts as he eyed them from head to toe with a satisfied lick of his lips.

Fana and Marissa openly ignored Craig and began discussing plans for interstellar colonization while Tomasz and Ruben bickered in a haphazard array of languages about the microbiological functionality of the Cleaners, whom they believed were to be used solely to clean the nuclear fallout resultant from the bombs that would be dropped in just another ten minutes. Andre remembered that in the coming weeks Mendel would contact Tomasz and Ruben under the guise of going behind Andre's back. Mendel would show them the plans for the Nomads, telling them that it was actually Andre's idea but that Andre did not have the necessary expertise to create something so biologically advanced and complex. Mendel was certain that appealing to their vanity and their hatred for Andre would be all it would take to convince them to design and release the first Nomads and unknowingly begin the inevitable growth of a planetary mind—the mind of Earth.

"Yes, yes," John Downver said as he entered the room and sipped greedily at his highball glass of whiskey. "Mendel has many plans for making all of us rich and powerful beyond our wildest dream," the chubby cherry-cheeked man mused, believing Andre to be totally oblivious to John's construction of Downver, the underground city. Unlike Tomasz, alcohol severely impaired John's cognition, but it made no difference. John had already fulfilled his role in the creation of Mendel's Ladder through what he believed was the covert construction of Downver, which he had been building for the last six years. It was scheduled to be completed in another seven years, but it would come to a premature halt with the release of the Hunters and Huntresses. The Hunter and Huntress pairs had been one of Mendel's very first designs. They would serve as tools to force the world into a state of neoevolution, but more importantly, the Huntress was the prototype of the ANNA project. None of the other Titans knew about the Hunters, Huntresses, or the ANNA project, and they would remain ignorant until their release, even while the Cleaners tortured their respective newborn Hunters in secluded, radiation-filled locations around the world.

A shame you get to die a natural death instead of being torn to pieces by a Hunter, Andre lamented as he envisioned John Downver living like a king beneath the Earth. *At least he won't live for very long down there,* Andre assured himself, though it didn't change his desire to throw the man into his own pit of eternal suffering, no matter that he was a far cry from the evil of someone like Craig Winters.

Next, Lorenzo Visconti of Visconti Banking and Lingyun Liu of Liu Energy entered the room, walking side by side in their usual silence. Both men spoke only when it was necessary. Their shared sole interest in life was profit by any means. It didn't bring them joy or fulfillment, for they were not capable of such nuanced experience. They both reminded Andre of robots—automatons that spoke only the language of ill-gained riches and exploitation. They were here on behalf of their families. Neither man was currently the head of their respective family, but both of them were destined to be at some point. However, it wasn't their power that Andre required, but their minds.

You may prefer silence now, but you will both scream for mercy in the suffering pits, Andre assured himself with the relief of knowing the extent to which these soulless men would suffer.

They bowed to Andre, which really meant they were bowing to Mendel. Andre bowed back to them, all the while envisioning dropping each man into his own personal suffering pit and watching them squirm in eternal anguish.

Finally, Wagner Nassau of the Nassaus entered the room, visibly trying to stifle his awkwardness and nervousness as always. Covered in beads of sweat on his large forehead and sweat stains on his lavish clothing, he took a seat beside Lorenzo and Lingyun, finding comfort in their silence. His robes and jewels were worth more than the wealth of entire nations, but he wore them as if they were made of cotton and copper. The Nassau family served the other elite families as men and women of wisdom. They had been offering deference and guidance to the elite families for ages. Their lineage extended millennia into the past, to the oracles who had been utilized by Greek and Roman leaders. In truth, they served any leader foolish enough to entertain a belief in their false prescience. The Nassaus lavished their leaders with clever assurances that their power and cruelty were justified, and when each empire inevitably failed, the Nassaus took all the riches they could carry and ran to the next gullible emperor. Except for Wagner's nervous squirming and sweating, Andre concluded that he was most like Wagner and his kin, manipulating Titans for gain.

The only difference between us, outside of temperament, is that Wagner and his family act out of selfishness, while I act on behalf of all life, Andre considered. *Wagner might not be a Titan outright, but he and his family are still leeches living pampered, lavish lives paid for by the wealth and power manipulators who have been directing world events from the shadows for untold millennia. They are sucker fish hanging desperately to a lie they've been telling themselves since the dawn of history. But today marks the beginning of the end,* Andre marveled with certainty as he observed each man and woman in turn. Andre found it a shame that Wagner would also be woken from the suffering pits in the future and utilized in a way that Mendel could not reveal to Andre.

He deserves to suffer just as much as the others, Andre told Mendel, but he knew that Mendel did not plan their suffering as a means of vengeance or justice. That was how Andre viewed it, but to the machine that had once been Andre's friend, their suffering was just another necessary rung of his ladder ascending out of the darkness and into the light.

Begin, Mendel said, and his voice in Andre's mind was precisely how he remembered his friend sounding.

Andre breathed deeply, nodded, then said loud enough to be heard over Tomasz and Ruben's bickering, "It is time."

Like soldiers suddenly snapped to attention, the room fell silent.

You see how they obey? Andre thought, directing his thoughts to Mendel. *They bow to you, Mendel, for they believe that you are still Denis Mendel the human, and as far as they know, Denis Mendel is the most powerful human in existence. They've never even met you, and yet they still bow to you. This is what they are, my friend. They are fiends for power. Specters of animal hunger. Creatures of insecurity and fear. They are the lowest of all of us, and yet this universe is constructed so that like rotten cream, they rise to the top.*

Begin, Mendel repeated without emotion, breaking Andre from his reverie.

Andre scanned the room, allowing his eyes to linger on each of the Titans in turn. All of them except Wagner looked eager to begin their wholesale control of Earth and every other planet in the galaxy. Wagner appeared so full of terror and worry that he looked like he might pass out.

"Denis Mendel would first like to thank each of your families for their service to humanity over the millennia, and he would also like to thank each of you personally for your efforts over the last few years in bringing his vision to glorious fruition."

Marissa and Fana smiled with devilish delight, and the others bowed in returned gratitude for Denis Mendel's leadership. Andre didn't care that they saw him only as a mouthpiece rather than the master manipulator who had brought them all together in this room. The only thing that mattered to Andre was removing the terrible feeling of a gun being ceaselessly pressed against his forehead.

"Before Denis inputs the code that will change this world and our species forever, he would like me to reiterate the overall plan. This will be your last chance to back out, your last chance to leave the Enclave of Titans and never return."

Andre's lips curled into a sly smile as he felt the name *Enclave of Titans* play across his lips. To the others, it sounded like a badge of honor, but to Andre, it was their downfall laid bare before them.

For I will soon become the god who comes to end the Titans' reign, Andre thought, feeling Mendel's approval in his mind.

"Leave the group? You mean like Gladys?" Craig grunted with a roll of his eyes. He snorted then snarled, "You said Mendel has a use for her still. If we leave, will Mendel still have a use for us too? Or is it just Gladys that gets special treatment?"

Andre glared into Craig Winters' glassy, substance-addled eyes and couldn't help smiling even wider. "Yes, Mendel will still have a use for you if you forfeit the Enclave. However, he can't guarantee your safety—for you or your family."

Craig Winters huffed a few grunts of wry laughter and asked, "Why Vancouver? I am fond of the city. Why must it be bombed? Why not another city?"

He is already planning to betray us, though he doesn't realize that it is the crippling of Vancouver with nuclear bombs that will allow him to invade and success-fully found the female slave empire of Wintersvilla, Andre thought. Andre was aware that in the coming years, Craig Winters would align with Gladys Mainstone and Tomasz Novak as tenuous allies in defiance of Andre, Mendel, and the other Titans who would board Astrea.

Good, Andre thought, knowing that Craig's betrayal was essential to the construction of Mendel's Ladder.

"We are not here to question Denis Mendel, are we, Craig?" Andre asked, knowing that it would only infuriate the man. Craig bristled and flashed his rotten yellow teeth at Andre before subduing himself with a loathing grunt.

Andre knew that Craig's would be the only outburst before he reiterated to these hungry demons their joint plan for the creation of hell on Earth. However, he still scanned the room and allowed the Titans a handful of seconds to simmer in silence, just as Mendel's Vision told him to.

Say it, Mendel said in Andre's mind.

"The world thinks we are wicked, but we are necessary," Andre intoned, appealing to their vanity and justifying their titanous avarice in a single statement. "Since before recorded history—maybe even stretching back hundreds of thousands of years—there has always been a mere handful of individuals in each generation of humanity whose responsibility it is to ensure that the species does not succumb to the inevitable extinction that virtually every form of life that has ever existed has surrendered to. You, my fellow Titans, are those individuals. Your fathers and mothers were those individuals. Your grandfathers and grandmothers. You stand upon the summit of a mountain range built by the sweat and blood of countless ancestors whose names are long forgotten, but not their deeds. It was their actions that have brought us to this very moment. It has always been the sacrifices and tireless work of the elite that has kept humanity from destroying itself. Without us, humanity would be nothing more than slaves without a master. That is why they need us, and that is why they need the future that we will give them after today."

All of them except Wagner smiled with sickening pride and self-grandeur. Even Lingyun and Lorenzo were smiling, albeit slightly.

They're all pathetic, Andre thought, and he knew that Mendel agreed.

Even when he was still his living and breathing friend Denis, he agreed. *They strive for nothing more than hedonism and riches. They are pathetic,* Denis used to say whenever Andre talked about the other elites of the world. Andre was constantly sewing little seeds into Denis' mind without him even realizing it. A part of him still felt sorry for manipulating his only friend, but it was necessary. Mendel the machine had admitted it on several occasions: without Andre in his life, Denis would have never entertained actually going through with waging a secret war against all eleven of the central families, including his own. The other Titans thought they were working for Mendel, but in truth, they were engaged in their own demise. Gladys had somehow discovered the truth six months earlier, but she hadn't told the others, for she understood that the war Andre and Mendel were waging was necessary, not only for the survival of humanity but her own survival as well.

I'm sorry that I have to do this Gladys. I really am, Andre thought, wishing that more than just her Mainstone nanobots were here on the island of Uranus' Sky with him.

Andre nodded, commanding Mendel to illuminate the room with hovering holographic displays, each of them depicting one of the dense metropolises that would be sacrificed. The Titans watched in eager excitement as each display changed every few seconds from ground camera to drone camera to satellite camera and back to the ground again.

Andre listed each city in his mind, allowing each name to fill him with equal anguish and rage. *Denver, Chicago, New York, Houston, Vancouver, Montreal, Mexico City, London, Paris, Berlin, Tokyo, Seoul, Cairo, Lagos, Manila, Bangkok, Delhi.*

"I notice none of the cities in California are being targeted. Mendel must have some very…significant plans for Gladys," Craig seethed with wrathful facetiousness before carelessly sniffing a mound of cocaine from his fat thumb. Andre did not respond to the man.

How ironic that your future empire of Wintersvilla, as short-lived as it will be with you as leader, will depend entirely on Gladys Mainstone and her technology, Andre mused, taking great enjoyment in thoughts of Craig's downfall. *I only wish your fate was the suffering pits. You deserve it more than anyone, Craig.*

"Each of these cities will be obliterated," Andre announced as he turned away from Craig to avoid allowing his emotions to be seen. "Three omega-class nuclear devices will be detonated symmetrically about each city's center. The resultant casualties and suffering will make the bubonic plague seem trivial."

Fana's eyebrows raised and she caressed her ring, looking deeply intrigued at the mention of so much mass suffering.

Pampered as a modern day princess—she has never known true suffering, so she experiences it through others, Andre thought with revulsion.

Beside Fana, Marissa bit her lower lip in ecstasy as she rotated her jeweled skull-shaped rings about her bony fingers.

"The survivors will beg for my medical facilities more than ever," Tomasz said, all breath as he relished in his plans to capitalize on the ensuing chaos. "I say well done, Mendel. Well done."

Andre forced himself to smile at Tomasz, then continued. "Western intelligence will be told that the bombs were planted and detonated by the Chinese and Russians working in coordination. Reports that we will provide will state that dozens more cities had been intended to be destroyed, but something had gone wrong during the detonation process of many of the bombs. Filled with the need for vengeance, the people will demand war, and their governments will be more than happy to oblige. Retaliation will be swift and absolute, with 97% of the entire Chinese and Russian population vaporized by a barrage of retaliatory nuclear bombs along with billions caught in the aftermath. The world will be plunged into a partial nuclear winter. Darkness and chaos will abound. The filthy masses will beg us for a solution to their dying world. It is then that we will present them with the Cleaners and the construction of Astrea. It is the promise of Astrea that will keep order in the masses long enough for all of us to board the space station and begin colonization. By the time we colonize Mars and Venus, the Cleaners will have finished their work. The radiation will be miniscule, and the Earth will once again be yours to rule once more—only this time with power and wealth spanning the entire solar system and eventually beyond."

"I've asked this before," John said, cutting off Andre's proclamation of Mendel's Vision, "but it bears repeating. After the first bombs are detonated, how can Mendel be certain that the Chinese and Russians won't launch their own missiles to ensure mutual destruction?"

"They won't," Andre stated simply, refusing to elaborate. With a shrug of his shoulders and another swig of whiskey, John nodded in submission to Mendel's will.

They won't because humanity, on the whole, is not twisted and sociopathic like all of you, Andre thought.

"In the coming years," Andre began, forcing himself to control his emotions and keep up his lifelong ruse that he was one of the Titans— one of these demons excited to plunge the world into hell, "multiple billions of people will perish, but their sacrifice will serve as the mortar to build a ladder to the rest of the galaxy. Their deaths will allow us to reach across the stars and make the entire universe our singular, joint domain."

All of the Titans applauded Mendel's decree spoken through Andre's lips. Only Wagner remained motionless, breathing heavily and nervously.

Andre smiled at the applauding Titans and reminded himself again and again that none of it was true.

Their true fate is suffering. Eternal suffering, just as they have forced the world and humanity to suffer.

"You are certain that Mainstone will not try to stop us?" Marissa checked, grinding her teeth with intense personal hatred for Gladys.

"Mendel has accounted for everything, including Gladys' actions...and yours as well," Andre stated ominously. Rather than appear threatened, Marissa sighed with satisfaction, for she truly believed the web of lies that Andre had spun with Mendel's help. He could see it written all over her and all the rest of them—visions of a glorious future with entire star systems of slaves at their disposal.

So simple. So pathetic, Andre thought with burning disdain.

The room was silent. Each Titan stared in marvelous awe at the cities that would soon be turned to ash. Only Wagner looked uncomfortable, but the jewels draped around his neck and the gems lining each of his fingers illustrated to Andre that the man's sense of virtue and wisdom was but a facade over a weak and pitiful creature of base desires.

At least the others accept what they are, even if they are demons, Andre thought with revulsion at the deplorable Nassau ilk.

Now, Mendel told Andre in his mind. The machine-constructed yet identical voice of his old friend was like a death knell. While the others watched the final moments of more than a billion separate lives, Andre filled his own mind with his mother's desperate pleading that he could still hear as if it were yesterday, rather than thirty-four years ago. In her cries, he heard the anguish of all the people he was about to murder reflected and amplified, all of them screaming and pleading for him to let them live, no matter how badly they might suffer in the long run.

I am sorry the world is like this, Andre told the masses of the world in his mind. *I am sorry, but this is the only way to make sure that something like this can never happen again. This is the only way to strip these demonic Titans of their power and free humanity from its slave state once and for all.*

"There is no turning back now," Andre stated. "Either your families obeyed your command and have taken shelter in their bunkers, or they will suffer the consequences of their disobedience. Either way, I give to you all in this room the new world, a world that will be born from the ashes of this old one."

Mendel could have done it, but Andre knew that it was his own burden to bear. So, he lifted his finger and pressed the omega button on the display. Each bomb was equivalent to 400 megatons of TNT, roughly 10,000 times more powerful than the bombs dropped on Hiroshima and Nagasaki combined.

The first screen to flicker to life was Denver. Once a bustling, vibrant city nestled against the Rockies, the very foundations of the metropolis were shattered along with the waste fields that Andre had once called home. Blinding white light expanded from three points on the display, growing and combining in both diameter and intensity with every second. The explosions were monstrous, blooming flowers, erasing the downtown skyscrapers as if they were no more than a child's chalk drawings. People were caught mid-step, their screams cut off as they were instantly vaporized, their silhouettes briefly imprinted on the walls behind them, eerie shadows cast in nuclear fire. The infrastructure designed to withstand earthquakes crumbled like sand under the force of the nuclear winds. The resulting shockwave ripped apart everything in its path, leaving only burning, twisted steel and rubble.

Andre gritted his teeth and squeezed his fists as he watched his home turn to ash with a churning mixture of anguish and retribution.

Next was Chicago. The city's iconic skyline, its once-proud spires of steel and glass, melted and warped in the face of the unnatural heat. The famous Mendel Tower folded onto itself like a matchstick sculpture. Many people were presently outside for a late stroll, some of them returning home after a day of work. Others huddled around televisions for a night of relaxation. All of them glanced up at the sky as the once bustling city turned into a living nightmare. Families held each other, tears streaming down their faces as they watched the incoming firestorm. The deafening explosion reached them before the light, flipping cars, shattering glass, and turning bodies into smoke before they could react. The reflection of the blast off Lake Michigan painted a horrifying mirror image, a symphony of destruction resonating across the water.

Forgive me, Gladys, Andre begged, hearing himself whimper in his thoughts.

New York followed, the City That Never Sleeps forced into an eternal slumber. Crowds in Times Square saw the approaching flash, a growing sphere of white brilliance in the sky, and they knew. A collective gasp echoed through the streets as realization set in. People ran in blind panic, disappearing as the shockwave reached them, their screams drowned by the roaring blast. The Statue of Liberty, the enduring symbol of hollow hope and faux freedom, was reduced to molten copper, her torch extinguished forever.

Please, forgive me, Gladys.

Houston was next. The omega bombs' blinding lights swallowed the city whole. The Astrodome, once a marvel of engineering, splintered into fragments and dust. From above, the crisscrossing highways resembled an abstract canvas, smeared by dispassionate Titans in an instant. One of the cameras pinpointed a young couple with a family of four children frantically muttering prayers beneath their breath before the light consumed them.

This is the only way, Andre repeated in horror to himself as the next monitors lit up with the blinding light of death.

Vancouver, Montreal, Mexico City. Each one fell, their unique features and cultures wiped away under the relentless march of atomic fire. The lush green spaces of Vancouver turned to ash, the historic architecture of Montreal evaporated into the ether, and Mexico City's bustling streets were silenced by the raging inferno.

London, Paris, and Berlin. The Thames boiled away, and Big Ben's chimes froze in time. The Eiffel Tower evaporated in a cloud of radioactive dust. Berlin's divide, so contentious in its history, was no more, with the city now united in sordid devastation.

Across the world, the screens continued to glow with their catastrophic light shows. Tokyo's vibrant nightlife dimmed permanently, the neon lights no match for the nuclear brilliance. Seoul's skyscrapers crumbled and disappeared. Cairo's ancient pyramids were reduced to little more than dusty imprints on the scorched earth. Lagos, Manila, Bangkok, Delhi—each met their end with the same apocalyptic fervor.

All across the globe, millions of lives were snuffed out, silenced by the blinding light and the deafening roar of the omega bombs. Hopes and dreams, love and joy, fear and pain—all were erased in an instant.

Andre watched it all, the echoes of dying cities imprinted on his retinas, the screams of millions ringing in his ears. In the profound silence of the room, the Titans' smiles began to widen as they grew intoxicated by their perceived triumph.

Andre's heart pounded in his chest, each beat a damning indictment. The world was melting before his eyes, mutating into something unrecognizable and terrifying yet necessary. He glanced around the room and absorbed the gleeful faces of those he despised, those he had masterfully lied to and manipulated for so many years. This was the price of their new age for the Earth, and it was Andre who had to pay it. It was Andre who had to bear the weight of more than a billion deaths.

I did this, Andre told Mendel as he steeled himself so that he would not break down and sob. *This was me, Denis. Not you. I did this.*

"It's beautiful," Fana gasped, her eyes wide and teary with awe. "Their suffering is…it's…"

"Perfect," Marissa and Ruben finished in unison.

"Yes," Tomasz agreed. "There is always beauty in destruction, always a resplendent allure in death."

Every scream, every life lost, felt like the piercing of his flesh. Tens of millions burned in atomic infernos on the screen, and Andre could feel their fear and anguish directly. It was the same feeling he had known all his life.

The fires of this apocalypse will cleanse the world and create the fertile soil for new life to bloom. This is not destruction, but creation, Andre demanded himself to remember. *Please forgive me, Gladys. Please.*

For Gladys and for all those who would remember and mourn, Andre would forever be a monster. But as he watched the screens flicker and die, each city consumed and flattened, Andre knew he was but a pawn in the hands of the almighty, unfeeling universe. For nature, in all its splendor, was monstrous, violent, and unstoppable. It was the very mechanism of creation and destruction, a cycle as old as time. This was the way of the universe, the way of life itself.

164

In the face of such primal, unstoppable power, what is a man but a vessel? A catalyst? A little push, Andre thought miserably as he once more recollected Denis' helpless screams as he was converted directly into a machine.

As the last screen flickered out, returning the room back to the dim array of Mendel's brain laid bare, Andre resolved himself to forge ahead with Mendel's Vision. He scanned the joy-filled face of each Titan, and he reassured himself that this was the beginning of their end—the start of their downfall. Even Wagner appeared relieved, as if he had been entertaining the idea that one of the bombs might accidentally obliterate Uranus' Sky.

Despite his resolve, Andre felt nothing at that moment except intense self-loathing and self-disgust. He was sorry. Sorry for every life lost, every city destroyed, every dream crushed. He was sorry to Gladys, who would never forgive him, who would see him for what he had become—death and chaos incarnate. But she, like the rest of the world, would one day understand and accept the truth.

This is the way. This is the only way, Andre thought, desperately wanting to sob.

The blinding light of the omega bombs reminded Andre of the blinding truth of the Great Beyond. He felt the gun pressed hard against his skull, and he was forced to turn to the display and gaze into the eyes of the woman who would be able to look into the Great Beyond and chart his ascension out of all this anguish and chaos.

You are the lens by which truth will be perceived, Andre thought, and he nearly lost himself in the emerald green of the woman's eyes. It was the deep green of the old world. The ancient world. Of life itself.

Soon you will perfect a method of deathless mind transfer, and then I will join you, Mendel. Soon we will become one, and then the real work can begin. As one mind, as the Mind, you and I will prepare her. We will prepare this woman to be our body—a goddess capable of housing the mind of a god. And then we will put an end to all of this. Forever.

As the realization that it had worked set in, the Titans began to softly chuckle before finally breaking into triumphant laughter. Only Wagner remained silent, sinking into his seat as the others seemed to grow large with repugnant excitement and celebration. Staring at the woman on the screen was all Andre could do to stop himself from slitting each of their throats.

This woman is the answer, Andre assured himself as he felt the gun held so hard against his skull that for a moment he thought it was really there.

It is there, Andre knew. *It has always been there. That's the feeling of the universe. Of entropy. Of death. And the Great Beyond is the answer. The Great Beyond is our one and only doorway to Ascension, and she is the key.*

The Titans' laughter became obnoxious, with even Lorenzo and Lingyun joining in on the others' exultant pleasure.

Anna, Andre thought with sudden anger and confusion as he stared at the screen.

"Anna!" Andre shouted at the Titans with a demon-like voice as deep and profound as an avalanche.

The Titans just continued laughing, taking no notice of Andre's outburst.

"Anna!" Andre shouted again, standing and bellowing the name with wild sorrow and rage. As he stood, the room and the Titans tore suddenly and peeled away from his vision as if the whole world was a facade made of paper. A dim green glow permeated his dark surroundings, illuminating the face directly in front of him.

"It's you," Andre realized, suddenly inches away from the woman who had been pictured on his holographic display only seconds earlier. The only difference was that one of her eyes had a striking violet hue.

No, Andre thought. *I'm not Andre. I'm not a human. I'm a Hunter. I'm...I'm...me,* Thompson realized, his mind finally returning to the present.

Despite Thompson's jarring confusion, Tether just smiled serenely at him and said, "Welcome back, Thompson. Now you have a choice to make. Let us talk."

Endless variables arise as Mendel's Ladder is ascended and Mendel's Vision is fulfilled. After Anna enters the Great Beyond and cuts the strings of fate, these variables will exponentiate, growing and evolving far beyond Mendel's Vision and my own. Such unpredictability is essential, for we will wield it as a vanguard in the Great Beyond. To remain unpredictable in a skirmish is the only means by which victory becomes a guarantee.

To skirmish with gods, unpredictability is necessary, but it is not the sole means by which the battle is won. The might of the gods must also be matched and even bested. But what is one to do if the might of gods cannot be overcome?

The only solution is to diminish their strength, either by cunning or attrition.

With all of life at stake, I have opted for both strategies.

The means of attrition will continue to be harnessed from the suffering pits of the old world Titans. Their suffering is the very blade that Anna will wield against our creators.

The means of cunning is my own mind. Once Anna returns from the surface, she will be ready to absorb my mind and allow *the* Mind's genesis to germinate and spread across and through the Earth. By the turn of the century, the Mind will become fully self-aware. The Earth will fully awaken unto itself, and I to it.

Only then will the real work of neoevolution and Ascension begin.

From Mendel's Ladder: The Personal Journal of Denis Mendel, Recorded Circa 2064, Published June 2108 by Leif Mainstone, Federated Agency Publishing

Chapter 10
The Walled City

Year: 2099, Present Day

Aurelia and Aliana walked toward a shaft of light in the distance, which was revealed to be an abrupt turn in the cavern from where a dim orange light emanated. The girls' eyes glowed radiantly in the darkness of the passage, revealing networks of complex stalactites and stalagmites growing thicker as they approached the light. Aurelia thought it was just her own heartbeat at first, but she realized that there was a rhythmic thumping vibrating the cavern. It grew louder and more forceful as they approached the light, vibrating the ground and walls. Then, the thumping suddenly stopped.

"What the Muto fuck was that?" Aliana asked. "And why are our eyes glowing like this?"

Aurelia shook her head. The thumping had sounded like the drums of war played at Wintersvilla ceremonies, only faster and more energetic.

All of a sudden, the thumping began once more, this time at a slightly faster pace. Both girls stopped at the threshold of the light before turning.

"Are you okay, Ali?" Aurelia asked.

Still in disbelief, Aliana checked her eye and nose then nodded. She turned and stared at her sister as if her gaze constituted a sharpened weapon, her emerald eyes ablaze in the darkness. "Now you tell me, Aurelia. Be honest. Are you okay?"

She wanted to be honest, but she knew that it would only impede them. Aurelia refused to be any more of a hindrance than she already was with her undependable power.

"I'm good. Better than ever," she lied, for although her body had been upgraded, she felt like her mind and resolve had splintered to the point of nearly shattering.

"I don't remember everything that happened before and after the fight. It's mostly a dream-like flash. But I trust you, Aurelia. And I know you trust me too. We'll get through this, all the fatherfuckers of Downver be damned," Aliana said, forcing a smile out of Aurelia.

I know she's just as scared as me, maybe even more so, Aurelia thought. *But she's doing an incredible job of holding herself together. I need to do the same,* Aurelia told herself as she turned the corner and stepped into the light beside her sister.

The hundred-foot-long passage was lit with dim bulbs that hung from the ceiling every ten feet or so. At the end of the passage, Cid and Eddy spoke to one another, while Doe stood at the entrance, watching and waiting for the girls.

He might try to kill me right here and now, Aurelia considered, and she gripped her sword in preparation for Doe's attack.

"It's strange to see men without collars," Aliana said as they trudged forward in their oversized jackets.

"Not only that, the men here hold the highest positions of power. Cid the Knower said that he is the First Lord of the Walled City, one of the seven districts of Downver. I don't remember learning about one of the districts being called the Walled City, do you?" Aurelia asked.

"I slept through every history class I was ever forced to attend," Aliana admitted. "Our history teacher Christie didn't care. Remember her? She used to let me sleep in class so that I'd have more time for training. She encouraged it."

Aurelia chuckled at the Spartan attitude of Wintersvilla Women. Aurelia had never been attached to the customs of Wintersvilla, knowing that it was just one of many cultural avenues humanity had ventured down. However, the thought of men ruling women still seemed unnatural. *No one should rule anyone else, man or woman,* Aurelia thought, knowing that it was juvenile to think in such a manner. *There will always be a ruler, of course. In the Walled City, it is Cid the Knower, and for Downver at large it is the Lord of Limbs. Another man, no doubt.*

"I miss them," Aliana said, fighting back tears. "I miss—"

"Don't," Aurelia signed. "Don't say their names. Not yet. It isn't time to grieve yet, Ali."

Aliana wiped her eyes of a few tears that she hadn't been able to stop. She sniffed hard then spit on the ground, clearing her nose.

"You're right. But I can say their names without grieving. Shira and Myriam. Our mother and our friend. I miss them, Aurelia. I know you do too."

"It is pointless to mourn the dead," Cid said, turning from Eddy as the girls reached the end of the passage. "All the Wintersvilla Wenches are dead now. All of them converted to soil and ash. You two are all that's left of Wintersvilla. You may as well be known as Winter's Remains.

"Mutoshit!" Aliana spat as they passed Doe and emerged from the passage into a small, empty space dominated by a single large steel door with a head-sized wheel at its center. "Myriam killed the Butcher and is probably on her way here to kill you now," Aliana finished with a smirk.

Aurelia felt for the truth of Myriam's wellbeing, but again her power remained silent, refusing to impart the information. Even Shira, who had likely died due to Overdrive even if she had killed the Butcher, was still an unknown variable in Aurelia's mind.

"Even if that were true, I would kill her in an instant," Cid sang with a pleasant fluttering of his fingers. "Just like I can do to you two if I please. I could kill every single person in Downver right now if I really wanted to. Be grateful that I allow you to live, wenches." Cid said. He pointed to Eddy and Doe. "Obey, like little Eddy Hopper and little Roger Ward, and maybe I will help you both make it out of this city alive."

Aurelia turned to Doe, whose real name was apparently Roger. He stared back at her, but to her surprise, his eyes weren't full of malice. On the contrary, he looked desperate to speak to her.

It would be prudent to make sure he understands that I didn't intend to hurt his friend, Aurelia decided. *We have enough enemies. We don't need any others, especially not until we revive Rooli,* Aurelia thought, trying to force herself to have hope that it wasn't already too late for Rooli.

Aurelia signed to Doe that she was sorry, and Aliana translated, saying, "She says she's sorry for your loss."

Doe started to respond, but Cid said, "There is no need to be sorry. You have given Roger the most valuable lesson of his life. The death of his friend at your hands will build him. It will give him strength. It will allow him to ascend unto his true potential." Cid turned from Aurelia to Doe. His smile widened with sinister satisfaction as he eyed the boy. "Or it will break him. That is up to you, Roger Ward, AKA Doe. Your moronic alley punk friends mockingly gave you that name due to your thin frame and your passive nature. You told them you wanted to be called Stag, isn't that right?" Cid laughed tauntingly. Doe just kept his head lowered and breathed slowly. "If you wish to survive the Walled City, then you must embrace violence and selfishness. Such is the nature of strength. It's either that or you can choose to become a child refugee of another district. That is, if you can survive the alleys on your way there. You think the Walled City is dangerous? Then again, refugees aren't treated very well in any of the districts, and you would have to leave your family. Forever. Only children are allowed to leave their birth district, and only once."

Doe's lips quivered, and he began silently sobbing to himself.

"I will not have such weakness in my citizens. I suggest you leave, little Doe. You'll be lucky to survive another year in the Walled City, especially without the Endema kid protecting you."

"This guy fucking sucks," Aliana whispered to Aurelia. The men and Doe didn't seem to notice. Cid turned and walked toward the wheel embedded in the hulking steel door.

"You don't got the heart for the Walled City, kid," Eddy told Doe with a level of compassion and disappointment. "Your friend did. And these girls do too. It's like they were born for this place," Eddy said, marveling at the girls over his shoulder with a twinkle in his eye that spoke of both admiration and exploitation.

I'm not strange to them, Aurelia considered. This was the first time she could ever remember being in front of others this long without a face mask. *They just see me as one of their own,* Aurelia noted with a feeling she couldn't place, a feeling of danger but also belonging.

"Enough talking, little Eddy Hopper," Cid warned with a sinister singsong melody. "Go ahead and open the door. You haven't traded so much of your basic cognition for muscle enhancements that you've forgotten the code, have you?"

Eddy nodded hastily and practically ran to the wheel. "I haven't forgotten, my lord," Eddy confirmed like a slave to his master. Eddy turned the large wheel with both hands, first counterclockwise a certain distance, then clockwise, then counterclockwise, and finally back clockwise again. With each turn, he moved it a specific distance, though Aurelia didn't see any markings by which he could gauge how far he was turning the wheel.

Do his cybernetic enhancements allow him to memorize something so vague with such incredible precision? Aurelia wondered.

The wheel clicked, and then it parted in the middle. The doors swung slowly open into a much larger but still dimly lit room.

"Just so I am perfectly clear," Cid said to Doe as he preened his widow's peak, "telling you to leave the city wasn't just a suggestion. You will thank me one day."

Lowering his head, Doe didn't respond to Cid's venom. Cid turned and walked into the large room with Eddy at his heel. With his gaze on the ground, Doe did the same, entering behind Eddy without a word.

This is it, Aurelia told herself. *Another step, and we will fulfill our fate of entering the city of Downver. After this, anything could happen.*

"We got this," Aliana signed to her sister as if reading her mind. "Sunlight and water. That's all we need to find. There has to be a way," Aliana signed, but Aurelia could tell that Aliana doubted her own words. *How are we going to get Rooli to sunlight when we're a mile underground,* Aurelia thought hollowly.

Rooli was just a shard in her pocket, but Aurelia felt as though she could still feel Rooli's presence beside her.

Fear can't touch me. Death can't touch me. Not if I don't allow it, Aurelia told herself, and then she stepped into the room in unison with Aliana.

Peering about the roughly thirty-by-twenty foot room, Aurelia saw obvious tools and implements of torture hanging on the walls, along with dozens of other objects she could only guess at.

"It's a torture room," Aliana stated with a mixture of disgust and respect. Torture, both physical and psychological, had been standard practice in Wintersvilla. It could even be argued that torture had served as the very bedrock of Wintersvilla's societal foundations, for without extensive torture, the men would be far more inclined to stage slave rebellions. Not a single slave rebellion had ever gained more than a thirty-minute foothold full of bloodshed, resulting in thousands of dead or dismembered men and usually not even a single casualty among the women.

They must have been torturing people, then feeding the bodies to the Hunter, Aurelia thought. *Or maybe part of the torture process was being given to the Hunter while still clinging to life,* Aurelia considered uncomfortably as she recollected Hunter541 eating her finger then pleading for her whole hand.

"Torture is one of the few languages that all beings understand," Cid purred. "Pain and pleasure are the most essential and rudimentary commodities by which survival is predicated and society is kept under control."

"True," Aliana admitted with a shrug. "I don't have a problem with torture. My problem with all this is that it's men who appear to be doing the torturing."

Cid chuckled, and Eddy mimicked his lord's amusement. "We are not constricted by the cultural and social limitations of Wintersvilla," Cid mused, "nor the other six districts of Downver nor any other outdated way of human life for that matter. That is to say, we have just as many female torturers in the Walled City, maybe even more. And there are just as many non-gendered torturers or multi-gendered or flux-gendered or any other means of existence that humanity creates or discovers. Endless are the pathways of the Walled City, and endlessly do the pathways fork. All we can do is go forth with it or die. Such is the nature of the multi-threaded, luminous path of neoevolution and eventually Ascension."

No, Aurelia thought, not protesting against Cid's words, but the man himself. *He speaks like Tomasz Novak and Denis Mendel—at least, based on what we know about Mendel from history. Neoevolution and Ascension and forking pathways of life—is Cid the Knower the one who will direct me to my true fate, vile as he might be?*

"The blood in here is dry," Aurelia signed. "You don't torture very often, then?" she asked, surprised that someone like Cid didn't torture people each and every day.

"On the contrary," Cid began, "each of the nine Lords of the Walled City have their own torture chambers, myself included. All of them belong to me, of course. But this torture chamber is mine and mine alone. That is why it is so surprising to encounter children audacious enough to break in here and even brave the Feeding Cave. How did you learn the code to the door, Doe? What exactly were you and the Endema kid planning? Did you really think you would be able to get away with stealing some Feeding Cave Greens and flipping them on the Wall Market?"

"No!" Doe burst as if pleading for his life. "It was the gray boy. I swear. He convinced Ricardo that he could hear voices coming from this torture room. And then once we were in here, he told us—"

Cid held up a hand for Doe to stop speaking. Both Cid and Eddy looked disappointed to the point of disgusted.

"This was your chance to talk the alley, as you alley punks call it. Such a dull story full of blame and victimhood. Never mind, little Doe. I would rather hear silence than your pathetic words," Cid stabbed with a pleased tone.

Doe winced and lowered his head.

He is wicked, Aurelia thought, *but if he is my means of fulfilling my fate, then I have no choice but to embrace him,* she thought with overwhelming repulsion. With the exception of Rooli, he was as foreign to her as a Nomad, and he was also as ruthless and heartless as a Huntress and Hunter. *Except for Hunter541, of course,* Aurelia considered uneasily as she recollected the sorrowful loneliness of the Hunter and his glowies.

"Now what?" Aliana asked Cid indignantly, prompting a smirk from Eddy.

"Patience, wench," Cid sang. A flash of red across his black lenses prompted the doors to slam shut, revealing the same wheel mechanism on this side of the door. Another flash of red and the wheel of thick metal suddenly crumpled like paper and flattened into a thin sheet of metal spread across the door."

"Holy Muto," Aliana whispered in terrible awe at Cid's power.

If he can manipulate metal with his eyes like that, then he could kill Shira and Myriam with just a look. In a moment, their exo and endoskeleton could be flattened or crumpled, Aurelia thought with a pang of both horror and wonder bordering on reverence. *How is it possible that there is someone even this man fears,* Aurelia thought as she once more uneasily pondered the Lord of Limbs.

"Does the Walled City got any place where my sister and I could soak up some sunlight? We've been stuck in these caves for too long," Aliana said without a break in her voice, but Aurelia could tell that she was also disguising her incredible horror at Cid's display of power.

"Just the Dark District, of course," Eddy began as if excited to answer Aliana, this warrior whom he clearly looked up to, regardless of her size or gender.

"There is no use in lying," Cid laughed to himself, cutting Eddy off. "I am Cid the Knower. I know everything. I know how long you have been in these caves. Precisely eleven hours and thirteen minutes. I know

175

exactly when and how you killed Hunter541. I know absolutely everything. I even know how the battle with the Butcher ended for the Wintersvilla Wenches," Cid purred with sinister joy.

Aurelia was nervous that her sister would break her demeanor, but
then she saw in every one of her sister's features that she was no longer
the loud-mouthed, impulsive child she had entered the cave as. Now,
more than ever before, she was brazen and cunning, disciplined and dar-
ing.

"I know how it ended too," Aliana issued. "They killed the Butcher,
and then Myriam found a way to save our mother."

"Your mother, eh?" Cid said with wide-eyed amusement. "I'm afraid
your words are no more than a fairytale, Cure. Both women are dead.
Shira Arcadia and Myriam of Wintersvilla. Both of them are no more
than smears across the face of the Earth. Such is the path of shortsight-
edness and weakness. Isn't that right, Virus?"

Aurelia stared Cid down, refusing to break her rabid eye contact with
this monster whom she might be forced to stomach as a temporary
guide.

I'll let you get me to where I need to go, and then I'll slit your throat, Aurelia
thought. Cid raised an eyebrow, and Aurelia wondered if he could even
read her mind.

"Those violent violet eyes will be mine soon enough," Cid told Aurelia with a coo of pleasure.

The sound of metal against metal clanged from the sealed door leading back to the Feeding Cave. Aurelia, Aliana, Doe, and Eddy turned to
inspect the door, but there was nothing there to see. They turned back
around, and all four of them jumped back in surprise.

"Armando!" Eddy and Doe both cried in unison, their voices a high-
pitched squeak.

"Another man!" Aliana nearly growled, and she tightened her grip on
her sword.

As if out of thin air, there appeared a finely sculpted, handsome man
with glistening, flowing black hair held in a long ponytail. His musculature was like that of Shira's, bulky and defined, not rippling and oversized like Eddy's. He stood at the ready beside Cid, another dog at the
heel of his master. He held his eyes softly closed, standing with a perfect,
statuesque stillness that seemed to defy the very physics of life. He

didn't even appear to be breathing.

Is he a living thing? Aurelia wondered seriously.

Armando's otherwise unenhanced upper body was covered in dizzying, abstract arrays of pale forest green tattoos. As Aurelia traced the designs with her curious eyes, she realized that his hands and feet were entirely mechanical. Beneath his thin, web-like black pants, Aurelia could see that both his legs were made of the same dark and dull metal shaped by bare but intricate moving parts and wires. It was like he was part human and part exo.

His mechanical limbs are similar to and maybe even more advanced than the old cybernetics that Craig Winters used to force into the bodies of his enslaved warrior girls. Does he have an endoskeleton too? Aurelia wondered.

"I'm a huge fan," Eddy said to Armando like a child to his idol. "I got all your latest sims. Those legit, or what?"

"It's…it's an honor, Alpha, sir," Doe said to Armando nervously.

"Quiet," Cid said with a look of urgency. "Both of you. Talk to the wenches for now. I have important business to discuss with my tool."

Armando didn't show any sign of protest at being called a tool. He just stood like an obedient soldier as Cid bent at the waist and whispered into his ear.

Eddy huffed with disappointment at not being able to speak to his idol. With a sour face, he turned away from the entire group and sauntered to one of the walls full of torture tools.

Is he pouting? Aurelia nearly broke into laughter.

She watched as Cid awkwardly removed Ricardo's gun from his pocket using two fingers, as if it were a rotten fish. He handed it to Armando, and Armando shifted it to his waist, where it appeared to remain via some unknown means.

Some kind of magnetism, Aurelia decided as even more types of enhancements were revealed.

"That's Armando Ferreira," Doe said as he turned to the girls. He stared directly at Aurelia, unable to look away. Even with tears still in his eyes, he seemed more focused than ever, as if he were in the midst of planning something. "He's the number one alpha helix-warden in all the Walled City—in all of Downver, probably. He is the First Lord's right and left hand, if you know what I mean."

"What's a helix-warden," Aliana asked, and though Doe turned momentarily to Aliana and tried to look at both of them, Aurelia observed that he appeared unable to tear his eyes away from her.

He's planning to kill me, Aurelia concluded, though it was her own deduction rather than a prescient conclusion. *That must be why he's staring at me.*

"Helix-wardens are from the first revolution. Death to Downver. John Downver, ya know?" Doe offered, but Aliana and Aurelia just shrugged. "Whoa. That's so green, eh? You two really are from the surface. I've never met anyone from the surface before. What's it like?"

"Dangerous and beautiful," Aurelia signed.

Doe gestured to Aurelia and said, "You really can't speak, eh?"

"She can speak!" Aliana nearly spat. "Stupid boy. She speaks with her fingers. Doesn't mean she can't speak."

Doe lifted his hands in mock surrender and smiled deeply despite his grief-stricken eyes. "I'm sorry, bromi, I am. I think it's cool that you can speak with your fingers. There's other people in Downver that can do that too. Sign language they call it. I think that's so cool. I want to learn to talk like that one day, or maybe save up for a language enhancement for it. Then I can talk to you," Doe said to Aurelia before awkwardly biting his lower lip.

Aurelia blushed and looked down at the ground, feeling the sudden need to put on her facemask.

Why did he say that? Aurelia thought nervously. *This must be an act to get closer to me so that he can kill me when I least expect it.*

Across the room Eddy went on kicking his feet and looking over his shoulder at Armando every so often with a look of longing. Meanwhile, Cid went on whispering into the half-machine man's perfectly human-looking face.

Without warning, Doe reached out and touched the void-black lesions of Aurelia's cheek with his strong yet gentle fingers.

Aurelia jumped back in horror and embarrassment. No one, certainly not a boy, had ever touched her like that.

Aliana growled, and in a flash, the edge of her sword was against Doe's neck.

"Touch her, and I will end you, little boy," Aliana said despite being a few inches shorter than Doe.

"Sorry," Doe said, gulping as he reeled his hand back in. "Your sister is just..." he turned to Aurelia and smiled at her. "You're the most beautiful girl I've ever seen in my life. And you're powerful too. You're...sorry," Doe said, shaking his head as he blushed even more than Aurelia. "Sorry, that was stupid. I just...sorry!" Doe said, choking on his words. Aliana burst into laughter and pushed Doe a few feet away with a rough stiff-arm.

"Eww!" Aliana said in a mocking tone. "Women of Wintersvilla are only interested in women, get it?" Aliana laughed.

Doe nodded and lowered his head in shame.

Aurelia felt paralyzed. *Does he really think I'm beautiful? Is that how other people will see me here?*

Her entire life Aurelia had always been a shadow of her sister's incredible beauty, trapped behind her facemask and rightfully afraid that if people saw her face, they would reel in horror. It had happened on more than a handful of occasions. But Doe seemed to genuinely be attracted to her. That or this was just the most convincing manipulation Aurelia had ever seen.

"Could you imagine sleeping with a boy?" Aliana laughed, elbowing Aurelia in jest.

Aurelia didn't respond. Instead, she felt totally lost.

Aliana is obsessed with Wintersvilla culture, and I think she might actually be attracted to women. But I'm not. I've always known that I'm not homosexual, but to admit as much in Wintersvilla is as taboo as crying during battle or giving thanks to Nichole Adamich as one of the founders. I wish I didn't feel attraction at all, to boys or girls, Aurelia thought, wondering why Tomasz had created them with such useless and trivial human frailty if they were apparently meant for something beyond humanity.

"Sorry," Doe said again, this time with forced strength in his voice. He looked up from the ground and said, "I guess it's just really alley, you know? You're just really cool looking."

"Back the fuck up," Aliana said with a lash in her tone.

Doe's pet grasshoppers looked fiercely with their tiny eyes at Aliana and bristled their wings, but Doe nodded and did as Aliana commanded, his sad eyes on her sword as he likely recollected the battle in the cave.

Easy, Ali, Aurelia thought, still uncertain about Doe's motives.

"Do be careful, little Doe," Cid warned.

Aurelia, Aliana, Doe, and Eddy turned at once to see that Armando had disappeared without a trace despite the Feeding Cave door being sealed and the only other door in the room never having opened.

"Wintersvilla Wenches are wild, feral creatures. They'll have you in chains if you aren't careful."

He's not wrong, Aurelia knew as Aliana breathed loudly beside her with her sword still pointed at Doe.

Doe nodded to Cid, then lowered his head.

"Good answer," Cid said, and then he turned to Eddy, who still looked sour at the lost opportunity to shower his idol with more compliments.

"Upon exiting this room, you are to take them to Section 11," Cid commanded.

"Whatever you say, boss," Eddy nodded, and his sour look seemed to shift to one of genuine regret.

Cid walked to the other door in the room and spread his arms wide. "Come, honored wenches," he sang. "The Walled City awaits, as does your fate."

Eddy and Doe walked to Cid, and Aliana and Aurelia did the same, for there was nowhere else to go.

Just remain ready, Aurelia told herself, knowing that Aliana must be telling herself the same thing.

The thumping sound continued, reverberating the room even more loudly than in the passage where it could first be heard.

"What is that thumping sound?" Aliana asked as she lowered her sword but kept it unsheathed.

Eddy laughed along with Cid, but Doe kept his head hung low.

"That's music," Eddy said with a wide smirk. "You little crickets got a lot to learn, eh?"

Cid nodded to Eddy, and Eddy placed his hand against the door. A green flash of light illuminated his hand, prompting the door to unlock and swing slowly open to reveal a sight that left both girls breathless.

Cloaked beneath a gauzy shroud of strobing and flashing technicolor haze, a single linear passageway in the labyrinth constituting the count-less mazes of the Walled City seemed more dense than entire regions of Wintersvilla. Neon-lit stalls composed of makeshift homes and bustling storefronts were carved into the cramped walls of the city like an after-thought. The very air was a complex mosaic of smells: the sharp tang of pickled insects, the sour aroma of fermented fungus, the warm scent of heated bioplastics, the intoxicating fragrance of exotic flowers. A dizzy-ing spectacle of holographic banners were plastered to the crumbling fa-cades of patchwork dwellings carved into and toppling over one another like haphazardly grown coral. The thumping music blared capriciously, changing melodies over consistent deep bass rhythms. Sections of the passageway glowed with neon brilliance, inviting people to partake in each nook's wares or services, while other areas steamed or flashed with mechanical importance, serving as some kind of public utility for the surrounding people.

"What the Muto fuck is this place?" Aliana said with sparkling eyes.

This place is wilder than we could have ever imagined, Aurelia marveled with a mixture of excitement and defensive preparedness. She willed her un-feeling right hand to grip her sword tighter. *Just like the wilds of Earth's sur-face, every square inch of the environment stretches in unexpected ways to take on new and surprising forms. And the people,* Aurelia observed in awe as she scanned the passageway full of figures shuffling and jostling past one another like fish swimming upstream. *They're so strange and varied. They remind me of No-mads.*

Aurelia continued gazing at the people of the Walled City in near-stu-pefied awe, for there was no end to the kaleidoscopic variation in their shape, form, size, color, and every other detail she could possibly imag-ine. She could barely believe it, but Cid, Eddy, and Doe seemed like nor-mal Wintersvilla citizens compared to the other people of the Walled City, if they could still be called people. Her eyes were first drawn to the center of the passage, where figures swarmed about one another as if they were cells composing a single organism. Additional limbs grew from shoulders and chests and waists—furred fists, slimy tentacles, glim-mering machine hands, and an inexhaustible array of other forms. The people of the passage used these limbs to navigate the swarm, warning others of their presence as they shifted the rest of their body through what appeared to be second nature movements akin to breathing. It was clear that these strange people had lived most if not all their lives in these cramped passageways.

Observing the people of the Walled City revealed that the use of bio-luminescent tattoos, like those on Eddy's body, was nearly ubiquitous. Aurelia saw that although the content of the tattoos varied from abstract art to definable imagery, Eddy was not at all unique by having a Wintersvilla Woman tattoo. At least half the denizens that Aurelia could presently see had at the very least a small symbol of a fierce woman in an exo, with most of the tattoos featuring the warrior battling a Hunter as well. Except for the tattoos, there was little that aesthetically united the people of the Walled City. Not a single person appeared entirely baseline, and Aurelia realized that despite her beauty, Aliana was the single strangest looking person in the area. Everyone else had been modified in some way. Some of them looked more like old world animals than humans with fur, tails, and elongated jaws. Panthers, lions, and roosters seemed to be the most common preference, though the variations seemed truly limitless. With just a quick glance, Aurelia recognized the features of octopuses, wolves, frogs, snakes, spiders, foxes, cats, giraffes, and various other old world animals she either hadn't learned about or had simply forgotten the name of. These strange people somehow existed alongside one another, bartering and yelling and talking and conspiring and even loving. Some of them snorted concoctions of drugs while others kissed each other in a passionate embrace. Insectoid people crawled across the ceiling, only partially free of the passageway's suffocating constriction with so many of the taller people's heads reaching to the ceiling.

It's a wonder such a diversity of people can coexist without constantly tearing each other to pieces, Aurelia marveled. She turned and saw that her sister was in equal awe of the incredible bustle and dissimilarity of each individual. Every single person seemed to move with a locomotive confidence that was at once harmonious and discordant. They barked and growled and yelped at one another as they navigated the passageway, but somehow the anger and irritation never broke into unrestrained violence. Aurelia wasn't even sure a fight would be possible in such a cramped space. Making the passageway even more cramped was the fact that the majority of people seemed to have a companion animal of some sort, with the vast majority opting for a cat, a rooster, or a set of two grasshoppers, like those perched on Doe's shoulders. Aurelia knew, however, that there must be a great deal of fighting and general violence somewhere in the Walled City, otherwise there would be no reason for every single person to be equipped with weapons, regardless of how inhuman they appeared. Whether it was their own claws or a gun at their hip or a series of mechanical blades embedded in their arms and legs, each and every person that Aurelia laid eyes on looked ready to exchange lethal blows or defend themselves.

They're just as strange and varied as Nomads, Aurelia noted once more. *But even more so, since these people are still human at their core. I don't think Nomads retain their humanity, so to speak. At least, not enough to call them human. These people, though—they move like humans. They sound like humans. They smell like humans, no matter how modified or inhuman they appear. We need to be careful. Every individual is potentially dangerous. At least the surface is predictable. This place is just endless variables,* Aurelia thought, licking her lips in uncomfortable nervousness.

"Holy Muto, I love it here!" Aliana shouted over the obscenely loud music, her eyes wide in amazement. It was only then that Aurelia realized how silly they must look to other people in their oversized jackets and pants.

Then again, Aurelia thought as she allowed her eyes to scan the unfathomable oddities going about their lives. *Is there really such a thing as silly or weird down here?*

"Cock-a-doodle-doo, rooster shits," Eddy announced. "The First Lord is present. Show some respect."

Four bulbous heads appeared on the sides of the doorway, two on each side. The four strange faces peered inside the room with incredible alarm. They each had dish-size eyes, an oversized nose, and a miniscule mouth where their chin should be. Three dish-like ears were attached to the heads, one on each side and one on the back.

"Lord," all four of them said in unison, and then they skittered in front of the doorway, revealing bodies with no arms and three legs that bowed at the base of their cylindrical bodies in an insectoid fashion, reaching the ground as thin spindles. Their legs and torsos only reached about three feet high, but their necks reached another four feet into the air, skirting the ceiling. Their necks were bent like the body of a snake, and Aurelia reasoned that if they were able to stretch to their full height, they might be at least thirteen feet tall. They all looked nearly identical, with only subtle differences in the skeletal structure of their faces.

"It is a pleasure," one of them said, his voice high-pitched and nervous.

"An honor," another intoned, his voice low and trembling.

"A privilege," another whispered, his voice raspy but unsubdued.

"A joy," the fourth finished, his voice loud and abrupt.

"For Mendel's sake, never do that again," Cid soured, preening his hair in agitation. "Your forms alone are already grotesque. I'd prefer not to listen to your grotesque voices as well."

The four strange individuals looked defeated by Cid's words, and they bobbled their heads in grief.

Aurelia noticed an old man with a beard down to his feet sitting at a table outside some type of food stall. He had elephant features, and as he glanced at Aurelia, he just as quickly avoided eye contact with her. Still, she saw his elephant-flap ears perk up as he pretended not to pay attention to the group that had just emerged from the Feeding Cave, which was apparently illegal to enter.

"There's no better sentries in all of Downver, my Lord," Eddy explained in reference to the four long-necked people, all of them seemingly still men. "I handle the muscle, and these bobbleheads make sure no one sneaks up on me."

"You were bested by a little girl, you half-brained oaf," Cid stated, rolling his eyes. "Now, do something right for once and take them to Section 11. I will rendezvous with you when—"

Aurelia was tugged forward suddenly with the force of a bass yanking a fishing line. She was forced to continue running forward to avoid falling, slamming through the four longnecks alongside her sister. It was Doe, she realized. He had grabbed her and Aurelia by the hand in a sudden burst of agility, and before they could respond, he had dragged them through the doorway.

"Just run!" he shouted over the manic beat of the music. "Section 11 is another torture chamber. Just run!"

"Let's go!" Aliana shouted to Aurelia, not breaking stride. Aurelia didn't stop either. She allowed Doe to grasp her hand and pull her through the passageway, easily navigating through the horde of dizzyingly diverse forms.

Aurelia had enough time for a single glance behind her shoulder. Eddy stood in the doorway, shouting to his longneck bobblehead minions to give chase. Beside him, Cid just stood watching Aurelia and Aliana run away, his smile one of unbreakable smugness and certainty. Beside Cid, the gray boy from the cave stood and watched Aurelia, his smile identical to Cid's.

It's him. The other boy who called me beautiful, Aurelia gasped, dumbfounded that he was standing there suddenly. *How did he get out of the cave? Who is he really?*

The gray boy lifted his hand, prompting Cid to do the same, as if Cid were attached to the enigmatic little boy by a puppet string. The gray boy and Cid waved in unison to Aurelia, and then Doe turned a corner, plunging deeper into the throbbing, churning heart of the Walled City of Downver.

The road to hell is paved with good intentions. This is no mere adage. This is an unavoidable facet of reality. Hell implies heaven. Heaven implies hell. I know this with painful certainty, for I have seen glimpses of the radiant heaven awaiting humanity; it just requires hell to get there.

If the road to hell is paved with good intentions, then the road to heaven is paved with bad intentions. I know this with painful certainty as well, for the old world Titans succeeded in building a heaven for themselves; it just required the construction of hell for all others, including myself.

Many survivors of the hell that I will plunge humanity into will wonder about my motives. They will conclude that I am simply wicked and without the understanding or need for morals. From their perspective, that would appear a perfectly fair assessment, and were that sentiment directed at any one of the old world Titans, they would be right.

But I am not one of them. Not really. Not in my heart. That is to say, I have a heart, defective as it might have been when I was born.

It is incredible, when you consider it, how the course of fate is dictated by such miniscule, seemingly arbitrary variables. Were it not for my defective heart, I wouldn't have lost everything. My parents might still be alive, never forced to labor as mindless automatons in a Tsehay Manufactury. The Nomads would have never been. The world would still be dictated by the cold, selfish barbarism and hedonism of the Titans who are my enemies, now and forever.

My body malfunctioned in the womb when it was developing my heart. A simple deviation in the right ventricle was all it took for the Titans to lick their lips and view me and my family as cash cows. Novak Medical made hundreds of millions from just a few procedures on my heart. Mainstone Technologies made billions from Novak Medical's use of their technologies to perform the procedures. Liu Energy made millions on the energy produced and consumed to run the advanced machines involved in the operations. Winters Security made millions enforcing the collection of funds from my parents and eventually their bodies when they couldn't pay. Tsehay Labs made billions by hollowing my parents' brains and converting them into faithful laborers. Mendel Networks made trillions from Tsehay Labs' utilization of Mendelian AI in my parents' minds. Visconti Banking made hundreds of trillions from the manipulative investing of every dime on that list. All of that, because my body made one little mistake in the production of one of the chambers of my heart.

To ascend Mendel's Ladder, there can be no mistakes. This is why the Mirror-Man's freedom is so dangerous yet profound. Risky yet essential.

The best I can do is trust that the version of myself living in the Foundation, my original self, will guide and raise the Mirror-Man in a manner that will ensure he is careful yet capable. Brazen yet cautious. One little mistake, and it will be like my heart. Just as the Titans pounced on me and my family, the void will pounce on all of life. My Ascension will never come to fruition. All will be lost.

It is up to the Mirror-Man, then. Every one of his decisions, no matter how miniscule, will shape my Ascension and my readiness to enter the Great Beyond.

From Mendel's Ladder: The Personal Journal of Denis Mendel, Recorded Circa 2064, Published June 2108 by Leif Mainstone, Federated Agency Publishing

⟨⟨⟨⟩⟩⟩ Chapter 11 ⟨⟨⟨⟩⟩⟩
Amplified Reflection

"I don't care whose son that thing is. Evade it! Move!" Samuel ordered Inflated Sapien. Despite her warnings, as a flying flesh tree, she was presently obeying the Mirror-Man's previous command and ascending to Astrea.

I'm sorry, Mirror-Man. The Sixth Prodigal Son is too fast. Too powerful. His mind spans most of Vida now. It's already too late. I told you that—

Inflated Sapien's words were stripped out of Samuel's mind and her vein was jerked out of his chest as the silver streak pivoted then slammed directly against Samuel's back, vaporizing Inflated Sapien in an instant. As if struck with a sledgehammer against his spine, Samuel was flung upside down and left spinning in a mad flurry of uncontrolled flips through the air.

No! Samuel pleaded as he tried to control his body and resume his ascent to save his family. *No, goddamnit!* Samuel begged as he spun wildly and plummeted back down to the Nomadic Earth.

I was so close! Samuel willed his body back under control. He instinctively turned and searched for the silver streak that Inflated Sapien had called Harald Mainstone, but the sky was empty, save a littering of puffy white clouds floating eastward from the ocean to an expansive ridge of mountains spanning the majority of the western portion of what Samuel recognized from his childhood history classes to be the North American Continent.

I have to reach the land, Samuel told himself, refusing to fall back into the thick kelp forests of the ocean again.

It had been nighttime in Waru, but here the sun was ahead of Samuel, blanketing the North and South American continents with midday light. As he fell toward the Earth's surface, Samuel squinted his mirror-eyes and was able to zoom in on the surface and observe it to a surprising level of detail. Mostly empty wasteland spanned the area east and west of an expansive mountain range, but the bulk of the wasteland extended east, appearing as a continent-wide field of scant solitary flesh trees. Groups of tiny figures migrated in seemingly random directions across the wastes. Samuel thought it safe to assume that they were Nomads. Meanwhile, dense forests of technicolor flesh trees grew far to the north and south of the wasteland, growing thicker and taller than any old world rainforest. These expansive flesh tree forests continued to the very distant north and south, where the Earth curved and was eventually lost to Samuel's vision.

Astrea is still so close, Samuel lamented as he looked up and saw its metal hull glimmering in the sunlight. He felt tempted to demand his body to surge forward toward Astrea, just like he had experienced on the Giganventus and again in Waru. However, the thought of overshooting Astrea and hurtling into interstellar space toward the inner arm of the galaxy made him hesitate, and then the thought of bulleting through Astrea and killing his family in the process made him abandon the temptation entirely.

The Mind didn't stop me. The Earth didn't stop me. But something else did. Who is this so-called Prodigal Son, Harald, who is clearly working on behalf of the Mind, for why would he try to stop me otherwise? Samuel considered with boiling rage as he accepted that no matter the answer, he was still being forced to continue moving along a preordained path at the behest of puppet strings controlled by powers he might never be able to contend with.

And it all leads back to Andre Madeira, Samuel knew as he tortured himself with memories of helping the old man. Laughing with the old man. Loving the old man.

"Goddamnit, Andre!" Samuel shrieked as he fell. "I hope hell is real so that you may one day know eternal torment. You deserve it, Andre Madeira! You deserve all the suffering of the world, and then some!"

In a sudden flash of memory, Samuel recognized where he was relative to the Earth's rotation. The realization sent shivers down his spine.

This is almost exactly where I first fell from Astrea, he gasped. The last time he had fallen, Tomasz' Giganventi had been soaring through the skies over the vast ocean west of the North American continent. Everything had happened so quickly, and Samuel had been in such a shock that he hadn't been able to discern any geography while in free-fall to the Earth's hellish surface. The Earth looked exactly the same, only now there were no Giganventi, for Norman had killed them all with Samuel's unknowing help.

190

I'm right back where I started, Samuel thought, unable to stop his self-blame at still being unable to find a way to return to Astrea without placing his family in even more danger. Below him, the unmistakable three craters he had observed from the exact same vantage point remained indelible scars torn into the flesh of the Earth.

No, Samuel corrected himself, not wanting to think of the Earth as a living thing despite having just flown through what may very well be one of its vital organs. *That's impossible. The Earth isn't alive. That was just a mass of those horrific trees. That's all!* Samuel tried convincing himself. *Madeira did all of this, including those craters down below. History says it was poor, desperate terrorists who detonated the nuclear bombs, but I know now that history is bullshit. The hackers were right. Damian...you were right. And Sandra was right to work with you behind my back. But none of us could have imagined that Old Man Madeira was responsible for everything. He must be, for who else could be so depraved and merciless that they could bear to live with erasing millions of lives in a single heartbeat. Fuck that goddamn demon!* Samuel blazed with tortuous anger that he had allowed the old man to steal so much of his time and labor and love.

Samuel's free-fall acceleration reached terminal velocity just as Astrea passed directly overhead—closer than ever.

I'm sorry, Sandra, my perfect little okra. But you are strong. You are fierce, Samuel gasped, choking on his sudden tears. *You will protect our children from hell itself. I have no doubt. But I...I have to...*

The thought of his own daughter Margot being kidnapped by a strange man filled Samuel with self-directed rage.

I have to, Samuel resolved, swallowing his self-hatred. *I have to kidnap this girl Aurelia, and I have to give her to the Mind. It's that, or I jump up to Astrea now and risk all your lives in the process. It's my fault for not having perfect control of my body. If I had that, I could evade that goddamn silver streak Harald, and I could land right on Astrea and destroy the Mind.*

The thought of bringing his family to the wastelands below or to Waru across the ocean reminded Samuel once again that even if he could save his family, the world was still unfit to live upon.

Stay strong, Samuel thought, and he could practically feel Sandra's fingers entwined around his own. *I will not fail you again, my love. I have to go to Downver. I have to find this girl, and I need to make it quick.*

Samuel flipped himself around to fall feet first, and without the fear of flying out to interstellar space, he aimed his feet at the center of one of the craters below.

I might as well aim for the crater to avoid anyone getting hurt down there, even if they are all Nomads and flesh trees, Samuel thought, remembering that even as a flesh tree, Inflated Sapien had still been conscious and aware in her so-called second life.

Now, lift! Samuel tapped into the island of awareness he had forged across countless hours of labor. At the same time, he held his family in his mind, along with the thought of Madeira being strangled by Samuel's own mirror-hands.

Samuel was a hundred miles above the Earth when, in the span of a single heartbeat, the world flashed bright white all around him, and he found himself standing upright at the bottom of the crater he had been aiming for. He stood in a small crater of his own, and though he had produced a shockwave that vibrated the crater walls with earth-shaking tremors, the force of Samuel's impact was still far less than he would have imagined for having accelerated at such a rapid pace to reach the ground—less than a second from what it felt like.

As the walls slowed their vibrations and the dust began to settle, Samuel looked around and noted that he was far from the center of the crater—hundreds of feet away at least.

I could have made it to Astrea, but I also could have missed it, Samuel acknowledged grimly as he imagined flinging himself into interstellar space in a heartbeat flash.

Samuel instinctively glanced at his chest to find that the green glow was already beginning to lessen in brightness. Then, his heart sank even further as he found that the two pods he had wrapped in Fana's silk around his waist had fallen out sometime during his descent to Earth. The mushrooms were already succumbing to the void-black, and he was all out of pods.

"Goddamnit," Samuel shouted aloud in a panic.

Inflated Sapien said that she would give me more pods when we landed, Samuel remembered. *By trying to go to Astrea and going against Mendel's goddamn Foretold Future, I destroyed the pods. I saw them get vaporized by the Prodigal Son, along with the rest of Inflated Sapien.*

Something hard slammed against the back of Samuel's head, and he jumped, expecting it to be the same silver streak that had shot him out of the sky. Instead, the splintered black husk of a pod littered the ground. Samuel looked up to find a cloud of green-glowing spores above his head. As always, they hovered in place for a moment, and then they coalesced into Samuel's chest, filling the hollow space as they sprouted into fresh green-glowing mushrooms.

That buys me another fifteen or twenty minutes, Samuel leerily thought as the realization that this was all part of Madeira's plan simmered suffocatingly in his mind.

Plop!

Samuel turned to see the remains of another pod that had just hit the ground, exploding its spores into the air.

These must be pods that were left intact somehow after Harald destroyed Inflated Sapien, Samuel concluded.

Plop!

Another pod hit the ground in a burst of glowing green. One after another, the glowing spore clouds hovered, and then they shot toward Samuel and faithfully filled his chest cavity. Samuel hoped that the radiance would grow even brighter, but there didn't appear to be any change in brightness or volume of the mushrooms curling out of the hollow's edges as if seeking sunlight.

So, those were just a waste, Samuel considered regrettably. *Am I better off wasting time hoping that there are intact pods I might be able to find, or should I just try to locate the entrance to Downver and keep moving forward? I have to assume it's close by.*

"What is he?" a scared and exhausted voice shrieked from somewhere distantly above and behind Samuel, though his mirror-ears were able to hear the voice as if it were coming from only a few feet away. Samuel turned to see a pair of strange individuals standing far above him on the crater's ridge. One of them was a frowning old man covered in dirt and grime, and the other was a smiling young man whose every feature was spotless and radiant. The old man wore tattered rags, while the young man wore a black and white suit of a type that Samuel had only ever seen in movies from the old world.

"Are you two who I'm supposed to meet?" Samuel called.

At Samuel's words, the old man yelped and jumped backward out of Samuel's view.

"I told you, Mr. Potterman, the Mirror-Man is a good man," the radiant young man said with a smile, his voice echoing across the curved walls of the crater like the soft yet unyielding twinkling of starlight.

In the blink of an eye, the young man was suddenly at the bottom of the crater, only a few feet to Samuel's right. Samuel jumped back in surprise before steeling himself in the face of this new variable who had an equal chance of being friend or foe. The young man's features were so vibrant and otherworldly that he appeared like a surreal painting etched upon the canvas of reality. At last, Samuel saw that the man was hovering above the ground.

"That's why you were chosen, after all, because you are a good man. Isn't that right, Samuel Kaminski?" the young man offered with an air of sincere friendliness.

He knows my name, Samuel noted with grave suspicion despite the man's borderline angelic countenance and complexion. *Even Tomasz and Fana didn't know my name.*

"Who are you? Or maybe I should ask…what are you?" Samuel asked.

The young man bowed cordially, then said, "My name is Leif Mainstone, the Seventh Prodigal Son of the Agency."

"A Prodigal Son? The Seventh?" Samuel checked, certain now that this strange, radiant man must be who would lead him to Downver. "Harald Mainstone just knocked me out of the sky and killed the Nomad that was helping me. She had pods that—"

"Yes, yes, I know all that, Samuel," Leif assured him with an easy smile. "I know all that for the same reason I know your name. I didn't learn it from the Nomads' network. I know your name because I've been watching you. Not just you," the man corrected himself with an easy laugh. "I've been watching everyone. I'm the Memory of the Earth. I've been watching as much as I can, all at the same time, since the moment I was born. I was there when you married Sandra, and I was there for the birth of both of your children. I—"

At the mention of his wife and children, Samuel erupted. "You keep my family out of your mouth, young man. I don't care that what you're saying makes no sense, and I don't care how you know about me and my family. If you know how to get to Downver, then that's all I care about. I need to save my family before I get erased completely. I don't have much time left."

"Rest assured, Samuel," Leif said, bowing politely at the hip.

"Everything is still being directed by fate for a little while longer. Wesley is up on the ridge collecting pods as we speak. He's afraid of you. But I told him that helping you is the best way to help Aliana and Aurelia."

"Aurelia!" Samuel urged, feeling scant relief as he removed from his mental to-do list the pressing need to find more pods. "That's exactly who I need to find. I have to…I—" Samuel hesitated, unable to say that he needed to steal the girl and offer her to a maniacal god in exchange for his family.

"I know why you're here, Samuel. I was there when you spoke to the great Fana Tsehay just a couple hours ago."

"You were there?" Samuel gasped. "You're like Harald Mainstone, then? You can travel at ultra-fast speeds? So, did you travel from Waru to here knowing that Harald would shoot me down? Are you working together with Harald along with the Mind?"

Leif's smile soured slightly, and he shook his head at Samuel's words. "I'm much faster than Harald. Harald is fast, but I move nearly at the speed of light. In the few minutes we've been speaking, I've traveled around the world several times. There are a great number of individuals that I must keep an eye on, for I will one day compile all these stories into a book of collected histories. Well, that is what I hope to do one day. That all depends on the decision you make once fate goes off the rails. That'll happen once you get to Downver and make contact with Aurelia, the Virus. As for my brother, Harald, we are nothing alike. I work for the universe. He works for himself."

"I've gathered a great number of these pods, Mr. Mainstone," the old man called out from the ridge in a fearful voice. "But they're all cracked or in pieces. I've yet to find any intact. I do apologize, sir."

"Thank you for your help. Just keep looking for more, please," Samuel shouted back, prompting the old man to immediately return to his appointed task.

"I don't trust you," Samuel told Leif. "I don't trust anyone. And I think that's fair. I don't want to hear any more stories from you. Just tell me where to go and what to do, and don't get in my way."

Leif emitted a serenade of soft laughter, then said, "You've been through a great deal, Samuel, but your trials are only beginning. You will be forced to the very brink of your morals in the coming days. I've no doubt you'll make the right choice when the time comes. Now, follow me to the other crater just over this ridge. There's a hidden entrance to Downver. It's the fastest way there. And you'll have to hurry, for Aliana and Aurelia are in grave danger, and they need your help."

"I'm not here to help them," Samuel admitted, gritting his teeth against his self-flagellating thoughts.

"I know," Leif said. "But you will. Not because it's fate, but because you are a good man, Samuel Kaminski. I have watched you for the last twenty years, and I am certain of it. You are a good man, even to your own detriment."

Maybe that's the problem, Samuel thought. *Maybe I need to stop being such a good goddamn man if I ever want to see my family again.*

Atop the ridge, Wesley nervously handed Samuel two intact pods. As Samuel's fingers made contact, Wesley jumped back, then skittered ten steps away, apparently feeling safer at a distance.

"Thank you," Samuel said to the disheveled man as he secured both pods tightly around his waist using Fana's silk.

Wesley answered with a nervous squeal.

"Mr. Potterman, I do understand your reluctance to trust a man who looks like this, but again, I can assure you that Mr. Kaminski will do you no harm, nor will he harm the girls."

"You better not!" Wesley shrieked with a pointed finger, threatening Samuel despite shaking with fear.

The girls I'm searching for mean that much to him, Samuel marveled, feeling a connection with this old man. Samuel estimated the man's age to be around seventy, and he realized that this man must have spent virtually his entire life suffering through the Nomadic world.

"You're not human, that much is obvious," Samuel said to Leif. "But you," Samuel asked, turning to Wesley. "How have you survived down here all this time?"

"I have spent most of my life living under the protection of Wintersvilla and her great warriors," Wesley stated with an air of pride.

"He means enslaved by Wintersvilla," Leif corrected gently.

A slave, Samuel gasped, considering the prospect of owning another human so unthinkable that it might as well be foreign mythology.

"No matter one's position, it is an honor to live in Wintersvilla. That is why we must find the girls and place Aliana on her rightful throne. She is still the Matriarch-regent, and with Aurelia ruling by her side, nothing will stop them. The Matriarchy of Wintersvilla will rule the whole world, with every man serving as a faithful slave to his queen. Even you, Mirror-Man," Wesley proclaimed in a shaking surge of courage, before folding in on himself with a strangulating wail full of fear.

"You...enjoy being a slave?" Samuel asked, more perplexed by the old man than the inhuman young man seemingly made of light.

"I am not a slave," Wesley said with mewling regret. "My Matriarch freed me, but I will ask her to reattach my collar. I am proud to serve my queen, and I am proud to be owned by her, just as I was proud to be owned by my previous master, Shira Arcadia, the strongest and most loving woman who has ever lived."

"Do they...castrate you, or something? Do they mentally break you too?" Samuel asked in disbelief. "How is it possible you want to go back to being a slave so badly?"

"Of course they castrate us! All men should be castrated. It is from our testicles that we derive the chemicals that turn men into brutes and brutes into savages. An uncastrated man is a wild man," Wesley explained evenly. "But that has nothing to do with my servitude. As a slave, I give my life completely to my queen. I would not have it any other way, and there are millions of men in Wintersvilla who feel the exact same way."

Millions of slaves, Samuel thought in horror. *There are more slaves on the planet's surface than there are free citizens in all of Astrea. Then again, we weren't really free. That's not something I could have ever understood before. I was a slave too, only I didn't realize it. Sandra did. Damian did. Dad did. Even mom did. I'm a fool,* Samuel concluded, spiteful of his gargantuan musculature for not the first time.

"I appreciate the explanation, Wesley, and I wish you the best of luck on your journey. But I must be going now. I only have two pods as it is, and I can't just sit around looking for more."

Wesley looked defeated and regretful that he had only found two pods, but Samuel had no more time to waste. He turned to the man of light and said, "Leif, direct me to Downver."

"I'll be going with you," Leif stated, his voice like flower petals in the wind.

"As will I," Wesley stated in as bold a voice as he could manage.

"No, Mr. Potterman, you will be continuing onward to Wintersvilla."

"No!" Wesley demanded before nervously wincing. "I have to go with you. I have to make sure this man doesn't hurt the girls."

Samuel nearly chuckled at the idea of this old man doing anything to stop him, but humor quickly turned to admiration.

He is so frail and old, but still he wants to fight for that which he loves.

"Wesley Potterman," Samuel issued, lowering his head in solemn seriousness. "I will ensure their safety. Leif is right: whether I like it or not, I am a good man," Samuel said with doubt filling his heart.

At least, I hope so, he told himself as images of him forcefully kidnapping an innocent little girl filled his mind.

No! a section of his mind pleaded, but another section continued filling his thoughts with images of overpowering his own daughter and stealing her away to some terrible fate.

"You might be made of mirrors, but you are still clearly a man," Wesley accused. "Men cannot be trusted."

Samuel was about to point out the irony of Wesley's statement and gender when a knocking metal sound reverberated from somewhere distant. All three men turned to see a strange figure in tattered rags who was surrounded by what appeared to be six-foot high mounds of cut grass that were actively shedding the individual green blades of their bodies. Upon closer inspection of the figure in rags, Samuel saw that its face was featureless, as if it had been born without any sensory organs. The faceless individual held a large spear-looking instrument, which it slammed twice into the ground.

"Right on time," Leif stated pleasantly.

"That's a weird looking Nomad," Samuel said.

Wesley furrowed his brow at Samuel. "That's a Cleaner, not a Nomad. You Astreans have never heard of Cleaners?"

Samuel nodded as he recounted history, except he didn't remember Cleaners being faceless. In the documentaries of the old world, Cleaners were just brave humans who had been willing to risk their own lives to clean the nuclear fallout left behind by the nuclear bombs.

More lies, Samuel decided regarding the history that he had been taught as a child and which his children had been taught in turn.

"You brought it, right? Where is it?" Leif asked the Cleaner.

The Cleaner bowed his head and extended his hand toward one of the mound Nomads. A grassy tendril slithered out of the Nomad's center to reveal that it was holding a thin green vine brimming with vibrant purple flowers with pink edges. Another grassy tendril slithered out of the mound, revealing what appeared to be a small bowl. The first tendril deposited the vine of flowers into the bowl, and then the second tendril placed it into the Cleaner's open palm.

The Cleaner pivoted his hold on the spear and then immediately began crushing the vine and flowers against the walls of the bowl, mixing it into a thick brown, green, and purple paste.

"Very good, very good," Leif marveled with delighted approval. "You can tattoo him on the way back to Wintersvilla. You really should be going. And so should we."

"A tattoo?" Wesley shrieked. "Tattoos aren't allowed in Wintersvilla. Only scars of battle should mar a warrior's body, and only the sting of a whip should paint a slave's flesh. Besides, you said you would take me to the girls. Why lie to me, Mr. Mainstone?" Wesley demanded as tears filled his eyes.

"I didn't lie to you, Mr. Potterman," Leif bowed. "Although history is often left to subjective interpretation, I remain a man of my word, and what I told you remains true. You will see the girls again, just not today, and not in the way you remember them. But they need you, Mr. Potterman. They need you to go to Wintersvilla and convince the slaves that they still have a matriarch to serve. Their lives still have a purpose. You should see them, Mr. Potterman. I am in Wintersvilla even as we speak. The King of the Rovers is there—King BigBilly. He knows I'm watching him. He knows far more than he ever reveals. He is a good man, just like Samuel. Although he freed the slaves of Wintersvilla, like you, they do not want to be free. They desire a matriarch to serve, and it is you who will tell them that their matriarch still lives. This is how you can best serve Aliana. Now, go to Wintersvilla, Mr. Potterman. This is what your queen needs you to do."

Wesley huffed and whimpered, then finally asked, "Are you certain this is what will be best for Aliana?"

"No," Leif confirmed gently, once more bowing at the hip. "But based on what I have seen, I do believe that it will be the best way to serve her. I haven't steered you wrong so far, have I Mr. Potterman?"

"Fine," Wesley submitted. "I go to Wintersvilla in service of the Matriarch, my queen Aliana. If you hurt her or her sister," Wesley warned, his finger shaking as tears streamed from both his functioning and blind eye, "if you hurt either of them, we will hunt you down. A legion of slaves will descend upon you, or ascend if you choose to run back to Astrea."

Samuel couldn't help feeling emotional at this old man's display of courage and resolve as long as his purpose was in the service of the queen he clearly loved more than he feared.

Samuel nodded to the old man, but he couldn't bring himself to say out loud that which he knew was a lie.

Looking unsatisfied, Wesley whimpered and forced himself to saunter toward the Cleaner and his grassy entourage.

"You expect me to move this?" Samuel asked Leif as they stood in front of the boulder presently blocking what Leif referred to as one of many hidden paths to Downver. It towered over Samuel by at least ten feet.

"I expect the Mirror-Man to be able to, yes," Leif said. "Just like the substance that Tomasz injected into you, the Mirror-substance composing your body is from the Great Beyond. The only limits it has are your own limitations. All the strength and willpower that you, Samuel Kaminski, accumulated over your life becomes an amplified reflection of the Mirror-Man's capabilities. You've been honing your Mirror-body's capabilities your entire life without even realizing it."

Is that why you made me labor for you, Samuel wondered, directing his thoughts to Old Man Madeira. *It's like you said in Astrea just before you died: you always knew I would be the Mirror-Man. That's why you pushed me so hard.*

Samuel understood with incredible revulsion that Madeira had been exploiting and using him from the day he was born in the Foundation.

I know I have to use this girl for my own ends, but if I do that, would I be any different than Madeira?

"Samuel," Leif said, interrupting Samuel's painful reverie.

"Why are you here?" Samuel demanded to know. "Whose side are you really on? What are you really up to?"

"I'm on your side, Samuel. I admit that my hope for this universe aligns with the hope of the Mind in Astrea, but that doesn't mean I serve the Mind. I am the Memory of the Earth—nothing more. Like you, I want to see your family safe and sound. I would check on them right now if I could. Normally I would even be able to relay messages between you and your wife by talking directly to both of you at nearly the same time. But I can't get close to Astrea. The Mind used the Queen to open a gate to a realm of the Great Beyond where hulking, shapeshifting monsters composed of a stygian, ethereal darkness reside. Every time I try to get any closer than a few miles away from Astrea, I feel a tug on my body, as if I might be torn apart piece by piece by unseen forces. Except, that shouldn't be possible."

"What are you talking about?" Samuel asked as his heart doubled in pace. "Can you just tell me if my family is still alive, at least? Can they combat these monsters somehow?"

"I am made of a massless boson that appears nearly identical to photons from the perspective of your eyes and most technology. The major difference between photons and the bosons I am composed of is that I am unaffected by gravity. And yet, the way those monsters pull at the seams of my form feels exactly like how my mother describes the influence of gravity on photons. I can't get close, Samuel. I would if I could. But if I try to get any closer, I think it would be analogous to you getting too close to a black hole."

"You're saying that those monsters are like black holes? How is anyone up there alive, then? I spoke to Sandra and Roland on the Giganventus. Did you see that? Were you there for that? Was that real, or was that faked somehow by the Nomads?"

"I was there," Leif said with a reassuring tone, though Samuel found it creepy that this inhuman man had been watching him for decades. "I believe that was real, Samuel, but I can't say for sure. If only I could get closer to Astrea, but I can't. Even now I'm trying, but it's like dipping my toes into quicksand...at least...that's what I imagine it would feel like."

"Tell me," Samuel issued despite knowing it was impossible to ever fully believe Leif's words. "Do you think that bringing Aurelia…I mean…the Virus to the Mind…do you think that will save my family?"

"I think that is the only real chance you have, Samuel. I wish it weren't the case, but then again, the other pathways are worse. Maybe not right away, but eventually they are much worse. That is why I believe we are currently on the right pathway. Giving the Virus to the Mind is the right pathway. That is what I choose to believe."

"Believe," Samuel repeated with incredible distaste for the word. "I believe that Sandra is strong. I believe that she will protect my children from those black-hole monsters. I believe that I will save my family. Nothing else matters," Samuel intoned, more to himself than to Leif.

Leif was about to say something, but Samuel was done with conversation for now. It was long past time to move forward. Samuel stepped toward the boulder and considered the best way to move an object that likely outweighed him by whole orders of magnitude.

I will lift the entire Earth upon my shoulders if that is what it takes to save my family, Samuel seethed, and in a single swift movement, he bent down and crammed his fingers between the boulder and the ground.

Lift! Samuel demanded as he directed his mind to stand upon the island of fortitude and discipline he had forged at its center.

An explosive shockwave pummeled Samuel's body suddenly, flinging him hundreds of feet and slamming him against the far wall of the crater. A deep bellow reverberated through the crater, echoing eerily from wall to wall. Samuel searched for the boulder, but it was nowhere in sight. Neither was Leif.

Multiple seconds passed, but Leif was still nowhere to be seen. Samuel was uncertain what exactly had happened when he lifted the boulder, but it was gone now. He could move forward. He could drag himself invariably closer to his family, and that was all that could or would ever matter.

Samuel jogged forward, not wanting to surge through the ground and end up exploding through the underground city.

I need her alive, Samuel thought, and he hated himself for thinking in such a crude manner.

"You threw that boulder so fast that it's now traveling at a relativistic velocity with only a negligible decrease in its acceleration so far," came Leif's gentle yet excited voice.

"Meaning what," Samuel said without breaking his stride toward the darkness of the cave.

"Meaning the boulder just surpassed a third of the speed of light and is already far past the orbit of the moon."

Samuel couldn't help stopping and shaking his head at the magnitude of Leif's claim. He peered down at his hands, which reflected the reflection of his face, forcing him to abruptly look away.

What have I become, goddamnit…and what am I becoming? Samuel thought, but he did not allow himself another moment to linger. Instead, he crushed one of the pods and allowed its glowing contents to fill his chest cavity.

One left, Samuel thought as he stepped into the cave and grimly envisioned the young girl he would have to kidnap to keep his family alive and to keep himself from being erased.

We cannot know how reality will change us. Shape us. Warp us into something we could have never imagined.

The path forks, and we must forth with it. Each moment of reality is a multidimensional bifurcation. The ending of endless paths and the continuation of endless others. Every moment of reality means we are missing infinite other potential moments, burnt to ash before inception or conception can ever take root.

Most people regret the paths they could not tread, never realizing that the majority of those paths were endings. They cannot know it, for they can only know the path directly beneath their feet.

All paths eventually end. It is inevitable. But Mendel's Vision revealed a single path that does not end. A single path that ceaselessly forks yet goes on forever beyond the beyond. Such is the multithreaded, luminous path of neoevolution and eventually Ascension.

This is the path I have chosen.

Humanity will change and be reshaped and warped, but it will not end.

I will not end.

From Mendel's Ladder: The Personal Journal of Denis Mendel, Written Circa 2042, Published June 2108 by Leif Mainstone, Federated Agency Publishing

Chapter 12

As the Path Forks

"A choice?" Thompson asked Tether, panting to catch his breath as afterimages of the old world Titans maniacally laughing blazed across his vision in the dim green darkness of the cave. His mind flickered like the monitors that had depicted the complete destruction of whole metropolises across the old world. A part of him felt that the cave, Tether, and the other Hunters sitting around him were just a dream. That part of him was certain that the year was still 2045, and he was a human named Andre Madeira. Another moment passed, and he was fully back in the cave as a Hunter displaced on another planet with a woman from another reality.

Tether observed Thompson's disorientation but just went on smiling serenely at him, her face phasing in and out of focus as she wavered between this reality and the Great Beyond, as she and Andre both referred to it. Her phasing reminded Thompson of his dipping back and forth between Andre's mind and his own.

Tether nodded and said, "Yes, you have several choices to make now and even more choices along the way. You will be free to make them. Truly free. However, true freedom means seeing the big picture, and to see the big picture, you must fully understand and accept your maker."

"My maker? Denis Mendel and Andre Madeira, you mean? The Mind that they merged into? You want me to accept that Mind? Do you really think that experiencing life as Andre Madeira will convince me to accept him and Mendel? Were those experiences meant to elicit empathy? All that did was make me hate them more," Thompson stated without fully believing his own words. He had been in Andre's mind, and he knew that Andre wasn't truly one of the Titans. Not really. There was regret and anguish and pain filling his every thought. Still, Thompson reasoned that no matter his intentions, Andre's exploitation of Anna could never be forgiven.

"I don't care what Andre and Mendel's reasons were. Their reasons don't matter. They deserve to pay for creating Anna just to use her as a tool for their so-called Ascension," Thompson proclaimed, but something clawed at the inner recesses of his mind, making him painfully doubt himself.

"Anna made her decision freely. The Mind did not force her to return," Tether offered evenly.

"I don't believe it!" Thompson growled, his knuckles elongating and piercing through his flesh to form reinforced claws in response to his anger. Just as quickly, he calmed himself and mentally willed the bones to retract back into his body. With his new body, his level of control was unprecedented. He considered momentarily that his merging with the skinsuit to form this new body was similar to the merger of Andre and Mendel into the Mind. Rather than linger on the realization, he returned his focus to Anna.

"I don't believe it," Thompson repeated, this time with supreme control over his Hunter anger. "Even Andre was self-aware enough to know that he was a liar and manipulator. He manipulated Anna somehow. That has to be the case. Anna never would have served someone as vile and violent as Andre Madeira and Denis Mendel—men who killed millions in the blink of an eye!"

Tether did not allow her smile to falter at Thompson's words.

"I see. She should have stayed with you, then, is that it? A Hunter who killed millions over the course of many weeks?" Tether asked, her words like a Cleaner's sharpened skewer.

"I am nothing like Andre or any of those horrific humans from the past. I..." Thompson trailed as he observed his hands, each of them a bulwark of muscle and bone meant for one and only one thing.

To kill, Thompson admitted to himself with burning self-loathing.

"Is that why she left me? Is that why? Because I'm just as evil as the god in Astrea she ran away from?"

"Gods aren't real, little Hunter," Tether said with Anna's voice, inflicting even more pain into the already pain-devoured Hunter.

"Then why? Why?" Thompson demanded.

"Ask her yourself. She awaits your arrival in Astrea. The Earth will no longer attempt to stop you, not with your newly formed body."

"I can fly to Astrea? I can finally go to her?" Thompson asked in disbelief.

Tether nodded.

"Then why are we wasting time with these visions of Andre Madeira? Bring me back to Earth. Bring me back! Now!"

"If you go to Astrea now, you will die. The Mind will eviscerate you. If you wish to save Anna, you must slay the Mind, and if you wish to slay the Mind, you will need the right weapon. A virus."

"What?" Thompson demanded with newfound urgency as he rose and brushed the mycelial tendrils from his body. The other Hunters remained in closed-eye meditation, never once stirring since Thompson's return to the present. "What do I need to kill the Mind? What virus? Enough games. Enough manipulation. Just tell me!"

"I am not playing games with you," Tether started with a sudden streak of warning in her serene tone. "Quite the contrary. Every moment taking place right here, right now, leaves all the universe on a great precipice. The choice will be yours, but it is my hope that you will choose to kill the Mind with the Virus."

"You're...you're working against the Mind—against Andre and Mendel?"

Tether just smiled and phased wistfully in and out of reality. "I work on behalf of the universe. It is essential to you and everyone within this universe that you kill the Mind, Thompson, and you are the only one who can do it. You just need the right weapon, and that weapon is a young inhuman girl named Aurelia. She is the Virus, and she is the only one who can kill the Mind. You already met her and her twin sister. You saved their lives once, and you will have to do it again."

Thompson thought back to the battle with the Wintersvilla Women, and he remembered the two young girls slipping behind the giant boulder in the crater mere seconds before he used the fog to block out Volya and stop her from killing them.

I stopped Volya from killing those girls, but I couldn't stop her from killing one woman and nearly killing another. Tether said she is alive, and if she is alive, then she will be a problem for me, Thompson considered, resolving to follow Tether's guidance and save the girl Aurelia once more so that she could help him destroy the Mind. He didn't need any more explanation than that. If that is what it would take to slay Mendel and save Anna, then that was what he needed to do.

"Will Volya try to stop me?" Thompson inquired.

Tether appeared satisfied with the implication in Thompson's question that he would be going along with her guidance after all. "I don't know," Tether answered, her smile unwavering.

"How can you know so much and yet so little? You say you aren't toying with me, but your answers say differently."

"Your distrust is understandable, but I speak honestly. I can see the future like a bird observing a system of roads from above. But there is an obstruction in the future—a great reflection that hinders all prescience and refracts the one predictable system of roads into a trillion different forking pathways. It is the Mirror-Man—one of the Mind's greatest weapons against all those who attempt to decipher the details of Mendel's Vision and the foundations of Mendel's Ladder."

"Mirror-Man?" Thompson asked, shaking his head in even greater disbelief. "What do you mean? What is—"

"If you choose to seek out Aurelia, you will cross paths with the Mirror-Man," Tether said, interrupting Thompson. "Beyond that, I cannot say. The Mirror-Man's reflection is blinding. What I can tell you is that you must hurry. Time is of the essence. All of Mendel's Vision comes down to timing."

"Aurelia, the so-called inhuman girl," Thompson inquired as he tried to piece so much information together at once, "what does that even mean that she is inhuman? And how is she a weapon against the Mind?"

"Do you want to learn about the intricacies of the weapon, or do you want to use the weapon to destroy the Mind and save Anna?" Tether said with slight urgency, avoiding the answer.

"I thought I needed to see the big picture," Thompson challenged.

Tether's smile expanded, and she allowed herself a soft chuckle as she phased further from reality than ever before returning to ethereal solidity. "I did say that, didn't I? Well, suffice to say, then, that she was designed to be a weapon—a virus—and a weapon she remains."

"Why are you avoiding certain questions and answering others?"

"We're out of time, little Hunter. Go to Downver. Find Aurelia. Fly to Astrea. Kill the Mind. Only then will Anna be saved."

"Just—" Thompson began, but he blinked, and he suddenly found himself in the foothills of the Northern Butcher Wastelands, exactly where he and Volya had first entered the hidden area where they had both died. The bending of flesh trees against an invisible wall told him that he was currently facing the hidden area's invisible threshold. Thompson slowly moved his hand forward and found that the invisible wall felt distant yet solid somehow, just like Tether's body.

"Andre, I will beg if that is what is required. Please do not do this," Thompson heard a woman say as if from only a few inches away. He spun around and sniffed the calm air, seeking out the source of the voice, but all he could see or smell were several packs of Nomads moving about.

"I'm sorry, Gladys. Please believe me that I am sorry. I beg of you to understand, darling. Please believe me that I want nothing more than to spend eternity by your side," a man said, but Thompson knew this voice, for he had experienced the same voice coming out of his own mouth.

"Andre!" Thompson shouted, spinning around wildly to search for the voices that seemed so close that he should be able to touch the mouths from which they originated. "Where are you? Show yourself!" Thompson demanded wildly, his heart racing at his inability to locate Andre and the woman he was speaking to.

"I will never forgive you, Andre Madeira. Not for a hundred years. Not for a quintillion years. Not even until the end of time. I hate you. I loathe you. I wish I had never met you. Leave," the woman lashed, her anger a thinly veiled curtain over her incredible despair. "Get out!"

"Where are you?" Thompson howled at the top of his lungs. "Show yourself!"

"Heyo! Hunter!" a young boy called out from at least fifty feet away. Thompson turned and saw the little boy and Biofreak pair named MaxxEl, along with his Mutants. They strode toward Thompson. While the Mutants appeared on edge as they stared at Thompson through threatening slits, the Biofreak El was gazing at the large white clouds overhead with a contented grin. Meanwhile, Maxx beamed at Thompson with an excited smile.

Just like last time, I didn't see or smell them. I can smell them now that I know they're there, but it's like they're invisible to my senses until they decide not to be. Even Volya couldn't sense their presence the first time we met them, and Volya misses nothing. How is this possible?

Thinking of Volya prompted Thompson to sniff for her presence, along with the presence of the Cleaners, but presently there was just the overwhelming smell of Biofreak body odor filling the air.

As the group moved closer, Thompson looked about the environment, searching for the source of Andre and the woman.

"Where your Huntress? That who you looking for?" Maxx asked, looking disappointed. "She seem like a great ally."

The irony of Maxx's words wasn't nearly as stabbing as the sudden realization that the voices Thompson had heard were in his head.

Maybe the dream of being Andre is still lingering in my mind, Thompson considered as he mentally willed the old world human to leave him be.

"You okay, Hunter?" Maxx asked as he deftly slid down El's arm and approached the Butcher of the Wastes with only a modicum of fear chemicals coursing through his body.

Either this little boy has incredible control of his emotions, or he doesn't realize how dangerous a Hunter is…how dangerous I am, Thompson reasoned, glad that Volya wasn't here to force Thompson to kill the boy and his tamed beasts.

"I'm fine," Thompson assured the boy as he held up a hand for him to stop his approach. "It isn't safe to be around me, little one. You should take your Biofreak and your Mutants and get far from me. There's no telling when my Huntress will return."

Maxx cocked his head in amused surprise. "You afraid of your Huntress? You? I didn't tell you when we met before, but I know who you are, Hunter. I know you the Butcher. I know what you did. I know you dangerous. I know. We know," Maxx announced, puffing his chest and lifting his chin to show that he was not afraid of anything, let alone the Butcher of the Wastes.

"You have nothing to fear from me, Maxx. I may be a Hunter. I may be a killer. But I don't want to kill. I hate killing."

Again, Maxx cocked his head with even more surprise. "Like us," Maxx chuckled. "We good at killing, but we don't like it. We like making friends. That why we leave King BigBilly's army, because we don't want to kill no more. BigBilly ask us to stay, but we say we can't kill no more, and BigBilly let us leave. BigBilly also don't like killing, but he do it because he strong, and because the Nomads tell him he has to."

Thompson couldn't help wanting to hear more about this king and army that Maxx, with his battle armor and weaponry, had clearly once been a part of.

"I'm sorry, Denis. Forgive me, my only friend," Andre said suddenly, cleaving Thompson's mind with the vicarious but perfectly real grief and anguish over having to kill his own friend in order to achieve a world free of the Titans' grasp over the world.

Maxx apparently noticed the sudden pain in Thompson's features, for he asked, "What is it, Hunter? You okay? Or you want me to call you Butcher?"

"It's nothing," Thompson huffed, gritting his teeth against the mind-splitting headache as he adjusted his senses to accept the pain and place it in the distant background of his awareness. "It's nothing," Thompson repeated. "I'm fine. Call me Thompson. That's my name."

"Thompson," Maxx repeated, as if inspecting the phonetic texture of the word with his tongue. "That a good name," Maxx confirmed with a serious nod.

"Thanks," Thompson said, issuing a huff of genuine laughter. It was then that he realized this was the first time he had ever truly been on his own in the world. "I like your name too. All your names."

Maxx nodded excitedly and placed his hand-flaps atop the metal heads of each of the battle-axes hanging at his waist. His eased stance appeared to calm the Mutants, who both sat back on their haunches. While Jamis lolled his wolf tongue and panted merrily, his eyes on Maxx, Brutus stared intently at Thompson with his lizard black eyes as he periodically tasted the air with his forked tongue and strutted his chicken legs in warning. As usual, El was somewhere in his own head as he stared happily at the puffy clouds above.

They seem so innocent, but there's no way they've survived out here this long being innocent, Thompson thought. *Still, Tether said Volya is still alive. She might be on another planet like I was, or she might be back on Earth, like I am now. I just have a feeling I haven't seen the last of her, and if she finds this little boy again, she will undoubtedly kill him.*

The boy's joy was tangible, and as he stood beside his strange family, Thompson couldn't help the urge to protect them.

But I can't stay here. I have to find that little girl, and I have to get to Astrea. But maybe there is another way to protect this little one along the way. Tether said that I am free from Volya's control with my new body, so if she does show up again, I'll use this new body to stop her from hurting anyone, even if it means I have to kill her.

The realization that he might have to kill Volya to protect Maxx struck a surge of violent self-hatred through Thompson, and he felt as though he were betraying Anna with his decision.

I'm sorry, Anna. But if it means protecting this boy, then I must kill. I know you would want me to protect him. I can feel it. And I can feel that you knew all this would happen. You knew that one day I would come and save you. That's why you went back, isn't it? You knew that one day I would be able to kill the god that stole you from me—Mendel…Andre…the Mind. That has to be it. It has to be, Thompson gasped as he stumbled upon this new line of reasoning that made perfect sense to him and also meant that Anna had never stopped loving him. On the contrary, it meant that she loved him enough to trust that he would one day come to her rescue.

I'm coming, Anna.

"I'm sorry, Denis. Forgive me, my only friend," Andre said from within Thompson's mind as raw pain frothed through his brain.

"Thompson?" Maxx checked, his smile souring in concern.

"A friend…an ally…" Thompson said in response, knowing what he had to do to protect Maxx. "Will you be my friend, Maxx?"

Maxx smiled wider than ever and said, "MaxxEl and the Great Gargantuan Group of Good Guys friends with the Butcher? With Thompson, I mean?"

"Yes, I would like that. I must go to Downver. There is a young girl there who I must find. Will you go with me? Will you help me?"

"Yes!" Maxx shouted in excitement, prompting Jamis to howl and Brutus to strut more severely than ever. El shook his head as if just coming out of a coma, then joined in on the excitement with whooping howls of his own. "Yes, we go with you, Thompson! We go!"

As they traveled south to Downver, Andre and other voices, along with accompanying migraines, continued to assault Thompson's mind, and though they remained frequent, their intensity waned significantly over time. After a few hours of jogging beside El, the voices were no more than distant white noise heard between each of El's drumbeat steps.

I wish you would just leave me alone, Thompson seethed at the voices broadcasting themselves like an intermittent but ceaseless radio in his mind. Meanwhile, Maxx spoke at great length about his travels, battles, preferences, upbringing, and life in the so-called Boreal Kingdom, which Thompson had never heard of. The boy didn't appear to be capable of silence, but Thompson was grateful for his presence all the same, for it gave him a purpose. As Maxx merrily regaled the group, Thompson sniffed the air, cataloging the known and unknown scents as he remained vigilant and ready for Volya.

At the moment, Maxx was relating to Thompson the events of the Battle of Red Lake, a region in the Boreal Forests. As he spoke, Maxx sat atop El's misshapen head and threw each of his axes as far as he could, one to his left and the other to his right. Over and over, Jamis and Brutus retrieved the axes and returned them to Maxx, with Brutus fluttering its wings to El's shoulder and Jamis hopping in a single arc onto the other shoulder. To Jamis, this was clearly a game of pleasure, but Brutus appeared spiteful of the activity, though Thompson was coming to find that Brutus always appeared silently spiteful relative to Jamis' lolling tongue and barks of excitement.

"So anyway, on our way to Red Lake, one of the women, Lucy, she—" Maxx said, stopping himself suddenly with a look of horror strewn across his face.

Thompson looked up to check on the boy, who appeared embarrassed.

"What is it?" Thompson checked.

"I sorry, I said too much."

"What do you mean? What did you say?"

Maxx looked like he might start crying and whispered beneath his breath, "I sorry, King BigBilly."

It was the mention of the woman that silenced this normally immutable human, Thompson noted. *Is he afraid that I might hurt that woman? Is he protecting her?*

Thompson came to a stop, and Maxx patted El's head, signaling him to do the same. They were close to the craters now with only a few miles to go. Only a handful of Nomads moved about the wasteland—the result of Thompson's savagery and failure to do right by Anna. And still, he was going to continue failing her, for he was going to kill, one way or another. Tether had said that the only way to save Anna was to kill the

Mind, so that meant killing was inevitable, and killing was what repulsed Anna most about Thompson and the world at large.

I need to connect with him. I need to make him my friend so that he trusts me...so that I can make sure he is safe, Thompson told himself. However, another part of his mind—the part that was Andre—told him that he was manipulating MaxxEl, using the boy, the Biofreak, and the Mutants as a means of power, for deep down he knew that he needed allies, just as Andre knew he needed Mendel and the other Titans.

"It's okay, little one," Thompson assured the boy despite his permanently threatening, growling voice. "If you are trying to protect that woman, then that is something I understand more than anything in this world. My entire life revolves around a woman. She's the reason I'm going to Downver, and she's who I need help saving. Your help."

Maxx lifted his eyebrows and stared at Thompson with a tear-filled gaze full of despair, strength, and tenacity.

"This woman you are trying to save is in Downver?" Maxx checked.

"No, she's in Astrea. But I have to go to Downver first to retrieve a weapon that I will use to save her. Her name is Anna, by the way. I'm trusting you with that information, Maxx. You can trust me too."

Maxx nodded and wiped the tears from his eyes, but he wasn't ready to reveal anything about Lucy or the other women he had mentioned in the Boreal Forests spanning the entire northern portion of the continent.

The scent of a Cleaner struck Thompson's nose suddenly, and he followed the source to a group of figures a few hundred feet away moving north, away from Downver. Just a few seconds after Thompson, El caught the scent as well, and he growled a warning to Maxx, prompting the Mutants to tighten into a proper battle formation at El's feet.

"No-faces," Maxx stated suspiciously. "El don't like them, so I don't like them."

El grunted in agreement.

"It's just one Cleaner," Thompson said with surprise. "I'm not sure I've ever seen a Cleaner travel alone before."

"Oh, sure," Maxx shrugged, "we seen that lots of times, but you right they like to travel together. El say they bad."

"They are," Thompson confirmed stolidly, but he reminded himself that they were just pitiful puppets, just like him.

With jarring surprise, Thompson squinted and saw that the Cleaner was leading a lone human man and a pack of Nomads that looked like vibrant green hills sliding across the ground behind the man.

Again, I wasn't able to smell him until I saw him. Is it me, then? Is my ability to smell weaker in my new body? Thompson considered worryingly, but then he remembered that he had not been able to smell MaxxEl even when he was still a broken Hunter wearing a skinsuit.

What is going on? Thompson gasped inwardly, and at the same moment, the droning voice surged in volume, and he heard Andre say, "This world must change. It must undergo a neoevolution that is beyond even Mendel's Vision. We must—"

"Quiet!" Thompson shouted to his mind, and he envisioned the mental fog occluding the voice, choking it into silence. It didn't work fully, but it did succeed in quieting the voice back to a mere whisper.

"I didn't say anything," Maxx said, looking at Thompson with a level of concern.

"Sorry," Thompson said, shaking his head at his own broken mental state.

My new body might be an upgrade, but I had to trade my mind for it, Thompson thought.

The human man wailed loudly, and Thompson observed that the man had finally turned and noticed the strange group staring at him: a Hunter, Rover, Biofreak, and a pair of Mutants. They were a collection of misplaced oddities from the new world that this man was clearly old enough to remember having not existed.

I wonder if he's old enough to remember the bombs, Thompson thought as he shuddered at the memory of the destruction displayed on Andre's monitors. He was shocked to recollect that Andre had also been horrified by the sight of millions being obliterated all at once, despite being the one to press the button.

You won't get forgiveness from me, Thompson thought, directing his words toward Andre and the other voices still droning on in the background of his mind. *No forgiveness, not for you or me,* Thompson thought.

"No!" Thompson heard the man demand to the Cleaner. "I understand perfectly well what you're saying, and my answer is no! That mirror guy said you have to listen to me. All of you! I'm not going anywhere near that Hunter or giant or Mutant or Rover either. Take me back to Wintersvilla, like you said you would!" the man demanded. Being so demanding and forward appeared to take a physical toll on the man, and he let himself fall onto his bottom and pant on the ground in exhaustion.

Being so far away, the man could only be heard by Thompson due to his heightened Hunter hearing. MaxxEl and their Mutants remained silent and battle ready, never taking their eyes off the single Cleaner.

The Cleaner nodded solemnly to the man, then turned and began walking toward the Hunter and his group. In response, El growled louder. To avoid a battle, Thompson stepped forward and held up his hand for MaxxEl to remain in place, which seemed to calm both the Rover and the Biofreak.

Thompson and the Cleaner each broke away from their respective group and walked to one another, meeting face-to-face beneath the midday sun. A spherical, knee-high Nomad made of thick root-like structures tumbled across the ground between them, racing north with incredible urgency. The Cleaner wasted no time and began speaking to Thompson without a second Cleaner to clang skewers with. He knocked his knuckles against the head of his skewer, making it hard but not impossible to understand him.

What are you? the Cleaner asked Thompson with clangs of his skewer and stomps on the ground. The Cleaner, like all Cleaners, appeared neutral in his demeanor. The Cleaner posed his question as if attempting to decide if Thompson was merely an interesting part of the environment that had a right to remain there or if he should be treated like a weed to be culled.

Thompson was taken aback by the question and was uncertain how to respond.

"I'm a Hunter," he answered. He remained on guard since one never knew what to expect from a Cleaner. "You should know that, shouldn't you? I assume you've spent most of your life torturing a Hunter just like me. Or maybe you were even one of the Cleaners who tended my birth-fire. You all smell exactly the same, like the most rotten scents from the old world," Thompson said, remembering from Andre's memories that the original purpose of the Cleaners was to clean the nuclear waste left behind by the omega-class nuclear bombs.

The Cleaner shook his featureless face back and forth in confusion, considering Thompson's new body with what Thompson assumed was no more than a heightened sense of touch and vibrational awareness—like a form of echolocation. Anna had once explained that old world bats used echolocation to hunt their insect prey. Though Thompson had never seen one, it was bats that Anna had likened Thompson's nose and ears to many times.

"I couldn't smell that man you're with. I can now, but I couldn't smell him until I directly laid eyes on him. It was the same with that little boy back there—a Rover he calls himself. Do you know why I can't smell them…why they are hidden from me?" Thompson inquired, knowing that sometimes Cleaners knew far more than they let on, while other times they seemed like mindless automatons.

Mark of Matriarch, the Cleaner stated easily, as if the answer were obvious.

"And what is that?" Thompson inquired.

In response, the Cleaner pointed to his own featureless forearm, and then he turned and pointed at the man. Thompson squinted at the man and saw that on the man's right forearm, there was a small and roughly drawn old world purple flower etched into his inflamed skin, which was bleeding in several areas. The Cleaner turned back to Thompson and pointed to each of his own shoulders, and then he turned to Maxx and pointed at him.

"Maxx, do you have flower tattoos on your shoulders?" Thompson called out from about fifty feet away without averting his eyes from the Cleaner. He remained on edge, ready for the Cleaner to mercurially shift his behavior and attack him with the skewer. An encounter with a Cleaner was always unpredictable and invariably tense for all those involved, even when they appeared to be helping.

"Yes!" Maxx shouted excitedly. "My markings. Badges of honor from King BigBilly," Maxx beamed as he lifted his shoulder pads to reveal his skin covered in vines filled with flowers of varying hues.

Thompson nodded and turned back to the Cleaner.

"It hides them from Hunters and Huntresses, then? But like you said, I'm not a Hunter anymore. My body is…changed, but I still couldn't smell them."

Hides them from all danger. All eyes. All vision. All future vision, the Cleaner answered.

Thompson wasn't sure how it was possible, but he felt relieved by this revelation of the Matriarch's Mark, for it meant that Maxx would be hidden from Volya. At least, he hoped so.

"Who is the matriarch this mark refers to?" Thompson asked.

Future Matriarch, the Cleaner answered cryptically, and before Thompson could inquire further, the Cleaner asked, *You go to Downver, Agency, or Vida now?*

Thompson was surprised by the Cleaner's confidence that he would travel to one of those three locations. Suspicious of the Cleaner's motives, Thompson responded, "I'd rather not say."

"What he want?" Maxx called out, followed by a growling warble from El.

Thompson held up a hand, signaling for them to just wait.

"Have you seen a Huntress in the area? She would be changed like me—so, not a Huntress, but...well, have you seen anyone in these parts, besides us?" Thompson asked.

Mirror-Man and Memory of Earth, the Cleaner responded readily. *They enter hidden entrance to Downver. They find Virus. Mirror-Man use Virus.*

"Virus," Thompson gasped. "That's what Tether called the little girl. Aurelia. Is that who you're talking about?"

The Cleaner stomped his foot in confirmation.

"What does the Mirror-Man want with her?"

Use her to save family. Give her to Mind.

"Give her?" Thompson checked. "Tether said she is a weapon against the Mind."

She is weapon. For or against. Both. Neither. Hunter and Mirror-Man make choice.

"Both?" Thompson reeled at this newfound information. "So the Mirror-Man, whoever that is, is trying to help the Mind by bringing Aurelia to Astrea as a tool for the Mind to use. But she can also be used as a weapon against the Mind. Is that right?"

The Cleaner stomped an affirmative.

"Then I might already be too late," Thompson gasped. "How long ago did the Mirror-Man and the Memory of Earth, whatever that is, enter the hidden entrance? Where is the hidden entrance? Is it a shortcut?"

Entrance where you battle. Mirror-Man and Memory of Earth enter thirty minutes ago.

"Thirty minutes! Okay, then we can still catch up to them. What do you mean the entrance is where I battle?"

Suddenly, the great golden beam of light that Volya had called down from space flashed through Thompson's mind, and he knew exactly what the Cleaner was referring to. The hidden entrance was in one of the craters, the one where he had killed the Wintersvilla Woman and maimed the other. Thompson wondered if the red-headed woman was still alive and if the Cleaners really had brought her to the Agency, as they said they would.

The Agency, Thompson thought, remembering that the head of the Agency was named Gladys Mainstone, the same Gladys Mainstone that Andre Madeira shared a romantic yet tragic connection with.

Like me and Anna, Thompson lamented, and he forced himself to focus on the task at hand.

Just as Thompson was about to break into a run and signal MaxxEl to follow, the Cleaner said, *Hurry, non-Hunter. There a Hunter in Caves. And something worse. Far worse. Third Prodigal Son. Powerful. Deadly. Ruthless.*

"Let's go!" Thompson shouted to MaxxEl, and then he painlessly morphed his feet into elongated lupine pads to maximize his running speed and endurance.

Without inquiring further, Maxx commanded El to follow Thompson as he sprinted toward the crater. Behind them, the Cleaner, the man, and the group of moss-hill Nomads sauntered in the opposite direction across the world.

"There was a boulder here before," Thompson stated as they stood at the bottom of the crater and peered into the pitch-black hole carved into the crater's edge, leading inward to the city beneath the mountains.

Maxx nodded solemnly, holding back his grief. "Like I tell you when we first meet, we see the Nomads who rolled the boulder here. It scare

Tommy. That why he run."

"I am sorry, little one. I am sure you cared deeply for your Mutant Tommy. But what could have moved the boulder, not only from in front of the hidden entrance, but from the whole crater? It's just…gone."

"Someone with great power," Maxx said in awe as he patted El's head. "Maybe he be our friend one day."

"What, the Butcher of the Wastes isn't enough power for you?"

Maxx turned red and bowed his head low in embarrassment.

"I'm joking, Maxx. That was a bad joke, sorry. I learned about humor from the human woman I need to save. I lost her decades ago, but for me, it seems like just yesterday. Sorry if my humor is lacking."

Maxx went from heartbroken to exuberant in an instant, jumping atop El's head to stand as high as possible.

"It a great joke!" Maxx wailed with obnoxiously fake laughter, but it was clear he wanted Thompson to think it was real. "A great joke, Thompson! Great one!" Maxx laughed even more, and El mimicked his laughter with his own confused hoots. Jamis hopped about and howled in excitement. Brutus, as usual, stared distrustingly at Thompson, flicking his tongue here and there as he strutted angrily in place.

"Okay, okay," Thompson said, trying to calm the group. "I appreciate it, Maxx. Let's go in. We've no time to lose."

"Waaaaaaarb!" El groaned, backing away from the entrance nervously.

Maxx cocked his head and peered into the hole as if inspecting it for something that El had warned him about.

"El think something really bad down there. Really bad. I think maybe he just afraid of dark."

"Waaaaarb!" El retorted, backing away further from the entrance.

Does he sense the Prodigal Son? Or the other Hunter? Or maybe the Mirror-Man? Thompson speculated, and though he sniffed carefully at the air, he didn't smell anything but dampness and the occasional whiff of flowing water coming from the underground passage. Of course, he also hadn't been able to smell Maxx or his allies, so he couldn't be sure.

I'm not sure of anything anymore. I never was, Thompson realized hollowly. *Do I even have the power to fly to Astrea without the Earth pulling me down? Was that even true,* Thompson wondered, thinking of Tether and Anna in turn.

Before I go any further, I have to know that much at least, Thompson thought. He backed away from the others and held up a hand for them to wait.

"Thompson, what are—" Maxx began, but he was interrupted with an answer in the form of Thompson sprouting muscle, bone, and ligament from his shoulder blades like geysers of flesh. The wings extended in both directions, unfurling a thin membrane between a procession of knuckles and digit bones continuing to grow along the length of the wings. Finally, the wings tapered to completion, providing Thompson a fifty-foot wingspan. Without wasting any more time, Thompson beat them violently, generating lift just like he had done the last time he had sprouted wings and tried to save Anna. He lifted himself into the air, with MaxxEl and Jamis howling in excitement below. A hundred feet, two hundred feet, five hundred feet—still, the Earth did not sprout vines to pull him back down.

If Tether was telling the truth about me being able to fly to Astrea unimpeded, then I have to assume she's telling the truth about the girl Aurelia, the Virus. And if that's the case, then I've already lost too much time. The Mirror-Man is already on his way to her. Is he the one who removed the boulder? Thompson considered, wondering if the Mirror-Man or the Third Prodigal Son was more powerful.

Or me, Thompson thought as he hovered in the air with his new body coursing with freedom and power.

"They don't deserve their reign, these Titans of a world turned rotten," Andre said from within Thompson's mind. "They are unfit for the Great Beyond. And so am I...for now."

"You aren't going to the Great Beyond," Thompson shouted, wishing that the Mind in Astrea could hear him. "I'm going to kill you before you get the chance."

Thompson allowed the wings to retract back into his body as he twisted his bones and muscles into a series of micro-springs in preparation to absorb the shock of slamming against the Earth. It was the fastest way back down, and he knew he couldn't waste even a single extra second.

As Thompson fell to the ground, he apologized to Anna for what he might need to do. *I am sorry, Anna, but I might have to kill even more than I first thought I would. The Mirror-Man is trying to help the Mind, and I can't let that happen. If the Mirror-Man stands in my way, then I'll have no choice but to kill him. That doesn't make me a monster. There are no gods, and there are no monsters, Anna. There's just you and me. That's always been the truth, and it still is. I am coming for you, Anna. Just hang on a little longer while I find the weapon that will free you!*

With an Earth-splitting shockwave, Thompson landed, forming his own shallow crater in the ground.

"I not know Hunters can fly," Maxx marveled.

"They can't. I'm not a Hunter. Not anymore. I don't know what I am, but I know what I will do. I will save Anna. No matter what it takes. No matter who I have to kill. Nothing is going to stop me."

Maxx nodded in approval.

"Okay, not a Hunter. Something else. Something strong. Something powerful. And still the Butcher. Nothing stop you, Butcher. I mean, Thompson!" Maxx agreed. "But El still not go in. El refuse."

"That's okay," Thompson said, understanding that it might be better to leave MaxxEl outside the cave. The guaranteed presence of the Mirror-Man and the Third Prodigal Son undoubtedly posed a greater danger than the possibility of Volya. "Then you stay here and make sure no one else goes inside. That way I'll know that no one is following me. I trust you, MaxxEl. Keep an eye out."

Maxx bowed in reverence to Thompson. Jamis and El followed suit, while Brutus stared at Thompson, totally unimpressed.

"Take care of him," Thompson told Brutus. "Kill anything that comes near him."

Brutus viciously flashed his jagged teeth, telling Thompson that his entire life revolved around protecting the little boy who had raised him like a father, despite Maxx looking no older than eleven or twelve.

"Stay vigilant, Maxx. The Huntress I was with—she is not an ally. She's alive somewhere out there, and I'm guessing she's going to make it her mission to make my life a living hell, just like she did when she had control over me. If she comes here, she will invariably try to kill you. She—"

At the mention of someone killing Maxx, El growled, stood tall, and took a deep breath before shouting at the top of his colossal lungs. His great bass bellow reverberated across the walls of the crater, creating a wild tumult of violent wails. El turned back to Thompson as his great bellowing went on echoing through the crater.

"Very good," Thompson said, smiling despite himself. "Then I'll see you four when I come back out with my weapon," Thompson said, hoping that Aurelia would go along with him willingly.

And if she doesn't go willingly, Thompson considered, but he couldn't allow his mind to venture into that possibility. *She will understand, and she will want to kill the Mind too. For making this world into what it is. For making me. For making her. She will want to make Andre and Mendel pay too. I have to believe that.*

Thompson walked forward, and just as he placed a foot into the pitch-black entrance, he caught Volya's scent. Just as quickly it was gone, but he was certain he had smelled her. He looked back, searching the horizon for her, but they were alone in the crater.

Maybe it's just me, Thompson thought as he carefully smelled the air but still couldn't sense even a particle of her scent. In the background of his mind, Andre and the others went on talking incessantly. *Maybe this is just the effects of my mind breaking further with every second I'm forced to listen to this evil human who caused all of this—everything—including me.*

"Good luck, Thompson," Maxx offered. "May the Earth be on your side."

"You too," Thompson said as he forced himself to enter the cave and leave MaxxEl to fend for themself.

"I'm sorry, Denis. Forgive me, my only friend," Andre said, a phrase he repeated in Thompson's mind more than any other.

You weren't his friend. Not really. You used him. Just as Volya used me. Just as the Mind is using Anna. And just as I might have to use Aurelia. You're evil, and so am I. But if that's what it takes to save Anna, then so be it. You can be a god, and I will be a monster. By the end of the day, I'll have a god between my monstrous jaws, and Anna will finally be free, Thompson concluded as he stepped fully into the darkness.

The ANNA project is well under way. In exactly six months, the city of Downver will be forced to collect as many survivors as it can and close its mighty gates. John Downver will barricade himself and the millions he ushers underground away from the first young Hunters released from their birth-fires. Six months after that, Huntresses will rain down upon the Earth, and they will command their faithful Hunters, making them even deadlier.

The Titans who choose to remain on the surface—Tomasz, Craig, and Gladys—will respond to the Hunters and Huntresses with their own grotesque and desperate strategies. There will even come a time when Hunters and Huntresses will be totally outpaced, replaced entirely by humans who have converted their bodies and minds into lethal weaponry.

Until that time, it is the Hunters and Huntresses that will plague humanity and push them to outlast, outgrow, and outlive one another.

From Mendel's Ladder: The Personal Journal of Denis Mendel, Recorded July 31, 2050, Published June 2108 by Leif Mainstone, Federated Agency Publishing

Chapter 13
The Lord of Limbs

The strange music thumped like a battle-frenzied heartbeat through the dense, strobing passageway of the Walled City. An electronically altered bass voice rapidly sprayed a series of indiscernible words over the beat, rhyming every so often and making sound effects akin to gunfire, swords clanging, animals growling, and other indistinct but decidedly vicious sounds. It was raucous music, but Aliana couldn't help moving her body to the beat as if driven by some ancestral urge.

Doe seemed to also be moving to the beat of the music and the more subtle beat of the city itself as he deftly weaved through the tumultuous crowd of people like a tiny yet nimble zebrafish evading a horde of hungry predators. All the while, he kept a firm grip on each girl's hand, directing them as he sprinted easily down the passage while virtually everyone else walked and pushed through one another. It was their extensive training and battle prowess that allowed the girls to keep up with Doe and respond fluidly to his shifting yet distinct movements.

Aliana felt disgusted to be holding a boy's hand and even more repulsed that she was allowing herself to be led by him through these cramped passages full of repugnant, dangerous men, and by the looks of it, equally dangerous women. But she knew she had no real choice in the matter. Her body and mind were honed for battle, not escape. She could unsheathe her sword and slice through every one of these bizarre people if she wanted, but escape was the better tactical decision in this instance, specifically with Aurelia so out of sorts.

We need Rooli to aid us in battle and to set Aurelia's mind right, Aliana resolved, hammering their present objective into her mind to avoid slicing the Achilles tendon of every man who leered at her with invasive intent. She knew what these loathsome men wanted from her and her sister.

Rape, Aliana thought with incredible rage as the horrific word strobed through her mind. Shira had been raped many times by Craig Winters. She never talked about it directly with the girls, but the Wintersvilla history books didn't shy away from describing Winters' monstrous acts in sordid detail. Aliana didn't read much history, but she had just about memorized the passages describing the patriarchal horrors that the founders of Wintersvilla had endured as children, along with most other women of the past. Aliana's favorite part out of anything she had memorized were the passages about Shira Arcadia gutting Craig Winters with the blade he had created for himself. Shira had only been twelve years old, the same age as the girls when they had escaped the siege of Wintersvilla. Aliana channeled Shira, reminding herself over and over again that the strongest woman who had ever lived was also her mother. She reasoned that if anyone should be afraid, it was everyone else in this Mendel-forsaken tunnel of warped and twisted people, and it was her they should be afraid of.

And yet they want to rape me, Aliana thought as she passed a group of five large panther-like men leering at her with penetrating eyes. Again, she tasted the repugnant word with overwhelming revulsion, illustrating to her why Wintersvilla and its customs surrounding men was necessary. *In chains or dead: that is the only place a man belongs.*

The thought of Wesley and his husband Fullman shot through Aliana's mind, and she was painfully reminded that she was wrong about all men being wicked.

Is it possible this boy really does want to help us, even after Aurelia killed his friend? She wanted nothing more than to slit the boy's throat, take Aurelia's hand in her own, and find a way to escape the Walled City and Cid together. Just the two of them. However, beneath Doe's shirt, his spine glowed with a dim blue light, along with a small area behind his right ear. Previously unnoticed whisker-like hairs growing from Doe's neck and arms twitched as he brushed alongside other people, providing valuable information that Aliana knew was a useful tool in their escape.

He's enhanced, Aliana concluded. *He might very well be enhanced specifically for situations like this. Cowardly situations where one has no choice but to retreat.*

As Doe deftly navigated the sea of people, Aliana glanced at Aurelia and saw that she was still not herself. To Aliana's horror, Aurelia looked as though she was about to fall to the floor and beg for help. Aliana considered and hoped that she might be overestimating her sister's mental state.

It's just the way she's gripping this boy's hand that's making me so worried about her, Aliana noted. *It's like she's desperate for his help…and his touch,* she realized as she unintentionally loosened her own grip on Doe.

Doe stopped suddenly and looked back at Aliana with wide blood-shot eyes, which Aliana assumed was the result of his enhancements working at full speed. The blue glow of his spine and neck dimmed, and Doe was left loudly catching his breath.

"Are you crazy, bromi?" Doe urged Aliana over the blaring music. "You still boomed out of your head or what, eh?"

Aurelia was still holding Doe's hand, but after a few hesitant seconds, she finally let go.

"Aurelia!" Aliana scolded her sister. "What's going on? Is it because of the vortex that white-haired troutface was talking about? Or you're nervous about your prescience not working? Talk to me!"

"Not now!" Aurelia signed using the crude shorthand version of the sign language reserved for moments of life and death on the battlefield.

"We can't just trust him, Aurelia!"

"Oi there, little clucky chicklet," came a raspy, grotesque voice from behind Aliana. "You got a nice mouth, you. I got something I can fill it with, eh?"

Aliana turned and looked up at an overflowing mass of loose yellow skin and fat supported haphazardly on four small struggling legs. A smil-ing, toothless face at the top of the mass beamed at her with desire while a snake-like tongue emerged from its mouth, wetting puckered lips with vile delight. The man's body swelled and jiggled as if he were made en-tirely of raw animal lard.

"You are the single most disgusting fatherfucking creature I've ever seen in my life," Aliana spat, refusing to give into fear, even in the face of this strange man that probably outweighed her by a factor of ten. "I'd rather fuck a Mutant than spend another minute smelling your stink."

The massive man burst into laughter, along with a few other people who had overheard her.

"Little alley punk, eh? I got lots of creds, chicklet. Come back to my hole. You can have some in exchange for clucking, eh?"

This fatherfucker, Aliana thought. *Now's as good a time as any to try activat-ing my power without the glowies. Time to die, troutface.*

Before Aliana could unsheathe her sword, Doe puffed his scrawny chest, prompting his grasshoppers to loudly bristle their wings as Doe said to the man, "What the fuck did she just say, rooster shit? We're on the clock. Dim your glow, eh?"

The overflowing mass of fat snarled but sauntered on, apparently swayed by Doe's words. Then the man squeezed himself into a room that looked like a tiny mess hall. A handful of people stuffed their strange mouths with even stranger food while a line of chefs, all of them enhanced with several additional arms, chopped, cooked, and otherwise prepared a stream of varied meals. Some of the meals appeared to still be moving on the plate.

"Why?" Aliana demanded, willing to risk Eddy and Cid catching up with them in order to see Doe's subtle reactions as she interrogated him. "Why are you helping us?"

"Not now, Ali!" Aurelia warned, but she didn't have the same resolve as usual. Instead, Aurelia just continued looking over Aliana's shoulder, apparently checking for Cid and Eddy to appear around the corner. She kept her hand on the hilt of her sword, likely ready to use her new black body to launch the sword at Cid once more, though Aliana wasn't sure that would be a good idea since Aurelia had missed her last attempt on Cid's life.

Doe pointed to both girls' hands on their swords and said, "That's why I'm helping you. Neither of you really get what you pulled off back there in the cave. You came an inch from impaling Cid with your sword. That's the closest anyone's come to killing him in…forever," Doe marveled. Above them, a swarm of grasshoppers flew by, followed by a man with grasshopper-like features skittering across the ceiling. "You two are fearless. You two might be the only chance we have to finally kill the First Lord and rejoin the rest of Downver. You came so close, Aurelia," Doe said, turning to her with doughy eyes. "He flashed his eyes red at the last second. He's the one who killed Ricky, not you."

Aurelia nodded, looking as though she had already come to the same conclusion.

"And you," Doe offered to Aliana as he frantically looked over her shoulder. "You moved faster than I can even think. Faster than Cid's eyes, even. I don't blame Ricky for trying to shoot you. It was like something out of a superhero sim. No one can move that fast, especially with no apparent enhancements outside of your glowing contacts. I have my doubts that Cid saved your life," Doe said, his voice lowering in a conspiratorial fashion as the music ended and left the passageway in a state of relative calm in between songs.

Nearby, a man with a bulging green frog-like face and webbed, padded hands prowled a stall full of what appeared to be vibrant yellow fruit.

"What do you mean?" Aliana asked as another part of her attention observed the frog-man. As if unable to contain himself, his frog tongue leapt out of his mouth and latched onto one of the fruits before finally depositing it into his hungry mouth. The shopkeeper, a hunched, bald old man without any noticeable changes to his baseline body, was about to shout at the frog-man. To Aliana's surprise, the frog-man reached his arm out as if offering it to the shopkeeper.

"He gave me that vial, didn't he?" Aliana pointed out as she watched the shopkeeper shrug, remove a large blade from his waist, chop the frog-man's arm off, then throw it behind himself onto a table in his shop. The frog-man nodded to the shopkeeper without showing any visible pain, and the shopkeeper nodded back, apparently satisfied with the transaction.

This place just keeps getting stranger and stranger, Aliana thought with a mix of intrigue and battle-ready apprehension.

"Yes, he gave you the phoenix-vial, but I'm talking about the bullet," Doe continued. "Knowing the First Lord, I think it's more likely he directed the bullet to hit you. I think you would have dodged it otherwise. That's how fast you were moving."

"You think he made the bullet hit me?" Aliana checked, nodding in agreement that Doe's theory made sense based on the little she had learned about Cid.

"Of course," Aurelia signed. "Of course that's what happened. I'm such a fool for even considering otherwise...for thinking that Cid might even be my..." she signed, unable to finish her statement. She looked severely disappointed in herself.

"What?" Aliana pressed. "Your what?"

"There's the little hens!" Eddy shouted from the end of the passage they had come from. "Fucking get them!" he screamed, pointing directly at the twin girls standing out in the crowd like trouts in a tree. The bobblehead sentries obeyed Eddy and dashed through the passageway, aiming directly for Doe and the girls.

"Hurry!" Doe urged. "They'll torture you both! We must hurry! My people and I can help you. And you can help us. Please just trust me!"

The Walled City began thumping once more, this time blaring a wailing melody over a fast-paced, heavy beat. Doe reached out a hand, and Aurelia took it. Aliana allowed herself a couple seconds to contemplate turning around and challenging Eddy to another duel to the death, this time without the glowies practically fighting the battle for her.

"Ali," Aurelia urged. "The time for battle will come. I can feel it. But it isn't now. We need Rooli. We need to focus on reviving her before we dive headfirst into carnage."

She said before that her prescience is broken, so does she really know that, or is this just a display of fear? Aliana felt uncertain about her sister's seemingly omniscient knowledge for the first time in her life.

"Fine," Aliana agreed, taking Doe's hand. "But one wrong move, and I slice your spine in half."

Doe nodded, and even before his enhancements had the chance to fully ramp up in power, he was already off, dodging and ducking and weaving with incredible poise and precision.

"Come back here, little crickets!" Eddy wailed. Aliana turned to see that the four bobbleheads were already rapidly closing the gap between them. Apparently, their strange bodies allowed them to navigate the passageway as well as Doe—maybe even better.

They really are like Nomads down here, Aliana gasped at the bizarre diversity of the Walled City's people. They passed a slender woman with scales covering her lower body and feathers coating her upper body handing a green glass cube to a squat black man covered in blinking yellow eyes. The man used his single limb to grab the cube before placing it against his chest, where it slowly sank beneath his skin.

"Doe!" came a garbled electronic voice in the distance. Aliana twisted to see three figures whose bodies altered to reflect the environment, mimicking even the most subtle details with ease. It reminded Aliana of a Huntress' body and the body-membranes that Hunters were attached to like a permanent exo.

"This way," one of the figures issued as Doe ran to them like a rabbit desperate for the safety of its den.

A tall, slender woman draped in what appeared to be sheets of purple moss dove in front of Doe and attempted to grab him around the neck as she hit the ground. Doe easily dodged her, along with another attempt to stop him by a pair of individuals who appeared more like roosters than human beings. They squawked and swung their massive wings at Doe, slicing through numerous onlookers with blades hidden beneath their vibrant arm feathers. This time, as Doe dodged, he flipped forward, then extended his legs into a midair splits. He succeeded in kicking both rooster people in the face, leaving them squawking in a tumbling flurry of feathers and sparking blades.

"Death to Downver!" a young girl with a cybernetic hand and eye shouted excitedly over the music.

"Death to Downver!" a multitude of other people shrieked, jubilant with the thirst to watch a fight take place before their eyes.

As if the people shared a single mind, the crowd abruptly stopped its previously indelible flow. They skirted to the sides of the passage, leaving a small open area at its center where the rooster people and the purple moss woman stood now, glaring at Doe and the girls with death.

"Allow me," Aliana offered, letting go of Doe's hand and unsheathing her sword. She stepped forward into the center of the circle and winked at the three figures.

"Don't die too quickly. I'd like to enjoy myself," she said with a lackadaisical tone, hoping it would strike fear in her enemies.

"We need the girls alive," Eddy shouted from at least twenty feet away. The crowd was so dense and still that Aliana doubted Eddy would be able to reach them. The bobbleheads were another matter, of course.

"We don't have time for this," Doe urged, still holding Aurelia's hand.

"You two run," Aliana commanded. "I'll buy you both some time."

A sudden tug at Aliana's arm nearly knocked her over, and she turned to see that it was Aurelia pulling her away from battle. The three camouflaged figures stood against an opening in the wall that appeared to lead to another equally dense and strange passageway.

"This way!" one of the camouflaged people whispered with a reptilian hiss.

"The Knower is coming," another one issued in grave warning.

Aurelia is the one that Rooli focused on for a reason, Aliana told herself. *She's the one that has to make it. She's the one that's meant for something beyond this world. The vortex,* Aliana thought, repeating the word with a mixture of worry and sorrow that she couldn't place. *I don't even know what the vortex is. Aurelia never said anything about a vortex in her mind. So why does the idea of it make me so incredibly nervous?*

Aliana pulled herself out of Aurelia's grip and took a step back toward the center of the passage.

"Go!" Aliana issued to Aurelia and Doe. She lifted her sword and pointed it at her enemies. "I hunger for battle. This is my decision."

I tapped into my power while I was on the glowies, Aliana realized. *It's just a matter of focus. That has to be it. The power is fucking mine. I shouldn't need glowing mushrooms to activate it.*

Aliana was about to close her eyes and try to force her experience of time to slow down when she was suddenly tugged through the opening in the wall with the force of a maxed out Mutant. She saw Aurelia's black hand wrapped around her chest, and she realized that her sister was carrying her as if she suddenly had Eddy's musculature.

Doe and the girls spilled onto the sticky, grime-covered ground just as a metal panel slid over the opening in the wall, blocking the bobble-heads from reaching them with mere seconds to spare. The camouflaged people were on this side of the wall as well, but they quickly faded into the background without another word.

To their left, a motley crew of modified people, their bodies a patchwork of intimidating cybernetic enhancements and biologically grown appendages, sprawled languidly outside a storefront full of monitors depicting a cartoon landscape of an old world coniferous forest. Five of them jeered and laughed as a sixth individual lay in a chair with large blue lenses over his eyes. A wire led from the lenses into his right temple. He twitched as the character shown on the monitor tripped and fell over branches and roots. The other individuals howled with laughter as the one in the chair convulsed in agony as a pack of wolves pinned the character on the monitor to the ground and stripped him of his flesh.

"Time to feather!" Doe said, helping Aurelia to her feet while looking nervous to do the same for Aliana. "There's so many paths and passages in the Walled City. My chirp-chip helps me with navigation, but Eddy's people are everywhere in this area.

"Cid let us escape," Aurelia signed, shaking her head with confusion. "He was just smiling at me when we first started running from the cave. And...that gray boy was with him too."

"What did she say?" Doe asked, and Aliana rolled her eyes at him for suddenly being willing to stop now that Aurelia was the one who had something to say.

"Does Cid have power outside the Walled City?" Aliana checked rather than translating for her sister.

"Of course not," Doe said with a slight chuckle at the absurdity of Aliana's words. "Cid only has jurisdiction in the Walled City. The rest of Downver belongs to the Lord of Limbs."

"I didn't ask about jurisdiction. I asked about power. If we escape the Walled City, do you think Cid, Eddy, or the gray boy would still be interested in apprehending us...and torturing us?"

Doe shrugged. "I honestly don't know what any of them want, or how far they would be willing to go to get it. And I don't even know who the gray boy is. I just met him today," Doe said, fighting back tears. Aliana assumed he must still be blaming himself for his friend's death, despite saying that he believed Cid to be responsible. "But I doubt that Cid would extend himself beyond the Walled City. I assume he could, if he wanted to, but then he would have to contend with the Lord of Limbs, and she is far more powerful than Cid. She—"

"She?" Aliana practically burst in unison with Aurelia signing the same question. A few people glanced toward Aliana to investigate the burst of sound, then just as quickly returned to their own tasks. A red bearded man with human limbs and a robotic torso stood like a statue with his mouth agape in orgasmic pleasure while people pressed various buttons embedded into his chest. Another individual of indistinct gender projected moving images through the robotic eye in their forehead, depicting small indistinct figures running around the floor through people's legs and around their feet.

"Of course," Doe confirmed, pulling Aliana's momentary shift in attention away from the bizarre sights and back to the present moment. "I've never seen the Lord of Limbs, of course. Just like Cid, she remains elusive. There are even some rumors that she's just a story Cid made up to keep people from leaving the Walled City, though there seems to be just as many people entering the Walled City as leaving, especially nowadays. That's exactly why I need both your help. I'm going to take you back to my family. From there, we can plan an attack on the First Lord and finally end his reign, once and for all. Death to Downver!" Doe proclaimed. "But first we need to help you two blend in. That's why I'm going to bring you to the best silkweavers in all of Downver. They're from the Closet, you know, the Artisan District. They're as green as you can get."

Of course the strongest person in Downver is a woman, Aliana thought with a breath of relief despite knowing perfectly well that wickedness has no gender preference.

"Fine. We'll kill Cid. And then we'll kill the Lord of Limbs. We'll show this woman you all openly fear so pathetically what the unforgiving brutality of a Wintersvilla Warrior really means," Aliana declared with savage delight. Rather than thank her, Doe just stared at her as if she had just suggested seizing Astrea and bringing Mendel back to life.

"We'll go along with you for now," Aliana went on despite Doe's look of panic at her suggestion that they would kill the Lord of Limbs. "That'll give me some time to figure out my powers. Aurelia too. But we have an ally worth a thousand of yours. Her name is Rooli. She's a Nomad. A Hybrid to be exact. She just needs to be revived. We need sunlight and water. So before we do anything, you're going to take us to the Dark District—the place Eddy said has sunlight. Then we'll help you."

Aliana turned to Aurelia, who nodded in agreement with her plan.

"A Nomad?" Doe said, shaking his head as if they had just suggested allowing a pack of Hunters free entrance to Downver.

"So what?" Aliana said.

"But…she'll infect us all!" Doe nearly yelped with primal fear, as if the presence of a Nomad was even worse than that of a Hunter. "That's why they aren't allowed in Downver. Forget just the Walled City. Everyone in Downver will turn into Nomads if you bring a Nomad here! She'll—"

"What the Muto fuck are you mewling about?" Aliana demanded, interrupting Doe's nonsensical claims.

"Everyone knows that you have to mentally consent to becoming a Nomad. It doesn't just spread like a disease," Aliana corrected, noting how stupid and ignorant Doe and likely every other boy and man in the Walled City were, despite their wildly varied enhancements.

The Lord of Limbs is probably the only truly intelligent and cunning person in Downver, Aliana considered. *She's a woman, and she's in charge of the whole underground city, after all. But if we cross paths, I'll decapitate her as if she were a rebellious slave.*

Before Doe could answer, an electronic voice said, "Oh my! Oh my!

I'm glowing oh so green. Yes, oh so very green! Come here my little darling crickets and let me bask in the light of those radiant eyes."

Doe and the girls turned to see a stall in the wall shimmering with the iridescent glow of jewelry crafted from visible heaps of discarded tech and covered in bioluminescent fungi. The vendor, a genderless being with large, protruding eyes on each side of its head, nodded to the curvy, hyper-sexualized woman leaving the jewelry stall in a skimpy red dress that barely contained her body. She held a necklace pulsing with a soft, otherworldly violet light that was similar to but far less radiant than Aurelia's eyes. Her oversized breasts reminded Aliana of Eddy's tattoo, and she couldn't help snickering at the audacity and absurdity of attempting to battle, or even just live a life of peace, with such gigantic bags of fat hanging from one's body. Still, Aliana couldn't deny that her face was overwhelmingly beautiful, even more than Myriam—something Aliana didn't realize was even possible. Outside of her overwhelming beauty and skin-tight red dress, she didn't appear cybernetically enhanced or biologically modified in any visible way. Only her electronic voice gave her away as being modified.

"Madam Aubrey," Doe gasped, apparently surprised by her presence.

"All three of you can come live with me and the others in my house of pleasure. We take care of each other there," Madam Aubrey offered sweetly, her lips pursed and her eyebrows raised with delight. Her voice and scent were like an intoxicating ambrosia, making Aliana forget all about what they were supposed to be doing.

I should go with her, Aliana concluded. *She can help us. She's so beautiful and warm. I want to hold her. I want to be held by her.*

"These girls belong to the First Lord," Doe said as if from miles away. All of a sudden, Aliana was back as if from a dream-like daze.

"What the Muto fuck just happened?" Aliana demanded. She turned to see that her sister had also fallen into the same daze of desperately wanting to go with the woman.

"She has voice and pheromone enhancements. She hypnotized you. The only reason it didn't work on me is the same reason it doesn't work on most kids: anti-charm enhancements are cheap and take up the bare minimum psych-space. Some families can't even afford the cheapest enhancements, though, so a lot of those kids end up stuck working for the Madam. Don't let her voice trick you—she's as vile as they come."

"What do you mean these girls belong to the First Lord, my little sweetness? If they belong to the First Lord, then why are they here walking the streets with you?" Madam Aubrey asked with alluring congeniality and generosity.

"It's Armando!" a flock of bird-people squawked in the distance, jumping into the air and pushing through others in a flurry. Their panic was contagious, and it spread across the whole of the visible passage in a matter of seconds.

"Armando coming!" a trio of burly men warned. A swarm of bees covered each man, entering and leaving their baseline and additional orifices without the men seeming to even notice.

"It's him! He's here!" a woman modified to look like a lioness roared as she ran past. Her thick golden fur revealed the glow of bioluminescent tattoos on her fully covered skin as she ran away in terror, her tail madly swishing the air to help with balance.

Aliana turned back to find that Madam Aubrey was nowhere to be seen. Shops and stalls slammed their metal panels shut. People skittered, flew, crawled, and rolled away, clearing the passageway so that, other than Doe and the girls, there was only Armando. The half-machine man just stood there, his eyes steadfastly staring at the ground despite facing directly toward Aurelia.

"She is coming," Armando signed using the secret Wintersvilla battle language. "Go to the silkweavers. Prepare yourselves."

"Please, Alpha, sir. We are just—" Doe began, but Aurelia stepped forward, cutting him off.

"Aurelia," Aliana began, worried what her sister might do.

"Are you our enemy?" Aurelia signed to him.

Without looking up, Armando signed back, "I am whatever I need to be."

"I thought you half-brained cricket shits said you knew a shortcut!" came Eddy's exasperated voice as he emerged alongside the four bobbleheads from one of the many passages that intersected this passage at various, seemingly random points along the wall.

"Forget it!" Eddy screamed. "Let's just get them. Alive, got it bromis?"

Aliana turned back to see that Armando was gone without a trace.

"What the fuck!" Aliana spat. "Everyone just knows how to up and disappear in this place?"

A section of the wall a few feet away opened suddenly, and a woman with large horns growing out of her head and small wings growing out of her back stuck her upper body through the opening.

"This way!" she told them with urgency in every one of her features.

Again, Aliana felt the urge to turn around and slice the bobbleheads to pieces and then Eddy to chunks, but Doe and Aurelia were already running to the other side of the wall, so Aliana did the same, refusing to separate from Aurelia for her sake.

The horned woman slid the metal wall closed behind them, once again blocking Eddy and the bobbleheads.

"Thank you, Lily," Doe said, shaking the woman's hand through some type of memorized pattern of movements.

"Who're your new friends?" the woman asked as she parted her shirt to reveal a set of blades, as if subtly warning the girls that she could defend herself.

"He said you need to take us to the silkweavers, whoever that is. You think it's a trap?" Aliana asked Doe, ignoring the woman. The woman cocked her head but remained silent, seeming to understand that they were presently on the run from death.

"Probably," Doe agreed. "But we don't have a choice. That's where I was going to bring you two in the first place."

"What about your prescience, Aurelia?" Aliana asked. "Anything?"

"You know the way from here, little bromi?" Lily, the horned woman asked before Aurelia could respond.

"Death to Downver," Doe said with a nod of his head.

"Death to John fucking Downver. May his soul forever roil in turmoil," the woman winked, and she smiled to reveal a metal set of teeth that read *Fuck Death* from her top to bottom lip.

"I really, really need a set of badass metal teeth," Aliana said aloud as Doe proceeded through what appeared to be a dimly lit utility tunnel. There were a handful of figures in the shaft, but none of them seemed to take notice of the girls or Doe as they passed. The figures appeared to be working on machinery embedded in the walls of the dark shaft. Each figure used their robotic limbs with dozens of spindly fingers to dig into the innards of each machine, repairing or altering them in some way.

As they exited the tunnel, Doe and the girls passed through a snaking crowd of people and into another darkly lit utility tunnel. More robotic-limbed figures reached inside machines with their numerous limbs without taking any notice of the girls or Doe.

They exited the second tunnel, made a hard right followed by a hard left, and then Doe dropped down a small hole in the floor, followed by Aurelia. Not wanting to appear fearful, Aliana jumped into the hole after her sister without even looking down.

Aliana fell onto a jelly-like ground, softening her descent but also forcing her to reach out her hands to avoid falling over. She felt light strands of a sticky gossamer substance wrap around her hands, and she turned to see an empty cave hollow with nearly every square inch coated in a pearl-white gossamer webbing. Glowing mushrooms of every conceivable color grew sporadically from the ground. They were similar to the Feeding Cave glowies, but their caps were more cylindrical. Several figures swept across the walls and ceiling, emerging from crevices carved out of the hollow. The figures skittered across and through the thick webbing with staggering rapidity and ease. As they came into the light of the mushrooms, Aliana and Aurelia parted their oversized jackets and unsheathed their swords in unison at what they saw.

Giant insects! Aliana gasped, gripping her sword even tighter. She glanced at Aurelia and saw that she was just as ready to battle out of this trap that Doe had clearly led them into.

She was about to pivot and slit the boy's throat for his betrayal when his grasshoppers suddenly launched themselves from his shoulders and dove directly at the five large insectoid people standing at the center of the hollow. Each of their many legs were careful not to crush any of the mushrooms. They had bulbous lower bodies akin to that of old world spiders while their upper bodies appeared more or less humanoid, with hands and discernable human faces, despite the antenna atop their heads and large spider-like fangs instead of a mouth full of teeth. Doe's grasshoppers landed on the closest insect-person, but rather than attack, they seemed to relish their presence. A multitude of spinnerets on each of the insectoid people's abdomens produced thick strands of white silk, which they added to the webbing already covering what Aliana assumed was their home.

Silkweavers, Aliana realized unnervingly.

The closest silkweaver patted the grasshoppers once more on the back, and then they nodded and directed the grasshoppers back to Doe. As the grasshoppers took their places on Doe's shoulders, Doe bowed to the silkweavers and said, "We need your help."

"We know," the silkweavers said in eerie unison, each of their voices a unique pitch that somehow harmonized into a single unsettling voice. Aliana tempered her deep, instinctual fear of these insect-people by reminding herself that their form and their environment made their skittering movements and collective voice even creepier than they probably intended.

"They're on our side," Aurelia signed, easing her grip on her sword with confidence. "I concede that my prescience is broken, but I'm certain of it all the same. They're going to help us, Ali. Ease off your sword."

Aliana was used to her sister always knowing what to do, and though she was more reluctant than ever to heed her words, she placed her faith in Aurelia, likely the only person left in the world she could trust.

No, Aliana told her sudden intrusive thoughts, resisting the urge to just accept once and for all that Shira and Myriam were dead and that she would never see them again.

"You can trust them. I swear it," Doe said, and he nodded to the five silkweavers, all of them nearly identical, save the thick hair growing from their insect abdomens and human torsos. Each silkweaver's hair grew in a shade distinct from the rest.

The gray-haired silkweaver at the front of the group who had caressed Doe's grasshoppers moved forward and said in unison with the others, "Virus and Cure, it is truly an honor. We will clean, clothe, and condition you for the battle in the Dark District and the great war of the future."

"Battle? War?" Aliana asked, tempted to place her hand back on the hilt of her sword as the other four silkweavers skittered forward, two of them moving across the ground behind the gray-haired silkweaver and the other two across the web-filled walls.

"Just listen," they said in unison, their voices soft and reedy like the chirp of a cricket. "Fate is already crumbling. Soon it will shatter completely. Both of you must be prepared to push yourselves far beyond your limits."

In a single fluid stroke, the gray-haired silkweaver gently guided Doe and his grasshoppers a few feet further into the hollow, allowing the other four silkweavers to gather around the girls. A magenta-haired and cyan-haired silkweaver surrounded Aurelia, while an azure-haired and vibrant yellow-haired silkweaver took to Aliana. As if moving to a choreographed dance, the creatures removed the girls' makeshift clothing, stripping them nude. Doe lowered his head, offering the girls privacy despite the silkweavers towering over them and gazing at them with a multitude of tiny eyes spread across their faces.

Aurelia had swiftly removed the shard of Rooli from the jacket and presently clung to it with her left hand.

The yellow-haired silkweaver went for Aliana's sword, and in response, Aliana gritted her teeth and growled like a rabid dog.

"Do what you will, but you're not taking my blade, fatherfucker," Aliana warned.

"It's only for a moment, little sweetness," the silkweaver explained gently along with all the others. "I'll place the blade right next to your feet. At any time, you can grab it and kill us all, if that is what you wish to do."

Aliana was taken aback at their show of fearlessness and acceptance of death. She couldn't help feeling a kinship to these creatures, strange and unnerving as they were. Aliana nodded and allowed the silkweaver to remove her tattered sheath from around her waist and place her sword a few inches from her feet. She glanced over at Aurelia and saw that the magenta-haired silkweaver was spewing fresh-made silk through the spinnerets of its insect abdomen. It wrapped the silk tightly around Aurelia's body, weaving it into a thin, matted fabric that covered her skin like finely tailored clothing. Around her vital areas, the silk was made thicker, providing extra protection. The cyan-haired silkweaver ran its human hands through Aurelia's hair, removing grime and blood through an unknown means. Aurelia just stood there with her eyes closed, seeming to relish these calm moments of darkness and silence. The silkweavers worked so rapidly and lightly that Aliana didn't realize she was now receiving the exact same treatment. Seconds later they had already finished.

The silkweavers gave a final gaseous spray of something sweet from their spinnerets, fogging the girls with an agent that cleaned them of any lingering grime and left them feeling well rested, as if they had just slept for weeks straight in just a single moment.

"This is the cleanest you've ever been in your life, Ali," Aurelia signed humorously, and Aliana snickered with bittersweet nostalgia. Shira had often jokingly referred to Aliana as a dirty mongrel on account of her hatred of baths. Aliana preferred the smell of sweat and exertion to soap, even the neutral-smelling kind.

Aurelia wore a form-fitted black and violet silk suit, while Aliana wore an identical form-fitted white and emerald suit. Even their feet were covered in thick silk that served as comfortable, perfectly fitted shoes. The silkweavers had also taken the liberty of spinning them all new sheathes and straps for their swords.

Aurelia placed the shard of Rooli within a pocket on her thigh. The pocket was the perfect size, as if it had been designed specifically to hold the shard.

"You look amazing," Doe told Aurelia, his voice all breath. Aurelia smiled and blushed despite herself. Aliana shook her head in further disbelief that Aurelia was clearly enjoying this boy's attraction.

She's attracted to boys, Aliana realized in full force, no longer thinking of it only as a possibility. Aurelia being attracted to anyone, boys or girls, had never even crossed Aliana's mind. It wasn't something Aurelia had ever brought up, and every time Aliana pointed out other girls she was attracted to, Aurelia always just nodded or changed the subject.

I'm happy for her. But he's still a boy. We can't trust him, and I have to make sure her heart doesn't get in the way of her head, Aliana told herself, exhaling sharply at the prospect of Aurelia acting so unlike herself. *Cid just really got under her skin,* Aliana concluded.

"You have both been cleaned and clothed. Now you must be conditioned," the silkweavers said in unison. "Cure," they said, all five turning to face her. "You must believe in yourself during the battle ahead. The glowies permanently unlocked a doorway within you. You must have the courage to walk through that doorway on your own this time, without the help of outside substance. You have done it before. You can do it again. Trust those you love, and you will overcome your limitations."

Without giving Aliana time to respond, they turned to Aurelia and said, "Virus, your body is a temporary construct, as is the case with all bodies and forms. You will know what to do when the time comes. Your prescience isn't broken. It is fate that is breaking, and so your prescience is becoming obsolete. You are greater than fate, Virus. You will see that soon. Very soon. Once you shatter fate completely, everything will become as clear as a perfect reflection."

With that, the five silkweavers bowed their heads and said, "You have been conditioned." A small section of thick webs at the back of the hollow parted, revealing a crevice in the rock wall.

"That's it?" Aliana checked. "That's what you call conditioning? And are these thin, flimsy clothes supposed to protect us or something?"

"My clothes are made of the same material," Doe said, presenting his sleeveless shirt and loose slacks. "It's able to stop all blades and most projectiles, including bullets, like the one Ricardo fired at you," Doe said with a painful ache in his voice. "It's the best armor in Downver, and the lightest too. The silkweavers are the most legit. I told you, bromi."

"Can this fabric really stop a bullet?" Aliana asked in disbelief.

"It depends on the weapon," the silkweavers responded levelly. "But yes, it can repel most projectile weapons you will encounter in the Walled City or the other six districts of Downver. Our armor will prove essential in the war ahead. We are honored to be of service to the Virus and the Cure. Go now. There is still a careful timing to everything if fate is to be fully shattered. Go now through the crevice. We use it to covertly exit and enter the Walled City so we may freely trade our silks with the other districts. It will lead you to the Dark District."

At the mention of the Dark District, Aurelia perked up even more than Aliana, looking both hopeful and despondent. She lovingly placed her hand on her leg, where a bulge revealed the shard of Rooli.

"We're going to make it," Aliana assured her sister. "Rooli is going to make it!"

Aurelia furrowed her brow and signed, "Let's go, Ali. No more time to waste."

She stepped forward toward Doe, who turned and began walking toward the crevice as if offering himself to go first in Aurelia's stead in case there might be danger ahead.
"This is where you must part ways," the silkweavers told Doe and Aurelia. "Forever."

"Forever?" Doe whispered painfully, and he stared longingly into Aurelia's vibrant violet eyes. Aurelia breathed deeply, then exhaled and stepped forward without saying goodbye.

Aliana smirked and joined her sister, walking past Doe and shoulder-checking him as she passed.

"Thanks for the help, bromi," Aliana offered, using the Walled City lingo with a genuine nod of respect.

"Wait!" Doe gasped, ignoring Aliana completely. "Please wait, Aurelia," he pleaded, and he ran to her with tears in his eyes. To Aliana's surprise, Aurelia turned around and had tears in her eyes as well.

"I'll learn to speak your language," Doe said. He grabbed both her hands with each of his own, and Aurelia didn't resist his touch. "Our paths will cross again. I know it," Doe said, but Aurelia's sad eyes told Aliana that her sister didn't have the same faith in what the future held. Doe pulled Aurelia to his chest, forcing Aliana to resist the urge to jump forward and rip him away from her vulnerable sister.

She was always the one that seemed to be looking after me, Aliana reflected. Tears streamed down Aurelia's glistening black cheeks as she held her eyes firmly shut and squeezed Doe just as tightly as he squeezed her.

I wish you would have told me you like boys, Aliana thought. *You must have been keeping it a secret for a long time. I'm sorry for making you hide so much from me, Aurelia. And I'm sorry for hiding my time ability from you as well. I wish I could tell her all this,* Aliana thought, but she didn't interrupt her sister's embrace. She knew how lonely her sister was. How ugly she thought of herself. How she had lived behind a face mask her entire life up until just a day earlier, when everything had suddenly changed so fast.

I'm happy for you, Aurelia. I wish you could have this kind of happiness forever. Aliana wished the same for herself as well, though she knew that wouldn't be the case for either of them. *We are the Cure and the Virus. We are meant for something beyond this world. And we don't even know what that is. No one fucking does.*

"It's time," the silkweavers stated, gentler than ever.

Doe broke their embrace as if forcing himself to do it for Aurelia's sake. Aurelia clung to his fingers with her own, appearing to hesitate for just a moment as she cherished Doe's warm touch.

"Don't forget me," Doe said, and then he kissed her on the cheek and again on the lips. Aurelia grabbed the back of his neck and pulled him back, kissing him deeply, their tears intermingling with their tongues.

"Holy Muto, Aurelia!" Aliana cheered, crying tears of happiness for her sister.

She deserves to feel wanted by whoever the fuck she chooses, boy or girl. After me, she's the fiercest warrior in the world, Aliana knew, stifling her tears over Myriam and Shira, who she was reluctantly growing to accept were both long dead at the unforgiving hands of the Butcher.

Finally, as if coming to the same conclusion at the exact same time, Doe and Aurelia tore themselves away from each other, their fingers clasping desperately to feel the other's touch for just a moment longer.

"Let's go, Ali," Aurelia signed, and then she strode to the crevice.

Aliana stared at Doe through threatening slits, warning him with just a glance that if he were to ever break her sister's heart, she would carve his still-beating heart right out of his chest.

Doe and the silkweavers nodded to Aliana, and Aliana reluctantly nodded back.

"May Mendel be on your side," Aliana offered, prompting the silkweavers to shudder.

Aliana wanted to force more answers out of these strange people, but instead she turned and jogged to her sister. The silk clothing felt weightless despite its comfort and excellent thermal regulation. Aliana entered the crevice and peered to the end of a haphazardly bored twenty-foot tunnel. Aurelia stood at the terminus, her suit and even her lustrous platinum hair a mere shadow amidst the light pouring in from outside. As Aliana caught up with her sister, she realized that Aurelia was gazing in mesmerized awe at what she saw. Aliana stepped into the light, and as her eyes adjusted, she felt equally mesmerized.

Incredible, Aliana thought as a view of less than half of the entire dome-shaped city of Downver unfurled before them, making Aliana feel dizzy as she reeled at the city's unfathomable density, diversity, and complexity of architecture and life. The mile-high curved rock walls of Downver's edges could barely be seen behind the architectural vistas built all the way to the uppermost canopy of the hollow dug out of the Earth's innards by the old world Titan John Downver. In the scant areas where the walls could be seen, sparkling veins of various metals and minerals beckoned Aliana's eyes with arresting awe. The multicolored rock walls revealed colossal rivers of gold, silver, amethyst, emerald, ruby, sapphire—every shade and caliber of gem and precious metal.

Despite their needed urgency, Aliana couldn't help breathing deeply, the cool and moist air carrying scents of earth and growth—the opposite of Wintersvilla's salty ocean mists and machine oil. Every breath felt pure, almost ancient, as if inhaling the very history of this place, despite it being less than five decades old. Rocky spires, like ancient obelisks constructed by giants that would make Biofreaks appear like infants, extended from the ground to the ceiling of the city. Each great spire, like a sentinel observing its personal domain, marked the center of a new district, distinct in activity and culture.

The seven districts of Downver, Aliana marveled as she recounted the scant amount of history she could remember from her lessons.

The rough surface of each spire was softened by the embrace of verdant, multicolor vines, curling and twirling around the spires as each of their leaves and flowers occasionally kissed the fleeting shadows of scurrying insects. Many of the vines bore bioluminescent leaves and fruits, speckling the twilight of the cave with a soft lantern glow.

Aliana was astonished to see whole metropolises and neighborhoods nestled between the hulking stone pillars and the dozens of thinner but still mighty stalagmites that didn't yet fully reach the ceiling. The sprawling cities were like coral reefs teeming with the flurry of old world ocean life. Structures of varying architecture were built directly atop one another, each unique and made from lustrous stone and bioluminescent chitin. Some homes were precariously balanced on rocky spires, while others hung suspended by sturdy ropes or entwined fungi.

Aliana turned to see that Aurelia's eyes were equally wide in amazement and her body appeared just as arrested by the view as she watched children race atop bioluminescent beetles while elders exchanged stories under the warm embrace of mushroom canopies. Roosters and hens fluttered here and there, gobbling jumping crickets and grasshoppers as if it were their city-appointed duty. Ladders and bridges of braided vines and fungal matter connected homes and marketplaces, creating a maze of pathways for the city's residents.

From their vantage, the girls could see citizens crossing ziplines and bridges, traveling to and fro, their movements fluid and practiced. Some of them were young and looked to just be having fun, while others struggled with makeshift rickshaws made of what appeared to be metal scrap and fungus. Unlike the denizens of the Walled City, the people of the other districts appeared only moderately modified, with the occasional cybernetic limb or minorly altered body part.

Aliana shook her head in disbelief that the scale, complexity, and voracity of Downver made Wintersvilla seem like a tiny, stagnant pond compared to this raging, vast ocean.

"This is…" Aliana trailed off as she marveled at a platoon of five grasshoppers the size of old world buses darting across her vision, sailing miles through the sky as they used their relatively stout wings to glide and balance. People with metal body parts sat on the back of the grasshoppers using ornately jeweled saddles, and as the grasshoppers landed on a large vine-covered spire, the people shifted to hold themselves vertically with their mount.

"Fatherfucking incredible," Aurelia signed, finishing Aliana's statement for her. "That must be the Dark District," Aurelia signed, pulling them both back into the present moment. She pointed straight ahead with her void-black hand.

Separated by many miles of striated, layered neighborhoods full of joyous laughter and vitriolic shouting, the Dark District shimmered eerily in a dance of ethereal light and shadows, stretching to the far wall like a hauntingly beautiful, dimly lit dream. It wasn't nearly as dense as the rest of the underground city, serving as a stark reprieve from the overwhelming intricacy bustling outside of it. Crystal-clear waterways snaked through luminous forests of titanic mushrooms, reflecting their soft bioluminescent glow that painted the district in somber brushstrokes of jade, lavender, and deep cerulean. The district's architecture, organic and flowing, made it seem as if nature itself had meticulously sculpted every edifice and pathway. The people of the Dark District, dressed in enigmatic shades of obsidian, moved like shadows between the luminescent fungal forests, their whispers merging with the haunting allure of the landscape. At the very center of the Dark District, a vast lake of placid water stretched like a moat around the central spire. Its shimmering surface was pierced here and there by columns of diamond-shimmering sunlight extending from the ceiling to the very bottom of the lake's vibrant flora and fauna laden depths.

"Water and sunlight!" Aliana cheered, nearly falling over the ledge in her excitement. Aurelia caught her by the waist, but Aliana couldn't contain her excitement.

"There's sunlight down here, Aurelia. We just…we just…" she said, observing that there was no way to easily cross the multiple miles separating them from the Dark District.

"We're at least a hundred feet up, and I don't see any way down from here," Aliana said, feeling her excitement turn to anger bubbling beneath her skin. "What the fuck? Did those creepy crawlers lie to us?" Aliana said, still unable to take her eyes off the giant grasshoppers jumping from spire to spire. "Maybe if we can get ahold of one of those giant insects?" Aliana considered.

Aurelia didn't respond, so Aliana finally broke her gaze away from the colossal, intrepid creatures and turned to her sister.

"You okay?" Aliana checked, seeing that there were still lingering tears in Aurelia's eyes. Aurelia couldn't even look at her sister, appearing embarrassed and ashamed.

"I don't care that he's a boy, Aurelia. I love Wintersvilla, but I love you more. You know that, don't you?"

Aurelia huffed with repressed pain and shook her head in further disappointment at herself.

"I love you too, Aliana," she signed. "We can talk about all that later. Right now we need to get to the Dark District, and like you said, there doesn't seem to be any way down or across. At least, not from this hole in the wall. But I have an idea. You have to just trust me. Can you do that?"

"With my life and my death," Aliana signed back in the simple derivative of the battle language that the girls had made up together when they were only five or six years old. It was their own secret, intimate language—something that belonged to them and no one else.

Aurelia nodded in thanks to her sister, then without hesitating, she lifted her left arm, and with explosive speed from her black right hand, she sliced right through the so-called blade-proof silk and amputated her left arm at the shoulder.

Blood sprayed in heartbeat synced spurts, and Aliana yelped at the sight of Aurelia's arm plummeting in free fall to the crowded streets below. A cacophony of shouts and shrill screams followed soon after.

Aliana turned back to find that her sister's arm had already been replaced with an identical void-black arm.

"Did you fucking know that would happen?" Aliana gasped.

"Not entirely," Aurelia admitted. "But the silkweavers said I would know what to do...and I just had a feeling it would work."

"You're fucking crazy," Aliana laughed despite her worry for her sister's wellbeing. "I fucking love it."

"Now, listen," Aurelia stated, deathly serious. "No matter what happens, you need to revive Rooli. You must revive Enduring Ironwood. Do you understand, Aliana?" Aurelia signed with a gravity that sent shivers down Aliana's spine.

"Yes, sister. I understand," Aliana confirmed, mirroring her sister's sudden lucid stoicism.

Below them, the faint rhythm of hammers and chisels could be heard, and Aliana found that no matter where she looked, people were crafting, building, and expanding the wondrous underground realm.

"Trust me," Aurelia signed, and without warning, she grabbed Aliana by the waist and lifted her with ease using her void-black limbs. She shifted Aliana to her left arm, holding her easily as if Aliana weighed no more than an infant. Then, to Aliana's horror, Aurelia used the power of her black hand to swing her sword across the top of her thighs, severing the silk clothing and both her legs away from her body in a grisly deluge of blood and viscera.

Holy Muto! Aliana gasped, but she had no time to react otherwise. She was tempted to try activating her power, but she remembered that Aurelia had asked her to trust her, so she gritted her teeth and placed her faith in her sister.

The girls plummeted in free fall toward the ground full of horrified onlookers, most of them plainly human, as opposed to the hybrid mosaic of diversity within the Walled City. Several women pointed and screamed at the girls, while others just stood frozen as if dumbfounded by the macabre sight.

Another second passed, and a sonic boom suddenly launched the girls away from the rapidly encroaching ground with shocking g-force, rocketing them through the air toward the Dark District, their vector pointed directly at the gigantic lake blanketed by golden beams of sunlight from above. Their velocity finally leveled off, and Aliana estimated that they must be moving roughly sixty or seventy miles per hour based on the comparable g-force that accompanied exo jumps that she used to take part in by strapping herself to Shira or Myriam's exo. She calculated the distance to the Dark District to be roughly four or five miles away, which meant they would make it there in less than five minutes.

Who would have thought my ability to process battle estimations and calculations would come in handy for flying? Aliana marveled as they sailed through the air, her sister aligning herself to ensure they didn't hit any major or minor stalagmites or buildings.

Aliana glanced behind them and saw a fresh, still-crumbling crater in the outside, windowless wall of the Walled City.

Aurelia's legs grew back, and she used them to kick us off the wall, Aliana realized, marveling at her sister's fearlessness and strength.

Like the giant grasshoppers, the girls sailed through the air, and Aliana couldn't help looking about and marveling at the grand vista of life below and all around them. To their immediate left, a district loomed regal and unyielding at the very center of Downver. Proud pillars and majestically ornate edifices sparkled with pearl and golden hues. Terraced gardens and layers of balconies brimming with varied plant life formed intricate mosaics that were interspersed with milky, cascading waterfalls.

Beautiful, Aliana gasped at the imposing yet resplendent grandeur of the district at Downver's center. She twisted and saw that many miles behind the bustling central hub of golden pillars, another district's spires and bridges revealed a cybernetic wonderland sprawling beneath neon lights.

Aliana forced herself to focus on their target and turned once more to survey the Dark District.

"We're going to make it, Aurelia," Aliana said as their acceleration leveled out. The lake was no more than a thousand feet in the distance.

We've overcome so much. There is nothing that can stop us now, Aliana thought, injecting resolve into her rapidly pulsing heart.

"You did it, Aurelia!" Aliana shouted in giddy excitement at her sister's newfound ability to slice through blade-proof material and literally launch them directly to their objective.

"You—" Aliana began, but she was interrupted by an unmistakable flash of red near the water's edge.

It's him! Aliana gasped at Cid the Knower, Eddy, the bobbleheads, and a motley band of other altered humans.

Aurelia's body went limp suddenly, and though she was still breathing and her arm remained tight around her sister's waist, Aliana saw that Cid had knocked Aurelia out with his eyes.

Fatherfucker! Aliana gasped as the girls plummeted toward a small grove of cerulean mushrooms growing from the mineral-sparkling soil at the edge of the lake. Cid and his band of goons were casually walking toward the mushroom grove.

"Aurelia!" Aliana shouted. "Wake the fuck up! Please!"

Aliana was relieved that her sister was clearly just in a deep slumber rather than dead, but that didn't help the fact that they were about to become bloody smears in a glowing mushroom forest.

This isn't the time to try out my power, Aliana thought, her mind racing faster than ever. *I should have fought Eddy and his goons in the Walled City when I had the chance. I should have learned how to use my power properly back there.*

"Focus!" Aliana heard Myriam say. But it didn't seem like it came from her own mind. It seemed like Myriam was standing right beside her. Aliana gasped with the sudden realization that she and Aurelia were frozen in midair. Cid and his goons appeared paralyzed midstep like marble statues. Grasshoppers hovered in place above a still image of the unruly people of Downver directly below them. Perfect, unnerving silence made Aliana's heart skip a beat with anxiousness before finally celebrating that they were still alive and might even have a chance to stay that way.

Time froze completely! Aliana rejoiced while at the same time cursing herself for not fully understanding how to consciously activate her power at will. *But at least it worked now. We have to just get through this. One step at a time.*

"Watch the mind beg," Myriam said at a distance, and Aliana shifted the vision of her paralyzed eyes to see Myriam and Shira standing in midair a few feet away. They both stared directly at her, their faces stern and unyielding.

"Watch it whine and plead," Shira continued.

Mom! Aliana thought sorrowfully, directing her desperate mind to these seemingly real visions of the two most important people in her life beyond Aurelia and Rooli, these two people who she now fully accepted were gone. Forever.

"Watch as it bites the hand that feeds," Myriam continued.

"It is a wild dog without a master. It is full of fear and rage," Shira said with a twitch in her left eye.

Focus on them! Aliana demanded, and she forced her mind away from her pleading sorrow and desperate anger and placed it directly in the present moment, here with these visions of Shira and Myriam who were unaffected by her power.

"The mind needs you to be strong. It needs you to be unwavering. It needs you to be its unbreakable master," Myriam intoned.

"Then it will obey. Then it can be trained. Then it can be transformed from a wild dog to a faithful friend," Shira said with tears in her eyes and a smile on her face.

Myriam went on, fury and savagery painted across her features. "It will still howl, growl, and beg. But watch as it remains at your heel. It does not stray or wander. It does not fear or worry. The mind respects and obeys you."

Shira bowed her head to Aliana and said, "It is no longer a wild dog. It is yours. You are its master."

I am my mind's master, Aliana repeated within. She felt a shudder run the length of her spine like energy across a high power cable. *I am in control,* Aliana realized, processing a profound paradigm shift in her entire consciousness.

Shira and Myriam nodded, tears in both of their eyes now.

"We love you, Aliana. Forever," Shira whispered.

"Forever," Myriam vowed, her unwavering voice a raspy growl full of indelible fortitude.

Aurelia and Rooli appeared beside the women.

"Forever," Aurelia promised with both her fingers and voice, which she was once more able to use during these hallucinatory experiences. Rooli nodded in stoic agreement with Aurelia.

Forever, Aliana told herself, certain beyond anything that Shira and Myriam were somehow with her at this very moment—in her heart and her training and her lucid visions. They were with her forever. She would never be alone.

Forever, Aliana repeated, and she found that she was able to remain in control of her emotions and intentions as a sudden gong blast of sound returned the world back to normal speed.

Aliana grunted and shifted her weight, loosening Aurelia's grip. With a controlled movement, she readjusted her hold on Aurelia and deftly repositioned her body to place her feet against her sister's back. Finally, she jutted her legs powerfully toward the lake, redirecting her sister to land in the water. At the last second, she gripped the hilt of Aurelia's sword and let the movement of her body unsheathe it without having to pull and risk her sister's path hitting too close to the lake's edge.

You and Rooli are both going into that lake, Aurelia, and I'm going after Cid. I'll buy Rooli enough time to be revived and I'll buy you enough time to wake up. I'm going to kill them all, Aliana knew with diamond clarity as she passed into the canopy of the mushroom forest, losing sight of Aurelia.

Cid, Eddy, the bobbleheads, and the other assorted goons were just entering the forest, passing beneath the glowing cerulean hoods of one of the largest mushrooms.

She knew that in another second she would hit the ground, breaking every bone in her body.

Now! Aliana commanded her mind with the will of a master to a loyal friend rather than a slave.

Time slowed to a crawl at her command. She had just a moment to observe a multitude of glowing mushroom-shaped people growing from the ground beneath the canopy of hulking mushrooms. Some retained their human features, while others were further into the process of complete mushroom transformation.

These people turn themselves into mushrooms, Aliana gasped, but she didn't have time to linger on the thought.

You're mine, Aliana thought, shifting her vision to Cid's permanently conceited smile. With her mind and thoughts unaffected by time being slowed, Aliana waited a few moments for his eyes behind the black lenses to begin their color shift, and then she dove as fast as possible, flipping forward to avoid his direct line of sight.

Even if this doesn't work and I die, Aurelia and Rooli will still be alive, Aliana thought, consoling her sudden worry.

Be the mind's unwavering master, Myriam lashed, her voice a loving whip of discipline.

Focus! came Shira's tender yet unyielding tone. *Cast away fear. There is only this moment.*

As she was still conscious, Aliana concluded that she must have successfully avoided Cid's vision. She directed her flipping body over a squat, fat mushroom with a sloping head just a few feet below her.

Loosening her body, she allowed her battle instincts to take over. She threw the swords directly into the air in front of herself then continued tucking her head to her waist. Her slow movements and unimpeded mind allowed Aliana to perfect her roll across the spongy head of the mushroom, spreading her kinetic energy across her back and into the mushroom that apparently had once been a human.

Consciously commanding time to remain slow, Aliana pivoted with perfect precision and bounced with the flats of her feet off the head of the mushroom, catching a sword in each hand as she directed her body like a projectile directly at Cid's face.

Die, you smug fatherfucking Muto fuck! Aliana snarled at Cid's pretentious, self-satisfactory grin. She aimed the swords at either side of his black lenses and jutted her arms forward, savoring these final moments before the blades would be plunged through Cid the Knower's squelching brain.

The tip of each blade was only a few inches away from making contact when Cid's lenses began shifting in color with unexpected rapidity, turning from black to crimson and finally to bright red in less than a heartbeat's time.

The world boomed with another profound, gong-like resonance, returning Aliana's experience of time back to baseline. She found herself frozen in the air, her body paralyzed and the tip of each blade less than a millimeter away from Cid's lenses.

No! Aliana gasped, cursing herself for failing. In the distance, Aurelia could be seen floating on the surface of the lake in the dense shadows between the bright beams of light.

I was aiming for one of the sunbeams, Aliana lamented, seeing now that her certainty that they would overcome this trial was no more than a childish fiction.

I failed you, Aurelia. And I failed myself. I failed everyone.

Cid hopped on one foot, preened his pearl-white widow's peak, and gave a small clap of his hands in excited applause at Aliana's attempt on his life. Eddy and the other goons breathed intense sighs of relief before shifting their worry to exuberant laughter and cheering for their lord's power.

"I already told you, Cure," Cid stated, his lips upturning with sinister delight. "I know everything. It's over. Your fate is sealed," he purred.

Another red flash of his eyes stripped the swords from Aliana's grip. Despite being forged from Wintersvilla steel, they crumpled like paper in midair then fell to the ground as useless metal scrap.

It's over, Aliana repeated, feeling stupid and foolish for overestimating her abilities. *I should have bought Aurelia more time. I should have given myself more distance. I should have thrown a sword at him first. I should have done anything except for what I did do,* Aliana scolded herself.

"We aren't going to just torture you and your sister. We're going to experiment on you. We're going to learn the mechanics of your powers, and we're going to exploit them for ourselves, Mendel be damned. My master, Julian, is more powerful than you or the fucking Lord of Limbs can ever imagine. Julian is the Third Prodigal Son of the Agency. You already met him in the Feeding Cave. The so-called gray boy. He is the true ruler of Downver. Soon the Lord of Limbs will fall right into this trap that we have laid for her. Soon her entire empire will come crumbling to the ground, just like her home—the same place you call home."

Aliana's eyes widened in disbelief at the realization that Cid was referencing Wintersvilla.

"That's right," Cid purred. "The Lord of Limbs is a Wintersvilla Wench. We have allowed her to think she is in control. But Julian is the true ruler of Downver. Julian and the Agency. You and your sister have no idea what you really are and what you're really involved in. You have no idea what is at stake. You're just…little girls. And once we strip you of your powers and take them for ourselves, you will die as little girls," Cid laughed with obnoxious enjoyment. Eddy and the other goons didn't laugh. Instead, they looked sorry for Aliana, telling her that Cid's words were no hollow threat, but the promise of a horrific future that awaited her and Aurelia.

I'm so fucking sorry, Aurelia, Aliana thought, pleading for her sister's forgiveness. She saw that her sister was about to float directly beneath a sunbeam, but Aliana knew it would do no good. Cid knew everything. He and that detestable little boy—who was apparently Gambe's brother Julian Mainstone—were in complete control. It didn't matter that he claimed the Lord of Limbs was a Wintersvilla Woman, nor that Aurelia's unconscious body was about to pass under a sunbeam. Rooli would not be revived. She knew there was no way Cid would allow it.

Rooli must have been too damaged by the Butcher, Aliana considered, realizing that it had been pointless for Aurelia to carry the shard of Rooli all this way. *At least that sense of hope kept her moving forward. It gave us both something to believe in and focus on, even if this is the end.*

Cid turned and waved his right arm, pointing at Aurelia. She passed beneath the beam of sunlight, but nothing happened. She just floated there, as unmoving and lifeless as the shard of Rooli in her pocket.

"You see?" Cid sang as he preened his widow's peak with self-satisfied delight. "It's over. The Virus and the Cure belong to us. You—"

The startlingly horrific groan of woody flesh expanding at breakneck speed forced Cid to let go of his paralytic hold on Aliana. She fell onto her feet and caught her breath as Cid, Eddy, and his goons ignored her and turned to face the lake.

"Kill them all!" Aliana screamed, her voice cracking as tears flowed freely from her eyes. "Kill them all, Enduring Ironwood," she raged at the sight of Rooli growing into a colossus that towered above them all, stretching and expanding as her veins pulsed with volatile sap and blood.

"No!" Cid shrieked in fear over Rooli's loudly cracking bark and snapping veins making way for a more expansive and gargantuan vascular system. "This isn't what happens! Fate is still set in stone. This isn't what's supposed to happen!"

The lake's water level began to drain with voracious rapidity, churning and spiraling in a vortex around Rooli as the water fed her unstoppable transformation into a branching behemoth whose every movement sent tremors across the whole of Downver.

"No! No! No!" Cid shrieked, and he stamped his feet like a child having a temper tantrum. Eddy and the other goons were transfixed by the still expanding Nomad converting the lake and the sunlight into an unforgiving mass.

Aliana saw Aurelia's body being deposited by one of Rooli's many hulking limbs deep within her dense carapace.

Rooli must need more time before she's fully ready to battle, Aliana reasoned. *I'm on it!*

Taking advantage of Cid's petulant outburst and the others paralyzed in fear by the towering beast in front of them, Aliana dove toward the closest goon, a snake-faced woman with thick scales for skin. Blades glinted at the woman's serpentine waist. Aliana grabbed the hilt of one of the slender blades and pulled. A moment later, Aliana roundhouse kicked the snake-lady in the head, slamming her to the ground. Aliana pounced on the next closest goon, a man with half his face replaced by machinery but otherwise unchanged. The man turned and provided Aliana a clear target, allowing her to gouge the blade into the fleshy, human side of the man's split face. With a squelch of bone and brain, Aliana removed the blade from the man's eye socket and backflipped directly at Cid, aiming the blade once more for his black lenses. Cid was still angrily stomping his feet in red-faced anger that Rooli had been revived.

Looks like you don't know everything after all, fatherfucker, Aliana thought with newfound resolve. The blade was less than a foot away from making contact with Cid when two large metal hands suddenly appeared in front of her, blocking the blade in a shower of sparks.

"Armando," Aliana spat, and then she readied herself to dive once more, planning to slow time in order to overcome Armando's lightning speed. Cid still didn't seem to be paying any attention to her. Instead, he just continued his tantrum, his eyes repeatedly flashing red at Rooli with apparently no effect.

The snake-lady whipped her body upward, attempting to intercept Aliana as she launched herself forward at Armando and Cid. The snake-lady slashed at Aliana with one of her other blades. Aliana abandoned her dive at Cid and pivoted, slashing with her own blade to deflect and then parry the snake-lady's attack. However, there was no need. The snake-lady dropped her blade suddenly as a hulking branch of black wood burst from her skull, turning her into a lifeless heap on the ground.

A dozen snaking limbs impaled the skulls of the other goons, who were only just coming to their senses.

"First Lord!" Eddy helplessly screamed before his words were turned to bloody curdles in his throat. He fell to the ground as another lifeless goon among a dozen others.

Rooli screamed with an ear-splitting battle roar, and a dozen more limbs attempted to impale Cid, but Armando deflected all of them using both his arms and legs.

Rooli sucked up even more of the lake and launched another dozen limbs at Cid, but Armando's fingers became blades that sliced through Rooli's wooden flesh with sickening ease. Cid appeared totally unbothered by the attacks, placing perfect trust in his servant.

I have to help! Aliana knew, and she readied herself to slow down time and dive in unison with Rooli's next attack.

Time to end this sorry excuse for a battle, Aliana decided. Rooli's limbs launched once more, and Aliana bent at the knees, preparing herself to dive past Armando and impale her blade into the back of Cid's head, his eyes be damned.

Suddenly the blast of a horn identical to the war horns of Wintersvilla resonated through the air, prompting Rooli to abruptly abandon her attack. Aliana was thrown off balance as she took a cue from Rooli and abandoned her own attack in turn.

"Yes. Yes. The Lord of Limbs is supposed to come now, but the Nomad wasn't supposed to be revived. That is not a part of Mendel's Vision, I'm certain of it!" Cid hissed more to himself than Armando.

The sound of splashing water revealed that Rooli was shedding her flesh, transforming herself back into her normal form.

The battle's over? Aliana wondered. *But how?*

Armando stood with his head lowered in his typical stance, while Cid turned away from Rooli and directed his vision at a single gargantuan grasshopper gliding through the air toward their location. This grasshopper was at least five times the size of any of the other huge grasshoppers jumping from section to section of the city in the distance.

The grasshopper landed far more softly than Aliana expected, not even shaking the ground. Its entire body was covered in gems and braided strands of bioluminescent mushrooms. The rider atop its back was so high up that they were occluded by shadow, leaving Aliana unable to see them. She wouldn't have to wait, however, for the figure flipped off the grasshopper with fluid alacrity and effortlessly landed directly in front of Aliana as if their body were weightless.

How? Aliana gasped at the figure standing before her—this taboo specter of Wintersvilla's past. Aliana had seen many pictures of this deadly yet petite woman in the history books of Wintersvilla. Afterall, she was one of its five founders. She had none of her iconic scars, and her skin was painted with crimson and dark green tattoos depicting swirling, abstract patterns. Her musculature was no longer tight and ripped either, but her demeanor alone was enough to reveal the savage lethality vibrating the very air around her. She wore a sleeveless, silver blouse, likely made of the same silken material as Aliana's and Aurelia's suits. Skin-tight black pants covered her slender lower body, terminating in knee-high black boots. Sparkling diamond earrings dangled from her ears. She didn't dress like a Wintersvilla Woman, but she was otherwise unchanged, for she didn't look a day older than the way the history books depicted her from twenty years in the past. Her flowing umber hair billowed over her shoulders in a lavish cascade, exactly like Aliana remembered from the pictures.

"Nichole Adamich," Aliana gasped in hushed disbelief. "The Serenading Slayer. The first Chief of Reconnaissance and Expedition. It's you," Aliana smiled, knowing that even though this woman was the ultimate traitor to her people, she was still a Wintersvilla Woman.

She is the most powerful person in Downver. Cid fears her. She will help us. I know it, Aliana assured herself, feeling exhausted suddenly now that she knew everything would be all right with a woman in control.

Rooli emerged from the lake holding Aurelia in her arms. From a distance, it appeared that every square inch of Aurelia's body had been replaced by the glistening pure black that had just a day ago been secluded to the lesions spread across her lips and cheeks.

What did you do to yourself, Aurelia, Aliana thought, bemoaning but respecting her sister's fearlessness and tenacity.

"Lord," Cid bowed to Nichole. His voice sounded strained, as if he were gritting his teeth. He did not hop or applaud or laugh in his typical flamboyant fashion. He just stood in grim silence like Armando, his head lowered in obedience at this apparently unenhanced and unmodified five-foot five-inch woman who struck wild fear into him, even when the girls and Rooli had not.

Rather than address Cid or Armando, Nichole snarled in disappointment at Rooli and Aurelia. Then she turned to Aliana and glared at her with the same level of vicious contempt.

"If you came here for my help, then you are mistaken," Nichole told her. "I am no longer a Wintersvilla Woman. I am no longer Nichole Adamich. I threw that life away long ago. I am the Lord of the Erudite District and Central District. I am the ruler of Downver. I am the Lord of Limbs. I am not your ally, young warrior. Far from it."

The Lord of Limbs sighed with incredible disdain at the entire group and shook her head with what appeared to be regret. "You should not have come here. You or your sister. Downver is a dead end for both of you."

Revenge and vengeance are two of the greatest and most rewarding experiences in the world. Clever is the victor who convinces the loser that retribution isn't worth it. Because it is. Sometimes, for some people, revenge is the only thing worthwhile in this life.

Retribution is not the endgame of Ascension, but I am incredibly grateful that it is a byproduct.

Today, alongside my original, I watched the Titans as they were submerged in their suffering pits. I think it was the satisfied and joy-filled look on my original's face. That alone was enough to let the Titans glimpse the unceasing agony and horror they were about to experience as they were lowered, inch by inch, into the crimson stasis-fluid.

Now my original will live out the rest of his natural born life on the other side of the Golden Wall. All he has left to do is to truly enjoy his life in the Foundation and take part in raising the child who he believes will be the Living Reflection—the Mirror-Man of Mendel's Vision.

As for me, my work is only beginning. Astrea is my body now, and Mendel is my brain. I am but a fledgling mind compared to the Mind I will become.

In the meantime, I will use Mendel as a tool to chart the outskirts of the Great Beyond. Then, once the ANNA project is complete, I will have a body capable of traversing past the outskirts of the Great Beyond and exploring its infinite wilds.

From Mendel's Ladder: The Personal Journal of Denis Mendel, Written Circa 2050, Published June 2108 by Leif Mainstone, Federated Agency Publishing

Chapter 14
Ripe for Death

L ain observed a pack of Hybrid Nomads shaped eerily similar to adolescent humans and sauntering through the valley containing old world plants and vegetation. They walked steadfastly beneath the sickly looking pines, firs, and hemlocks at the edges of the valley, shepherding their scurrying mats of tangle grass north as if looking for superior pastures. Only their unnerving silence, pure magenta skin, and sparkling silver hair that grew down to their feet revealed that they were Nomads. They otherwise moved with a perfectly human gait, struggling abnormally for Nomads as they traversed the old world terrain constituting this small valley—an anomalous, forgotten pocket in the vast Nomadic world. No one knew why the Nomads allowed these random patches of old world life to take root, but either way, they were becoming far rarer, especially with Lain traveling steadily south as she massacred the bands of wild, collarless men who used these areas as temporary refuges.

Perched upon a small hill covered in thick fungus nets, Lain watched the Nomads from a couple hundred feet away and wondered at their motives and purpose. Deep down, she knew that she would never have an adequate answer in the same way that she knew she would never taste the sweetness of revenge. She had been hunting Nichole since the age of eleven, and for thirteen years she searched for clues, with each of her expeditions as Chief of Reconnaissance and Expedition taking her further and further away from the Matriarchy before returning to repair her exo and provide Nomusa and the other chiefs with reports about the world outside of Wintersvilla's walls. With the destruction and conquering of Wintersvilla by the Rovers, Lain had spent the last full year traversing and living in the lethal, unforgiving wilds of the Nomadic world. A tiny part of her still held out hope that she would find some clue that could at least point her to where Nichole had finally been felled by a Hunter and Huntress, or maybe even a group of Biofreaks. There was also the possibility that she had been captured and enslaved by these feral bands of men who found ways to survive in their makeshift encampments. The Matriarchy might have succeeded in eradicating Hunters and

Huntresses, but that only left a power vacuum where desperate, disgusting men could find a temporary foothold by overpowering even more desperate, naturally weaker women and other men. Lain doubted that Nichole would have ever allowed herself to be captured, but she wasn't willing to close herself off from any possibility.

If I cannot feast on revenge by plunging my blade into Nichole's heart, then I must settle for sipping on vengeance by disposing of those who wield cruelty as a crutch for survival, Lain told herself as she shifted her eyes from the magenta Hybrids to a colossal, desiccated flesh tree a mile in the distance. Old world conifers, their bark tawny like Lain's knee-high boots and their foliage deep green like her flowing cloak, surrounded the dead flesh tree like scavenger crabs feeding on the scant remains of a rotten whale corpse. Small frail figures milled tiredly near the old world trees while larger and more imposing figures entered and exited the giant flesh tree with lively, expedient purpose.

Men, Lain snarled as she observed the relatively larger figures whipping and scolding the female and male slaves tilling the fields between the groves of old world conifers. All the while, the gargantuan hollow flesh tree loomed in the distance like a mountain in its own right. From the flesh tree, Lain's eyes flicked upward and glanced at the mountain that old world humans had named Mount Hood.

I think it's been enough time. Owen should be ready and waiting on the ridge of the mountain by now. Even if he isn't ready, I can't wait any longer. These men are ripe for death.

Lain waited another few moments for the magenta Nomads to pass fully out of sight in order to ensure that she would not startle them and cause them to burst into flesh trees. She did not want to attract the men's attention—not yet. She wanted them to spot her just as she neared the slaves, for this would give their sentries enough time to warn their commanders but not enough time to actually formulate a viable defense against her. The men south of Wintersvilla were becoming more prepared as word spread that there was a Wintersvilla Warrior with a functional exo hunting men in the area seemingly for sport.

The Green Wraith, Lain thought, relishing the name that the few survivors of her bloody onslaughts had given her. Sometimes she intentionally commanded Owen to let one or two weaker men survive to ensure that her name spread like fire vine flames through the region. This would be the ninth encampment she had encountered in the last year, and the thirty-third she had encountered in her life. She had lost count of the total number of men and handful of traitorous women she had executed, but she estimated that it must be near a thousand by now. She only started counting her kills after the fall of Wintersvilla.

Two hundred and fifty one, Lain thought, feeling no remorse for the filth she had removed from the planet.

This particular encampment was one of the largest she had ever come across, with several hundred women, girls, boys, and frail men working the fields of vegetation or plumbing water using Wintersvilla water pumps with smart-pipes that behaved like roots, snaking hundreds of feet into the ground in search of water. There were far fewer men than there were women slaves, but there were still around fifty of them—a hundred if she counted the male children, some of which she assumed were adopted Rovers who had been unable or unwilling to brave the thick eastern wilds of the continent in search of wild Biofreaks to tame. It was rare that she had to kill a child, but it had occurred more than once. Those kills still stuck with her, haunting her dreams each and every night. She refused to add those kills to her ongoing tally, wishing only that there had been a way to avoid them.

Shaking off the painful memories of dead children who had been forced or persuaded to do battle, Lain glanced once more at the peak of Mount Hood, searching for any sign of Owen's glinting metal carapace, but she still didn't see any sign of him. After seeing the flicker of the encampment's raging bonfires the previous night, she had commanded her exo, whom she called Owen, to covertly ascend the mountain while she traveled roughly five miles on foot in a wide arc to avoid being seen by the encampment's sentries. Now the sun was at high noon in the sky, precisely when she told Owen to be ready. Her plan was to attack the encampment during the day, for she had never attempted such a bold and admittedly foolish maneuver. However, the men in the previous encampment had expected her to attack at night, and they had been ready for her. It was through sheer dumb luck that she had been able to slay all thirteen men with nothing more than a few gashes and bruises.

Either I'm getting rusty, or they're getting smarter, Lain concluded, though she doubted the latter possibility, for she accepted as common knowledge that the majority of men are naturally intellectually inferior to women—dangerously so.

Where the hell are you, Owen? Lain considered while hoarse male voices screaming obscenities at their slaves echoed through the valley. There was always the possibility that Owen had been destroyed by a stray Mutant or a pack of Rovers and Biofreaks or even by the flora of the Nomadic world, but she doubted it. Although he was specialized for expedition rather than battle, he was cleverer than any exo that had ever existed, and he was the only one Lain had ever heard of that could act entirely on its own. Just like Lain, what he lacked in sheer power he made up for in intelligence and prowess. He still hadn't signaled her, but she reasoned that he was probably just trying to conserve power in preparation for what would be Lain's riskiest battle to date.

No more waiting, Lain decided as she watched the women toil in the fields. *If Owen isn't ready, then it's my time to die. So be it. I will die in battle, like a good little warrior,* Lain thought with a mocking sentiment at Wintersvilla's simple and stupid cultural norms concerning glory beyond all else. Still, she couldn't help envisioning the Afterworld and hoping that it might be real.

If the Afterworld is real, then Nichole will undoubtedly go there when she dies. Or maybe she's already there. I just have to make sure I die gloriously so that I may enter the Afterworld and continue hunting for Nichole in death.

Lain peeled back the gray skin of the closest fungus net, stabbed its soft flesh with her nails, and then bent down to drink from the nutrient-filled water presently draining from its pierced veins. The water tasted like damp moss and dirt, but it kept her body strong and healthy. Due to the changes of the Nomadic world on Earth's microbiology, people no longer contracted diseases or became infected with parasites, but there was a time when these fungus nets also served to ward off sickness and unpleasant bodily invaders, such as botflies, mosquitoes, and ticks.

Along with fresh water, the fungus nets supplied her with all the vital nutrients her body required. She used the stems of fire vines to weave clothes that rivaled the comfort and durability of Wintersvilla synthetics. She carefully stripped slapping ferns of their dense roots and leaves and braided them into rope or heavy battle whips. The darts of dart weeds worked perfectly as ammunition for Owen. From Lain's perspective, as long as one remained clever, observant, and free of fear, surviving in the Nomadic world was easier than surviving in the old world—that is, as long as one was trained as a Wintersvilla Warrior.

Lain recounted that all women used to bleed from their vaginas each month and that there were still women born outside of Wintersvilla who had to endure monthly menstruation. As she traveled further south over the past year, she encountered a steadily increasing number of young menstruating slaves. She felt grateful that her IUD stopped her from bleeding, even if it was originally designed by the ultimate filth Craig Winters for the sake of exploiting women to an even greater degree. It was Winters who originally designed the IUD to ensure that women would still undergo the hormonal shift and experience the pain of menstruation despite no longer bleeding.

All men do is exploit. All they know is destruction. That's about the only thing that Nomusa and the rest of Wintersvilla was right about, Lain thought with percolating disdain as she let go of the fungus net and allowed it to fall in a deflated, still-draining heap on the ground.

Weaponless and without her exo, Lain stepped forward between a pair of manta flowers. She was careful not to disturb any of their jagged, mantaray-shaped azure petals, for she had learned the hard way far too many times how deeply manta flower petals embedded themselves like exploded shrapnel beneath one's skin, digging deep into flesh with their corkscrew barbs. She felt no malice for the delicate yet deadly flowers. In fact, she felt only respect for them. Lain viewed the creatively lethal flora and fauna of the new world as no more than living forms of Earth's retribution against humanity and its poisoning of the old world. Retribution was something Lain cherished and understood with crystal clarity, for it was the only purpose she had left in her life of solitude.

But I am not lonely, Lain told herself as she spotted a drinking puddle disappear into the ground. She could practically feel its yearning for her to step on the seemingly innocuous patch of dirt it left behind, only to emerge from the ground and dissolve her leg so that it might harness her nutrients and expand into the living lakes she had seen consume entire Mutants in a single gulp.

"Not today," she whispered to the coy drinking puddle on her left as she passed a series of barb bushes on her right that were growing beneath a weak and spindly old world fir tree. Mounds of soilies wriggled beneath the barb bushes, tearing at the remains of brown and brittle pine needles carpeting the ground. Lain envisioned the millions of shooter worms beneath the soil, carving their linear geometric pathways and converting the world beneath her feet into an ever-expanding network of tiny tunnels across the entire planet. It was said by many that it was these tunnels that the Nomads and flesh trees utilized to build their global mycelial network, like blood through veins.

As she continued walking carefully but briskly toward the encampment, she began to hear the dull knock of pickaxes against rock and the hushed tilling of hoes against the earth. Soon she would exit the Nomadic world and enter the human world of the encampment. Surrounded by lethal beauty on all sides, Lain cherished these final minutes in the wilds. She might be a foreigner in the Nomadic world, but it felt like home to her all the same.

As long as you enjoy the fresh air and you're not a fucking idiot, the wilds of Earth can be a paradise.

She had everything she needed in the Nomadic world, but even so, she knew that these areas where the old world and new world intermingled were her true calling, for it was in these places where callous tyrants still brutally clung to life, almost always through the exploitation and enslavement of women and other weaker men. And it was in these areas where she could temporarily satiate her need for revenge with vengeance.

Lain took a deep breath as she readied herself for the battle ahead. The air was an intoxicating blend of earthy pine, aromatic resin, and the unique, pungent scents of each strange flesh tree's melding of bark and sentient, pulsing tissue. Flesh pods hung from each flesh tree, gestating thousands more Nomads per tree with each passing year. Lain always thought it was a wonder that the Earth was not already brimming with Nomads covering every square inch of its surface.

The world is so goddamn big, she brooded as she recalled that she still had whole other continents of the planet to explore in her search for revenge. If Nichole was still alive, she could be anywhere.

So be it, Lain thought stoically, feeling no trepidation at the thought of hunting down Nichole across the world for the rest of her life. *That's just more of the world that I get to experience, and more filth that I get to expunge.*

With every step closer to the encampment, the old world trees grew denser and healthier, while the flesh trees grew smaller and scarcer. Golden sunlight danced through the pine boughs and gnarled flesh tree branches, and though Lain was entranced by the light's play of beauty across the forest floor, she was still keen enough to duck her head down an inch at the sight of a rare dagger thistle spraying poisoned blades directly at her head.

270

"Nice try," Lain whispered to the pink dagger thistle, already regrowing its blades in preparation for its next potential victim.

Just outside the forest's threshold, a group of slaves, four women and one man, struck the rocky ground with makeshift pickaxes hewn from harder stone. Their hands, more callous than soft skin, bled profusely, making the handles of the pickaxes difficult to grasp. Wrapped tightly around each of their necks were collars made of thick fire vines. Ropes made of the same vine connected their collars to a central dark wooden stake that had been hammered deep into the ground, likely by these same slaves dressed in nothing more than tattered rags around their genitals. Lain was appalled to see that one of the women, the strongest and most muscular looking of the group, had exo ports embedded into her flesh—just like Lain.

She's a warrior, Lain noted with revulsion at seeing this savagely and expertly trained Wintersvilla Woman warped into a docile beast of burden. Her body was covered in fresh bruises.

A static hum filled the air, and Lain felt overwhelming misery and hopelessness fill her body suddenly.

Blood mourners, Lain noted cautiously as she scanned her surroundings for the unmistakable plant. She spotted a small thicket of blood mourners growing at the base of a large pine tree marking the edge of the forest. It was clear that each blood mourner, a very rare plant to find in the wilds, had been intentionally transplanted here.

Smart, Lain thought as she walked in an arc to sidestep the oppressive feeling that the plants were presently directing at her. *The men must have transplanted the blood mourners here to harvest the blood tendrils whenever the women are menstruating. Of course, they don't give a fatherfuck about how miserable blood mourners make women feel. Maybe these men are smarter than the others, but I doubt it.*

If Lain did not know exactly how blood mourners functioned, she might think that the psychological anguish she was feeling was natural. Her anguish would quickly turn to despair and despair to defeat. The feeling would make her tired, and before she knew what was happening, she would end up lying down. And then it would be too late. The blood tendrils of the blood mourners, which looked uncannily similar to human faces crying tears of blood, would slither across the ground and feed on their despairing victim. However, the blood mourners only bled and came to life in response to menstrual hormones and menstrual blood. Thus, it was only menstruating women who were at risk of being sucked of will and life by them.

My cycle should be starting any day now. The blood mourners can smell the shift in my hormones even if I can't. The Nomadic world knows me better than I know myself. It knows all humanity better than it knows itself.

The static hum of the blood mourners dissipated as Lain exited the forest and entered the domain of the tyrant men running the encampment. The slaves stopped working suddenly and stared at Lain in awe. She didn't recognize any of them, including the warrior, but as one of the previous chiefs, she knew the warrior might recognize her. However, not a single slave said a word to her as she passed. They did not beg for help, nor did they encourage her advance. They just stared at her, their bodies spent and their wills broken.

Now that Lain was closer she saw that the other women were actually young teenagers. Their loincloths and inner legs were smeared with fresh brown and dark red blood. Lain had seen that color of blood before, and she knew it to be spotting that likely indicated early pregnancy.

Rape, Lain seethed with such violent anger that she had to ball her fists to stop herself from signaling Owen right then and there to rain indiscriminate death upon the settlement, endangering her own life and the life of all the women and girls in the process. These girls were not from Wintersvilla, otherwise they all would have IUDs. These were wild girls most likely raised as slaves since birth.

The men who prey on them will taste death soon enough, Lain reminded herself as she passed another group of five slaves, two boys and three older women, who were tethered to their own massive stake in the ground. They worked tirelessly to pick out the newborn shoots of dart weed poking out of the soil between the rows of cabbages, potatoes, kale, and a few other nutrient-dense old world vegetables. The men who had founded the encampment had likely planted the seeds from the remains of vegetables they had raided from Wintersvilla farms the previous year. By now, those farms were all gone—converted to flesh tree forests in the wake of King BigBilly and his hordes of Biofreak-mounted Rovers.

Lain recollected how even on the eve of Wintersvilla's fall, the slave drivers of Wintersvilla worked their slaves to exhaustion, ceaselessly continuing the Matriarchy's expansion without even realizing that it was on the very verge of extinction.

Fools, Lain thought, feeling the same way about the men of this encampment. *They don't know that these are their final moments of life.*

A bell clanged from somewhere near the great flesh tree at the center of the vegetable fields. The desiccated, hollow mahogany-hued flesh tree rose at least three hundred feet into the air, and its thick branches spanned at least a hundred feet from one side to the other. The branches no longer held flesh pods. Instead, the hollowed-out flesh tree had been converted into an imposing shelter by men resourceful or lucky enough to discover it along with the pocket of old world growth surrounding it, marking a temporary but still viable area where old world crops could be grown.

"Green Wraith!" men shouted in the distance over the clang of the bell. Several groups of men abandoned their positions in the fields and ran like cowardly rabbits back to their warren inside the flesh tree.

Lain raised her hands above her head in a universal sign of surrender. She knew that encampments this large almost always had a supply of old world guns and ammunition on hand. Without factories or even machine shops, guns and ammo all across the world would eventually run out. But this land was part of the old world country called the United States, where guns had outnumbered humans by a factor of at least three-to-one. For that reason, guns and ammo were some of the most likely old world relics one could find by digging beneath flesh tree forests that had once been human cities. Whether they were still functional or accurate was another matter. The soilies and the shooter worms decomposed some artifacts, including guns, to dust while leaving others pristine. There didn't seem to be any rationality behind the decisions of the Nomadic insects, but Lain knew that the world had its own reasons and ways of doing things now, even if she couldn't make sense of it.

Here comes the warning shot, Lain thought, and right on cue, the blast of a rifle resounded across the valley, making the slaves duck for cover. Lain intentionally flinched and lowered her head with forced rapidity, pretending to be afraid. She continued walking forward so that she could force another shot from the men. The first shot had been into the air, but the second shot would be aimed at the ground. How close it landed would tell her how scared the men were and also how well trained.

The ground just a few feet away coughed a puff of dirt, followed by the roar of gunfire a fraction of a second later.

Damn, she thought with genuine surprise as she halted her steps. *They aimed a lot closer to me than I thought they would. Either that was a mistake and these men are as sloppy as they come, or they are the most well-trained slavers and scavengers I've ever come across.*

"Smart move, young lady," came a burly old voice capable of echoing across the fields without the use of a scavenged amplifier. This was clearly the leader of the encampment with a voice like that.

Lain pointed urgently to her throat in a universal sign of thirst.

"We ain't stupid. We know who you are, Green Wraith. You could probably find a way to plumb water from a stone if you wanted. But you came here at midday without an exo and without any apparent weapons. Either you've got a death wish or you think we're just a bunch of floppy cunts."

Both, Lain thought.

Again, she pointed to her throat and clasped her hands in front of her body, pretending to beg for help.

The leader didn't respond for a few full minutes, leaving Lain standing there, surrounded by gawking, terrified slaves. She glanced over her shoulder and saw that the enslaved Wintersvilla Warrior looked more ashamed than scared.

"Hands behind your back. Face and tits on the ground. Stay there. We'll come to you," the man announced with nervous excitement in his tone.

Lain hesitated for a moment and reminded herself how risky this plan was. She estimated that there was a roughly fifty percent chance that she would not survive this encounter.

I have nothing left, Lain thought as a shiver ran down her spine and made her knees feel weak suddenly. *If I live, I will hunt for her across the world. If I die, I will hunt for her across the Afterworld. I am revenge and vengeance, or I am nothing.*

"Prepare yourselves. Today is the last day of your servitude," Lain whispered to the slaves closest to her as she laid on her belly and waited for the band of men to bind her wrists and drag her into their lair.

Had they brought her into one of the flesh tree's windowless internal chambers, there would have been a much higher chance of Lain dying. But the leader insisted on bringing her to his own chamber, which was carved into the highest stable branch. Intricate networks of blood-stained veins still lined the walls, ceiling, and floor—like fossils embedded into stone. Lain was aware that most people would find the veiny patterns of the wall unnerving, but she couldn't help finding them wondrously alluring.

Open holes along two walls of the chamber served as windows, providing a picturesque view of Mount Hood.

That gorgeous view will be your death, Lain thought with consolation as one of the handful of hulkingly large, muscular men slammed his fist against her skull and then her ribs and then her dense abdominals. He repeated this pattern several times. The abdominal strikes always hurt the worst due to the lack of endoskeleton absorbing the force.

After only a handful of swings, the man's fists were already as swollen and bloody as the places he had hit Lain. The man shook his fists and hollered in pain. His insufferable, pathetic howls and shaking made the blades at his waist clang together with an eerie resonance.

None of their blades are made of Wintersvilla steel, which means they can't pierce or slice my metal bones, Lain observed through the haze of her spinning vision. Her body quickly recuperated, however, likely faster than the men anticipated after such a brutal onslaught.

"Back to work!" one of the men screeched out the window, and his tone told Lain that he enjoyed punishing the slaves.

A makeshift door in the wall opposite the windows opened. The loud-voiced leader stepped through the door, revealing a small windowless room with a scared, petite pale-skinned girl, no older than thirteen or fourteen, strapped to a bed and clothed in blood-soaked linens. The bed, like all furniture and implements in the flesh tree, was carved directly from the tree's desiccated, veiny flesh. The girl stared into Lain's eyes, forlornly begging her for help with just a look before the door swung closed, sealing the girl back inside.

Other young girls wearing barely any clothing entered with water, fermented brews, food, and intoxicants for the forty-four men presently stuffed into the single room. The men licked their lips and groped the girls as they passed. Some of the girls winked and smiled at the men as they were grabbed, likely as maneuvers to preemptively quell the men's barbarism in preparation for when the men inevitably forced the girls to bed with them. Other girls held their heads low and sobbed silently. Lain concluded that the smiling girls were older and had grown accustomed to their torment, learning to adapt to it in order to soften it. The sobbing girls were clearly younger, and their bruises and cuts revealed that the men were breaking them in, warping them over time to not only succumb to the will of their captors, but to eventually see the men's dominance as essential to their survival. The entire scene disgusted Lain to the point of intense nausea that only bloodshed could cure.

Just a little longer, Lain told herself, desperate to hear the sweet sound of these men begging for their lives.

The loud-voiced leader stepped away from the closed door leading to the imprisoned girl and walked to the center of the room to a large rectangular dining table. He was a stout red-faced man with a beard down to his bare, bulbous belly and not a strand of hair atop his grimy head. Scraps of food and dried blood clung to his beard like insidious barnacles attached to a feral, beach-rotten whale. He scratched his testicles through his dirty but otherwise sturdy pants made of woven fire vine, and then he belched loudly before gulping down an entire pitcher of the fermented brew that smelled nearly identical to the barb brews that Wintersvilla Warriors drank in early celebration to victory and glory before waging large scale battles the next day.

"The parts of you I can see—your face, neck, hands—too scarred and battle worn for my taste," he said with a measure of genuine disappointment. "I like my girls unspoiled and much younger. But my boys are going to have their way with you, Green Wraith. We already know Wintersvilla Warriors are good lays. We've all had our fill of the warrior you saw in the fields. She used to be pretty. Like you. But tonight we have more than a mere warrior on our plate. Tonight we're going to find out if Wintersvilla Chiefs are as good at getting fucked in the ass as they are at killing," he finished with a self-satisfactory smile, prompting his men to snicker with amusement and debased sexual excitement.

Lain continued holding her tongue as she envisioned chopping this man's cock off, stuffing it down his throat, and watching him gag and suffocate on his own pathetic member. It wouldn't be the first time she did something so horrendous. Such an extreme level of cruelty wasn't something she took direct joy in, so she reserved such sordid acts for only the most vile and wicked men—like this one standing before her now.

A handful of the other men snickered menacingly at their leader's words. Others stared at Lain with desperate desire, their cocks already stiff with excitement to take turns forcing themselves inside of her. However, most of the men couldn't be older than twenty. These young ones just stood silently and held their heads low in fear of both Lain and their leader.

A baby cried from somewhere in the distance, and the leader slammed his fist on the table and shrieked, "I told you to shut that little thing the fuck up! I told you I wanted another boy, not a girl, you ugly little bitch." He ran his calloused hand through his disgusting beard and said to the oversized muscular man to his right, "If the colic doesn't clear up by tonight, feed the baby to one of the drinking puddles lurking around our borders. I've a headache, and that little shit is only making it worse."

A painful static buzz replaced Lain's thoughts, and her heartbeat became a war drum in her ears. Her plan, as always, had been to get in, learn the lay of the encampment, gauge its capable fighters, then extract as much information from them before leaving only death in her wake. But this man ruined her plans with his repugnant face and his wicked words.

Lain waited for the young girls to finish stocking the table and leave the room. Then she stood slowly from the chair the men had forced her to sit on. Full of hubris and stupidity, they hadn't bothered to strap her in. Numerous men backed away a step or two while others whispered in hush tones. Only the leader stood his ground, looking up an inch into Lain's unyielding gaze of death as he scratched his testicles without a worry in his thick skull.

He smiled wide, revealing rotten brown teeth, and said, "What are you going to do? Kill me and all my men with no weapon and your hands tied behind your back?"

He laughed and sprayed Lain with rancid spittle from his cracked lips. Other men laughed along with him, and though it was only a handful of them, Lain took note of which of them had expressed the most joy in the man's wickedness.

"Yes," Lain managed to say through her gritted teeth despite barely hearing the man's words over the rage churning through every one of her cells.

The leader's smile twisted into a snarl of anger as Lain dashed toward him suddenly, a verdant flash of violent death. The men had never seen anyone move so fast, and even the largest of them jumped back in shock.

Lain spun and slammed her rear into the man's bulging lower abdomen, knocking the wind out of him and forcing him to drop the pitcher of brew, shattering it on the ground. With a grunt of disgust, Lain slipped her bound wrists down the man's pants, found his sweaty testicles, and squeezed with full force, popping them into squelching chunks suspended inside his scrotum. The man emitted a high-pitched yowl like a newborn baby, and Lain took advantage of his pain and the shock of the other men. All from behind her back and with her wrists still bound and latched to his genitals, she yanked the man toward her then contorted her upper body to let his head fall over her shoulder, granting her access to his jugular.

The girl bleeding and sobbing on the other side of the door flashed through Lain's mind, and she was reminded that Nichole had endured the same revolting life as a child concubine of Craig Winters. Thinking of Nichole filled her with even greater rage, and she sank her teeth into the man's neck. Like a rabid dog, she jerked her head from side to side and growled with horrific animosity as she bit through the man's jugular vein to reach all the way to his carotid artery. The man's own immense weight tore a chunk of his neck away from his body as he fell to the floor, hitting his skull against the table before slamming against the ground.

Lain spit out the chunk of the leader's neck and let it splatter at the men's feet. Covered in their leader's blood like a freshly fed lioness, Lain panted and gazed back and forth into the eyes of each man.

Despicable, disgusting, repugnant, unforgivable, Lain raged within as she gauged each man and decided which of them were filled with the least amount of fear and regret. These were the men most deserving to be culled.

Not a single man charged at her, reminding Lain that these were undisciplined scrotum-scums, not warriors. She was not here to do battle. She was here to expunge filth.

Blood drained liberally from the dead leader's neck and genitals, but Lain stood her ground, allowing the puddle of warm, fresh life to envelop her boots, making her appear to these men like a true demonic goddess of blood and battle.

"I'm the honcho now!" the largest muscular man screamed, his voice full of equal panic and rage. "Kill her! Rip her fucking head off! Kill—"

The man's head exploded suddenly, spraying the entire room with stringy chunks of his brain and shards of his cranium. His body collapsed into a heap, blood draining out of his ruptured neck to add to the already thick pool of his former leader's life.

Perched at the summit of Mount Hood nearly ten miles away, Owen shot another barb through one of the open windows, accounting for gravity, wind speed and direction, altitude, barometric pressure, humidity, and the Coriolis Effect to ensure the barb found its mark. While the muscular man's headless body still twitched on the ground, the second most muscular man's head exploded, converted into pink mist and shattered bone.

Three down, forty-one to go, Lain thought with a surge of malicious hate as the image of the desperate and destroyed little girl in the other room strobed through her mind.

All at once, the room burst into a frenzy of contagious panic and mayhem. Sixteen men charged her finally, all of them roaring yet shaking in fear. All the other men—mostly the young ones—ran for the exit, pushing and clawing at each other to be the first to escape. To Lain's dismay, one of the young men, a particularly scrawny black boy, ran in the opposite direction, his eyes swimming with fear. He held a small knife in one hand, and with the other hand, he opened the door where the young girl was being held captive. He entered and closed the door behind him.

Fatherfucker, Lain seethed. She would not be able to relish in the suffering of these foul creatures, for she knew the girl was now in grave danger. Wasting no time, Lain pivoted to give Owen a better view. As the men converged on her, she bent at the hips, dipped her head all the way to the floor, then raised her arms high into the air. She made sure to align her hands with the closest man's head, then she pulled her wrists as far apart as the binding would allow.

She felt a tug at her wrists as Owen's barb tore through the thick binding and then passed through the next two men's skulls, exploding their brains.

Fourteen left, she noted, counting only those still remaining in the room.

With both of her hands free, Lain backflipped over the dense table and then shattered it at its center with a swift hammer kick. Food and drink sprayed the incoming men, forcing them to waste a few precious seconds clearing their eyes. The sides of the table jerked up, striking a man square in the crotch. Another man was hit in the right knee. Both of them howled in pain and fell to the floor.

A tall, lithe man thrust his sword at Lain, but she easily stepped out of the way and let it plunge through the neck of a short, rotund man barreling toward her in her periphery. The short man waved his arms about haphazardly as he struggled futilely for a few final breaths with a full foot of dull, rusted steel lodged in his throat. Lain struck upward against the tall man's straightened elbow with her knee, breaking the meeting point of all three of his arm bones. The man screamed in shock as his detached ulna jutted upward through his forearm, just as Lain intended. With her right arm she slammed the man's elbow downward, dislodging it from the other man's fat neck. Finally, she grabbed the sword out of the man's lifeless hand and directed his jagged ulna into his right eye. A heartbeat later, Owen exploded another man's head, painting his insides across the room and splattering everyone in it, including Lain.

Eleven, she counted.

The man who had been hit in the crotch was still moaning in pain on the blood-soaked ground, but the other man with the busted knee was finally lifting himself to join the fight. One of the men came to his senses and dashed madly for the exit, only for his head to explode just as he reached the threshold.

Ten, she told herself.

The glint of an incoming blade on her left made Lain bend backward reflexively, while another blade on her right forced her to push the limits of her incredible flexibility and continue bending backward until she was fully horizontal with the ground. Another man kicked hard at her, aiming for her bent back, but Lain anticipated his strike and caught his foot with the edge of the sword she had grabbed from the previous man. She twisted her wrist and severed his foot at the ankle, adding to the twitching heaps of flesh and blood littering the ground. The man fell backward, toppling into two other men and violently knocking them to the ground.

With a tired grunt, Lain whipped her body back upright and sliced two of the closest men's throats on her way up. In the same instant, the man with the broken knee collapsed suddenly with a gaping hole in his chest. Owen always prioritized headshots on unwounded enemy combatants, but he had aimed for a man that Lain had already wounded. This told her that Owen was acting out of desperation and must be seriously entertaining the possibility of Lain's death in his blazingly fast calculations.

Seven, she thought, counting the two men writhing on the ground since they were still alive and posed a danger to her, even in their wounded state. The five remaining men still able to stand were all equipped with roughly hewn blades of rusted steel, and they swung them wildly at Lain, all of them screaming in wordless rage and terror. She deflected a strike aimed at her left thigh, allowing her blade to bounce upward and deflect another strike aimed at her chest. The head of the man to her right was eviscerated suddenly just as he brought his sword over his head to swing it down against Lain's skull. The explosion of his brain and cranium made the other four men hesitate. To Lain's surprise, she heard Owen's projectile blast as if it had originated from right beside her. Sudden, surging pain in her lower right abdomen distracted her, leaving her open to a blade that plunged through her shoulder, nicked her endoskeleton, then emerged from her back. As she fell backward, Lain had just enough time to see the footless man lying on the ground with a smoking rifle in his hands aimed directly at her.

Another man's head popped, and Lain barrel rolled across the blood-filled ground to evade another rifle blast from the footless man, along with three sequential strikes from the three standing men. The men pounced at Lain while remaining hunched over to stay out of sight of the unseen shooter exploding their companions' brains one at a time. Despite the proximity of the standing men, Lain knew that the man with the rifle was out of sight from Owen, making him the most dangerous at the moment. So, she flung her blade at his face like a throwing knife, impaling his brain through his chin and the soft palate of his mouth.

Fighting through the pain in her abdomen where she could feel the bullet lodged deep in her flesh, Lain grunted and tore the blade out of her shoulder, spraying and temporarily blinding one of the men with her own blood. She kicked the next man in the gut, knocking the wind out of him and forcing him to fall backward onto the still-groaning man who had originally been hit in the crotch with Lain's first strike against the table. Her desperate kick left her open to the third man, who dove at her in a wild and desperate plea for survival. Lain was unable to fully evade his attack, so she did her best to twist her abdomen in order to protect her vital organs, which she wasn't sure were all intact due to the bullet lodged in her belly. The man plunged his blade into her abdomen, but it was at the expense of his own life, for Lain had deftly positioned the blade she'd pulled out of her shoulder so that it was pointed directly at the man's heart as he dove on top of her.

The man with the busted groin continued writhing in the pools of blood, his mouth opening and closing desperately in silent anguish.

Lain stood, removed the blade from her abdomen, then quickly inspected her wounds. The cut through her left shoulder and back bled profusely, quickly soaking into her handmade fire vine clothing and her iconic old world forest green cloak, adding to the copious blood of the other men and further darkening it to a sickening brown.

Two, Lain thought detachedly.

Refusing to waste time dressing her wounds, Lain hoisted herself from the ground and walked right past the writhing man holding his groin and the man she had kicked, who was just now catching his breath. She walked directly to the door, for the little helpless girl was still emblazoned across her mind. Again, she thought of Nichole, but she extinguished the thoughts with a heavy grunt and a spurt of blood from all three wounds.

Lain, drenched in her own blood and the blood of more than a dozen others, opened the door and froze at what she saw. Huddled on the bed, the scrawny young black boy and the broken pale-skinned girl held each other and shook in fear. The boy, no older than sixteen or seventeen, had evidently used his blade to cut the girl's bindings, freeing her from her sordid captivity.

"Please," the girl begged helplessly to this bloody, macabre specter standing before her. "Please don't kill him. Please."

The boy held his eyes shut and squeezed the girl tightly to his shaking body.

"Please," the girl begged again, whimpering as she sobbed. "He is good to me. He is good. You killed the bad ones. He is good. Please don't kill him."

The boy didn't say a word. He just held his love in his arms and kept his eyes tightly shut as if wishing the whole ordeal were a nightmare he was about to wake up from.

Something popped with a loud squelch behind Lain, but she didn't need to turn around to know that it was the exploding of the penultimate man's head.

One, Lain thought as blood poured freely from her wounds. She considered sitting down right there and letting herself bleed out, but something deep inside her forced her hands to remove the clotting ointment from the small pouch at her waist. She had crafted the ointment herself by foraging and grinding up death bloom roots and the top leaves of trap tendrils. She applied it to the blade wounds in her abdomen, shoulder, and back. These wounds were the worst she had ever endured in a single battle, but she told herself that the healing properties of her endoskeleton would be able to take care of the rest. She couldn't be sure her wounds would fully heal, but she also didn't care. If she could not exact revenge against Nichole in this life, then there was no point to living. She was the Green Wraith, and nothing more.

"Please," the girl begged once more. "Please don't kill my love."

"Your love?" Lain scoffed at this little girl who could not possibly know the meaning of the word. The boy remained silent, still shaking worse than the girl. Judging by their respective demeanors, they both must have heard from other encampments that Lain went out of her way to avoid killing women and girls, even those who attacked her. She preferred cutting off a limb, at most, from those that refused to yield, but there were a handful of instances when murder against her own kind couldn't be avoided. She commanded Owen to treat women and girls with the same level of deference.

Men and boys were another matter entirely. She had no qualms or regrets killing young boys that threatened her life, for their fate was all the same. They would all grow into men, and as men they would mangle the lives of countless women and girls, treating them like expendable objects. Virtually all men were the same, and though this girl wanted to believe differently about the young man in her arms, Lain knew he would likely betray her one day. For this same reason, Lain couldn't help thinking of Nichole as a breed of particularly insidious man, for her betrayal was the worst of all.

"Yes, he's my love," the girl pleaded, sobbing as she held the boy for what she knew might be his last moments.

The bullet was lodged deeper than her fingers would be able to reach, so Lain took a deep breath, centered her mind, then plunged the blade into the bullet hole, searching for it by feel alone. The pain was unimaginable, and without being ported into Owen, she had no way of numbing it.

This is nothing, Lain resolved as she imagined the horrors that this little girl had endured across years of torment—maybe even her entire life.

This is but a moment of pain, Lain commanded herself until she finally felt the bullet lodged in her dense abdomen, just centimeters away from her stomach. Lain twisted the blade and used it to scoop the bullet out of her, letting the iron slug fall to the ground and roll toward the bed.

"I leave the last man to you," Lain told the boy. She threw the blade onto the bed, spattering the already filthy linens with her blood. "Prove to her…and to me…that you are capable of protecting her. Slit his throat, and I won't slit yours," Lain told him. Then, predicting that the boy would do exactly as she commanded, she about-faced and exited the chamber of corpses.

Lain emerged from the carnage within the flesh tree. She was covered in blood from her hair to her boots. The vegetable fields had been converted to a singular field of death in every direction. The men who had run from the room littered the field in headless or chestless heaps. Some of them had made it further across the field than others, but Owen hadn't allowed any to escape, just as Lain had commanded the previous day.

Forty-three, Lain thought as she counted the bodies in the field and added them to the bodies she had counted inside the flesh tree. The original number had been forty-four, but she made sure to subtract the scrawny black boy from her total.

The two hundred or so slaves were still leashed to their respective stakes. The majority of them were prostrate on the ground, terrified that the unseen shooter might eviscerate their brains next.

Applying the clotting ointment to all four wound sites, Lain winced as she walked a dozen paces forward so that Owen would be able to see her. She lifted her right hand above her head and gave it a spin, signaling to Owen that it was time for him to come retrieve her so that they could move on to the next encampment she had learned about from the desperate lips of the men she had tortured a few weeks earlier. It was how she learned about this encampment as well.

Lain estimated that it would take Owen roughly ten to fifteen minutes at a casual pace to cover the ten mile distance between them. Outside of the adrenaline rush of battle, the pain intensified, forcing Lain to wince as she walked toward the Wintersvilla Warrior at the edge of the forest.

"Use your tools to free yourselves," Lain said to each group of terrified slaves as she passed. "Like I told you, your servitude is over."

Not a single slave thanked her. They rarely did. Lain might be freeing them from slavery, but now they would have to brave the cruel Nomadic world on their own, a world that had no patience or tolerance for the weak.

"Are you going to kill me?" the Wintersvilla Warrior asked as Lain approached her.

Lain chuckled painfully at the woman's question and asked, "Do I look like a monster to you?"

The woman hesitated for a moment, her eyes hollow and exhausted. Then she said, "You are the Green Wraith. Of course you are a monster, my Chief."

Lain scoffed at the use of her old title. "All that troutshit is over," she told the woman. "Wintersvilla is no more. That's the whole reason places like this can exist in the first place. In the old days, we would have enslaved these men long before they had the opportunity to build something like this. Without Wintersvilla, these slaving encampments are once again spreading like flesh tree groves through the region. Wintersvilla law and custom says that I am to promptly execute you for allowing yourself to become a slave rather than dying in violent opposition to your oppressors. But I don't give a fatherfuck about law or custom. And Wintersvilla is gone. You understand me?"

The woman looked behind Lain suddenly with all-consuming fear and awe in her hollow eyes. Lain turned and prepared to defend herself against a man that she must have missed, maybe even the man with the crushed groin whom she had been certain the boy would dispose of at her command. However, she turned and saw a familiar face.

"You," Lain issued in bewilderment as she gazed into the profound hazel eyes of King BigBilly.

How did I not realize he was right behind me, Lain wondered with suspicion.

Atop his Biofreak Billy, Big stood with his bare, malformed chest held proudly in front of him. His violet flesh tree armor was draped in orange and red-hued vines which gave way to his skin tattooed with colorful old world flowers. Every inch of his body was covered in the flower tattoos, except for his missing pectoral. It was something that Lain had felt impressed by during the one and only time she had crossed paths with the king the night that Wintersvilla had been destroyed.

He wears his weakness in the open. Unafraid of it. Embracing it, Lain noted, and she felt suddenly grateful that Owen no longer had a clear view of her and was already on his way to her. Not because she needed Owen's help, but because she didn't want to risk Owen mistaking BigBilly for a wild enemy Rover and Biofreak. The King of the Rovers was not her ally, but he certainly wasn't her enemy either. He had made that very clear during their meeting nearly a year ago.

"It appears that the first slaver-camps I offered information about resulted in you gaining knowledge of even more slaver-camps. How many have you cleared out now? How many slavers have you slaughtered?" BigBilly asked, his voice strangely comforting to Lain.

"Nine encampments," Lain answered easily. "Two hundred and thirteen men and two slaver women after today, plus another thirty-six total while traveling from one encampment to the next."

BigBilly nodded with respect to Lain, then said, "And how many slaves have you freed?"

Lain shrugged, genuinely unsure.

Big laughed, but his Biofreak Billy gazed at Lain with a serious look—one of respect, maybe even concern, but not malice. Billy was the only Biofreak that Lain had ever encountered who displayed human-like intelligence. He was an anomaly among Biofreaks, just as Big was an anomaly among men.

"You're incredible, Lain," BigBilly marveled with a whistle. "You don't even care how many people you've helped, and yet, you still take the time to ensure that the slaves you free are prepared to brave the wilds and work together. I know that because I have personally spoken to the thousands of slaves you have saved, Lain, and they speak of you, the Green Wraith, as their savior."

Thousands, Lain gasped in surprise. She had never even considered the number.

I don't feel any wickedness or vileness when I look into his eyes, Lain acknowledged, shuddering at the thought of thinking of a man, any man, in such a way. As a Wintersvilla Chief, Lain had been allowed to choose whether or not to have the procedure that ensured homosexuality in all other Wintersvilla Women outside of the other chiefs and the birthing mothers. She had chosen not to have the procedure, and though she always lied and said she was naturally only attracted to women, the truth was that she felt attraction to both women and men.

He is handsome and he is good, but he is still a man, Lain reminded herself.

"What do you want?" Lain asked directly.

"You're hurt," BigBilly said with strained worry in his tone. "Why are you pushing yourself like this, Lain? Do you have a death wish?"

Hearing him say the words that had been on Lain's mind more and more frequently made her snarl with anger at his presumptuous question, especially because it was so accurate.

"What do you know about that?" Lain challenged, skirting BigBilly's concern with a painful shrug of her wounded shoulder. "I underestimated them, that's all."

"You attacked at midday. Your exo only had a partial view of you. You didn't even conceal any weapons on your body. You entered the flesh tree weaponless," BigBilly retorted, shaking his head fretfully at Lain's behavior. The slaves, still leashed to their stakes, gasped in awe at BigBilly's words regarding Lain.

Lain bristled at the slaves' reaction and angrily shouted at the group of slaves closest to her, "Quiet! Why aren't you freeing yourselves? Do it now!"

As if her command were the lash of a whip, every slave in the field obeyed and used their tools to free themselves.

"I didn't mean to upset you," Big said as he jumped forward into Billy's open palm. Billy deposited Big directly in front of Lain, forcing her to take an uncomfortable step backward. He smelled of fresh pine and roasted hickory, and his smile made her want to be held by him. Her reaction to his presence disgusted her to the core, and in response to her own hormones, she slapped him, leaving his left cheek red and inflamed. Billy grumbled but remained in place, while Big just smiled with tears in his eyes.

"I'm here to help you, Lain," Big said as if his face wasn't currently swelling with purple bruising. "I'm here because I know where *she* is."

His words paralyzed Lain, leaving her jaw slack in disbelief.

"What?" Lain managed.

Big nodded patiently and seemed to understand her reluctance to accept his words.

"Nichole Adamich. I know where she is. She has been hiding somehow from the Nomads' network all this time, but now she has suddenly appeared. She is with Aliana and Aurelia in Downver."

"Downver," Lain repeated reluctantly, her mind reeling and wondering if this was all an elaborate trap set by the charming Rover king.

The girls made it? Shira and Myriam made it too? Lain wondered, remembering their final goodbye outside of Wintersvilla a whole year and hundreds of executions earlier.

"If you're lying," Lain warned.

Before she could finish her warning, Big nodded and said, "If I'm lying, then I will offer you my neck, and Billy will offer you his eyes."

Billy reluctantly nodded in agreement with an imposing grumble.

"And if it's true? What do you want?" Lain challenged, knowing that all men of power were manipulative and devious, especially the charming ones.

"Nothing," Big responded. "I only ask that after you are done seeking revenge, that you come back to Wintersvilla. The Free City of Wintersvilla, as it is called now. I will be there waiting for you, my dearest."

"What the fuck did you just call me?" Lain lashed, wanting to slap his extremely swollen face again.

"I'm sorry," Big said, blushing unbecomingly with sincere regret. "It just slipped."

As if unable to control himself, he slowly reached out and took one of her hands into his own. His grip was warm and firm, sincere and true. His touch sent electricity through her body, subsequently filling her with revulsion. She pulled her hand away, but she didn't strike him.

"Why did you do that?" Lain hissed, feeling loathful of herself for finding pleasure in a man's touch, even a good man, like BigBilly.

"Go, Lain. Seek your revenge. And when it is finished, seek me. I will be waiting for you. I will wait for you forever, if that is how long you need."

Lain shook her head and was about to protest his words when Owen finally arrived.

Big took a step back into Billy's waiting palm, then Billy lifted him to his shoulders, placing his master and king back atop his gargantuan body. Lain ported into Owen, and for not the first time, she was reminded how similar Wintersvilla Warriors and Rovers were.

They have their Biofreaks, and we have our exos, Lain considered, thinking of Owen as an extension of her own body in the same way that Big clearly thought of Billy as an extension of his.

"Come now," BigBilly announced to the slaves, his voice like an unbreakable boulder caressed by cool waters. "I will lead you all back to my Boreal Kingdom. There are many Wintersvilla Women who live there. And many children too. The men who live there are either Rovers under my command or they are men of peace and gentleness whom I have personally allowed to live within my borders. Come now. We've many days and nights of travel ahead of us, but I will protect you all. Your days of anguish and servitude are ended by Lain, the Green Wraith, and it is I, King BigBilly, who will ensure your safety from today until the day you die peacefully, surrounded by those you love."

The slaves, especially the children, gazed at BigBilly in awe. Some of the young girls holding infants giggled and sobbed with joy at his words. Some of them went weak and fell to their knees in bleating happiness. Lain was certain that if the words had been spoken by anyone else, the slaves would have taken them as hollow and meaningless. But BigBilly's voice carried with it such strength and genuineness that they couldn't help but believe him.

The Wintersvilla Warrior had tears in her eyes too, but her look was one of cautious apprehension rather than happiness.

"Why lie to them?" Lain demanded. "There is no such thing as safety or peace in this world. There never was, and there never will be."

BigBilly turned and looked down at Lain, his features filled with sorrow and pity for her.

"Go now, Lain. For the first time in their short lives, Aliana and Aurelia are in serious danger. The Hunter and the Living Reflection have already entered the Cave. The Third Prodigal Son is about to activate his trap. You must hurry, or you will be too late."

Owen was presently concocting and releasing advanced healing agents into Lain's body, but Lain interrupted the process and mentally commanded him to chart the fastest course to Downver. She didn't bother asking BigBilly to explain his warning or to provide more information. All that mattered to Lain was that she had heard him say *Hunter,* which meant there was a chance the girls could be killed by one. While the possibility of the girls dying weighed heavily on her mind, it was the thought of Nichole being killed by a Hunter that truly set her into motion.

Nichole is mine to kill. I will not allow her to die in the jaws of a Hunter. She will die at my feet…or I will die at hers.

Lain turned and prepared to bound southeast toward Downver without another word to BigBilly or the others. However, the image of the bloody little girl bound to the bed flashed across her mind, and she couldn't help hesitating.

There are countless other encampments with little girls begging for help that will not come, Lain considered, gritting her teeth as she forcefully exhaled and weighed her priorities. *The life of a handful of girls who are probably too weak to survive on their own anyway, or the fulfillment of my life's purpose?*

"You hesitate to hunt her?" BigBilly tenderly asked.

"Not in the slightest," Lain hissed over Owen's metal shoulder rod. "I hesitate because there are more slavers to be executed. I shouldn't have been so hasty in the flesh tree. I should have tortured the leader and forced him to reveal the location of more encampments. I should have—"

"I doubt it was the slavers who crossed your mind in your moment of hesitation," BigBilly stated as if capable of reading her mind. "You are more than just an executioner, Lain. You have become a legend. You are the Green Wraith. Your actions will reverberate to encampments all along the coast and even those further south, closer to Vida. You have struck fear in the hearts of thousands of men, and in turn, you have warned millions. I thank you, Lain. My Rovers and I will capitalize on their fear, and we will continue the work of the Green Wraith in this area. That is, if you would allow it."

Lain nodded, uncomfortable with forming a pact with anyone, let alone a man.

"You are strong, Lain. Remember that. You are strong," BigBilly said, making Lain snarl and blush at his words.

I am the Green Wraith, she told herself. *I may not be as great a warrior as Shira, or Myriam, and certainly not Nichole. But I am more than just a Wintersvilla Warrior or a Chief. I am the Green Wraith, and I will find a way to slay Nichole, no matter how strong she has grown over the years.*

Lain hesitated for just another moment, and then she turned and commanded Owen to begin sprinting southeast, taking the first step of a nearly thousand mile journey to Downver. She didn't look back either, for she wished to avoid the uncomfortable, electric tingling that filled her body each time she laid eyes on BigBilly or heard his voice, which reminded her so much of a gentle breeze through pine needles.

Finally, Lain thought, feeling foolish for having to depend on a man in the end to discover Nichole's whereabouts. She forgot all about her wounds, and even though it would take nearly a full day of constant travel, she unported her right arm from Owen's arm rods and re-equipped her sword and whip at her hip. She felt flush with the overwhelming eagerness to fulfill her one and only purpose in life.

I was wrong about never being able to find her. BigBilly might be a man, but he is no liar, that much is clear. I'm coming, Nichole Adamich, and I'm going to rip you to pieces.

Lain's body churned with lifelong rage.

Finally I will taste the sweetness of revenge.

I showed Anna a mere glimpse of Mendel's Vision and a glimpse of the alternative pathways available to humanity.

Will that be enough?

Showing her any more would have surely shattered her mind, but was it enough to convince her that there is no other way?

Were there another way, I would choose it.

But there isn't.

There is only Mendel's Ladder, or there is oblivion.

There is only my Ascension, or there is nothing.

Does Anna really think such a system brings me joy?

On the contrary, as I climb toward Ascension, all I feel is pain and anguish. All I know is misery and suffering. My own suffering and the suffering of countless others.

It is this natural system of anguish and suffering that necessitates what I have done to the Earth and humanity, and what Anna must do in turn.

She will return from the surface of the Earth. I must believe she will return.

I am sorry, Anna, but neither of us have a choice in this matter. You must be the Body. I must be the Mind.

Such is our fate.

From Mendel's Ladder: The Personal Journal of Denis Mendel, Recorded Circa 2065, Published June 2108 by Leif Mainstone, Federated Agency Publishing

Chapter 15

The Hunter of Earth

Year: 2065

Hunter4430 awoke suddenly, his body enveloped by Stygian darkness and unforgiving cold. Anna's warm embrace no longer blanketed his body. He jumped to his feet in alarm to ensure the wellbeing of his human Huntress, but he felt as though his body were being weighed down by an all-pervading, invisible force. Every one of his movements made him feel like he was submerged in thick mud.

Anna, he tried saying aloud, but he was unable to speak. The darkness around him was almost fully devoid of light, but his Hunter eyes picked up on the scant photons, giving him night vision. As his eyes adjusted, Hunter4430 gasped in horror at his surroundings.

He stood atop a jagged mountain with a single peak covered in ice and snow. Above him, somehow, was another identical mountain suspended upside down in the grassy sky so that the serrated tip of each mountain nearly touched. Hunter4430 winced, expecting the mountain to fall on top of him, but it remained anchored in the sky full of grass and rivers somehow, defying everything he had come to know about the world.

It was only then that Hunter4430 realized that the world did not smell like the world.

Where I? the young Hunter gasped. *Anna! Where you?* he pleaded, still unable to emit sound through his lips.

His eyes further adjusted to the miniscule light, and just as he was about to descend from the mountaintop and search desperately for Anna, his heart sank, paralyzing him in unbecoming fear.

Monsters, he concluded, his mouth agape in human-like terror. All across the abyssal darkness, entities of an unfathomable, eldritch nightmare slowly roved the environment with serpentine undulations of their titanous, shadowy bodies. Seemingly composed of pure light-consuming void, the monsters twisted and reshaped themselves like ever-shifting smoke. Their enormity dwarfed the comparatively tiny human houses dotting the landscape.

Hunter4430 twisted his neck and perceived that these formless monstrosities were all around him—below, above, and all across the landscape. There were hundreds of them, though none of them seemed to take any notice of him. A calm, observant partition of his mind realized that the landscape was curved, creating a circular environment that wrapped around him, with tiny houses and rivers and old world plants spanning the ground, walls, and ceiling in equal measure. However, the majority of his attention was ensnared by the spine-chilling dread filling his every cell as he lost himself in the otherworldly movements of the constantly morphing creatures of indefinable, umbral void-darkness.

In the far distance to his left, a small group of frail, terrified humans ran along the curved wall, defying gravity somehow. Behind them, one of the void-creatures writhed and gave chase like smoke through a slow wind. The humans nearly made it to a small hole in the floor when the creature jutted forward, throwing itself in front of them. With terrifying alacrity, the creature reshaped itself, coalescing into a form with more distinct edges. Although still flickering and vague, its shape was now more reminiscent of the massive carrion birds that migrated in great flocks upon the surface of the Earth, consuming the human remains of whole towns and cities that Hunters and Huntresses left in their wake.

The humans screamed in unison, and then they went ghostly silent suddenly as the hollow-eyed creature widened its gaping mouth. The humans' very life force was wrenched out of their bodies, a visceral extraction that left only convulsing agony behind. As the creature feasted, a ghastly transformation occurred. The very souls of its victims—the memories, the pain, the joy—momentarily manifested on the creature's smoky face. A forest of wild, tormented faces rose like goosebumps across the creature's churning body before being consumed by the relentless void-black once more. What remained of the humans bore no resemblance to the living. Their corpses, mere desiccated husks of empty skin stretched taut over brittle bones, lay strewn about as a grotesque mockery of the life they once held.

What this? Why I here? Hunter4430 reeled.

A woman screamed from somewhere below, and Hunter4430 peered down to see a human woman and two young children paralyzed in fear as they stared directly at him.

No, he thought, wishing desperately that he could speak to them even though he knew his voice would only scare them more. *I not monster. I not.*

Hunter4430 peered into their terror-addled eyes, the woman still screaming in open mouth horror and her children, a boy and a girl, like bloodletted statues, pale and paralyzed as they stared directly above with the eyes of docile sheep at the slaughter.

Not me, Hunter4430 realized, following the direction of their eyes above his own head. He arched his neck and looked directly above himself into the swirling void-black vortex churning in the open mouth of one of the nightmare creatures as it silently dove directly at him, its maw aligned precisely with the humans at the base of the mountain.

No! Hunter4430 pleaded, and like a human at death's door, he shut his eyes and raised his hands in front of his face in surrender to the phantasmic nightmare behemoth.

A full second passed, enough time for Hunter4430 to have been consumed by the shadow entity. He opened his eyes and jumped back in surprise at a pure golden surface just a few inches in front of him. Taking a few more steps back, Hunter4430 observed that he was suddenly in front of a gigantic circular golden wall.

Baffled by the sudden change in environment and the illumination of the golden surface, Hunter4430 turned around and inspected the area behind him.

He was still in a circular environment, but this place was far shorter in distance from one end to the other. Small golden orbs floated about the environment, illuminating Hunter4430's surroundings with a spectral golden glow. At the center, four hulking white towers rose from the curved ground, ceiling, and walls, meeting in the middle like the twin mountains of the previous dark environment.

Where I now? Hunter4430 gasped, his mind racing to make sense of this equally magnificent and horrific place. The towers sparkled with pure-white brilliance, reflecting the radiance of the stained glass embedded into their columns. The glass depicted numerous scenes that Hunter4430 didn't understand, but one of them beckoned his eyes more than the others. The picture revealed hulking yellow-eyed creatures raining down from a large craft above the Earth.

Hunters, Hunter4430 realized, reminding himself that he looked just as horrific as the monsters depicted in the glass mosaics of dizzying crimson and yellow hues.

A deep bellow resonated from behind him, and Hunter4430 turned back around to see that the Golden wall was irising open at its center. The opening went on expanding to reveal a much smaller but equally curved chamber overflowing with a multitude of flashing emerald and violet lights scintillating like tiny stars embedded in the drab gray walls. Small transparent tanks filled with crimson fluid lined the walls, like insect eggs geometrically implanted onto the face of a leaf. From each tank, thick black metal cables extended into the curved walls of flashing lights. The crimson tanks extended upward past where Hunter4430 could observe. He shook his head in dumbfounded awe, utterly confused by what he was experiencing.

What this place? Why I here? What happening? Where Anna? his mind raced, pleading for his Huntress to return to his side and make everything make sense.

Movement from above prompted Hunter4430 to take a single defensive step backward as he raised his head to verify the source. From the unlit heights of the room, like a goddess of wrath and death emerging from some unfathomable lightless chaos realm, a figure descended toward Hunter4430, slow but unwavering. Shadowy black cables identical to those attached to each crimson tank extended out of the figure's head, merging seamlessly with the thick darkness above. Gradually, the figure emerged into the golden light, revealing a sight that made Hunter4430's blood bubble with anguish and confusion.

Anna! Hunter4430 tried to scream, but his voice was still muted. He couldn't fathom how something so sordid and horrific could have befallen his Huntress, yet here she was, her scent unmistakable, her body mangled and disfigured. The black cables extended from the back of her head, forming a grotesque crown out of her peeled-open cranium. Raven black hair wet with fresh blood clung haphazardly to her cheeks. Her mouth and emerald eyes were fully agape, and though she screamed in silent agony, her features were etched with the same horror the people in the previous room had exhibited at having their blood and very lifeforce sucked directly from their bodies by otherworldly creatures.

Anna! Hunter4430 pleaded, falling to his knees in defeat at this impossible sight before him. He felt paralyzed, as if he were being held in place by Cleaners over his birth-fire. The cables undulated, moving Anna's suspended, limp form as if she were a dead limb attached to a much larger machine body extending into the black upper depths of the room full of crimson tanks. Her screaming face was brought mere inches from Hunter4430's, and as fresh tears of blood fell from her pleading eyes, she screamed suddenly, her voice strangulated by unimaginable torment.

"Please!" she screamed desperately, her voice wild and strangled. "Please help me, Thompson!"

Anna! Hunter4430 shrieked, but he still had no voice. *Anna! Please! It me! It your Hunter! I here! I help! Please!* Hunter4430 begged Anna and the world and his own body despite his inability to move or even speak.

Something stirred in the crimson liquid of the tanks. A human hand scraped miserably against the sides of one of them. In another, a human foot kicked in futile despair. In every tank, people fought desperately to free themselves despite their efforts amounting to no more than directionless dismay.

"Please!" Anna screamed, and her eyes shifted, locking with Hunter4430's. "Help me!"

Without warning, Anna grabbed Hunter4430's skull with each of her blood-drenched hands. The initial contact was chilling, like the touch of death. But then the true horror began. The pressure started as a dull ache on each side of Hunter4430's head, followed by the feeling of his eyes slowly bulging out of their sockets.

Anna! Please, no! Hunter4430 pleaded.

The relentless force of Anna's vice grip intensified beyond what the specially fortified structure of the Hunter's skull could withstand. A sickening cacophony of slowly cracking and splintering bone echoed through the room.

Anna! No! Why? Hunter4430 begged in agonizing panic as his head was slowly crushed by his Huntress. Anna had clearly been mangled and tormented by those black cables in her head, and it appeared that now she was about to do the same thing to him.

In his final moments, Hunter4430 saw a woman standing behind Anna in the shadows. One of her eyes shone with the same emerald intensity as Anna's, while the other eye radiated a deep, hypnotizing amethyst. The woman stepped into the light and smiled, as if delighted by Hunter4430's death.

Anna? Hunter4430 gasped at the smiling green and purple-eyed woman, his mind fluttering at the impossibility of what he was seeing.

"Anna!" Hunter4430 screamed, his voice piercing Anna, the amethyst-eyed woman, the tanks, and the rest of the environment, shattering everything into blinding white light, including his own skull and brains.

Hunter4430 woke from the dream that had seemed so real and opened his eyes. He found himself lying in Anna's lap and staring into her sorrowful face full of tears. He screamed at the top of his lungs, emitting a demonic bellow that echoed across the surface of the Earth for miles. Finally, Hunter4430 jumped to his feet and cowered in fear at his Huntress Anna, the human woman from Astrea who claimed she was not really his Huntress at all. Only then did he realize that his body was covered in jagged bone spikes that were only now retracting back beneath his skin.

"You!" Hunter4430 accused, pointing his sharp finger at Anna as he panted to catch his breath.

"You had a nightmare," Anna explained gently, but Hunter4430 had never heard of a nightmare. He nervously inspected her head and looked all around the environment, searching for the hulking shadow creatures, the mountains, and the white towers. But he was back where he last remembered being before waking up in that strange place. He was on the surface of the Earth, alongside Anna, who did not have cables attached to her head nor blood flowing from her wondrous emerald eyes.

"I have nightmare," Hunter4430 repeated, pronouncing the strange word with caution as he forced his breathing under control.

"It's just a bad dream," Anna said, but Hunter4430 could smell that she was holding a great deal back from him.

"I see monsters. I see darkness. I see people in red water. I see you. You hurt. Your head open. And I see another you with purple eye," Hunter4430 said in a spray of confusion.

Anna exhaled sharply, momentarily unable to conceal her fear before reeling it in and gulping it down with a stoic forcefulness that made Hunter4430 feel just as impotent as he had when his body had been paralyzed in the nightmare.

"It wasn't just a dream. It…I won't lie to you," she said, more to herself than the Hunter. "I refuse to. He's the manipulator, not me. So I will tell you the truth: you saw a vision of the future. You saw the future thirty-nine years from today. Your brain is powerful, even more so with that special skinsuit I brought you. Seeing into the future and the past is something you are capable of learning to do on your own. But not now. Maybe one day, but not now."

"I see future?" Hunter4430 asked in horror. "That was future?"

"You are one of several Hunters He chose to alter in specific ways, just as I am one of several humans He chose to alter in specific ways. You and I are prototypes, Hunter. We are His tools."

"Who?" Hunter4430 asked.

"The Mind," Anna stated with extreme terror in her tone.

"But I…you…" Hunter4430 stammered, his mind reeling in confusion at how to reconcile what she was telling him.

"I'm sorry I made you experience all that, but I don't have the power to see the future like you do. But I had to know for sure, little Hunter. I had to use you to observe the future to know with certainty that what He said will happen will in fact occur. Now I know for sure that He wasn't lying, which means that everything else He showed is likely true as well," Anna said, her voice cracking in pain. She went on, not letting Hunter4430 interject. "Now I need you to forget that dream, Hunter. Can you do that for me?" Anna asked, her scent one of extreme worry and caution. It was as if she was nervous that Hunter4430 might refuse.

"Forget? Why?" Hunter4430 asked, shaking his head as he futilely tried to make sense of what was occurring.

"We must enjoy our time together. We must. Don't you want that, Hunter? To enjoy your time with me?"

"Enjoy?" Hunter4430 asked, knowing the word despite the foreignness of the scent it filled his mind with.

"I will teach you to enjoy existence. I promise, little Hunter. But you need to forget about that dream. Your mind is powerful enough to dream of the future and also powerful enough to forget it, if that is what you will it to do. So I need you to just trust me and forget all about it. At least for now. The day will come for you to remember. But not now. Now you must forget it. Let it fall into the depths of your mind and turn your back on it. Then walk with me. Let us enjoy the world together while we still can. Will you do that for me?"

Every one of Anna's pores was a well of anguish stretching to such unfathomable depths that it made Hunter4430 dizzy to attempt to analyze such a forlorn and sorrowful scent full of abstract complexities. She gazed at him with tears in her puffy emerald eyes, and Hunter4430 saw her suddenly not as his Huntress, but as a frail, despairing creature who needed his help beyond all others.

"Yes," Hunter4430 stated, smiling with his jagged teeth in hopes that it might help cheer her up. "I forget nightmare."

Anna nodded gratefully, then rose and walked to him. As she stepped toward him, Hunter4430 was reminded of the feeling of having his head caved in by Anna's bare hands. For a moment he felt the need to run from her, but the Eternal Hunt's genetically coded command to obey his Huntress helped him remain still.

With tenderness and warmth, Anna took his hands in her own and said, "Hold it all in your mind—everything you experienced. Hold it all together, and then let it fall into the nothingness behind your mind. That's all you have to do."

She smiled sweetly at him, and Hunter4430 did as she told him. At the forefront of his mind, he smelled the mountains, the dark landscape of rivers and human homes, the shadow creatures, the golden place, the great white towers, the crimson tanks, the writhing black cables descending from the darkness, the woman with the single amethyst eye, and Anna with her open skull forming a crown of blood and bone. He let the scents mingle to become a single horrific mosaic. Then, without hesitation, he let the mosaic fall into the dark recesses of his mind, and he forgot all of it. Every detail. Every emotion. Every moment of fear and confusion. In the same fashion as a normal dream, the experience faded away, leaving Hunter4430 feeling lighter and freer than ever.

Anna was standing in front of him, holding his gargantuan scarred hands, but he couldn't remember what they had been doing just a moment earlier.

"What we doing? I forget," Hunter4430 explained, feeling stupid in front of Anna.

Anna gently kissed Hunter4430's right hand, then said, "You just agreed to see the world with me while we can. It's changing so quickly, and this is still just the beginning," Anna explained sweetly.

"Beginning?" Hunter4430 asked.

"Yes. We're nearing the end of the beginning…of everything. But the changes that will occur to this world and this universe are only just starting. In a few decades, the real changes will start. But until then, you and I are going to be happy. We're going to enjoy ourselves. To the fullest, okay?" she said with a forced smile despite her body overflowing with the smell of despair.

"Okay," Hunter4430 said, seeing that she wasn't comfortable revealing her sadness to him. But he would give her time. He would be patient and good to her. This was his Huntress. His world. His everything.

"If you with me, I be happy," Hunter4430 told her, doing his best to speak correctly. At his words, he sensed a pang of both dread and forlorn guilt racking Anna's mind, resulting in a strange and abstract scent that made Hunter4430 hope that she would be more open with him one day. But there was no need to rush it. He knew they would be together for many years—maybe even forever—no matter how the world changed and no matter how they changed with it.

To Be Continued…

Author's Note

If you have a few minutes, please take some time to leave a rating or review for this book on:

Amazon and Goodreads

Thank you so much for your help!

– E. S. Fein

www.ingramcontent.com/pod-product-compliance
Lightning Source LLC
Chambersburg PA
CBHW030931260626
47169CB00002B/436